Glittering parti...
passiona...

Regency

High-Society Affairs

They're the talk of the Ton!

A Reputable Rake
by Diane Gaston

&

The Heart's Wager
by Gayle Wilson

Regency

High Society Affairs

Regency

HIGH-SOCIETY
AFFAIRS

Diane Gaston &
Gayle Wilson

M&B™ and M&B™ with the Rose Device
are trademarks of the publisher.
Harlequin Mills & Boon Limited, Eton House,
18-24 Paradise Road, Richmond, Surrey TW9 1SR

First published in Great Britain in 2005 and 2004

REGENCY HIGH-SOCIETY AFFAIRS
© Harlequin Books S.A. 2010

The publisher acknowledges the copyright holders of the individual works as follows:

A Reputable Rake © Diane Perkins 2005
The Heart's Wager © Mona Gay Thomas 1995

ISBN: 978 0 263 86882 1

052-0310

Printed and bound in Spain
by Litografia Rosés S.A., Barcelona

A Reputable Rake

by

Diane Gaston

As a psychiatric social worker, **Diane Gaston** spent years helping others create real-life happy endings. Now Diane crafts fictional ones, writing the kind of historical romance she's always loved to read. The youngest of three daughters of a US Army Colonel, Diane moved frequently during her childhood, even living for a year in Japan. It continues to amaze her that her own son and daughter grew up in one house in Northern Virginia. Diane still lives in that house, with her husband and three very ordinary house-cats. You can find out about Diane's books and more at her website: www.dianegaston.com

Chapter One

April 1817

'Unhand her this instant!'

The woman's shrill voice carried easily in the evening air, reaching Cyprian Sloane's ears as he strolled down one of the paths through Hyde Park. He stopped in his tracks and groaned. Why had he not caught a hack on Bond Street instead of yielding to the temptation of a fine spring evening's walk?

'Release her.' Cultured and emphatic, the voice reminded Sloane of a scolding governess. Whoever she was, she was a fool for being in the park at this late hour.

'Go to the devil!' a man responded fiercely.

Sloane blew out a breath and pressed his fingers to his temple. No choice but to investigate. Gripping his silver-tipped walking stick, he automatically adopted the cat-like stealth of his former clandestine life.

He edged over to the bushes that hid the speakers from view, using the leaves and branches to obscure his own presence, on the slim chance he could walk on and not become involved. He peered through a gap in the leaves.

A man in an ill-fitting brown coat held the arm of a young, pretty blonde-haired woman who wore the bright red dress of a doxy. Her other arm was clutched by another young woman, the owner of the governess's voice. She was taller than the doxy, pleasantly slender, and respectably attired in a plain lavender dress. That her bonnet hung by its ribbons on her back and her brown hair had come partly loose of its pins attested to the intensity of her struggle with this ruffian. The man and the 'governess' played tug-of-war with the woman in the red dress, while another female—this one could be nothing but a maid, still in her apron and cap—bawled a few feet away.

'Miss Hart, do not let him take her!' the maid wailed.

It was like a scene in a bad play, and, God knew, Sloane had seen plenty of bad plays at Drury Lane Theatre this Season. At least this time he could do something to halt the melodrama.

He stepped into view. 'What goes on here?'

The characters all looked at him in surprise.

The man spoke first. 'This need not be your concern, sir. You may proceed on your way.'

Sloane's brows rose. He disliked being told what to do by anyone, but more so by an obvious scoundrel.

The 'governess', who was apparently the Miss Hart to whom the maid referred, took advantage of the man's momentary distraction and pulled hard, causing him to lose his grip on the doxy's arm. She quickly tugged the red-dressed girl behind her, making a shield with her body. 'Do not heed him,' Miss Hart pleaded. 'Help us. He would take this girl away!'

'She's my sister!' wailed the maid.

'Bugger you.' The man lunged at Miss Hart and tried to push her out of the way. She stumbled, falling to her knees, while the red-dressed doxy ran to hide behind her sister.

'Enough!' shouted Sloane, moving quickly. He crossed the short distance and grabbed the man by the collar of his coat, lifted him in the air and tossed him into the bushes.

Sloane extended his hand to help the woman rise. 'Are you injured?'

She shook her head as he pulled her to her feet, but her eyes flashed with alarm. 'Take heed!'

Sloane spun around, swinging his stick as he did so. The man rushed at him, but Sloane's stick struck him across the abdomen, and he staggered backwards. Putting a hand in his coat, the ruffian pulled out a knife.

The maid screamed.

Crouching, the man waved the knife, its long blade catching the last rays of the sun. 'You leave her to me, now,' he growled. 'I'll take her and be on my way.'

'No!' cried Miss Hart.

Out of the corner of his eye Sloane saw her start forward and held her back with one hand. Not taking his eyes off the knife, he turned his head slightly towards the girl in the red dress. 'Do you wish to go with him, miss?'

'I…I…' she stammered.

'Oh, say you do not, Lucy,' her sister cried.

Her words rushed out. 'I do not wish to go with him.'

The man glared at Sloane, but he too addressed the girl. 'You will come with me, missy. We had a bargain.'

Sloane let a cynical smile turn up one corner of his mouth. 'It appears the young lady has changed her mind.' He twirled his stick, then held it in two hands in front of him.

The man came closer, slashing the air with his knife, circling Sloane, who merely moved to evade him. The man scowled and spat out expletives. His performance was indeed worthy of Drury Lane. Sloane laughed at him.

Miss Hart still hovered too close. Sloane longed to shout

at her to stay out of the way, but he did not want to alert the man to her close proximity. The last thing Sloane wanted was for the man to slash his knife at her.

But the ruffian's attention was riveted on Sloane. The man inched in closer. Sloane twisted the handle of his walking stick, ready for him.

The man swiped his blade again. Coming up behind him, Miss Hart jumped on the man's back. He flailed at her, trying to shake her off, the blade of his knife coming perilously close to her skin.

Foolish girl! Sloane quickly released the sword hidden inside his walking stick, its deceptively innocent wooden sheath falling to the ground. 'Leave him to me, woman! Stay out of the way!'

She let go, falling backwards on to the ground and rolling out of range. The man charged Sloane in earnest, but Sloane checked the knife's blade with the steel of his sword. His opponent was undaunted and his blade flashed to and fro as Sloane's sword rang loud when it connected with the blade.

The maid screamed, but there was little to fear. This man might grunt and slash, but Sloane had been in fights much worse than this one. This one had even odds, at least.

Miss Hart jumped to her feet again and still she did not move out of range. Her presence merely distracted Sloane and this was not a time for distractions. Sloane parried the man's blows. Becoming bored, he bided his time until the opportunity came to knock the weapon out of the man's hand.

Their blades connected once again and the clash of steel rang out like an alarm, loud enough for someone to hear the commotion and to summon the watch. What ill luck that would be. Sloane had no desire to be detained, and even less desire to be discovered brawling in the park. No one would believe the disreputable son of the Earl of Dorton had happened upon this scene by chance. Rumours would fly, and before the rise of the next sun, the *ton* would have him cast back into the gaming hells and other sordid corners of London's underworld from where he'd emerged.

He'd be damned if he'd let this ruffian spoil the progress he'd made. After all, he was becoming well nigh respectable. Astounding what a fortune could do.

The ruffian, dripping with sweat, did not seem to perceive the folly of continuing to attack Sloane in every way he could. Sloane had seen all the tricks before. If the man kept this up, it crossed Sloane's mind that he would be late to dine with Lord and Lady Cowdlin and their very marriageable daughter, Lady Hannah, or that he might dishevel his perfectly tailored coat and snow-white neckcloth.

Sloane abandoned restraint. Snarling at the fellow, he kicked him in the stomach. *Deuce.* He'd been aiming lower.

'Go to the devil!' yelled the man, coming at him again.

Miss Hart charged up behind the man, the wooden sheath of her rescuer's sword in her hands. The deuced idiot! She'd get herself hurt yet. She swept the stick hard at the ruffian's feet, so hard it flew out of her hands.

The man tripped and fell forward. With a loud crack, his head struck a rock in the ground. He bounced once, then lay still, legs and arms splayed.

Well done, thought Sloane.

'Oh, dear! Have I killed him?' Staring at the prone figure, she picked up the wooden walking stick.

The girl in the red dress gaped open-mouthed and the maid, still hanging on the other girl's arm, turned her head away.

Sloane strolled over. Pointing his sword at the man's neck, he nudged the man's ribs with the toe of his boot. The man did not move. Sloane squatted down and felt the neck for a pulse. 'He's alive.' He stood again. 'But I'll wager he'll have the very devil of a headache when he wakes up.'

'Good.' She handed Sloane his walking stick and he sheathed the sword.

He raised his eyes from the unconscious figure to look directly into her face. A smudge of dirt on her cheek marred a fair complexion, flushed becomingly pink. Her dark brown hair draped her shoulders like a silken veil. She returned his stare. Her eyes were not blue, but, in the waning light of the evening, he could not tell for certain what colour they might be.

He raised one eyebrow. 'Miss Hart?'

There was a maturity about her that did not fit her youthful clear eyes and smooth, unlined face. He could not even ascertain her station in life by her attire and certainly not by her manner. She was not much like any other woman he'd ever met.

'Are you injured, ma'am?' he asked.

She shook her head and the veil of hair moved like waves on the sea. 'Nothing to signify.' She extended her hand. 'Thank you, sir, for coming to our assistance.'

He accepted the surprisingly firm handshake, giving her an ironic smile. 'I fear it is I who must thank you. You vanquished the fellow.' His gaze reluctantly left her to glance at the other two women. 'May I know what goes on here?'

'You have rescued this young woman from ruin.' Miss Hart swept her arm towards where the other two were still clustered.

Back to the melodrama, Sloane thought.

She referred to the young woman in the red dress. 'He would surely have snatched her away.'

'He did not snatch me, miss,' the girl protested. 'I made a bargain with him.'

Miss Hart turned to her, her voice incredulous. 'You could not have wished to go with such a horrible man.'

The girl rubbed her arms. 'But I did.'

'No, it is nonsensical,' piped up the maid. 'You have respectable work, Lucy.'

The girl simply lowered her head.

'Did he give you that horrid dress, Lucy?' the maid went on. 'You look like a harlot!'

This, Sloane thought, was probably just what she was…or intended to be.

Lucy merely responded with a mutinous look.

With a glance at Sloane, Miss Hart broke in, 'We will discuss this later.' She turned to Lucy. 'And we will find some other resolution than…than going with that creature. Promise you will have patience.'

The girl glowered at her, but finally nodded.

Sloane cleared his throat. 'I am delighted that is settled. Now, may I suggest we leave the park before the *creature* in question rouses? I suspect he will be none too happy when he does.' Sloane picked up the man's knife and tossed it into the thick undergrowth. 'I will escort you ladies safely to your destination, then I must be on my way.'

Miss Hart gave a dignified toss of her head. 'We must not trouble you further, sir. We have not far to go.'

Sloane frowned. 'I will escort you all the same. I have no wish to repeat this performance with some other fellow lurking in the bushes. The park is no place for women alone, you know.'

'Very well.' As efficient as a governess and clearly the leader of the incongruous group, she gathered the other two like wayward chicks.

Sloane followed the trio back to the path. They made their way quickly out of the park, returning to the quiet Mayfair neighbourhood where he'd been strolling a short time ago.

She turned back to him. 'There is no need for you to see us further.'

She did not wish him to know her direction. Perhaps he did not look as respectable as he thought. No matter. Something told him he was better off having as little as possible to do with this motley group.

All the same, a faint measure of disappointment teased at him. This ladylike virago, who scrapped as readily as the toughest rookery orphan, intrigued him.

'I do thank you again for your chivalry.' She extended her hand once more, and as he grasped it he looked into her eyes, the colour escaping him still.

He hesitated before releasing her hand. 'Goodnight, Miss Hart.'

'Goodnight,' she said softly then turned back to the other two and herded them quickly away.

Morgana Hart hurried her two charges past the sedate town houses on Culross Street, so close to the most fashionable residences of Grosvenor Square.

'We will discuss what to do in the morning, Lucy,' she said as they walked at a quick clip. 'When we reach home you must take a rest.' In Lucy's present mood, it made no sense to try to reason with her.

'You did not have to come after me.' The girl's voice was petulant, but she avoided looking at Morgana.

Morgana's maid stepped in front of her and brought them all to a halt. She leaned right into her sister's face. 'What would have happened to you if Miss Hart had not come after you? You ought to be grateful to her. I cannot understand you.'

Lucy folded her arms across the low bodice of her gaudy dress.

Morgana gave them each a push. 'Let us be on our way.'

She ushered them into the house through the servants' door. Tears stained Lucy's cheeks and Morgana wrapped her arm around the girl and brushed the hair from her eyes. 'Why don't you take some time to get cleaned up? Then, if you like, you can come to my room while your sister helps me dress.'

As Lucy ran up the back stairs, the door from the hall opened. Cripps, the butler, with nose lifted, gazed first at Lucy's retreating figure, then at Morgana.

Morgana stared back, but spoke to her maid. 'Amy, please go to my room and set out a dressing gown for me. I shall be there directly.'

Amy gaped at Cripps with frightened eyes. 'Yes, miss.' She bobbed a quick curtsy and fled up the stairs after her sister.

Morgana felt a sinking chagrin. When she had hired Cripps and his almost-as-taciturn wife as butler and housekeeper a month ago, she had hoped to thaw some of that chilly reserve of his, but all her friendly smiles and solicitous questions as to the Cripps' health or their contentment with her employment had been to no avail. The butler kept himself so contained, she'd been unable to take the measure of the man.

He would likely resent her interference in his responsibilities, but she could not risk him playing the strict upper servant and admonishing Lucy. The girl might run again. 'I have handled this situation, Cripps, entirely to my satisfaction,' she said in an even voice. 'You need not be involved.'

'Very good, miss.' He bowed.

She tried a smile, hoping it would ease his sombre expression. 'I suppose I have delayed dinner, haven't I? Were Grandmama and Miss Moore served?' Morgana had ordered a light supper to be sent up to the dowager Lady Hart and her companion in Lady Hart's room.

'Yes, miss,' Cripps responded, his tone bland but, Morgana

suspected, disapproving. 'I ordered Cook to keep your dinner warm.'

She made herself keep smiling. 'That was good of you, Cripps. You may have it sent up to my bedchamber.'

He bowed again and retreated towards the kitchen. Morgana sighed. Perhaps if she'd known more of the man behind Cripps's austere exterior, she might have sought him out to chase after Lucy instead of going herself.

But then she would not have encountered the magnificent man who came to their aid. She could just see him, dark brows and eyes peering from under the brim of his hat, so at ease with the violence, moving as gracefully as a dancer and as lethally as a charging lion.

Placing a bracing hand against her chest, she stepped into the hall and climbed the staircase to her bedchamber on the upper floor. Amy was there, smoothing out her dressing gown.

Morgana walked to the wash stand and caught sight of herself in the mirror above it. 'Oh, I look a fright!' Her hair was completely out of its pins, falling on her shoulders straight as a stick and her face was smudged with dirt. She stifled the urge to laugh. What must Cripps have thought of her?

Or, more significantly, what had the gentleman in the park thought?

She poured water into the basin and took a cloth to scrub her face, then Amy helped her out of her dress.

Why could the excitement of this evening not have occurred during one of the many excruciatingly dull days she'd endured this last month while awaiting her new wardrobe? Tonight was her first chance to experience London's many entertainments. She was to attend the opera in the company of her aunt, uncle and cousin, having been included in the invitation of the gentleman her cousin planned to snare as a husband. Certainly opera would seem tame after witnessing a man wield a swordstick as if it were an extension of his arm.

Amy worked at the strings of her corset. 'I do not know what got into Lucy's head, miss. I am sorry for troubling you with our problems, but what would we have done without you?'

Morgana looked over her shoulder at the girl. 'The thanks belong to the gentleman who helped us.' She smiled to herself. 'If he was a gentleman.'

In the mirror she saw a dreamy look came over the maid's face. 'He looked like a pirate to me, miss. A handsome one.'

'A very handsome one!' Morgana laughed. 'What a treat to be rescued by such a man.'

She made light of the incident for Amy's benefit, but in truth it had deeply affected her. She was appalled by the man trying to take Lucy away and stunned by Lucy's willingness to follow him. She was also stirred into a cauldron of excitement by the gentleman who had rushed in to help them. He was tall and dark-haired, like any good pirate should be, but in an impeccably tailored coat and fine linen. Like the stick he carried, he looked sleek and expensive on the outside, but, on the inside, hid a violence ready to be unleashed. She could barely catch her breath just thinking about him.

But she was not the sort to waste time mooning over a man, especially one she might never see again. Although perhaps he would attend the opera this night? Her cousin said *everyone* would be there—

Morgana caught herself again. It was foolishness to get worked up about something that might not happen. Her father had always told her so.

She changed the subject. 'Do you know anything of why Lucy would try to go off with that man? Did she confide in you?'

Amy shook her head. 'She's been a moody one for a long time, but she shares no confidences with me.'

Amy and Lucy Jenkins had come recommended to Morgana by her aunt's housekeeper, a relative of some sort. Amy proved to be a treasure, aged twenty, a very young but talented lady's maid. Lucy, on the other hand, two years younger, was another story. More than once Morgana had found her in a room, dust rag in hand, staring into space, looking…tormented.

She gave Amy a look of motherly reassurance she did not entirely feel. 'We shall discover what troubles Lucy. And then we shall solve it.'

Amy returned a grateful smile, full of a complete confidence Morgana did not share. Although Morgana was a scant three years older than her maid, she'd seen a great deal of the world at her father's side in his diplomatic posts on the Peninsula and lately in Paris. Affairs of a carnal nature between men and women, however, were still somewhat of a mystery. Could such desires lure Lucy to follow that disreputable man? Morgana had no doubt he would turn her into the sort of girl men purchase for an evening. The vivid memory of one such woman Morgana had spied in Portugal still haunted her, the hopelessness that had shown in her eyes.

Desperation and hunger might drive a woman to such ends, but Lucy had plenty of food and Morgana was a kind employer. Why would she choose to run off?

Morgana washed herself with rose-scented soap she'd brought from France, noting with some alarm bruises on her arms and legs. Luckily her clothes would cover them.

Amy helped her into a dressing gown and tied her hair back with a ribbon. She looked nothing like the person who had engaged in fisticuffs, but more like the baron's daughter she was.

There was a knock on the door. Amy answered it, taking a tray from the footman and carrying it over to a table.

Morgana pulled at a chair. 'See to your own dinner, Amy. And try to induce Lucy to eat something, too.'

'Yes, miss.' Amy curtsied. 'I'll be up directly to help you dress for the theatre.'

After taking just a few bites of her meal, Morgana pushed the tray aside. She was restless after the incident in the park, and thoughts of their rescuer all too easily filled her mind. She fancied she remembered each move he made, each expression on his face. It had been a strong face, long and lean, with piercing eyes, a Roman nose and what she could only think of as sensual lips.

She rose from her chair a bit too quickly, knocking against the table, clattering her dishes. She caught the wine glass just in time before it spilled. Releasing a relieved breath, she slipped out of her room and walked more carefully down the hall to visit her grandmother's sitting room.

'Hello, Grandmama,' she said as she entered the room. Her grandmother Hart, a tiny woman who seemed not much more than paper-thin skin hung loosely over frail bones, sat smiling in her winged-back chair.

Her grandmother's eyes lit up upon seeing her. 'Why, hello, dear.'

Morgana was not fooled. The dowager Lady Hart greeted everyone who entered the room in the same manner, even the footman who came in to tend the fire. Morgana leaned down and kissed her grandmother's cheek.

Her grandmother's companion, the faithful Miss Moore, well into her sixties, handed a cup of tea to Lady Hart. Lady Hart stared at it a moment before smiling up at Morgana again. 'Would you like a cup, my dear?'

'That would be very nice.' Morgana sat in a nearby chair.

The cup of tea trembled in Lady Hart's hand, still poised in the air. Morgana held her breath, not daring to speak until her grandmother remembered to take a very slow, shaky sip and to put the cup on the table next to her.

'Did you have a nice day, Grandmama?' Morgana nodded her thanks to Miss Moore, who had handed her a cup of tea.

'Oh, I had a lovely day, my dear.'

Morgana smiled. Her grandmother always had lovely days.

Morgana would not dream of telling her grandmother about the incident with Lucy, nor about the gentleman who came to their rescue. Not that it mattered. Her grandmother would not remember a word of the conversation the moment Morgana left the room. She did chat about attending the theatre that evening. Her grandmother smiled and said, 'Oh!' and 'How lovely' in all the right places.

It was good that Morgana's father and his new wife had gone straight to his new post in Naples rather than travel with Morgana to England. Her father knew nothing of his mother's failing memory, or of her increasing frailty. Morgana would withhold that information from him until he'd had more time to enjoy his newly wedded bliss, absent of family concerns.

In the meantime, Lady Hart made Morgana the very best sort of chaperon, giving the appearance of fulfilling the proprieties without any of its constraints. Morgana had become used to her independence. Had she been forced to reside with her mother's sister in the company of her prosy uncle and frivolous cousin, she was certain she would have gone mad.

Lady Hart's gaze drifted away, and Morgana realised she'd stopped following the conversation altogether. Dear Miss Moore filled in with interested questions. A few minutes later, Morgana kissed her grandmother goodnight and returned to her bedchamber.

Amy was already there, setting out Morgana's new sea-green silk gown. As she helped Morgana with her corset, she asked, 'Who do you think the gentleman was, miss?'

Amy must have had as much difficulty keeping from thinking of the gentleman as Morgana had. An image of him, sword in hand, came vividly into her mind. Morgana resisted a sigh. 'I do not know. Perhaps we will never know.'

She sat at her dressing table. Amy removed the ribbon that tied back her hair and combed it all on top of Morgana's head.

'Do not even attempt to curl it,' she told Amy, with exasperation.

Instead Amy plaited some strands with matching green ribbon and others with strings of pearls. She pinned the plaits in loops so that they resembled curls at the crown of Morgana's head.

Morgana smiled, pleased at the effect. 'It looks splendid!'

As she dabbed a droplet of French perfume behind each ear and on the underside of each wrist, there was a knock on the door and Lucy entered, now dressed in her grey maid's uniform, her countenance still like a June thunderstorm.

Morgana's brow wrinkled, but she tried to sound cheerful. 'Ah, Lucy, you look yourself again. Come fetch my gown.'

With a cloudy expression, Lucy gathered up the sea-green silk and helped Morgana step into it. Soon she had the bodice fastened, and Morgana turned to the full-length mirror in the corner of the room.

The silk draped beautifully and the tiny, luminous pearls at the neckline gave it some elegance, as did the lace covering the bodice and trimming the bottom of the skirt.

Her aunt's recommendation of Madame Emeraude's new shop on Bond Street had been a good one. The dress was exquisitely understated, a style that might not be the current fashion but suited Morgana much better than lots of flounces, flowers and lace. She'd been so fortunate that all the Paris dresses her father's new wife insisted she purchase had gone missing somewhere on her way to London. She hoped they were at the bottom of the Channel.

This dress had been worth the month she'd had to wait for a decent wardrobe. She turned to Lucy. 'Does it not look splendid?'

Lucy merely nodded, and the restless look came back into her eyes.

Morgana frowned as she fastened the earrings to her ears. Amy stood poised with her pearl necklace. 'Remember your promise to me, Lucy. No running away.'

The girl avoided Morgana's gaze. 'I remember.'

Before leaving the room, Morgana risked another quick glance in the mirror. Smiling, she reached for the paisley shawl that completed her outfit, with its deep greens and blues and long silky fringe.

With a quick goodbye to the maids, she hurried out of the room and down the stairs, pulling her gloves on as she went.

Cripps stood in the hall.

'Any sign of the carriage, Cripps?'

'No sound of it yet, miss,' he replied.

'I am determined not to keep my uncle waiting.' She again tried her friendly smile on him.

'Very good, miss.' He remained as stiff-backed as ever.

Morgana kept her smile in place, but it hid her disappointment. It would be so much easier if she knew she had Cripps's loyalty as well as his excellent service. She did so want them all to rub well together. 'I'll wait in the drawing room.'

Expression as bland as ever, he preceded her across the hall and opened the drawing-room door.

She walked to the window with its view of the street. No sooner had she done so than her uncle's carriage pulled up in front of the house. Suddenly nervous, she stepped back to view herself in the mirror above the mantel, fussing a bit with the neckline of her dress, but, remembering that her uncle had been suffering from gout, she hurried to the hall.

'I will meet them at the carriage,' she told Cripps, fancying he looked disapproving of a lady going out the door unescorted.

'I am ready,' she called, as Cripps closed the door behind her.

A tall gentleman stood next to the carriage in the process of assisting her uncle to disembark. Seeing her, her uncle paused. 'Come then,' he replied and disappeared back into his seat.

The tall gentleman turned towards her. Morgana stopped dead in her tracks. 'Oh!'

Standing before her, next to her uncle's carriage, dressed in elegant evening attire, was the gentleman from the park.

He, too, froze, but his look of surprise was replaced by a lazy smile that seemed to take for ever to settle on his face. Just as slowly he tipped his hat and came to her side.

'Allow me to escort you, Miss Hart.' His dark grey eyes kindled with amusement.

'Thank you,' she managed to reply, pulling her shawl snug around her shoulders and accepting his arm.

'It is a fine night, is it not?' His voice was as smooth and low as a viola. They were only a few steps from the carriage. 'A fine night for a walk in the park.'

'Oh, say nothing of that, sir. I beg you,' Morgana countered in a fierce whisper.

'My lips, dear Miss Hart—' the lips he referred to turned up at the corners '—are sealed.'

Chapter Two

Sloane handed Miss Hart into the carriage, to the cheerful greetings of her aunt, uncle and cousin. He climbed in after her and sat between the two young ladies, catching a whiff of Miss Hart's perfume, a faint scent but distinctly French and expensive.

She settled herself closer to the carriage window, which somehow caused his blood to race, more so than Lady Hannah's nearly imperceptible move closer to him.

Lady Cowdlin spoke. 'We must do the introductions, mustn't we? Morgana, may I present Mr Cyprian Sloane to you? This is my niece, Miss Morgana Hart. Her father is Baron Hart, you know.'

Sloane did know of Baron Hart, though the covert circumstances by which he was acquainted did not bear mentioning. It would cause more questions than he cared to answer.

He turned to the young lady. 'Miss Hart, is it?'

She did not miss his attempt at humour. 'Mr Sloane.' A smile tugged at the corner of her mouth.

Lady Cowdlin went on, 'Morgana is my dear sister's child, God rest her soul.'

'Ah.' He hoped the sound was appropriately sympathetic. The carriage lurched forward and they were on their way.

When Lady Cowdlin requested that her niece be included in the party, she'd not given the niece's name. Neither had Lady Hannah, though she'd chattered on about her cousin that very afternoon when, during the fashionable hour, he'd driven her in his curricle through Hyde Park. Lady Hannah had explained this was her cousin's second London Season. Hannah's mother had sponsored her years before, but the cousin 'didn't take.' Sloane had only half-listened to her account, attending more to how many of the *beau monde* saw fit to greet him. More each day. Two years ago none of them would have dared acknowledge him in public.

'Mr Sloane has been so good as to invite us to the King's Theatre, Morgana,' Lady Hannah said in a somewhat smug tone and unnecessarily, for Sloane was certain her cousin must have been told their destination ahead of time.

'Yes.' Miss Hart turned to him again so that their faces were very close. 'It was good of you to include me, Mr Sloane.'

'My pleasure.' He smiled.

The irony of his scrapping Hyde Park virago being none other than Lady Hannah's cousin made him want to laugh out loud. He contained the impulse, but found he liked sharing the secret with Miss Hart. It felt…wickedly intimate.

When she'd emerged from her town house, he'd first only been aware of a swish of green silk, then he'd recognised her. But instead of the look of an efficient governess, she'd had a regal air, as if her intricate hairstyle were a crown upon her head.

When he had offered her his arm, the torch at the doorway illuminated her face, and he at last discovered the secret of her eyes. They were light brown—no, that was not descrip-

tive enough—they were ginger-coloured, ginger flecked with
chocolate. With the frame of her dark brows and lashes, the
effect was remarkable. What's more, her eyes shone with
alertness and intelligence, as if they could not get their fill of
all there was to see. For that very brief moment he'd felt
caught in them, as if they also had the capacity to set a trap.

Miss Hart was a decided contrast to the classically beautiful Lady Hannah with her abundance of blonde curls, liquid blue eyes and blushing pink complexion. Lady Hannah,
fashionably petite and curvaceous, was like a sweet confection, while her taller, slimmer cousin brought to mind something with more spice—ginger, perhaps.

'Mr Sloane is seeking to buy a property in Mayfair,' Hannah continued to her cousin. 'Will that not be splendid?'

'Very nice,' Miss Hart agreed.

'We shall be neighbours!' Lady Hannah laughed, lightly
placing her hand on his arm.

'Mayfair is a big place,' intoned Lord Cowdlin.

Sloane knew Cowdlin was not at all happy about any proximity between Sloane and his daughter.

Lady Cowdlin piped up, 'Not so very big. He'd be hard
pressed to be farther than a few streets from our fine residence.' She gave a toadying smile. 'Why, we may be certain
to see him often as we are out and about.'

Lady Cowdlin undoubtedly favoured his suit, but then she
was probably not privy to tales told about him in the gentlemen's clubs and gaming hells. Still, Sloane was confident his
money would wear down Cowdlin's reservations, as would
his efforts to behave in an impeccably respectable fashion.

Lady Hannah leaned into his side. 'That will be so lovely,'
she purred.

Lady Hannah also made no secret of favouring his suit,
though the increasingly proprietary flavour of her flirtation,

so gratifying that very afternoon when she had sat by his side in his curricle, suddenly irked him. He'd not yet proposed to her, he wanted to protest in front of her cool, ginger-eyed cousin.

'Do you have a property in mind, Mr Sloane?' Miss Hart asked. It was the sort of polite question anyone might ask, but her gaze had flicked back and forth between him and her cousin.

'I have hired a secretary to search for me. A very bright young man—'

'Who is that, Sloane?' Lord Cowdlin interrupted. 'Someone known to me?'

Cowdlin probably thought he'd hired a man out of the rookery to handle his affairs. Sloane certainly knew such men, but he would be a fool indeed to mix that part of his life with his newly respectable one.

'His name is Elliot. I doubt he would be known to you, but he is extremely efficient.' Cowdlin would probably scowl in disapproval if he knew Elliot's background: the son of a man who had run London's most sophisticated smuggling operations. Now retired, he'd managed to get his son respectably educated. Working for Sloane was an opportunity for Elliot to join the respectable world. In that, he and Sloane had much in common.

'Ah,' responded Cowdlin without true interest.

The carriage soon drew up to the entrance of the King's Theatre. There was a long line of carriages behind them, signalling a large crowd. Sloane assisted the ladies from the carriage, Lady Cowdlin an awkward bulk, Lady Hannah all soft and melting in his grasp, and Miss Hart a mere formality, relying on herself, not his hand, to alight.

Sloane predicted Hannah would some day be a warm and responsive bed partner; it was one of the qualities that had fostered his interest in her. But he could not imagine what sharing a bed with Miss Hart would be like. His senses flared with a sudden curiosity to find out.

Sloane mentally shook himself. He was thinking like a rake, not a gentleman. In a very gentlemanly manner, he offered each of the young ladies an arm and allowed Lord and Lady Cowdlin to precede them into the theatre and on to the box he'd rented for the Season. It had cost a pretty penny, as had the boxes he'd rented in all the important theatres. These were investments, he told himself, the necessary expenditures of a wealthy gentleman of the *ton*.

His investment was already paying off. Lord Cowdlin had given up his own subscription to the opera this year, more evidence of his dismal financial situation. Lady Cowdlin and her daughter had been in raptures when Sloane offered his box to them. They insisted he must be part of their group or they could not possibly accept his generosity. Lord Cowdlin had been less enthusiastic about this invitation. No doubt that gentleman would prefer to find a wealthy son-in-law who did not come encumbered with a rakehell's reputation.

Sloane ushered Lady Cowdlin into the box. 'My lady, I would be pleased for you to take the front seats. The view should be excellent.'

Lord Cowdlin snapped to attention. 'What? What? You would sit in the back with my daughter?'

Sloane refrained from rolling his eyes. Did Cowdlin think him so big a fool? In such a public place, to sit in the dark with a maiden would surely compromise his efforts to raise his reputation from the depths it had sunk in the years he'd been on his own. Sloane was no fool. 'You misunderstand me, sir. I meant the front seats for all the ladies of our party.' He kept his voice deliberately bland. 'I fancy you and I will be less interested than the ladies in either the performance or the audience.'

'Oh,' mumbled his lordship. 'I beg your pardon.'

'I will sit in the back, Papa.' Lady Hannah batted her eyes. 'I do not mind in the least.'

Apparently Lady Hannah had fewer scruples than he. Either that or she was impossibly naïve.

Sloane noticed Miss Hart watching this exchange with those lively eyes. What was she thinking? If he sat in the back with her, he could ask. He fancied she was the sort who would tell him.

Lady Cowdlin seized her husband's arm with a dramatic flourish. 'I will sit with my husband, Mr Sloane. You young people must sit in the front seats. I insist upon it.'

And Lady Hannah insisted that she sit in the middle chair, Miss Hart on one side, Sloane on the other, to which arrangement Miss Hart acquiesced without complaint. She took her seat and immediately scanned the theatre, somewhat methodically, Sloane noticed. She slowly examined the house left to right, eyes lingering longer on certain boxes, watching certain people on the floor.

The theatre was filling rapidly, the expensively clad patrons taking their seats in the boxes, the less fashionable packing the floor below. The din of voices melded with the orchestra tuning their instruments, creating a buzz of general anticipation.

'Oh, look, Mr Sloane,' Hannah cried. 'There is Lady Castlereagh and her husband as well.'

Lord Castlereagh caught sight of Sloane as he took his seat. The gentleman acknowledged Sloane's nod. Castlereagh was one of the few who knew of Sloane's service during the war, when the government had needed a man to crawl around the city's underbelly, to sniff out traitors more interested in profit than patriotism. Sloane was compensated for his deeds by a portion of the spoils seized from those who betrayed England for French gold. The bounty had been the seeds of his fortune. Skill at cards had done the rest.

He was compelled to remain silent on those years, and to endure from those who recruited him the belief he had done it only for the money. Still, when he had asked Castlereagh to use his influence with his wife, one of the patronesses of Almack's, to issue him a voucher, the man had done so. Sloane's mere appearance in those hallowed halls had gone a long way to giving him entrée into the *ton*.

Sloane had forgone serious card play and other gaming, his quest for respectability being a more challenging game. Admittance to Almack's, however, had been like breaking a faro bank.

'Oh, I also see one of my dearest friends from school,' Lady Hannah exclaimed, her attention darting to the other side of the room. 'And my brother is with her! How nice. I have high hopes in that quarter.'

Sloane dutifully glanced in that direction.

Hannah turned to her cousin. 'Morgana, look, there is my brother Varney, and he is with Athenia Poltrop, my best bosom friend...'

Sloane no longer heeded Lady Hannah's chatter. He no longer thought of her cousin. His vision was riveted upon another box, where the erect, silver-haired figure of the Earl of Dorton entered, followed by his son, Viscount Rawley and his Viscountess. Last entering the box was a fine-looking young man Sloane could only guess was his brother's son.

What a friendly family party. How cosy for them all to attend the theatre together. Only one family member had been excluded from the familial tableau.

Sloane. The black sheep. The disreputable son.

He had no wish to be included in any of their activities, but one day they would not dare ignore him. One day he would have so much power and influence that his father would be forced to pay him respect.

'Who is that, sir?' Miss Hart's sharp eyes were upon him, obviously noticing the direction of his gaze.

Hannah answered for him. 'That is Lord Dorton and his son, Lord Rawley, and Lady Rawley. The young man is her son.'

'My father and brother,' Sloane finished for her.

Miss Hart's eyebrows rose a notch.

Hannah leaned over to whisper into her ear, but not quietly enough for Sloane to miss the words. 'They are estranged from Mr Sloane.'

Miss Hart darted a quick glance at him, one that did not linger.

The orchestra struck its opening chord, but the cacophony of voices from the audience did not subside one bit. The audience was too busy watching the spectacle of each other to bother with the opening of the curtain and the entrance of the first performers on the stage.

Morgana smiled to herself, taking in the disorder in the seats below, the ogling going on from box to box, the beautiful music and powerful, stirring voices. But all seemed mere background to the man who sat so near to her, Mr Cyprian Sloane.

Cyprian was an odd name, one she'd rarely heard except as another term for harlot. What would it have been like to grow up with such a name?

She stole another glance at him, pleased that her cousin sat between them so she could do so without him being aware. He'd said very little to any of them and still less to her, but she thought she perceived a hint of the man who fought with such restrained violence in the park. In a way, fighting in the park seemed a more fitting occupation for him than sitting in an opera box.

He was not quite focused on the stage, but still on the box where his father sat. There was a story there, she was certain. If she had the opportunity, she might ask him why he was estranged from his family. It was the sort of direct question she often later regretted. Such directness from a lady was not at all the thing.

She suspected it was one of the reasons she did not take with young men. It had been four years since she'd last been in a London theatre. She'd been nineteen, like Hannah, and it had been her come-out. But she'd ended that Season without a husband. She'd since decided she was glad of it.

Sloane shifted in his seat, and she stole another glance at him, seizing a few seconds to study his strong profile. His looks were faintly Latin, with his dark hair, strong nose and wide mouth.

She never would have guessed those gentlemen in the other box were related to him. She'd have more readily believed them related to Hannah. Lord Dorton, his son and grandson all shared the fair hair and complexion she saw so often in England and so rarely in Spain.

Sloane turned his head in her direction and she quickly averted her gaze, pretending she'd been watching the stage. She fancied she could feel his grey eyes upon her, and her pulse quickened.

For the first time in her life Morgana wished she were her frivolous cousin Hannah. She wished she'd been brought up in an English country house, with an English governess, attended an English girls' school, and learned to be thrilled with ladylike pastimes and housewifely pursuits.

But even so, would Cyprian Sloane be sitting next to her instead of her cousin?

She forced her gaze back to the stage.

The opera was *Penelope,* and Morgana thought herself

fortunate to be present at the soprano's début performance in the King's Theatre. Violante Camporese's voice proved rich and full, and Morgana set herself to focus her attention on the performance.

She managed tolerably well, and believed herself in complete mastery of her thoughts when the interval came. A servant arrived with refreshment, but soon nothing would do for Hannah but that she be taken to her bosom friend's box, and, because she could not go with Sloane alone, they all must go. So Morgana pushed herself through the crush of people all bent on calling upon someone else. She noticed one box with several gentlemen hovering at the door and made a mental note to figure out who was seated there.

When they knocked on the door to Miss Poltrop's box and the young lady saw who'd come to visit her, there were squeals of welcome and hugs between the two friends. The rest packed themselves in and, for a moment, Morgana had to squeeze by Mr Sloane, very aware of where every part of his body touched hers.

'I beg your pardon,' he said in his deep smooth voice, as if he, too, had noticed the contact.

Introductions were made. Lady Poltrop and Morgana's aunt were quickly deep in whispered conversation, and her uncle and Lord Poltrop just as quickly exited the box. While Hannah and her friend Athenia were giggling together, Morgana was momentarily at eye level with the knot in Mr Sloane's neckcloth. The man had to stand at least six feet tall.

'Do you enjoy the performance, Miss Hart?' he asked politely.

She had to tilt her head to look at him. 'Oh, yes. The drama and intrigue. Who is seated with whom? Who is cut and who not? The conquest by man of woman.'

His eyes crinkled in puzzlement.

She smiled and deliberately fluttered her eyelashes. 'You meant the performance on stage, perhaps? I was speaking of the entertainment in the boxes and on the floor.'

Then he did a marvellous thing that made her heart quite jump up and down in her throat. He laughed, a deep rumble of a laugh, complete with twinkling eyes and wide grin.

Hannah looked over. 'Mr Sloane, come talk with me and Athenia. We have great need of your company.'

Morgana's pulse still raced when he moved away without even a look back at her.

Her cousin Varney came to her side. 'Glad to see you out, Morgana.'

She was grateful he'd come to distract her. 'I am glad to be out at last.'

Varney glanced over to where Hannah stood clutching Sloane's arm in a lively, giggling conversation with her friend. 'What do you think of that?' He bent his head in their direction.

Morgana raised her brows. 'What am I to think? Are they to be engaged? Hannah has said she has hopes of it.'

Varney nodded. 'Oh, she has hopes, all right. He's flush enough, to be sure, but I still cannot like it.'

'Why?' Morgana could not help but ask.

Varney squirmed a little, glancing back at Sloane. 'A lot of talk surrounds that fellow. Some people say he was a smuggler during the war, in it for his own profit. He has a reputation as a philanderer and a card player—and not always in gentlemen's clubs.'

Morgana, too, directed her gaze at Sloane.

'I cannot think he is the man for Hannah,' Varney added in a gloomy tone.

Sloane looked every bit the part her cousin Varney described. She could more readily see Sloane at the helm of some smuggling vessel or seated at a green baize table staring at a hand of cards, than here chatting with two misses in their first Season. Morgana said what she was thinking. 'Does your father know of this talk? Why would he allow Sloane to court her then?'

Varney grimaced. 'Truth is, the family needs Hannah to make a good match. A wealthy one, that is. Sloane has been the best prospect thus far, and no one can complain of anything in his recent behaviour.'

'He is reformed, do you say?'

'*I* do not say it,' he protested. 'But others insist he is reformed. Castlereagh, for example. And the Marquess of Heronvale. Both are known to speak well of him.'

'Indeed,' she mused, more to herself than to him.

Lady Cowdlin roused herself from her conversation. 'Mr Sloane, I believe the performance is due to start soon. We must return to the box before there is a mad rush.'

Sloane responded with great affability, 'As you wish, my lady.'

Hannah clutched his arm, but spoke to her friend. 'Athenia, do walk with us. You have not had a promenade yet this evening. You and your mother can walk with us and Varney can escort you back.'

Varney hurried to Athenia's side, but Hannah insisted he escort the older ladies.

Sloane looked at Morgana. It appeared he was the only one who noticed she did not have a man's arm to hang on to. In any event, she could certainly walk the short distance to the opera box without assistance.

The corridors were every bit as congested as they'd been at the start of the intermission. Morgana dived into the crowd, trying to keep up with Varney and Sloane and the ladies on their arms. Sloane looked back once to check on her. If he looked back again, she did not know it. She became separated from the group by several men who had left the box she'd been curious of before. One young man gave her a very appraising look, which Morgana returned with a cool repressive one, just before she spied her uncle and Athenia's father coming out of the box as well.

Whose box was it who attracted her uncle and Lord Poltrop and all these other gentlemen? She pushed her way past, calculating that the box was five doors from Mr Sloane's. She'd gone no more than a yard when he came towards her in the crowd.

He gave her his arm. 'I ought not to have allowed you to proceed unescorted.'

She put her arm through his, thinking of how that arm so lethally had held a sword. 'I assure you I only had one illicit encounter,' she quipped. 'However, I am well able to take care of myself.'

He again gave that devastating smile and leaned down to her ear. 'I feared I would be compelled to break up another brawl.'

She could not help but laugh in return. 'You might recall exactly who ended that first brawl.'

They reached the door to his box and halted, each smiling into the other's eyes. 'I recall it,' he said, and for Morgana time seemed to stand still.

He opened the door, and the other ladies and Varney were crowded in the box saying their goodbyes. Sloane escorted Morgana to her chair and they were still standing next to each other when her uncle entered.

Morgana thought her uncle's complexion in high colour. She turned to check the boxes, counting carefully to discover who it was he and half the gentlemen in the house visited.

In the fifth box over sat a brightly clad, auburn-haired

woman holding court to several gentlemen who flocked around her. Her dress, while not scandalously low cut, none the less displayed to advantage her ample bosom. She looked the very paragon of fashion and gaiety. The woman caught Morgana's eye and smiled.

'Who is she?' Morgana asked Sloane.

He frowned. 'No one you should know, Miss Hart.'

Morgana glanced back at the woman. 'Why not? Is she a demi-rep?'

He drew her from the edge of the box, making her turn away from the audience. 'It would be best for you not to ask about such women.'

She pursed her lips. 'I am not missish, Mr Sloane, as you well know. My uncle and Lord Poltrop visited that box. I saw them. I would like to know who she is.'

He shushed her again, something that always raised her hackles ever since she'd been a small child. She gave him a direct stare and waited.

He returned the stare, much too long for her to be comfortable. Finally, he spoke, 'That is Harriette Wilson. She is a celebrated courtesan and not the sort of person a young lady of your station should know about.'

Morgana persisted, now more out of a desire to deflate his sudden prosiness than out of curiosity about the captivating Harriette Wilson. 'Do you know her?'

He paused, their gazes still locked. 'I am acquainted with her.'

She opened her mouth to ask him what he meant by that, when Hannah hurried over. Her friend had left, and she'd undoubtedly noticed her gentleman-of-choice had engaged in a brief conversation with someone other than herself.

The orchestra sounded its first chords and they all took their seats, Morgana feeling more stimulated by the brief conversation with Mr Sloane than anything else of that evening. She consoled herself that, since Sloane was Hannah's probable fiancé, she might have other opportunities to converse with him.

She peeked at him. He would make an interesting friend, and she could content herself with that. Her gaze wandered back to Harriette Wilson. No one in that box paid the least attention to the performance on stage. They were riveted on Miss Wilson, who exuded self-assurance and charm, as well as a frankly sensuous appearance.

Even Morgana could recognise her allure, though she could not explain it. Suffice to say the gentlemen flocked around her, even though she was not a young woman, perhaps even near her father's age.

Miss Wilson looked in the direction of their box, but not at Morgana this time. At Sloane.

What precisely had Sloane meant by being 'acquainted' with the celebrated courtesan?

Chapter Three

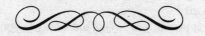

By the next afternoon, Morgana had quite settled in her mind that these frequent thoughts of Cyprian Sloane were entirely due to a month of inactivity and near social isolation. With the delivery of several dresses and more to come, she would soon have additional things to think about.

This night she would attend Almack's with Aunt Winnie and Hannah and was quite happy that her new peach muslin was finished and ready to wear.

Of course, Morgana wondered if Sloane would find it becoming on her. She squared her shoulders. She was thinking nonsense again. Besides, it was entirely possible he would not even attend Almack's.

Morgana donned her bonnet and walked out to the small patch of garden behind the town house, where Lucy, on her knees, was pulling weeds.

'Hello, Lucy.'

The girl gave her no more than a brief glance before turning back to tug at some raggedy green invader among a small patch of lavender. 'Good afternoon, miss.'

Morgana sat on the stone bench near where Lucy worked.

The afternoon was warm enough for the lightest wrap and the sky was overcast with milky white clouds. 'I thought now might be a good time for us to chat.'

Lucy tugged at another weed. 'If you say so, miss.'

Morgana sighed. She might be pulling teeth, not weeds, for how easy this would be. 'I do wish you would tell me—explain if you can—why you went with that man yesterday.'

'I met him when I was at the shops.' Lucy patted the dirt where it had loosened around the violets, not answering the question at all.

'Did he approach you? What did he say to you?' Morgana could not believe any girl would be so foolish as to allow such a man to speak to her.

'You have the wrong of it.' Lucy sat back on her heels and looked up at Morgana. ''Twas I spoke to him. I knew what he was. He's been about before.'

'You approached him?'

Lucy nodded. 'You'll want to know why, but I don't think it proper to tell a lady, such as y'rself.'

Morgana tried not to frown. 'I assure you, Lucy. I have lived in the world. You will not shock me.'

Lucy's eyes flashed sceptically. 'You'll not tell my sister?'

Morgana shook her head. 'I will not.'

Lucy shrugged. 'I suppose it don't matter if you do. You'll be letting me go after you hear what I done and then I'll be gone anyway and none of m'family will speak to me then.'

'I'm not trying to discover a way to be rid of you, Lucy.'

The sceptical look returned, as well as another shrug. 'Well, I'll tell you and we'll see.' She changed positions, sitting cross-legged at the edge of the flower bed. 'You were told us Jenkins girls was honest, clean girls and that's true enough of Amy.'

'But not of you?' Morgana tried to sound accepting of whatever the story would be.

'Nay, miss. I'm a bad girl.' She stared directly in Morgana's eyes. 'I've done it with men, you know. *You* know. Fornicating.'

Morgana remained steady. 'Go on.'

'More than once, miss. A lot of times, since I became pretty, you know. This man, he said I was friendly-like. He said he could tell that about me.' She paused. 'I didn't know how he meant that at first, but then he showed me.'

Oh, dear God. When had this happened? The girl was only eighteen.

'He gave me money for it,' Lucy added. 'So I did it again.'

Morgana closed her eyes for a moment.

'I won't tell you who it was, miss, so don't ask me,' she blurted in unnecessary defiance. 'Coming here didn't seem right, you see, after all that. You thinkin' I was a good girl and treating me and Amy so nice.'

Morgana reached out to the girl, touching her on the shoulder. 'Of course I would treat you nicely.'

Lucy pulled away, fat tears filling her eyes. She rose to her feet. From under her wide-brimmed garden hat her smooth complexion turned a becoming shade of pink. A breeze blew her simple maid's dress against her body, showing the lush shape of her figure. The bow of her mouth trembled and one tear slid slowly down her cheek.

Morgana could easily imagine what that man had seen in the girl. God help her, could Morgana witness another girl lost to such a life?

She could still see that young Portuguese girl who'd climbed over the wall into her father's property. Morgana brought her food and spoke to her in her halting Portuguese. Morgana had been thirteen and the girl of a similar age. As two children in a garden would naturally do, they played together. The Portuguese girl carried a rag doll and Morgana ran to get her doll as well. They'd spent a pleasant hour, feeding and rocking their dolls. Morgana impulsively traded her fine china doll for the girl's dirty rag doll, and she could still remember the light in the girl's eyes as she looked upon the gift.

Morgana had made a friend, one her own age. It had been an event so rare she could scarcely recall any others.

Then the housekeeper had discovered them and chased the girl away. As she scrambled over the wall, the doll fell from her arms and shattered on the ground.

She'd seen the Portuguese girl a year later, leaning out of a window, her breasts almost bare, her eyes hard and empty, while another woman, dressed equally shockingly, called to the soldiers in the street to come to have a good time.

Morgana stood and again placed her hand on Lucy's shoulder. 'Lucy, please do not do anything rash. Do not go back to that man.'

Through her tears, Lucy gave her a rebellious look. 'I already gave a boy a penny to take the dress back, but I dunno how long I can stay.'

'You may stay as long as you like, Lucy,' Morgana said quietly.

The girl shook her head fiercely. 'You don't understand, miss. I liked what the man done to me. I liked the money. Men pay lots of money. Why would I want to be hauling water and mucking out fireplaces and scrubbing and dusting all day when men give me more money for a few minutes of frolicking?'

It was true a maid's life was not an easy one, but what would be the cost of Lucy selling herself for a man's pleasure? 'There is no future for you with a man like the one in the park. That is no good, Lucy.'

'I won't go with that man, miss. Not after what he done, with that knife and all, but more I cannot say.'

Morgana had to content herself with that. Lucy whirled around and ran back into the house while Morgana turned, crossing her arms over her chest.

A man's face appeared through the bushes where the brick wall should be. She gave a startled cry.

'The mortar,' he said.

'Mortar?' Through a gap in the wall separating her garden from the one next to it, she saw a young man dressed in a dark brown coat and fawn trousers.

'The mortar must have been inferior. This part of the wall has crumbled.'

That fact was obvious now. She'd not spent enough time in the garden to notice before.

He smiled apologetically. 'I beg your pardon, miss. I...I did not mean to eavesdrop...'

'You heard everything?'

'I heard enough,' he admitted, blushing scarlet.

'Then I must ask for your silence.' She stared at him, attempting to assess his character.

He bowed. 'Aaron Elliot at your service, miss. I was examining the property. It is for sale. I must note the wall.'

Elliot? That was the name of Sloane's secretary. Her curiosity increased.

She extended her hand through the wall. 'I am Miss Morgana Hart.'

He shook her hand self-consciously, letting go quickly. 'Will your maidservant be all right?'

Morgana shrugged. 'I do not know. For the moment, I hope.'

'Poor creature,' he whispered, instantly endearing himself to her and leaving her certain he would not spread tales about Miss Morgana Hart's maid.

'I may rely on your silence, then?' She was already sure of his response.

'Indeed. You have my word upon it.'

She nodded. 'I thank you, sir.' She gave him a faint smile. 'I am pleased to meet you.' Then she turned and went back inside the house, entirely approving of Mr Sloane's selection of secretary.

She'd always believed that the quality of the servant reflected the quality of the employer, though what it said about her that she would wish to hang on to a maid who'd admitted such a moral lapse as Lucy had done, she could not guess.

Another thought crept in, one that put completely out of her mind the intention of informing Cripps about the wall. What if Mr Sloane purchased the property next door?

That evening Sloane surveyed the unremarkable décor and the predictable company, and lamented the sacrifices he must make in his quest for respectability.

Almack's. Was there any place so tedious?

Still, he crossed the room to pay his respects to the patronesses. Lady Castlereagh and Lady Jersey were keeping watch over their domain this night.

He bowed before Lady Castlereagh, not missing Lady Jersey's disapproving frown. 'Good evening, ma'am.' He turned to Lady Jersey. 'And to you, ma'am. It is an honour to be here this evening.'

He hoped his deference to the great Lady Jersey, who was known for her high opinion of herself and arbitrary opinion of others, would inch him towards her approval. Her frown eased just a bit.

'Good evening, Mr Sloane.' Lady Castlereagh offered her hand and he raised it lightly to his lips. 'I am so pleased you have come. Tell us, what do you think of our young ladies? Is there anyone to whom I might present you?'

Sloane gave his most polite, agreeable expression. 'I would

be honoured to be introduced to any young lady you think suitable.'

Lady Castlereagh turned to her companion. 'Who do you suggest, Sally?'

Lady Jersey puffed up in importance. 'You, sir, are acquainted with Lady Hannah, Cowdlin's girl. She is an unexceptionable choice for you, but we might also introduce you to Miss Simpson, Lord Kettleton's youngest. There is a tolerable dowry there, I am sure, though the family has launched three other daughters. Lady Kettleton is an annoying person, a bit common in her manner, but you could do worse in her daughter.'

'The girl is a shy little thing,' Lady Castlereagh added. 'But a nice well-mannered girl.'

He could not think of a young lady who suited him less than a shy, nice, well-mannered girl. 'If you both desire it, I shall be happy to make her acquaintance.'

Lady Jersey herself led him over to where Miss Simpson sat with her mother. Sloane saw the mother's flash of disfavour and the daughter's eye-widening fear as that notorious rake, Cyprian Sloane, approached her. The poor child had little to fear from him. He was reasonably certain he would make formal his interest in Lady Hannah, but to be *respectable* he must not appear to show favour until ready to declare himself. He was not certain precisely why he was not yet ready.

He bowed politely to Lady Kettleton and her daughter, and just as politely asked the girl to join him in the set that was at that moment forming.

With a frightened glance to her mother and Lady Jersey, Miss Simpson nodded and allowed him to lead her to the dance floor.

They took their places for the country dance near where

the musicians played in the balcony. Sloane leaned towards his terrified partner. 'I beg your assistance, Miss Simpson. Tell me if I make a misstep. I become a bit nervous in a crowd such as this.'

Her eyes widened even more. 'You become nervous?'

No, truthfully, Sloane never became nervous. And he hardly ever turned the wrong way in a country dance or trod on a lady's toes. He merely wished to put the girl at ease. If she saw him as less than an ogre—or less than a shocking rake—she might relax and at least enjoy the set.

'Does not everyone become nervous around so many people?' He tried to school his features into those of a self-conscious dancer.

Her eyes still mimicked saucers as the dance began, but she soon showed that she took his request very seriously. She quietly cued him on what step came next and complimented him when he made a correct figure. She was so absorbed in his performance, she appeared to have totally forgotten herself. As they moved down the line, the fear on her face had vanished, replaced by a rather sweet smile.

The set was long and boring, but Sloane congratulated himself on giving Miss Simpson a bit of confidence. When he finally returned her to her still-disapproving mother, she glanced around the room with more interest than fear. He bowed and bid her goodnight. As he turned from her, he saw Lady Hannah enter the room.

Rather he should say that he saw Miss Hart enter the room, accompanied by Lady Hannah and her mother, for it was Miss Hart who captured his gaze first. Because of her gown, he told himself. It was the colour of an evening sunset, the sort of soft orange that sometimes lights the horizon. Miss Hart's gown caught the eye more readily than a white one festooned with pink ribbons, flounces and silk flowers.

It might cause talk if he immediately approached them, so he walked to a corner of the room and stood at the crowd's edge. The two young ladies followed Lady Cowdlin to a bevy of dowagers and chaperons, obviously of Lady Cowdlin's acquaintance. Miss Hart turned to survey the room. She caught sight of him, hesitating a moment as she did. Sloane experienced a spark of awareness, but he would not credit that. It would merely be due to the high drama of their first encounter, that was all. A memory of danger and excitement often was accompanied by the same surge of emotions the real incident created. Why, he could not go down to the docks without reliving the macabre thrill of battling the French spy he'd been tracking, of the viciousness of the fight, and ultimate victory when his sword plunged deeply into the man's chest.

Blinking away that memory, Sloane nodded slightly to acknowledge Miss Hart. She smiled, and her gaze eventually travelled on.

A familiar young man he'd not noticed before walked over to him. 'Good evening, sir.'

Sloane was momentarily without speech.

The young man smiled. 'I am your nephew, David Sloane.'

Sloane shook his head, as if waking from a stupor. 'Yes, yes, I know who you are. I confess I am surprised…'

No member of his family had spoken to him or called on him or otherwise acknowledged his presence since he had arrived in town. He took a breath and extended his hand. 'How do you do, David.'

The young man accepted the handshake warmly. 'I am pleased to make your acquaintance, Uncle.'

This nephew had been a mere lad, not even old enough for school, when Sloane, then a youth himself, had last seen him. It had been during a rare holiday from school that Sloane spent with the family. He recalled his father being in some towering rage, the reason escaping him. Perhaps he'd been caught downing ale with the field hands at the pub, or had it been the time he'd overturned his father's new gig?

Did his nephew's memories of Uncle Cyprian include hearing the Earl's barrage of verbal abuse and his stinging lashes with a whip? If the young man were spared such memories, as Sloane was not, he was certain the Earl and David's father would have supplied other evidence of Uncle Cyprian's total moral collapse.

David smiled again. 'I had wanted to make myself known to you before, but I'd not found the opportunity.'

Sloane gave him a grave look. 'Your father and grandfather will not approve of your speaking to me.'

The young man laughed. 'I dare say not, but I assure you, I am not in agreement with them. Frankly, I think it does our family discredit to cut you off without a word.'

Our family? Sloane was amused at his nephew's words.

David's father had been born to the Earl of Dorton's first wife—the virtuous wife. Sloane's mother was not virtuous. She'd had a fairly public liaison with a dashing but impoverished Italian count, and, though the Earl of Dorton had declared Sloane his son, it was widely bandied about that Sloane was the product of that rollicking affair.

Indeed, the Earl, the man he *called* father, had branded him with the name Cyprian lest anyone forget what his mother was.

What he was.

From the time Sloane was old enough to understand these matters, the Earl had made certain the boy knew how good the Earl had been to acknowledge him as his son, how hard the Earl had tried to keep Sloane's mother on the country estate, how she ultimately left them both when Sloane was not yet three years old, running off to Paris with her count.

How she and the man who sired him got caught in the revolutionary upheaval there and, as titled persons, went to their deaths on the guillotine.

Sloane wrenched his thoughts back to this nephew. 'Your grandfather will be angry, I dare say.' And, like as not, would place the blame at Sloane's feet.

His nephew's eyes twinkled. 'I shall plead an attack of Christian charity. Grandfather will not dare argue on that score.'

Sloane could not help but laugh. 'I trust the Earl is in good health? And your father as well?'

The young man replied, 'My father is quite robust. Grandfather fatigues easily, although he will never admit to any weakness. Otherwise he is much as he has always been.'

Trying to still the flood of painful memories that suddenly assaulted him, Sloane asked other polite questions about the health of other relations who would, like as not, cross a street to avoid having to greet him. David answered just as politely, with an open countenance that led Sloane to think his sentiments might be genuine. The young man's looks were more poetic than manly, with features that in the father appeared weak, but in the son seemed kind. Sloane could not help but like him.

As they chatted, Sloane kept half an eye on Lady Hannah—and her cousin. The two ladies left the chaperons and were slowly promenading around the room, stopping to chat with Lady Hannah's 'particular' friends.

They eventually came near enough for Lady Hannah to feign surprise at seeing him. 'Why, Mr Sloane, how delightful to see you here tonight. You recall my cousin, Miss Hart.'

Sloane gave Miss Hart an amused glance. 'Yes, Miss Hart. I am able to recall our first meeting quite well, I assure you.'

Miss Hart's lips twitched.

Lady Hannah gave a tittering laugh, placing her hand

briefly on Sloane's arm. She turned to his nephew, waiting for the introduction.

Sloane obliged. 'Lady Hannah and Miss Hart, may I present Mr David Sloane.' He deliberately withheld their relationship, lest it put David in an awkward position.

His nephew bowed. 'I am pleased to make your acquaintance, Lady Hannah, Miss Hart. Mr Sloane is my uncle, you know.'

'Oh, is that not splendid!' Lady Hannah cooed, more automatically than genuinely. 'Tell me, are you gentlemen enjoying the assembly tonight?'

Enjoy would not be a word Sloane would attach to Almack's. His nephew answered first. 'I assure you, my lady. I begin to enjoy myself immensely.'

Lady Hannah blushed prettily and tittered again.

Not only poetical looks, Sloane thought in amusement, but a tongue to go with them. He glanced at Miss Hart, who returned a knowing smile.

'Are you gentlemen not dancing?' Lady Hannah piped up, with a flutter of eyelashes.

Undoubtedly this had been her objective all along. To work her way around the room to Sloane's side, so he could be the first gentleman to ask her to dance.

'The next set is a waltz,' she added significantly.

Before Sloane could open his mouth, David spoke, 'I would be honoured to be your partner, my lady. There is nothing I could desire more.' He accompanied this speech with a suitably earnest look.

'Oh.' Hannah blushed again, clearly pleased. 'Then I suppose we must dance, sir.' She turned to Sloane. 'Would you be so good as to ask my cousin to dance? I would not wish to leave her standing alone.'

Sloane disliked her ordering him around every bit as much as he had the ruffian in the park. He was not some besotted slave devoted to her every whim, but he gave an assenting nod.

David lost no time in whisking her on to the dance floor as the music started. Sloane turned to Miss Hart.

She gave him a level look. 'My cousin presumes too much, Mr Sloane. You are under no obligation to ask me to dance if you do not wish it. I am well able to walk across the room and rejoin my aunt.'

He understood the irritation in her voice, so like his own, but if she walked away from him, someone was certain to spread the tale that the notorious Cyprian Sloane had been rejected by a mere baron's daughter. That would cost him. Besides, should he allow Lady Hannah's presumption to stop him from doing what he longed to do?

He raised his brows to Miss Hart and spoke with deliberate exaggeration. 'And what if I have pined for just such an opportunity?'

She immediately caught his humour. 'Flummery, sir.'

He extended his hand to her. 'I would truly be greatly honoured, Miss Hart.'

Her ginger eyes were unreadable for a second. Then she accepted his hand with a very gracious smile. 'I confess, I long to dance.'

Sloane liked the feeling of leading her on to the dance floor and taking their places in the waltz. He put his arm at her back and she placed hers on his shoulder. He waited a moment to capture the beat of the music, then led her into the dance, twirling her to the music. With her height, he had only to bend his head a trifle to look into her face. Her eyes, softening into pools of golden warmth, were even more entrancing at such an intimate distance.

She followed his steps as if they were one person. He stopped even thinking of the dance, and merely allowed the music to carry them along. 'This is not so bad, is it, Miss Hart?'

She smiled, creating tiny lines at the corners of her eyes. 'It is better than a walk in the park.'

He laughed aloud and her smile widened.

He twirled her around twice more and she looked up into his face. 'I thought you were estranged from your family.'

He almost missed a step. Most ladies talked of trifling matters during a dance. 'That is one of the tales told of me. What others have you heard?'

She blinked rapidly and glanced away, but brought her gaze back to his. 'I beg your pardon, sir.' Two spots of pink touched her cheeks. 'I often speak before thinking. It is one of my most vexing faults. I did not intend to be so rude.'

He'd not expected that response. They swirled round the room in silence.

Her expression took on a determined look when she spoke again. 'The weather was lovely today, was it not?'

He laughed again. 'I concede defeat, Miss Hart. Spare me talk of the weather. You may grill me to your heart's content.'

Her eyes sparkled. 'May I?'

'Only if I may ask questions in return, such as, why were you in a tug of war with a scoundrel in Hyde Park?'

'Shh!' Her eyes darted to and fro as if searching for eavesdroppers. She raised them to him again. 'Now it is I who concede defeat. There is nothing left for us to speak of except the activities of other people, and I have no gossip at all to share, only being out in public these two days.'

He joined in her bantering. 'And I am loathe to talk of others lest they talk of me, though I have never been successful at stopping them.'

She made her eyes big, but they were dancing with mischief. 'Is there so much about you to be discussed?'

How unlike the frightened Miss Simpson, he thought, who needed protection from his disreputable self. Miss Hart was made of sterner stuff. But he'd known that from the first sight of her.

'We are at a stand again.' She laughed.

They went round and round with the music, in a companionable silence that did not entirely suit him.

His expression turned more serious. 'I was surprised when my nephew approached me,' he said. 'He is the first of my family to have done so in years.'

She answered quietly, 'I will not ask why, I promise you.'

Sloane's smile was not mirthful. 'Why he speaks to me? I cannot think why he should do so. Or did you mean why I am estranged? Why the respectable Earl of Dorton does not speak to his son? You will hear those stories soon enough, I am sure.'

She kept her gaze steady. 'Shall I believe them?'

'Some of them,' he admitted.

She nodded gravely, but with something that almost smacked of understanding. He must be careful. She could be like some of the women he met during the war, who could be as understanding as necessary in order to worm out confidences and sell them to the highest bidder. He'd been that high bidder some of the time. He'd learned to keep his mouth shut and reveal only what he wished them to know.

This was not war, with the lives of thousands of soldiers at stake, but rather his own personal campaign to conquer the *ton*. No matter how intrigued he was by this woman, he dared show her only what he wished her to see.

'You have not been in town long, Miss Hart?' A change of subject was always a good tactic.

A fleeting smile crossed her face. 'We are back to polite conversation, are we? Yes. Lately from Paris.'

'And did you like Paris?' he went on.

Faint lines creased her brow. 'I confess, I could not like the gaiety, as if all the horror of the past twenty-five years had not emanated from that place.'

Another response to render him speechless. He'd had the same feeling when visiting the city, both during and after the war, but he'd thought his reaction personal. She did tempt him to let down his guard. That would be all he needed. To let slip one of the shocking events of his life, what he had sunk to in the name of King and country—and before—so that she might inform her uncle and ruin his well-laid plans.

By the time the set had ended they were a gloomy duo, but both plastered smiles on their faces when Lady Hannah, David Sloane in tow, rejoined them.

Morgana only half-listened to the conversation between her cousin and her two admirers.

What had happened? One minute during that glorious waltz with Sloane they had been bantering as friends. The next minute he had retreated from her entirely. She had only asked one impertinent question, but had withdrawn it almost as the words left her mouth.

Maybe it had been her frankness about Paris. Perhaps she ought to have gushed over the beauty of the city, the delicious food, the fashionable gowns and hats. That was what Hannah would have done, and it was Hannah who had captured his interest.

Hannah and Mr David Sloane took no notice when Morgana backed away, but she caught Sloane staring at her as she walked over to two young ladies Hannah had introduced her to before the ill-fated waltz. When the next set formed, one of the gentlemen in their group asked her to dance.

She thought Sloane's eyes followed her as she stepped on to the floor.

Chapter Four

Two days later Sloane sat at his desk, gazing at the paper his secretary placed in his hand.

'Culross Street?' He glanced at the young man standing before him.

'It is an ideal situation, sir.' Mr Elliot spoke earnestly. 'Completely furnished, and in a manner that is presentable—if not in the latest style. There are servants eager to retain employment, and the owner is done up and desperate for cash.'

Sloane read the paper again. 'But Culross Street?'

Mr Elliot's brow wrinkled. 'I assure you, Mr Sloane, Culross Street is a very sought-after address. I took the liberty of making the agreement in your name—'

The young man stepped back as Sloane half-rose from his chair. 'You made the agreement?'

'As you gave me liberty to do, sir,' Elliot reminded him, with an indignant lift of his chin. 'If we had delayed, another buyer would have snapped it up, and I vow there were no other suitable properties in all of Mayfair. None that would allow you to move in directly.'

Sloane sat back down. Culross Street was a small one, to

be sure, but there must be at least a dozen town houses on it. What were the odds of being too close to Miss Hart? He began to calculate the numbers, as if this were a game of cards, but caught himself and waved his hand in impatience.

Decidedly easier to ask. 'Elliot, I am acquainted with a resident on that street. A Miss Hart. Can you tell me where this house of yours—I mean, *mine*—is situated in relation to hers?'

The young man beamed. 'Oh, yes, Miss Hart. She would be right next door.'

Sloane groaned.

'Is something amiss, sir?' Elliot blinked, clearly baffled.

Sloane shook his head. 'No. No.'

Nothing amiss. He was merely moving next door to a single lady, the cousin of the woman he intended to marry. What could be amiss? Only that someone was certain to attribute some lascivious meaning to the event and spread gossip. Why could Elliot not have put him next to some widowed viscountess or some such?

'You gave me authority to make this decision,' Elliot added defensively.

'Yes, yes.' Sloane rubbed his face and straightened in his chair. 'Well, it is settled and I am sure you have done well. We did not foresee this peculiar circumstance.'

'I have met the lady, sir, and she is perfectly respectable, I assure you.'

'You met her?'

'Quite by chance. I could not see any difficulty there.'

No, but Sloane could. He ought to have been wise enough to warn Elliot not to place him in any close proximity to a single lady of any age. But the cousin of his intended? Miss Hart, of all ladies.

Nothing could be done. He leaned back in his chair, balancing it on its back legs. 'When do I take possession?'

Elliot brightened. 'Today, if you like. The papers will be here for you to sign this morning.'

The chair nearly slipped out from under him. 'Give me a day or so. You may take possession today, however, and make sure all is in order for me.' Sloane needed a few days, if for nothing else, to alert the Cowdlins of his move. Would Lady Hannah dislike him living nearly in the pocket of her cousin? He was certain her father would.

'Come with me, Lucy.' Morgana practically had to drag the maid out of doors into the fine spring weather. She'd invented the excuse of desiring a walk in the park and needing a companion. Though it was not the fashionable hour, the park would be busy with other townspeople this fine day. A lady walking with her maid would not be remarked upon.

In some ways Morgana felt more kinship with her servants than with the few family members she possessed. The Cowdlins, including Hannah and Varney, treated her more as an obligation than a beloved relation, and her grandmother, the dear lady, could not even remember who Morgana was. It had not been much different growing up with her father. Baron Hart was always much too busy with some diplomatic crisis or another to attend to a little girl. As a result, Morgana had always formed attachments to the others around her, servants and governesses, short-lived as they were with her father's frequent moves. It seemed natural for Morgana to consider Lucy's problems as her own. She hoped to brighten the girl's mood and encourage her to stay.

But Lucy tied the ribbons of her bonnet with a desultory air. Determined to be cheerful, Morgana led the girl to the pavement. As they neared the corner of the street, a gentleman approached.

He tipped his hat. 'Good afternoon, Miss Hart.'

It was Mr Sloane's secretary. 'How do you do, Mr Elliot. How nice to see you again.'

Mr Elliot's eyes wandered to Lucy, and she, in turn, regarded him shyly from beneath her long lashes. Morgana did so like this young man. His expression towards the maid held nothing but kindness.

'My maid and I are going for a walk in the park.'

He touched the brim of his hat again. 'I will not detain you.'

Lucy lagged behind Morgana as they crossed the street and turned towards one of the park entrances. As Morgana had anticipated, there were plenty of people enjoying the fine day. Governesses letting their charges run about while they passed time flirting with young men. Shopgirls and workmen eyeing each other with interest. There was even the occasional curricle and cavalryman exercising his horse.

They walked in silence for a very long time. As they reached the Serpentine and stood gazing at the water, Lucy spoke. 'I think I'll be leaving your house, miss.'

Morgana turned to her. 'Oh, no, Lucy!'

The girl kept her gaze on the water. 'I cannot stay. I've been thinking about it all the time. I must go.'

'You cannot.' She felt like grabbing Lucy and shaking sense into her. 'The life you seek is no life for any girl.'

Lucy lifted a hand to her brow. 'Lots of girls is in it, miss. I heard of a madam who treats her girls fair well.'

A madam. Morgana cringed at the thought of Lucy in such an establishment, where men came to pay for favours. Neither love nor the creation of children would enter into the transaction. Why, Lucy might catch a disease, one that could kill her.

Morgana had learned about such things when she kept her father's house in Spain. She'd overheard plenty from the men who called upon her father and from servants' talk. And, of course, the memory of the Portuguese girl always hovered in the recesses of her mind.

She wanted to spare Lucy such a life, but what did she have to offer her in exchange? A life of hard work, no matter how kind she was as an employer?

'Lucy, what if I could procure some other sort of work for you?'

'Like what, miss?' Lucy asked, with little interest.

Morgana thought for a moment. It would be difficult to convince anyone to hire a maid to do another sort of job, but she could at least try. 'In a shop, perhaps.'

'And stand on my feet all day? I could not do it.' Lucy shook her head.

Morgana racked her brain to think of other jobs. For every one, Lucy gave an excuse.

A nurse? Lucy hated sick people.

A governess? Worse than a maid, Lucy vowed. Besides she was not good at learning.

A seamstress? It would ruin her eyes.

'What if I set you up in a business, like a shop of some sort?' Morgana was grasping at straws, but she could probably get her father to release enough money for a little shop.

'I cannot do sums, Miss Hart,' Lucy said. 'Besides, m'mind's made up on the matter. I'm going to go to the bawdy house.'

Morgana took Lucy's hands in hers and made the girl face her. 'I believe you are making a very bad mistake, Lucy.' She spoke in a calm but firm voice. 'It is not too late to live a virtuous life. I am happy to employ you and keep you as part of my household. I will not make you work too hard. In time you will meet a young man who will want to marry you—'

'No!' Lucy wrenched out of her grasp. 'There is no marriage for a girl like me. I want to go to the madam. She pays her girls well, I heard. That is what I want, Miss Hart. I want money and pretty dresses.'

It was no use. Morgana stared at Lucy for a long time, but could think of nothing else to say. Finally, she turned back in the direction they had come. 'Let us make our way home.'

They returned to the path. Walking silently a few steps in front of Lucy, Morgana waited while a carriage rumbled past.

Through the carriage window she spied the auburn-haired woman she'd seen at the opera. Harriette Wilson. The woman laughed gaily and happened to turn towards Morgana, giving her a smile of recognition and of something else—something rather smug and defiant, Morgana thought.

Next to Miss Wilson, Morgana spied a gentleman, but she could not see who it was. The carriage, however, was an expensive one, and the horses, matched bays, were very fine indeed.

After the carriage passed, Morgana could not make herself move. She was frozen by a thought flying through her head.

'Miss Hart?' Lucy asked uncertainly.

Morgana swung around and grabbed the girl by the upper arms. 'Lucy, I have an idea. A much better idea than you running off to that bawdy house!'

Lucy tried to pull away. 'I'm not staying, miss. My mind is made up.'

'Oh, yes! You will stay! For a while at least.' Morgana knew this idea was mad, but rather than consign Lucy to a life akin to slavery, she could set the girl free.

'You do not have to be beholden to a madam or a procurer or any of those sordid persons. You can be like that woman who just drove by!'

Lucy gaped at her as if she were indeed bound for Bedlam. 'I cannot be like her, miss! She was a lady.'

Morgana laughed. 'No, Lucy, that's the thing! She was not a lady. She was a courtesan!'

Lucy regarded her with a blank expression.

Morgana explained what a courtesan was. For the rest of the walk home, she talked about how handsomely gentlemen paid for the favours of such women. How courtesans could own property and fine clothes and jewels. She explained that a courtesan did not have to obey the dictates of a brothel madam. She did not have to take just any man into her bed. A courtesan could choose her gentlemen, and no one could tell her what to do. A courtesan could look gay and carefree like Harriette Wilson, not empty and hopeless like the Portuguese girl.

'But I do not know how to be a courtesan!' Lucy protested.

'I shall teach you,' Morgana said, her excitement building.

'You, miss?' Lucy cried in horrified tones.

'Well, I cannot teach you all of it,' Morgana admitted. 'But I know how to teach you to walk and talk and dress. We shall find tutors for the rest.' This was the right course, Morgana knew. How to precisely bring it all about was less certain, but she was determined to save Lucy from the bleak existence of a common whore. If she could not convince the girl to live a virtuous life, at least she could train her to be as gay and free and flush with funds as Harriette Wilson.

They had reached the house and Morgana stopped before the front door. 'What say you, Lucy?'

Lucy stared down at the pavement. As Cripps opened the door for them, she looked up at Morgana. 'I will do it, Miss Hart.'

Morgana grasped her hand and squeezed it, then she led the maid into the house past the butler, who, Morgana suspected, did not approve of her friendly manner towards a lower servant.

* * *

Sloane sounded the knocker to the Cowdlin town house. When he gained entrance, he handed his hat, gloves and stick to the butler.

'Shall I announce you, sir? Lady Cowdlin is receiving callers in the drawing room,' the butler said.

'Is Lord Cowdlin at home? If so, I would request a few moments of his time.'

Sloane was engaged to drive Lady Hannah and her insipid friend, Miss Poltrop, in the park. He'd deliberately arrived early to see Lord Cowdlin.

The butler bowed and made his dignified way up the stairs. Sloane cooled his heels. While he waited, a footman answered another knock.

His nephew stepped into the hall and handed the footman his card. 'Lady Cowdlin, if she is receiving callers.'

Sloane would have wagered his new home it was not the mother David had come to see.

The young man looked over and noticed him. 'Oh, Uncle. Good to see you.' He strode over and extended his hand.

Sloane accepted the handshake, but with an ironic twist to his mouth. 'Calling upon Lady Cowdlin, I hear?'

David responded with an abashed expression. 'I thought I might. And you?'

Sloane glanced towards the stairway. It was taking a devil of a long time for the butler to return with Lord Cowdlin's response. 'Lord Cowdlin first, I hope.'

David's brows shot up. 'Are you making an offer, Uncle Cyprian?'

'Not at the moment,' he replied. That ought to be his errand, but Sloane, who usually acted with dispatch over important matters, continued to drag his feet on this one. He told himself he hesitated only to give Lord Cowdlin time to accommodate to the idea.

A sudden thought occurred to him. He peered at his nephew. 'Are *you* making an offer?'

David shook his head. 'I cannot make an offer to any woman. At the moment, I have nothing but an allowance and prospects. It will be another three years before my trust provides me the means to support a wife.'

How like the Earl to have control of the boy's money for as long as he could. 'I see,' was all Sloane said.

The footman came for David long before the butler reappeared for Sloane. 'His lordship will see you now.'

Sloane followed the butler to Lord Cowdlin's library. He barely looked up from the papers at the desk in front of him. It was a rudeness Sloane would not let pass.

When the butler bowed himself out, Sloane approached the desk. 'You make no secret of your dislike, sir.' Sloane made certain he spoke these words in a casual manner.

Lord Cowdlin shot to attention. 'What? What?'

Sloane gave him a knowing smile. 'You do not rise to greet me. I assure you, sir, if you are so busy, you ought not to have received me.'

Cowdlin glared at him. 'Well, what do you want?'

Sloane made the man wait, but he stared at him until Cowdlin squirmed in his leather chair.

Cowdlin was no match for him. Sloane had sat across a card table from many a man just like Cowdlin, men who fancied themselves gamesters but who only had the skill to drive themselves into dun territory. Sloane would play his hand with Cowdlin with cunning and resolve. He would comport himself as a gentleman. 'I wish to do you the honour of informing you of my purchase of a property in Mayfair.'

'That is it? You waste my precious time to tell me you bought a house?' Cowdlin huffed with indignity.

'I came to tell you, before someone else bandied the story

about, that I have purchased the town house next door to your wife's niece.'

Cowdlin stood. 'What? What nefarious plans are you hatching, sir?'

Sloane gave him a level gaze. 'My secretary was charged with securing a property for me. He did as I'd wished and found precisely the place I required at the right price. The bargain was secured before he knew I was acquainted with Miss Hart.'

'You expect me to believe this?' Cowdlin barked.

Sloane slid into an ironic smile. 'No, I do not expect you to believe it. But it is the truth, and because of your connection to the young lady, I bring you the news first.'

'If I hear of any of your mischief towards my niece—'

'What sort of mischief, Cowdlin?' Sloane broke in. 'I am desirous to know.'

The short, round man stood and raised himself to his full height. 'You know very well what your reputation is, sir.'

'Ah…' Sloane pretended to relax. He strolled over to the library window and back again to Cowdlin's desk. 'The thing is, I do not know. What is my reputation, sir?'

'Why…why…why…that of a womaniser. And a bounder.' A bit of spittle dripped from Cowdlin's lip.

'Precisely what have I done? I am not aware of ill using any female, though I confess to having a man's needs. The ladies involved generally have not complained.'

'Well, there is how you made your money during the war. Smuggling. Bah! Answer that, will you?'

Sloane had no intention of breaking his word of silence about his war activities, not for this foolish fellow. He leaned casually on the desk, bringing his face closer to Cowdlin's. 'And, you, sir, did you forgo your brandy during the conflict? Did Lady Cowdlin or Lady Hannah never wish for French silk? How did you come by such items?'

'Well…!' Cowdlin began, but he looked down at his desk and fussed with his papers.

'Let me speak plainly, sir,' Sloane said. 'You are a man in need of money, with a daughter in need of a husband. I have the wealth you desire and am an eligible suitor. Can you afford to earn my dislike?'

To his credit, Lord Cowdlin met Sloane's gaze. 'Are you making an offer for my daughter?'

It was the perfect time to do so. Sloane had only to form the words.

He could not. 'I will make a formal offer if and when I choose to do so. But if you intend to refuse me, it would suit me well enough to be told now.'

Cowdlin averted his eyes. 'I do not refuse such an offer at this time.'

Sloane stepped back from the desk. 'Very well. With your permission I will then keep my appointment with your daughter and her friend to drive through the park.'

Cowdlin nodded.

Sloane bowed and strode out of the room.

He was more quickly admitted into the drawing room where Lady Cowdlin and her daughter received callers. Lady Cowdlin sat with Lady Poltrop on a sofa, the two ladies engaged in a whispering conversation, most likely the latest gossip of which lady of their acquaintance was sleeping with which gentleman. Lady Hannah and Miss Poltrop also had their heads together, watching David play at cup-and-ball. When Sloane was announced, Hannah looked over and waved happily. He paid his respects to the mothers and walked over to the younger group.

David gave an embarrassed laugh and set the child's toy on the table. Sloane felt suddenly very old.

'Are you ladies ready for a turn in the park?' he asked.

Hannah clutched at his arm excitedly. 'Oh, yes. It is such a fine day.' She batted her eyes coquettishly at David. 'It is a pity there is not room for you, too, Mr Sloane.'

David smiled. 'I would have been delighted for the company, but I must take my leave.' He bowed to each of the young ladies and then to Sloane. 'Good day to you, Uncle.'

After a long drive through the park, crowded with vehicles of all kinds, as well as riders and pedestrians, Sloane delivered Miss Poltrop to her door. As his tiger jumped on the back of the curricle and he and Lady Hannah started off again, the young lady exclaimed, 'I cannot believe you will be living immediately next door to my cousin!'

Sloane had imparted this information to the young ladies during the ride, eliciting happy squeals and exclamations.

'Do let us drive by your new house!' Hannah begged.

It was only a small detour, so Sloane turned down Park Street and was again on Culross Street. Lights blazed in the house next to Morgana Hart's; through the windows, Sloane spied servants hard at work dusting and polishing.

What would those servants think if they had seen some of the places he'd lived over the years? Would they be so fastidious? Sloane had slept in dingy rooms listening to mice scurrying and scratching within the walls. He'd even slept on the streets of Rome, when, as a young man, he had temporarily run out of funds during his wanderings.

'I think it will be lovely!' cried Hannah. 'Why, we might run into each other when I call upon my cousin. Would that not be a treat?'

'Indeed,' he said, keeping up the conversation. 'Do you call upon Miss Hart often?'

Lady Hannah gave a deep laugh and wrapped her fingers around his arm. 'I shall now,' she murmured.

When she allowed such a peek at the woman she was bound to become, Sloane wondered what was keeping him from formally proposing marriage to her. Her girlish giggles would eventually disappear, and then this hint of a woman would truly flower.

He slowed the curricle in front of his new home. In the window of the house next door, a face appeared.

'Oh, look! There is Morgana!' Hannah waved energetically.

Miss Hart's returning wave was less exuberant, and she peered at them with a puzzled expression.

Well, Sloane thought, she would know soon enough why his curricle had paused in front of her house.

Morgana stepped back from the window. No longer visible from the street, she still could see her cousin, blooming like a spring rose, seated next to the tall Cyprian Sloane, his fingers confidently holding the horse's ribbons.

How could a person feel such a combination of thrill and dejection? She simply must get over this tendency to moon over Mr Sloane and to flame with jealousy every time her cousin put her arm through his.

He was a man spoken for, even if he was the most interesting man she'd ever met. It would be ill mannered in the extreme to place herself in competition with Hannah. Morgana had enough difficulty maintaining the docile, agreeable manners prized by society. She would not be judged a man-snatcher as well.

She gave an audible groan.

As if a man like Mr Sloane would want her to snatch him. Hannah was the sort men wished to marry, all delicate and biddable. Not a harridan who scrapped with men in the park.

Or who all too often spoke her mind. Or one who must be asked to dance out of pity.

Morgana watched the curricle pull away, experiencing more conflicting emotions, this time relief and disappointment. For a few heart-pounding moments, she thought her cousin and Mr Sloane might call upon her.

'Stop all this foolishness,' she said aloud to herself.

She resolved again to tuck Cyprian Sloane away in her mind as merely a man with whom to engage in interesting conversation, a man she was bound to see often in her cousin's company. When he made his offer to Hannah, as Hannah insisted he would, Morgana would wish them very happy.

That was settled. She gave a firm nod and turned her thoughts to her most pressing problem. How to find someone to tutor Lucy in the skills of a courtesan. It was not as if such a person would advertise in the *Morning Post*. Where were they to be found?

Morgana needed a woman who could teach Lucy how to conduct the business, how to set prices and mode of payment. Morgana had no knowledge of such matters.

That lack of knowledge paled in comparison to her ignorance of how such women lured men in the first place. How did they display their 'wares'? She could not send Lucy to promenade outside Covent Garden. That seemed as sordid as lounging in a brothel. And when a courtesan entertained gentlemen, what did she do? Morgana knew what a courtesan would do in general. She simply did not know specifically how one went about it.

She needed an expert, someone like Harriette Wilson, to teach these skills. If she knew where Miss Wilson resided or how else she might contrive to speak to the woman, Morgana would summon the pluck to ask her to be Lucy's tutor. Such an opportunity might never come her way, however. She needed to do something now, or Lucy would lose faith in her and run off.

With sudden resolve, she marched from the drawing room in search of Lucy.

A few minutes later she and the maid were headed towards the shop where Lucy had made her contact with the world of the fashionably impure.

'I cannot think it proper for you to be seen out and about at this hour, Miss Hart.' Lucy needed to skip to keep up with Morgana's determined stride. 'A lady oughtn't to walk to Bond Street in the afternoon.'

True, at this hour young dandies and bucks tended to loiter in the street, waiting to accost any female who walked by with their catcalls and pinches.

'I think it the perfect time,' said Morgana. 'If we wait until the morning, think how many ladies will be in the shops. Do not concern yourself so. The veil of my hat quite obscures my face.'

'But a lady should not even talk of these matters, miss,' Lucy went on.

'Nonsense,' countered Morgana. 'How else am I to discover the proper tutor for you? Besides, you have spoken to these people, why shouldn't I?'

Lucy looked at her as if she were a doltish child. 'Because you are a lady.'

Lucy had told Morgana that the source of her information about the madam with the brothel had been none other than Morgana's modiste, the *ton*'s new darling of dressmaking. They hurried to Madame Emeraude's shop, which, if they had any luck, would be deserted at this hour. The ladies who might patronise the latest rage in dressmakers would more likely be proudly showing off the new creations in Hyde Park.

Morgana lifted the veil from her face as they entered Madame Emeraude's shop. No other customers were present.

Madame Emeraude emerged from behind a curtain leading to the back. 'Miss Hart?' She gave her a quizzical look. 'A pleasure to see you.' The modiste next examined Morgana's clothing. 'You are wearing one of my dresses! I hope you have been satisfied. Is the fit acceptable? Did my dresses emerge as you imagined them?'

Morgana smiled at her. 'Your gowns exceeded my expectations, Madame. I am now launched back into society with great success.'

Madame Emeraude beamed both with pride and relief, then she seemed to remember to be puzzled. 'What may I do for you at this…unusual hour?'

Morgana glanced towards the doorway. Even if no *tonnish* ladies walked through that door, a gentleman might, one escorting another sort of female to be dressed in fine clothes. 'May we speak in one of your private dressing rooms?'

The modiste gave her a puzzled expression. 'But of course.' She tossed a wary look when Lucy followed behind them.

Madame Emeraude led them to a room with brocade-covered chairs, the room where Madame Emeraude had previously shown her various fabrics and fashion plates, as well as some examples of her finely stitched creations.

'We are private?' Morgana asked as she sat.

'Yes,' the modiste replied. 'I am alone except for the girls upstairs.'

Previously Morgana had assumed those 'girls upstairs' were merely hard at work sewing seams and tacking on lace. But now she wondered if those girls were sometimes required to perform other tasks, the sort of tasks Lucy was prepared to perform.

'I will speak plainly, Madame,' Morgana began. 'You told

Miss Jenkins here that you knew the madam of a brothel where Miss Jenkins might be welcome—'

Madame gasped and threw Lucy a venomous glare. 'I did no such thing.'

Morgana gave an impatient shake of the head. 'I am not here to give you a scold. I want to know how to speak to this madam. I may require her assistance.'

Madame Emeraude's eyebrows nearly disappeared under her stylishly coiffed hair. 'You, miss?'

'I will not explain further, Madame, except to assure you my business with this person is not of her usual sort, nor will I bring trouble to her.' Morgana spoke in a confident tone, one she learned as a young girl of seventeen when she first assumed the management of her father's household. The appearance of confidence had been necessary to convince servants and tradesmen she knew what she was doing. Perhaps now it would convince Madame Emeraude—as well as Morgana herself.

She gave the madam a steady look. 'May I remind you I have spent a great deal of money in this shop and I plan to spend a great deal more; however, I suspect the ladies who have flocked to your door would turn their backs upon a woman who referred their maids to a brothel.' She paused to let her threat sink in. 'If you provide me with the information I seek and your word you will not speak of it further, I will not speak of it either.'

Madame Emeraude's eyes looked as if she were calculating sums. 'She is on Jermyn Street.'

Sloane turned the corner of Jermyn Street on his way to return the curricle and horses to the stable he'd rented. Out of the corner of his eye, he saw two women climb down from a hack. One looked suspiciously like the girl Miss Hart had been rescuing in the park, the one who had worn the red dress. He twisted around, but only the women's backs were visible as they walked into a glove shop. Calling to his tiger, he pulled the horses to a halt. His tiger hopped off and ran to hold the horses' heads.

'Take them, Tommy.' He handed the ribbons to the tiger and jumped down from his seat. 'See them stabled. That will be all I require of you at present.'

'As y'wish, sir,' his tiger replied.

Sloane, hands resting on his hips, stood on the pavement and directed his gaze at the glove shop door as Tommy drove the curricle away, the horses' hooves clattering on the cobbles.

He was a damned fool.

It was folly to believe the girl he'd only glimpsed had been Miss Hart's red-dressed companion. And more folly indeed to think it his responsibility to ensure the girl was not up to more mischief.

He walked slowly to the shop, swinging his swordstick, and slanting his gaze to peek through the window. Through the display of gloves of various lengths and colours, he glimpsed several ladies in the shop. One gestured angrily to the two who had arrived. He could faintly hear her raised voice. He sauntered past the shop and paused by a lamppost pretending to search his pockets.

The subterfuge came naturally to him. Many were the times during the war he'd had to watch and listen without anyone being suspicious of his presence. He used those same skills now and appeared to go unnoticed by the one or two men who walked by.

This was no innocent ladies' shop, he figured, but one that had rooms abovestairs with pretty mollies willing to entertain. Miss Hart's girl was up to the same larks, it appeared, though he still did not know why he bothered with the business.

He peered into a nearby wine merchant's shop, pretending to examine its wares, but keeping an eye on the glove-shop door.

The door opened, and the same two women came out, female screeches from the inside ringing behind them. They glanced around the street as if uncertain what to do.

Sloane approached. 'Pardon me, miss. Do you require assistance?'

He directed this question to the young woman he'd recognised correctly—Lucy was her name, he recalled. She did not answer him.

From behind a great deal of netting attached to the hat of the other female came a familiar voice.

'Mr Sloane!'

Chapter Five

'**M**iss Hart!' Sloane's stick slipped on the pavement, but the lady stood very composed while Lucy hid behind her and peeked about furtively. 'What the devil are you doing here?'

She lifted her chin. 'We were on an errand.'

He could barely make out her features through the haze of net. 'Are you mad? What errand would bring you to this street at this hour of the day? To this place?' He pointed to the glove shop.

'It is an errand of a private nature, sir.' Her tone of voice was excessively dignified. 'If you truly wish to be of assistance, you might procure a hackney coach for us. I do not see one about.'

He gave her a very stern stare. 'You would be lucky indeed to find one here. There will be an abundance of them on St James's, however, but that would require walking down that street past White's and Brooks's.'

Any respectable lady put her reputation in jeopardy by walking in this part of town at this hour. What the devil had she been thinking of?

Sloane leaned closer to her and spoke in a smooth, ironic

voice. 'Miss Hart, are you merely buffleheaded or must I consider you a *fast* woman?'

To her credit, she did not flinch from this query. If she blushed, it was obscured in gauze.

'Why I am here is, as I have explained, a private matter. If I must walk down St James's unescorted and unprotected, I will.' She pointedly shifted her gaze from him to her companion, 'Come, Lucy. Let us find a hack.'

With head held high, she strode off towards St James's Street. Sloane hesitated a moment. It was not his responsibility to extricate Morgana Hart from every foolhardy bramble she trod into. Let her suffer the catcalls and whistles of the young dandies lounging on the corners. Let her identity be exposed when one of those young bucks mistook her for a fancy piece and pulled off her hat. He started off in the other direction, but took no more than two steps before he turned around.

Even with his long legs, he nearly had to run to catch up with her. 'Miss Hart!'

She stopped and whirled around as if to confront an annoying pest.

He reached her side and pulled her by the arm to a doorway of a shop whose curtains were drawn. 'Wait here, speak to no one, and I will procure the hack.'

'Thank you, Mr Sloane,' she said with exaggerated politeness. 'That is very gentlemanly of you, but I do wish you would not call out my name in the street.'

He winced and looked about, fearing he'd exposed her, the very circumstance he hoped to prevent. Good fortune was with them. There was no one in sight.

'I will be but a moment.' He hurried off to where Jermyn Street met St James's.

Morgana leaned against the locked shop door and moaned as Lucy took a peek out of their hiding place.

Lucy tucked herself back in the doorway. 'I have caused you more trouble, haven't I, Miss Hart? You should not have come here.'

Lucy need not blame herself for Morgana's foolishness. Morgana patted the girl's arm reassuringly. 'Mr Sloane has saved us from trouble, hasn't he? He will find us transport and we shall be home directly.'

Morgana resisted the impulse to lean out of the doorway to watch him striding towards the corner. She ought to be mortified that he had discovered her in this part of town. What must he think of her now? First her skirmish in the park. Now this—this parading where no respectable woman would dare set foot in the afternoon. But frankly, she had been so relieved to see him.

The interview with the madam had not gone well. The woman had the gall to threaten Morgana with violence if she ever darkened her door again. Mrs Rice, as the abbess of the establishment was named, believed Morgana to be setting up a fancy house of her own. How appalling! Mrs Rice, furthermore, went into high dudgeon at the prospect of competition. She also accused Morgana of stealing her newest referral, Lucy. After such a disagreeable interview, Morgana had feared Mrs Rice would make good her threat and send some hulking footpad after them.

When Sloane appeared, her fears fled. She knew she could trust him to see to their safe return and to not speak a word to anyone of the incident.

'He's that man from the park, that's who he is. Isn't he, miss?'

'Yes, are we not lucky he has rescued us a second time?'

Lucy nodded in agreement. If the maid wondered why Morgana knew his name, she did not let on.

Sloane did not keep them waiting long. A black hackney

pulled up in front of them, and he hopped down to assist them inside.

When they were seated on the hack's cracked leather seats, Sloane rapped on the roof and the coach lurched into motion.

He faced Morgana, Lucy seated at her side.

'I thank you again for coming to our assistance,' Morgana said, sounding more genuine in her gratitude this time.

He peered at her from beneath the rim of his beaver hat. 'It is becoming a habit of mine.'

She could not help but smile, but quickly wiped it off her face when his expression remained grim.

He leaned forward. 'Do you have any idea what risk you took for your mysterious errand?' His gaze shifted momentarily to Lucy, who shrank to the corner of the vehicle.

'I protected my identity,' Morgana protested.

He lifted the netting away from her face. 'See how easy it is to expose you?'

She pulled it back in place and pretended to gaze out of the window at the passing parade of street hawkers and carriages.

She felt him shift position. 'If you are into some havey-cavey business, Miss Hart, I wish to know of it.' He gave a pause. 'Since we are to be neighbours.'

Her gaze flew back to him. Even Lucy straightened in her seat. 'Neighbours?'

He gave her the slow, lazy grin that made her heart do a flip. 'I have purchased the property next to yours.'

Morgana stifled a gasp. So it was true. Seeing Sloane's secretary two days in a row had raised her concerns—or was that her hopes?—that Sloane would move next door.

His eyes glittered with anger. 'I will be taking residence within a day or two.'

So soon? Could he not wait for renovations or something

equally time-consuming? No, he probably was in a rush to have a house to show off to a prospective young bride. Perhaps he would promise Hannah the pleasure of redecorating to her own tastes. Morgana closed her eyes and saw a horror of patterns, fringe and frills that no doubt her cousin would insist was all the rage.

She opened her eyes and gave a stiff smile. 'How splendid for you.'

He laughed—not the pleasant, open laugh of the opera, but a mysterious one. He leaned forward so there was no more than an inch between their faces. His voice turned very low. 'Does the prospect so displease you?'

Morgana's heart accelerated. 'I am certain you will make a tolerable neighbour.' She meant it as a jest, but the words came out stiff and prim. Why could she not possess her cousin's natural ability to bat eyes and to utter flirtatious nonsense?

His eyes became slits as he leaned back again. 'I will refrain from orgies and other rakish activities—will that prove tolerable enough?'

She opened her mouth to respond, but he continued, 'I merely ask the same of you. I would not much relish being blamed for whatever mischief you are planning in the future.'

Lucy gave a pained squeak.

'You be blamed?' Morgana cried. 'I assure you my affairs do not involve you.'

One of his eyebrows rose. 'Indeed? And is this not the second time I have pulled you out of a scrape?'

Morgana felt her face grow hot. At least he could not see her blush through the netting.

He gave her a level stare. 'When there is trouble around me, I am usually blamed for it. I would not much relish being blamed for whatever wild scheme you are hatching at the moment.'

Morgana resented his low opinion of her, even as she conceded the truth in it. She gave him her frostiest glare, although he would be unable to see it through the netting of her hat. 'I shall endeavour to please you, sir.'

That lazy smile slowly reappeared, and her heart lurched in spite of herself. 'See that you do please me, Miss Hart,' he murmured, his voice so low she felt it more than heard it.

She glanced towards Lucy, who was eyeing them both with a shocked expression. Morgana did not trouble herself to speak with him further, but she was aware of each breath he took, each move of his muscles.

When the hack pulled up to her town house, he jumped out to assist them from the vehicle. Lucy descended, mumbled, 'Thank you, sir', and hurried to the servants' entrance below, leaving Morgana momentarily alone with Sloane.

He gave his hand, still as strong and firm as before. He gripped her fingers, but let go as soon as her feet touched the pavement, stepping back as he did so.

Morgana took a quick breath and composed her disordered emotions. No matter what he might think of her, he had been her rescuer once again.

She looked up at him, his face shaded by his hat and the waning light. 'Thank you again, Mr Sloane,' she said softly. 'I am truly grateful for your assistance.'

He gave her a quizzical look, but eventually touched his hand to the brim of his hat and climbed back in the hackney coach.

Two days later Sloane stood at the door of the grey brick house, its exterior looking identical to those on either side. By God, he'd better not arrive home too addled from drink. He was liable to enter the wrong house. It would not help the awkward situation of living next to Morgana Hart if he barged into her home drunk as an emperor.

He glanced at her front door and pursed his lips, imagining stumbling up her stairway and flopping into her bed by mistake. No chance of that. He had long mastered control of vices such as gambling, womanising and drink. He might get foxed, but it would be in the privacy of his own home.

His own home. Now that made him feel like dancing a jig.

He wondered if the Earl had been informed that his scapegrace son had moved into Mayfair, *his* neighbourhood. Sloane wished he could have seen the Earl's face when told of it. Perhaps David had given his grandfather the information. Sloane hoped the boy would not be so foolish.

The more Sloane saw of his nephew, the more he liked him. He and David had engaged in a pleasant conversation the previous night at Lady Beltingham's rout, where Lady Hannah and her parents had also been in attendance. And Miss Hart.

He and Miss Hart had been civil to each other. She appeared to have conversed comfortably with other gentlemen. What might those men think if they knew she'd been parading near St James's Street?

She took too many risks. And she was brushing against elements of the underworld that could turn even nastier than they had already. The company of pimps and Paphians could become violent. And if she were on a quest of reformation, even merely the reformation of her maid, she was not likely to succeed. Once the underworld took hold, it was near impossible to escape. He ought to know.

He started towards his door, when her front door opened and she appeared. On Miss Hart's arm was an ancient-looking woman, all wrinkles and bones.

Miss Hart saw him immediately. 'Good morning to you, Mr Sloane.'

She looked as bright as the day's sunshine in a yellow dress and with a smile on her face.

He lifted his hat and bowed. 'Good morning.'

She continued in this friendly manner. 'Allow me to make you known to my grandmother.'

The frail lady looked as if she would crumble like some antiquarian artefact as she came down the steps and hobbled towards him, and he quickly raced down his and ran over to her to save her the exertion.

As if they were in the Prince Regent's drawing room, Miss Hart said, 'Grandmama, may I present Mr Sloane, who is to be our neighbour soon.'

Miss Hart's grandmother gave a toothy smile. 'Oh, how lovely to see you, my dear. Is it not fine weather today?'

Miss Hart continued. 'The dowager Lady Hart, sir.'

'A pleasure, my lady.' He bowed.

'Hmm?' Lady Hart she smiled again. 'It was so nice of you to call. You must do so again.' She looked up at Morgana. 'We are off to the shops.'

Miss Hart must have seen a look of bewilderment on his face because she responded with amusement. 'Yes, Grandmama. Off to the shops.' She leaned towards Sloane and whispered, 'We shall not make it further than the corner, you know.'

His brow cleared. The old lady must be a bit senile, that was it.

'Are you visiting your house, Mr Sloane?' Miss Hart asked. 'You will be pleased, I think. I've never seen such a marshalling of mops and rags.'

He could not help but return her smile. 'That is Mr Elliot's doing, no doubt. I'm afraid he approaches all tasks with great efficiency.' He gave her a careful look, so as not to miss her reaction. 'But I do not merely look at the house. I am taking residence at this moment.'

Miss Hart gave a small sound in the back of her throat, but quickly recovered her manners. 'How nice for you.'

He responded with a wink. 'I hope I shall be a tolerable neighbour.'

Two spots of pink appeared on her cheeks, putting Sloane in mind of how she might look flushed with passion. Such thoughts were not going to make living next to her easier.

Her grandmother twisted to look at a curricle that had passed by in the street. When she turned back towards Sloane, her eyes lit up. 'How delightful to have you call, dear. We are off to the shops.'

'Yes.' Miss Hart nodded shakily. 'We must be off.'

She and Lady Hart made slow progress. They had barely reached the pavement in front of the next house when Sloane called back to her. 'Miss Hart?'

Still holding her grandmother's arm, she looked over her shoulder. 'Yes?'

'May I be so bold as to inquire who lives with you?'

Her eyebrows twitched and she paused a moment too long before speaking. 'Lady Hart and her companion, Miss Moore.'

He continued. 'And who chaperons you?'

She maintained a perfectly bland expression. 'Why, my grandmother, of course.' Without waiting to see his response, she turned back and proceeded down the street with all the speed of a lame snail.

Sloane watched her with sinking dismay. Not only would he be living next to a single female about whom he harboured lecherous thoughts, he would be living next to an unchaperoned one.

There had been no invitations for that night, so Morgana was forced to remain at home. Ordinarily that posed no dif-

ficulty at all—she was perfectly capable of entertaining herself—but this night it was nearly impossible to refrain from
gazing out of the front window in the hope that she might
glimpse her new neighbour. Would he go out? Or would he
relish an evening at home in his new house?

And how long would it take for her to give him as little
mind as she did the Viscount and Viscountess on the other
side?

She had not yet seen him leave the premises, but the
thought of him walking around the rooms on the other side
of her wall was nearly as distracting as the window.

Her grandmother and Miss Moore had retired early, as
was their habit, so she was alone. She brought her mending
to the drawing room, but her eyes were too tired to focus on
the stitches in the flickering light. She picked up a book instead, but found it equally tiresome. She wandered to the
window and looked out. When she caught herself there, she
whirled about and determinedly marched away.

She settled at the pianoforte and played the music she
knew by heart. Morgana loved to play, loved the feeling that
the action of her fingers brought out the melodies. She did not
mind that her skills at the keyboard were passable at best. She
enjoyed the music anyway.

She played every piece of music she knew, from common
ballads to snatches of Mozart. Then she played them all over
again, but she remained restless. She rose and found herself
back at the window.

This time her vigil was at an end. She saw Sloane leave
his house and walk briskly down the street. Even though he
was no more than a shadow, she could not mistake that tall
frame, that gait so smooth and graceful, yet infused with masculine power. He soon disappeared into the darkness as if the
darkness were welcoming back a missing piece of itself.

She sighed. They had almost regained their friendly banter. It had been such a relief to converse pleasantly with him after their other recent cool encounters. In some ways it was easier to have him avoid her. But now that their relationship had regained some of its ease, she longed to be in his company again.

Voices sounded outside the drawing-room door, several female voices. There was a knock and Morgana swung around. 'Come in.'

The door opened only a crack, and Lucy poked her head in. 'Might I have a word with you, miss? If I am not disturbing you, I mean.'

Lucy actually wished to speak with her? This was puzzling behaviour indeed. 'Certainly, Lucy. Come in and sit down with me.'

Lucy lifted a plain mahogany chair from against the wall and moved it next to the sofa where Morgana had settled herself. Lucy perched primly on the edge of the seat.

The pretty maid finally spoke. 'Miss Hart, you remember how you said you would teach me to be a courtesan? And I would have a house and money of my own and pretty clothes?'

'I have not forgotten, Lucy. I have been trying to work out what to do next. Did you look through my *Ladies Monthly Museum* and read the article on comportment?'

Lucy nodded. 'Yes, miss, but—'

'I promise I shall discover how we may learn the other lessons we need.' Morgana held out a faint hope that she would have the opportunity to speak with Harriette Wilson. Miss Wilson could answer her prayers.

Lucy stood up suddenly. 'Miss, I've something I must tell you.'

Morgana's spirits plummeted, certain Lucy had decided to go to Mrs Rice after all. 'What is it?'

Lucy held up one finger, gesturing for Morgana to wait. She hurried to the door and opened it. She leaned halfway out of the room for a moment, then stepped aside. Three young women entered.

They stood in a line in front of Morgana. All were strangers to her. Two wore brightly coloured dresses. One showed revealing *décolletage,* the other wrapped a shawl around her. Morgana could not decipher the expressions on their faces. Wary? Eager? Defiant?

'Yes?' she asked cautiously.

Lucy joined the line. 'Miss Hart, these girls heard you talkin' to that Mrs Rice. The lady in the glove shop? They want to be courtesans. They want you to teach them.'

Morgana felt her eyes widen. 'But—'

Lucy gave her an imploring look. 'Please, miss. They said Mrs Rice is not a nice lady. They don't want to work for her no more. They want to be on their own, like you told me.'

What sort of Pandora's box had she opened?

One of the girls swiped a lock of red hair off her forehead. 'The shop ain't no good place to be, miss, begging your pardon for speaking. Mrs Rice, she makes us see as many customers as come. Sometimes we have to do as many as—'

Morgana's cheeks grew hot. 'Yes, I quite understand.'

The red-haired girl went on. 'We could do better on our own. Me and Mary, we talked about it, and, if you teach us how to be high-fliers, we'll be willin' to give you a portion of our money.'

'Oh!' Morgana knew her cheeks were flaming now. She stood. 'I think you misunderstood. I am not a…a procuress. I merely wanted something better for Lucy.'

'We want something better, too, miss,' the third girl said. She had raven black hair set off by skin so pale it was almost white, but her lips, perhaps tinted, were coloured rose. She gave a graceful toss of her neck. 'And we want it enough to pay you for it.'

'No.' Morgana shook her head. 'It is not possible—I cannot— It does not bear thinking of.'

'Excuse me, miss.' The girl covering herself with the shawl stepped forward. 'We do understand your hesitation. This must seem like an outrageous request on our part, but you are our only hope.'

Morgana was stunned. The girl spoke in cultivated tones. 'You sound…educated.'

She bowed her head. 'I have fallen on difficult times, miss.'

'Rose here and me may not be educated in books and all,' the red-haired one broke in. 'But we've had hard times, too, and the way I figure it, we're as deserving as some of those others that gets to be a fine gentleman's fancy-piece.'

The one with the shawl added, 'We have determined that it will be better to be under a gentleman's protection. If you are able to teach us how to achieve that, we would be grateful enough to pay you whatever you wish.'

'Not whatever she wishes, Mary,' her red-haired companion cried. 'Don't be daft. We have to save enough money to tell all the fellows they can go to the devil.'

'Don't use such language in front of Miss Hart!' Lucy broke in. 'I'm sorry I brought you here.'

Morgana held up a hand. 'Never mind, Lucy.' She gazed at all four of them. It was easy to see why the brothel wanted them. They were all pretty girls, with pretty figures, still in the bloom of youth. What might they look like a few years from now? Like…like the Portuguese girl, all used up and old before her time?

'Well, I'm sorry we came,' the girl shot back, 'because this lady's going to send us back, and I don't much fancy the beating old Rice's man is going to give us.'

A beating? Morgana turned away from them and walked over to the window where she'd so recently seen Sloane disappear into the night. She had not imagined beatings. She had merely pictured them climbing the stairs in the back of the glove shop and entering small bedchambers to await one man after another, night after night. Would she ever be able to look at herself in a mirror if she sent them back to that life?

'Nobody is going back,' Morgana said quietly.

Chapter Six

Two of the girls squealed and jumped up and down. The third sank into a chair. Morgana gestured for them all to sit.

'I cannot make any promises to you.' Morgana looked at each of them in turn. 'I have not been able to find a proper tutor'—an *improper* one, she meant—'but I can teach you to walk and talk and dress in a refined way. I can show you how to make economies and I can teach you the proper value of items.'

Their expressions were much more decipherable now. Desperation was gone from their faces.

Morgana went on. 'But there are things about pleasing men I do not know—'

'Oh, we know how to please men,' laughed the bold girl.

'Yes. Of course…' Morgana blinked, unable to hide her embarrassment. 'Well, then… Let me know who you are.'

The bold girl spoke first. 'My name is Katy Green. I'm from Derbyshire, at least I was until I came to London.'

She pointed to the dark-haired beauty, 'This is Rose O'Keefe. The new girl.'

'I am not really one of Mrs Rice's girls, miss.' Rose spoke

with a pleasing Irish lilt. 'I overheard these two talking. To be sure, says I, t'would be grand to come along.'

Rose was an enchanting vision of dark and light. In the proper clothes, she would cause heads to turn wherever she went. Her success as a courtesan seemed already a *fait accompli*.

Morgana gave an inward sigh. What sort of life was she offering the girl?

Better than Mrs Rice, she must remember.

'I am pleased to meet you, Miss Green and Miss O'Keefe.' She turned to the third girl. 'And you are?'

'Mary Phipps, miss.'

Morgana had a dozen questions on the tip of her tongue for this girl. What had happened to her? Why was she one of the girls in Mrs Rice's glove shop? How could someone, so like Morgana herself, be reduced to harlotry? But poor Mary's energy had been spent. Morgana would save her questions for later. There would be time enough. Mary and the others would be staying for a while.

'I am happy to meet you as well, Miss Phipps.'

Miss Phipps, looking ashamed, averted her eyes.

Katy gave her a kind, almost motherly look, although Mary was clearly the elder of the two. 'Mary is a bit quiet, miss. We'll have to liven her up. Men like spirit, I say.'

'Yes, of course.' Morgana cleared her throat. It would be a monumental task to transform quiet, subdued Mary Phipps into the likes of Harriette Wilson.

The enormity of transforming any of them into scandalous women who earned their livelihood by men's largesse descended upon Morgana like a sudden downpour. She mentally shook herself, thrusting away cowardice and determining to set herself to the tasks before her, one step at a time. That was how to battle self-doubt. Charge ahead. Perform the task. Save the deluge of emotions for later.

Was that how poor Mary survived? Did each of these girls set themselves to the task and suffer their emotions later?

Uncertainty came creeping back. Morgana curved her hand into a fist. Time to act. Worry could come after. She turned to Lucy. 'We must find places for everyone to sleep, Lucy. Is there room abovestairs?'

'We will manage, miss,' Lucy assured her.

'And tomorrow morning we must find other dresses. Plain ones. These will not do at all.'

'We must wear plain dresses?' Katy frowned.

'Yes, you must. In this neighbourhood, you must not attract any notice. I cannot tell you what trouble there would be if our…our courtesan school is discovered.'

'School?' laughed Katy. 'Fancy me going to school!'

'Please do not speak a word of it,' Morgana begged. Not only was the enormity of the task ahead threatening to engulf her, but the risks as well.

Lucy led them out of the drawing room, and Morgana rang for Cripps, who immediately presented himself.

'Cripps, we have three guests in the house.' She spoke in crisp tones. She knew she must think of some way to explain the girls' presence in the house, but that was a task she could put off for later.

His brows rose an infinitesimal distance. 'Very good, miss. Do you require me to rouse Mrs Cripps to make rooms ready?'

Morgana was equally uncertain of the housekeeper's opinion of their guests. 'That will not be necessary. Lucy will see to their lodging.'

His brows rose another notch. Lucy would have been the last of the household staff Cripps or his wife would have chosen for such a task. 'May I inform Mrs Cripps which rooms will be occupied?'

Morgana gave him what she hoped was a quelling look. 'We shall address such matters tomorrow.'

He blinked twice. 'As you desire, miss. How else may I serve you tonight?'

'I will not require anything else. Thank you, Cripps.'

The dignified butler bowed and left the room.

Morgana sank back on to the sofa. How would she explain all this to Cripps and his wife? And the other staff? And Miss Moore? She dropped her head into her hands. How could she explain the presence of these girls to respectable Miss Moore?

She sat erect again and lifted her chin. She would simply manage it. She must, because she would not be responsible for sending any of those girls to Mrs Rice, that horrid creature.

Morgana stood and resolutely walked out of the room and up the stairs to her bedchamber.

Sloane relaxed in the coffee room of White's, nursing a brandy and vaguely watching the other gentlemen. He wondered how many of them resented his ease and welcome here. He was a member and there was not a thing any of them could do about it, not even the Earl who had acknowledged him as a son. A legacy from a grandfather, a man with whom Sloane shared no blood ties, made it possible.

Years before, when the Old Club and the New Club merged into White's, the present Earl's father had arranged to have all his sons and grandsons and great-grandsons guaranteed membership for the next hundred years. The old man died before knowing that a rotten apple had appeared in the barrel.

As a young man Sloane had refused to set foot in White's. Anywhere his father was welcome, Sloane disdained, but now the wisdom of age prevailed.

If he was to take his place in society, he must appear where society gathered, and gentlemen of importance appeared at White's. This night he'd played a few sedate games of whist, careful to fold his cards before winning too much lest he be accused of fleecing the true sons of the *ton*.

In Sloane's darker days, his next meal had often depended on the turn of a card. The hungrier he became, the more skilfully he played, until he could count fairly well on living high as long as there was a nearby card game.

In fact, one marathon round of whist last autumn had deepened his pockets considerably. With such an abundance of riches, it dawned on him to change his game.

In these difficult economic times, wealth was gaining prominence over the elevation of one's birth. Soon nabobs and cits would amass enough wealth to buy all the power and influence his father's generation believed to be their birthright. Sloane, however, need not wait for such a day. Sloane had the status of birth, counterfeit though it was. He had more capital than his father. All he needed was a respectable reputation and nothing would stop how high he could rise.

He'd been scrupulous about his behaviour since making his appearance in the *beau monde*. All the *ton* knew of his past was mere rumour. If they had heard of some of the things he'd done to survive, or some he'd done in the service of his country, they would surely blackball him, but he'd given them nothing to remark upon these last months. What was more, he was in a fair way to contract a respectable marriage.

That thought did not conjure up an image of the delectable Lady Hannah. Rather, Morgana Hart flashed into his mind. Sloane frowned. Morgana Hart was unpredictable and much too apt to engage in ruinous escapades. Sloane could not afford to have her drag him down with her. He ought to avoid her.

Even though she lived next door.

Sloane took a sip, letting the brandy slide down his throat and warm his chest. Did her bedchamber share a wall with his? he wondered. Was she at this moment undressing for bed, perhaps sitting in a filmy shift, brushing her long silky hair? Sloane set his glass down on the table so sharply that some heads turned at the sound.

He must cease these rakish thoughts.

At that moment, three gentlemen entered the coffee room, one tall, but thin and slightly stoop-shouldered. Though this grey-haired man leaned on a cane, an aura of power still emanated from him. The two men with him were mere moons to this man's planet. He turned and caught sight of Sloane.

Sloane, glass in hand, met the man's eye and nodded.

His father, the Earl of Dorton, stood stock still.

Sloane knew what to expect, and the anticipation made him wish to laugh at the sheer predictability of it all. The Earl's gaze would gradually move away and he would turn his back, acting as if he had not even seen this unnatural son. He would do as he had done all of Sloane's life. Act as if Sloane did not exist.

Sloane was mistaken. The Earl marched directly towards him. Sloane's brother, Viscount Rawley, and his nephew, David, must have been equally surprised. They'd gaped open-mouthed at the Earl's destination.

Sloane stood, never straying from a direct gaze into his father's eyes. 'Good evening, sir.'

The Earl glared, but did not speak. Sloane's brother and nephew scrambled up behind. Keeping his eye on his father, Sloane turned the corner of his mouth up in the same insolent smile that in his boyhood used to earn him a hard slap across the face. His father's lips pursed in response.

'Would you care to sit down?' Sloane asked with an expansive gesture of his hand.

Without speaking, the Earl waved to his son and grandson to take seats. The Earl leaned heavily on his cane as he lowered himself into a chair. Sloane did not miss the effort. But the man who levelled a steely gaze directly at him was more like the one who used to strike terror in a young boy's heart.

No longer, however.

Sloane, with studied casualness, took a sip of his brandy, then asked, 'Shall I signal for more drinks?'

His father glared, his brother shifted uncomfortably and his nephew watched warily. Sloane took that as agreement and gestured for the server to bring more glasses. Sloane poured the brandy and handed each a glass.

He raised his drink in a toast. 'To this cosy family party.' None of them responded.

The Earl finally spoke. 'I want to know what your business is, boy, and I want to know now.'

Sloane gave an inward smile at the term 'boy.' He'd not been a boy since the age of ten, when this man made certain his eyes were wide open as to the circumstances of his conception. 'My business, sir?'

'You know what I mean.' He tapped his cane on the carpet. 'What are you scheming? I tell you, I'll not have you courting respectable young ladies and throwing your ill-gotten money around on respectable residences.' The Earl leaned forward. 'The word is out that you took Irwin for everything he's got. The man's all done up.'

'Irwin?' Sloane lifted a brow. Irwin had been the owner of the town house, the man who'd been desperate for cash. 'Your information is sadly amiss. I do believe my funds came to the man's rescue.'

David spoke up. 'That is true, Grandfather. Irwin lost a fortune at Madame Bisou's hazard table. Wasn't Uncle Cyprian at all.'

The Earl of Dorton wheeled on his grandson. 'And what do you know about that establishment?' He raised his voice. 'I'll not have you frittering away your allowance on cards and women. I can cut your monies in half, you know.'

Sloane felt a tremble inside, as if he were still the child who had so often received such a rebuke. 'Keep your voice down, sir.' He spoke with a low, steady tone. 'You make a spectacle of yourself.'

His father erupted. 'I make a spectacle of myself?' His voice grew louder.

Sloane leaned towards him across the table. 'Cease this at once, or leave this table.' Something in his eyes must have convinced the Earl, because the old man clamped his mouth shut.

Sloane leaned back and took a lazy sip of his brandy. 'That is better.'

The Earl looked about to explode. 'You are not welcome here, Cyprian,' he said through gritted teeth. 'Go back to whatever dung-heap you emerged from.'

Sloane's every muscle tensed. He'd not realised his father's barbs could still injure him. He'd be damned if he'd show it. 'As you have so graphically informed me, I was conceived upon and reared upon Dorton land, and I have no desire to return to it.'

'See here, Cyprian—' Rawley began, but Sloane quelled him with one glance.

'Good gracious,' cried David. 'Can we not converse in a civil manner? It would bring credit to us all if we presented the appearance of congenial relations.'

From the mouths of babes, thought Sloane.

David's rebuke had effect. Both the Earl and his son leaned back and sipped their drinks.

His father began again, in quieter tones. 'What are your

intentions toward the Cowdlin chit? Cowdlin's a friend of mine and I demand to know.'

Sloane bristled at his father demanding anything of him. He was about to retort in kind when he caught the pleading expression on his nephew's face.

He answered as mildly as he could contrive. 'I have made no offer for Lady Hannah at present, but Cowdlin will not oppose my suit. He approves of my fortune, if not of me.'

'Hmmph,' muttered the Earl. 'Then he is a bigger fool than I thought.'

'Oh, I am certain he is indeed,' agreed Sloane with equanimity.

The Earl of Dorton leaned forward again. 'You do not belong here, Cyprian. You do not belong among the quality. Go back to whatever cellar or…or gaming hell you came from, and leave decent people alone.'

'Grandfather!' David whispered in a shocked tone.

Sloane felt his body flinch, just as it used to when he was a boy. 'I do belong here, *Father*,' he said coolly. '*You* gave me the right when you acknowledged me as your son. As your son, I am invited to all the society events. I have vouchers for Almack's and a box at the opera. As your father's grandson, I am a member of White's. I have you to thank for all this, *Father*.'

For a moment his father looked like an old man, but the moment was fleeting.

When he stood, he looked as formidable as ever. 'I will not have you here, boy, do you hear me?' His voice was equally as strong. 'I will not have you here.'

With another flick of his fingers, the Earl signalled his son and grandson to leave with him. Sloane stood as well, making sure his father felt his eyes boring into him. As all three walked away, the Earl in the lead, David turned back and gave Sloane a look of sympathy.

* * *

'They are gone?' Mrs Rice looked up from her desk in a room above her glove shop.

The man, solid and stocky, brushed off the sleeves of his brown coat. 'We have searched all the rooms and they are nowhere to be found.'

'I sent them to the shops. Did no one see them return?' Mrs Rice laid down her quill pen, displeasure seeping into her voice.

'No one, ma'am.' He shifted from one foot to the other. 'The other girls think they ran off. There's some belongings missing.'

'Things of mine?' Her voice rose. 'I will not tolerate it if they have stolen from me.'

'Worthless trinkets, ma'am,' he responded. 'Their own trifles, the girls say.'

Mrs Rice stared vacantly. 'It does sound like they have run away.' She waved her hand at him dismissively. 'Well, search for them, Trigg. Bring them back. I will not have my girls coming and going at a whim. It vexes me.'

'As you wish, ma'am.' He turned and left.

Mrs Rice slammed her palm down on the desk and rose from her seat. With two girls short, she might have to turn men away this night. That was not good for business. She could kick herself for not having moved faster to bring that maid into the house before her mistress came calling. The termagant. That one had enough tongue for two sets of teeth, with all her talk about needing a tutor. A tutor for what?

At first Mrs Rice thought the lady was asking for lessons on how to set up a molly shop of her own, but that was too ridiculous for words. She'd since decided that a long Meg like that one probably wanted to learn how to get a man for herself.

It was a good thing, because she would not have made a good madam or a good molly. She'd talk the gentlemen right off the bed to run screaming down the street.

Mrs Rice gave a little laugh, the sound echoing off the walls of the room. Still, it would have been a lark indeed to see a lady of that one's ilk making her living on her back.

Mrs Rice wiped her eyes as her laughter subsided. She'd have another stab at the maid, if she got the chance, if Trigg could discover where she was employed.

And when she got those other girls back, she'd give them such a flogging they would never dare leave, at least not until they were too worn out to be of any use.

Chapter Seven

When Morgana woke the next morning, it seemed the very air was charged, as if the house were inside a huge electrifying machine, but Morgana knew any sparks that flew would be due to her own decisions. The porcelain clock on her bureau chimed six times. Morgana threw off the covers and was halfway dressed when Amy crept in, expecting merely to tend the fire.

Did Amy know of their guests? She must, but the girl did not reveal it. She did not even remark upon Morgana rising so early. Morgana meant to breakfast with her grandmother and Miss Moore, who always rose at dawn.

After breakfast she begged Miss Moore to take a walk with her. Miss Moore settled her grandmother in her sitting room with her maid for company, and the two ladies walked the short distance to the park, one of the footmen providing a discreet escort.

'Goodness, it is chilly this morning,' said Miss Moore as they crossed the park. 'It is fortunate Lady Hart did not come with us. It would be bad for her lungs.'

'Yes, indeed,' agreed Morgana, uncertain how to begin.

She'd tossed and turned all night, even rising once and wandering to the window at the exact moment Sloane returned to his house. Realising he would be undressing and climbing into a bed so close by had not helped her fall back asleep. But those wakeful hours did yield the semblance of a plan.

Morgana had decided that she needed to speak to Miss Moore before Mr and Mrs Cripps or any of the other servants. She had a reasonable expectation that generous salary increases would ensure the servants' co-operation and silence. But if prim Miss Moore could not be persuaded to go along with this scheme, Morgana did not see how she could proceed.

Morgana could not force a respectable lady like Miss Moore to endure a situation abhorrent to her. And she could not send Miss Moore away. With Miss Moore went her grandmother. Without her grandmother, Morgana would be forced to go to her Aunt Winnie's house, and the girls, Lucy too, would have nowhere to go except to Mrs Rice.

Morgana glanced back at the footman, who, enjoying the fine morning air, seemed uninterested in the conversation between the two ladies. Still, she spoke quietly so he could not overhear. 'I must talk to you, Miss Moore.'

Miss Moore gave her a fond smile. 'Is it about the three young ladies who are staying in the house?'

'You know about them?' Morgana glanced at her in dismay.

'Oh, yes.' Miss Moore nodded. 'Dilly told us first thing that there were three new girls. How did she put it?' Miss Moore paused, but there was a twinkle in her eye. 'The likes of which she'd never seen.'

Morgana inwardly groaned. Dilly, her grandmother's lady's maid, was an old retainer, nearly as old as her grandmother.

'Oh, I suppose everyone knows.' Morgana gave a helpless shrug. 'But I suspect they do not know the whole, and that is what I must tell you…'

Morgana explained to Miss Moore as well as she could. She withheld her plan to seek Harriette Wilson's assistance as a bit too much information, emphasising instead that the girls, Lucy included, would be lost to a terrible life unless Morgana helped them.

Miss Moore listened with an unremitting frown on her face that caused Morgana's spirits to sink. They had come to the banks of the Serpentine, where two graceful-necked swans glided through the water.

Morgana stole a glance at the lady's companion in her dark grey dress that matched the hair peeping out from her black bonnet. Miss Moore followed the swans with her eyes, but made no comment on the shocking tale.

Morgana blurted out, 'Oh, I know it is scandalous, and I know you must be wondering if I belong in Bedlam, but, please, Miss Moore, say something!'

Miss Moore continued watching the swans. 'I was a girl once, Miss Hart. As hard as that might be for you to believe.'

'Of course.' Morgana had no idea where this was leading.

'There were soldiers billeted in my town when I was young and green and foolish. When they sailed to the Colonies, I discovered I was with child. I was only eighteen.'

Lucy's age, Morgana thought.

'My parents would have nothing to do with me. They sent me away. If it had not been for your grandmother taking pity on me, I do not know what I should have done. She took care of me and made me her companion.'

Morgana's heart had thoroughly melted. 'What happened to your baby?'

Miss Moore's eyes filled with tears. 'I…I had had very little to eat. Sometimes I didn't have a roof over my head. Lady Hart found me at my lowest. She did what she could do, but the baby did not survive his birth.'

Morgana reached over and grasped the older woman's hand. 'I am so sorry.'

Miss Moore gave an embarrassed smile and blinked her tears away. 'It was a long time ago, but I well know what those girls of yours are facing. If you can give them a better life, a way to survive on their own, I shall help you!'

Morgana impulsively wrapped Miss Moore in a hug, blinking away tears of her own. 'I promise you, Miss Moore, you shall not regret it. You shall have a pension for life, I guarantee it!'

Miss Moore gave a little laugh. 'Oh, your grandmother arranged that years ago, before she became…feeble.'

Morgana wished she could have known the woman her grandmother had been. At this moment she was fiercely proud to be her granddaughter.

With the footman still oblivious, Morgana and Miss Moore walked back, arm in arm, quietly hatching plans of how to transform a maid, a harlot and a very ordinary girl into sirens of Greek legend. Rose O'Keefe, Morgana explained, would have no difficulty.

Sloane saw the two women from a distance. There was no mistaking Miss Hart's graceful posture and purposeful stride. He did not think he knew the other lady, but, if he kept to his course, his trajectory would put him on their path.

For a brief moment he considered turning the corner to avoid them, but he did not. He had little to do that morning. He had little to do almost every morning, thanks to the very efficient Mr Elliot. And Sloane was a man easily bored. At least Miss Hart would provide a diversion. She never bored him.

The woman who accompanied her was older than she and no one he recognised. When they came close enough, Miss Hart met his eye with a friendly smile. Sloane quickened his step.

'Good morning, Mr Sloane.' She was in high colour and he sensed an air of excitement about her, as if she were about to explode with good news.

Glowing as she did like a sparkling morning sun brightened his own mood—as well as bringing some baser senses to life. He touched his hand to his hat. 'Miss Hart.'

She introduced the lady with her as Miss Moore, her grandmother's companion. Miss Moore's face was nearly as flushed with excitement as Miss Hart's.

The hairs on the back of his neck rose. She was up to something. He narrowed his eyes at her. 'What are you about, Miss Hart?'

She responded with great exuberance. 'We have had a delightful morning walk in the park.'

He glanced from one lady to the other. 'That is all?'

Miss Moore averted her gaze and hid a smile. Miss Hart fluttered her lashes at him, all innocence. 'That is all,' she said brightly.

Fustian, he said to himself.

'Do you attend the *musicale* this evening, Mr Sloane?' she asked.

It was the sort of chitchat that made for conversation among the Mayfair set, but Sloane was not fooled. She was changing the subject.

He tilted his head and gave her a slow smile. 'You presume I was invited?'

'Oh.' Her cheeks gained even more colour than the brisk morning air had given them. 'I confess I did presume. It was bad of me to ask, I know. It smacks of lording it over another person who might not have received an invitation. I dislike that above all things—'

He laughed. 'Enough, Miss Hart. I am among those whose presence is requested.'

Her eyes danced with merriment. 'I did not know you were a jester, Mr Sloane.'

Her eyes, sparkling like the finest topaz, entrapped him. It took a moment for him to respond. 'I am many things, Miss Hart.'

She lowered her lashes, before meeting his gaze again. 'Well! I suppose we must not detain you, must we? I do hope you have a good day.'

Miss Moore, her smile softening, regarded him with a curious look. 'I am pleased to have met you, Mr Sloane. Good day to you.'

He felt suddenly reluctant to leave them, to leave the circle of sunshine that was Morgana Hart.

'Good day, ladies.' Sloane bowed to them both and proceeded on his way, resisting the impulse to look back.

Morgana, feeling breathless, set off at such a brisk pace that she had Miss Moore puffing to keep up. She slowed.

'What a handsome gentleman,' Miss Moore managed between breaths.

'Do you think so?' Morgana said stiffly. She laughed and entwined her arm in Miss Moore's again. 'Yes, indeed. He is a very handsome man. More like a Spanish guerrilla than an Englishman, do you not think?' And every bit as dangerous—to her heart.

Miss Moore chuckled. 'I do not have any notion what a Spanish guerrilla looks like.'

'Exactly like Mr Sloane!' Morgana laughed again, but her laugh soon subsided. 'He may be handsome, but he is also the gentleman Lady Hannah has her eye upon. I suspect he will offer for her soon.'

'Lady Hannah and such a man?' Miss Moore exclaimed. 'I cannot credit it.'

'Just so. She is the type all gentlemen want, you know.'

Much to Morgana's mortification, Miss Moore gave her a sympathetic glance. Morgana wanted to protest that she had no marriage aspirations. It was not necessary to feel pity for her.

Still, when she thought of the tall, exciting, valiant Mr Sloane, she wished, as she had never wished before, that she were a woman he would look upon to marry.

By the time they entered the house, Morgana had shaken off such nonsense. Why should Mr Sloane desire her for a wife when other men did not? It was nonsensical.

She and Miss Moore walked up the stairs to Lady Hart's sitting room, and found the elderly woman rocking in her chair, smiling pleasantly, while Dilly worked on some mending.

'You need not stay, Dilly,' Miss Moore said. 'I am sure you have much to do.'

'Very good, miss.' Dilly patted Lady Hart's hand before she walked out of the room.

Miss Moore sat in the seat Dilly vacated. 'What will you tell the servants, dear?'

Morgana remained standing, too restless to sit. 'I thought to tell Mr and Mrs Cripps exactly what I am about, and seek their advice as to the rest of the household.'

Miss Moore shook her head. 'Oh, no. No, indeed. I do not advise it.'

'Why not?'

Miss Moore's expression took on the same haunted look as when she recounted the sad events of her life. 'People do not take kindly to women who have lost respectability. If the household staff know who you have taken under your wing, they will fear the loss of their own reputations. Believe me, Morgana, they will leave your employ and they will talk to their next employers. You will be ruined.'

Morgana folded her arms across her chest and wandered to the window to look out on the garden. Lucy knelt among the flowers, pulling at weeds. She did not mind keeping her affairs private from prying eyes and gossips, but it seemed a folly to try to hide anything from the servants. They always knew whatever went on. Better to be forthright and hope for the best.

She watched Lucy, from this distance, looking so small and vulnerable. She might gamble her own future on the good-will of those in her employ, but she had no right to risk Lucy's or the other girls.

She turned to Miss Moore. 'What shall we tell them, then?'

'We shall tell them the girls are my nieces, come to London to learn town manners so that they might be employed.'

'That does not explain Lucy,' Morgana reminded her.

Miss Moore was undaunted. 'Everyone can see Lucy is unhappy. We shall tell them you have generously included her in the lessons, so that she might seek more compatible employment.'

Morgana gave Miss Moore a sceptical look. The story was preposterous. She took a deep breath. It would nevertheless afford the servants some protection, should the whole business fall apart. They could honestly say their mistress lied to them.

A few minutes later, with Miss Moore at her side, Morgana summoned Mr and Mrs Cripps. The butler and house-keeper listened to the concocted story with impassive expressions. Morgana had the sinking feeling they believed not a word of the unlikely tale. They did not even blink when she added that all the staff would receive bonuses because of the extra work entailed in having three more household guests.

* * *

By late morning, Cook, the footmen and maids were all given the false story. Morgana prayed the deception would hold.

She gathered her girls in the library where they could not be glimpsed from the street. Lucy had found dresses for them, and Morgana supposed she would need to concoct another story to explain why they had not arrived with luggage of their own. She bit her lip in dismay at the mounting lies.

At least the girls' appearance did not now give them away. They appeared as ordinary girls, ones who might indeed be nieces of Miss Moore. Except for Rose, who could not look ordinary if she tried, and who spoke with an Irish lilt besides.

Miss Moore walked into the room, Lady Hart leaning on her arm. 'Miss Hart, I hope you do not mind. But I should like to help.'

It had been enough that Miss Moore had not packed up and left London. Morgana had never expected her assistance. 'But what of Grandmama?'

'Allow her to sit among us. She will enjoy the liveliness, you know. It will be good for her.' Miss Moore helped Lady Hart into a chair.

Why not? thought Morgana. There was no risk her grandmother would remember enough to expose the truth.

'I should like to teach comportment and manners and proper speech,' Miss Moore said.

'I can teach music,' Rose chimed in. 'My father is a musician, and I have been trained on harp and pianoforte as well as voice.'

Mary Phipps looked up shyly. 'I...I used to be a governess. I can teach all manner of things.'

'That is splendid, Miss Phipps.' Morgana smiled at her. 'Perhaps you can look through the books here and find something useful.'

Katy laughed. 'Well, there is only one thing I know, but I can teach it, all right.' She gave a bawdy glance around the room. 'Might need one of those handsome footmen to help me.'

Miss Moore, who was a good deal shorter than the red-haired young woman, still effectively looked down her nose at her. 'Miss Green,' she said in clipped tones, 'you will behave like a lady here in this house. You aspire to be a high-flyer, attracting the best and the richest. To do so you cannot act like common Haymarket ware. You must not fraternise with the footmen. Do you understand?'

Oh, yes. Miss Moore would be an asset indeed.

Katy looked down at her lap, but with a hint of rebellion in her eye. 'Yes, ma'am.'

'It is Miss Moore, dear,' she said gently.

'Yes, miss,' Katy corrected herself.

Lucy hung her head. 'There's nothin' I can teach. I'll just be a burden on everyone.'

Morgana walked over and put a hand on Lucy's shoulder. 'You shall be in charge of supplies, Lucy. You managed to find everyone a proper dress and a bed to sleep in. In fact, I will prevail upon you to produce a trunk to be delivered, the nieces' luggage. Do you think you can contrive such a thing?'

Lucy gave a surprised glance, then wrinkled her brow. It took several seconds, but she finally responded. 'I could send to home for some of Amy's and my old clothes. Would that do?'

'That is an excellent idea.' Morgana had forgotten about her lady's maid. No matter what Miss Moore thought, Morgana simply must tell Amy the truth, though what the girl would say about it, she could only guess.

The day flew by with all of them talking and showing off their skills. When it was time for dinner Morgana led them to the main dining room. Lucy held back, insisting she ought not to eat there. Morgana acquiesced. There would be time enough to bring her abovestairs. To do so now would merely whip up the servants' curiosity.

The dinner was the most pleasant Morgana had passed in the house to date. When Mr Cripps and the footmen left the room, Morgana and Miss Moore drew the girls into the conversation, learning more about their lives. Rose talked of growing up in Ireland and of recently coming to London. Mary spoke of being the daughter of a country vicar. When he died, she'd become a governess. She did not disclose how she wound up at Mrs Rice's house. Katy, whose table manners needed the most improving, said she'd left Derbyshire to make her fortune in London and she'd go to the devil before she'd return there. Morgana's grandmother cheerfully picked at her food and smiled at them all. At meal's end, Morgana left the table in high spirits, confident that all would go well.

She retired to her room to dress for the *musicale*. As Amy worked on another braided style for her hair, Morgana told her the truth about the plan.

'Do tell me what you think of this business, Amy. Tell me if you think I've done right by your sister.'

Amy frowned as she concentrated on sticking hairpins in securely. 'It is not *right,* miss. I cannot say 'tis right, because it is not, but Lucy was ready to run off again, I know she was.' She gave Morgana a quick glance in the mirror. 'You stopped her from doing that. Going with one of those procuring fellows, I mean.'

Amy's point did not miss the mark. Morgana knew the better course was to convince Lucy and the others to lead moral lives, but, once fallen, could they rise again? Lucy had convinced her she could not.

Morgana watched Amy concentrate on her hair. She set her chin in determination. This *was* the only chance for Lucy. The only chance for all of the girls to change their lives.

Sloane surveyed the room where the guests to Lady Sedford's *musicale* loitered in groups, waiting for the latecomers to be announced and the programme to begin. Across the room stood his brother, Lord Rawley, who, without cutting him directly, was at least pretending he had not seen him. David gave him a friendly nod. At least the Earl was not present, although Sloane would have experienced a smug satisfaction if his father had witnessed him mingling successfully with Lady Sedford's set.

'Lord and Lady Cowdlin. Lady Hannah. Miss Hart,' the butler announced.

Sloane turned to watch them enter and greet the host and hostess. Lady Hannah looked as delectable as a dish of cream and strawberries in a white gauzy gown decorated with red ribbon. Her cousin wore a much plainer gown, one done up in gold fabric that nearly matched her eyes and glistened under the candlelight.

Averting his head so as not to be so obviously gaping, Sloane observed Lord and Lady Cowdlin stop to converse with friends. Lady Hannah seized her cousin's arm and propelled them both forward. Hannah glanced in Sloane's direction, pretended to glance away, whispered something to her cousin, and led her gracefully across the room, making it appear as if it were mere chance that they came to where he stood.

'Good evening, Lady Hannah, Miss Hart.' He bowed.

'How nice to see you here, Mr Sloane.' Lady Hannah

smiled up at him, showing her white, even teeth. 'You must sit with us. I insist upon it.'

Miss Hart also smiled, but her smile seemed distant, almost sad.

He turned his attention to Lady Hannah. 'Nothing would delight me more, my lady, but it might hint at partiality. I would not wish to make you the topic of gossip.' If Sloane were perceived to favour Lady Hannah to the exclusion of other eligible young ladies, he would be forced to make her an offer. He did not wish to be forced into anything.

A fleeting look of disappointment crossed Lady Hannah's face. She quickly recovered. 'I have it. You shall sit next to Morgana and that will seem quite unexceptionable.'

He opened his mouth to reply, but her attention had already flitted away.

'Oh, look,' she cried. 'Here comes your nephew, Mr Sloane. Perhaps he will join us as well.'

When the programme was about to begin, Hannah hurried them all in, and arranged the seating to her satisfaction. At one end sat Lord and Lady Cowdlin, then David, Hannah, Morgana, and Sloane. David made polite conversation with Lady Cowdlin, while Hannah looked about the crowd, waving to friends. Miss Hart studied her programme.

'Do you enjoy music, Miss Hart?' Sloane asked her.

She gave him a serious expression. 'You must not consider yourself obliged to make polite conversation, Mr Sloane.'

His brow furrowed. 'Are we back to not speaking, Miss Hart?'

Her face relaxed. 'Oh, no. I did not mean that. Goodness! I must have sounded cross. I am vexed at my cousin, not you. She treats me as if I were a doll to be moved about at whim.'

His lips twitched. He leaned closer to her. 'Confess, Miss Hart. You merely dislike being told what to do.'

She smiled. 'You have the right of it, Mr Sloane. It is one of my abiding faults.'

'Mine as well,' he admitted. 'Let us begin again. Do you like music, Miss Hart?'

Her ginger eyes came alive with expression. 'I do like it excessively, sir.'

'Do you play?'

She rolled her eyes, very unladylike, but charming none the less. 'Badly, therefore, never in company, but I do love to bash away for hours on my pianoforte.'

'Hmm.' He pretended to study the programme. 'I wonder how thick the walls are between our houses.'

She laughed softly. When he glanced at her again her eyes sparkled. 'And you, Mr Sloane, do you play?'

He could not help himself. He gave her a wicked grin. 'Not music, Miss Hart, but I play at other things very well.'

He watched, fascinated, as her pupils grew larger. Her smile changed from mirthful to inscrutable. Perhaps he'd gone too far. Reverted to his rakish ways. But she did have that effect on him. He averted his gaze.

Morgana looked away as well, resisting the impulse to fan herself. Had he been flirting with her? If so, it felt delightful. Very stimulating. She hoped her cheeks were not as flaming red as they felt.

She was glad Sloane did not dislike sitting next to her, though she still had no doubt he would rather be next to Hannah. Hannah had her head together with the younger Mr Sloane, who was obviously as captivated by her as his uncle.

It did not matter, Morgana assured herself, that Hannah drew the attention of men so easily. She was glad someone distracted Hannah from her chief prey. Morgana needed this opportunity to speak to Sloane. She opened her mouth again, but there was a signal that the music was about to begin.

Lady Sedford had achieved the coup of engaging Camporese for the evening. When the soprano stepped out in front of the musicians, she looked much taller and more slender than she'd appeared on stage at the King's Theatre, perhaps even as tall as Morgana herself.

Camporese reprised her solos from *Penelope,* to much applause. Morgana noticed that Hannah attended more to the guests than the music. Her uncle, quite the opposite, dozed, his chin drooping to his chest. Morgana smiled at that and glanced at Sloane, who caught her look and held it a moment before turning his eyes back to the soprano. The contact had been fleeting, but it somehow warmed Morgana all over. She did fan herself this time.

When Camporese finished her part of the programme, the room erupted into applause and shouts of 'Bravo' and the soprano gave a deep curtsy. Lady Sedford announced a brief interval and everyone left their seats to mingle. Morgana watched Sloane converse with Hannah and his nephew.

A gentleman and lady approached her. Morgana recognised them as Sloane's brother and sister-in-law, Lord and Lady Rawley. Her aunt presented her to them.

Lady Rawley gave her an inquisitive look. 'I see you are acquainted with Cyprian, Miss Hart.'

Remembering that Sloane was estranged from his family, Morgana regarded the woman with some interest. 'I am, ma'am.'

'What do you know of him, my dear?' Lady Rawley's question was phrased in ominous tones.

Morgana immediately leapt to Sloane's defence, though the notion he would need her protection was ludicrous. 'He is often in the company of my aunt's family. He is acceptable to them, and that is all I need know.'

Lady Rawley leaned in closer. 'My husband says there is

more to it, Miss Hart. Cyprian has the most shocking reputation. I implore you to beware of it and inform your cousin
before she makes a terrible mistake.'

Morgana's indignation caught fire. How dare this woman
presume to spread tales of Sloane to someone she had met not
one minute before? She would not stand for it!

She favoured Lady Rawley with her most innocent look.
'I fear Lady Hannah will demand the details before giving any
credence to my words. Would you please tell me exactly what
Mr Sloane had done to earn his shocking reputation?'

'Why…why he is a womaniser, for one thing,' the lady
responded.

'Indeed?' Morgana feigned interest. 'With whom has he
been linked? I am sure my cousin will wish to hear names.'

'I do not precisely know,' admitted Lady Rawley. 'But I
have it on good authority—'

'Oh, Hannah will not credit that at all, I'm afraid.' Morgana feigned being thoughtful. 'But I suspect there are many
gentlemen who claim success with the ladies. That would not
be enough to concern Hannah. What else has Mr Sloane
done?'

'I do not know, but it was very bad,' Lady Rawley said with
spirit. 'Something during the war, I think.'

Morgana pretended to consider this. 'I believe I must inform my uncle of this shocking information. He is responsible for Hannah, you know.'

'I am sure your uncle knows,' admitted the lady. 'Everyone knows.'

Morgana smiled. 'Then it must be a mere hum, because
Mr Sloane is invited everywhere. He even has vouchers for
Almack's.' She acted as if she were just struck by a thought.
'I suppose I could alert Lady Sefton or Lady Castlereagh. I
shall tell them you have informed me.'

Lady Rawley paled. 'No, no, do not do that. I would not trouble them. I am sure if Cyprian has vouchers, it must be quite all right.'

'Yes.' Morgana nodded firmly. 'I am certain such rumours are none of our affair.'

The guests began returning to their seats for the second half of the programme, and Morgana had an excuse to escape Lady Rawley.

When she again took her seat next to Sloane, he said, 'I see you met Lord and Lady Rawley.'

'Oh, yes,' she said brightly. 'Charming woman. She could not say enough about you.'

He laughed, that deep sound that seemed to resonate inside her like the bass notes of the music. 'I hope you defended my honour, Miss Hart.'

She looked him directly in the eyes. 'I did.'

Hannah leaned over her to ask Sloane something about the music. Soon the second half commenced, several selections from Haydn, guaranteed to please everyone.

It was not until the supper after the performance that Morgana found an opportunity to speak with Sloane again. He had not remained with their party for the meal, but joined some others, to Hannah's complete dismay. Morgana noticed him walk over to the buffet table to fill his plate and so joined him.

'May I assist you, Miss Hart?' he asked politely.

'How kind of you.' She seized this chance, keeping her tone casual. 'I have been meaning to ask you, Mr Sloane. There is a service you might do for me, if you would be so good.'

He cast her a suspicious look. 'What is it?'

'Nothing of consequence,' she assured him. 'I wish to contact Harriette Wilson, and I wondered if you might give me her direction so that I might pen her a letter.'

'Harriette Wilson?' His voice barely managed to remain a whisper. He moved closer to her and put a small round potato on her plate. 'Why the devil do you want to correspond with her?'

'Oh,' she said lightly, 'that need not concern you. I only need to discover where she resides, and because you are *acquainted* with her, I thought you would help me.'

'What are you up to, Miss Hart? Does this have anything to do with that infernal glove shop?' he asked in a fierce whisper.

'No,' she said, pointing to a small sausage, and again not entirely telling the truth. 'I wish you might forget that episode.'

'And the scrap in the park? And what else? I do not need to be involved in your schemes, Miss Hart.' He pointed to a parsnip and she shook her head.

'Then I am sorry I troubled you. I thank you for providing my meal.' She reached for the plate.

He did not let go. 'I will carry it for you.'

They walked across the room, both with stiff expressions on their faces. When Hannah spied Sloane, she insisted he join them, sitting him next to her, of course. He looked distracted and annoyed, even as he listened to Hannah's chatter.

Morgana, blood still boiling at his scold, could barely muster a word of conversation with her aunt, whose favourite topic of the moment was how splendid Mr Sloane was, and how kind he'd been to attend to her dinner. On the other side, her cousin Varney mumbled to her about how he did not care if Sloane was worth more than ten thousand a year, he did not like him paying his addresses to Hannah.

Lady Cowdlin leaned over both Morgana and Varney to speak to the Poltrops. A moment later she insisted to Sloane that he share their carriage after the musicale.

* * *

When the party had ended, Morgana stood at Sloane's side while they waited for the line of carriages to move.

Sloane pretended not to notice as Morgana tapped her foot impatiently. True, he was also tired of the wait, and Hannah's constant chatter had worn very thin. He could have walked home twice already and the carriage was not yet in sight.

What the devil was Morgana up to this time? He swore it must have to do with that female Lucy. Had not the altercation in the park shown her how dangerous the dissolute world could be? Harriette Wilson, indeed. Harriette was just the sort who would spread in every gentleman's ear that Cyprian Sloane's acquaintance Miss Hart had corresponded with her. He would be blamed for whatever mischief Morgana Hart was plotting.

The carriage finally pulled up. Even though he was thoroughly vexed with her, Sloane could not help but relish the feel of her hand in his as he assisted her into the carriage. He took the seat next to her, her perfume filling his nostrils, the heat of her body warming him. She sat stiffly and turned her head to look out of the window into the dark night.

When the carriage arrived at Culross Street and goodnights were said, Sloane helped Miss Hart from the vehicle. The coachman drove off and Sloane walked her to her door.

When she reached for her door knocker, he stilled her hand. 'Not so hasty, Miss Hart. I would speak with you first.'

Chapter Eight

Sloane doused the rush light, giving her time to enter her house if she chose. She did not. The darkness afforded some protection from passers-by, though it also gave the illusion of intimacy, as if a blanket wrapped around them both.

He stood close to her. The night breeze stirred a lock of her hair that had come loose from its pins. He almost swept it back into place.

He forced himself to get to the point. 'Tell me why you wish to correspond with Harriette Wilson.'

She did not flinch from him, but remained still, face up-turned to his. 'I seek some information from her.'

He disliked her evasion. 'What information?'

'That, sir, is private.' He could almost see her chin set in stubbornness. She turned to her door.

He grabbed her arms. 'I have a nose for trouble, Miss Hart, and I smell it now.' But what he really smelled was the exotic spice and floral scent she wore. 'I demand to know what mischief you are in this time.'

She did not pull away from his grip. 'I assure you, it is no mischief,' she said softly.

'You are flirting with a dangerous world, Miss Hart.' He leaned closer to make her heed his words. 'The glove shop may be respectable by day, but you can be sure it is not respectable at night.'

'I know this.' Her voice was low. It put him in mind of dark bedchambers rather than dark entryways. 'You need not worry.'

But he was worried. He told himself his only interest was avoiding blame for whatever her scheme was this time. He told himself he rued the day he had purchased property next to hers.

But, at the same time, she seemed pliant under his grasp. Her femininity was an intoxicating lure. It had been long since he'd tasted a woman's lips, or held a woman against him. Morgana Hart felt wonderful in his arms. He leaned closer and she rose on tiptoe. She placed her palms against his chest, her touch soft, but it filled him with heat. He wanted to slide his hands behind her and press her to his groin, to ease the ache that increased with each sweet breath that cooled his cheeks.

His arm trembled as he set her away from him, then released her. He sounded her knocker and stepped away, waiting until the door opened and she disappeared inside. She did not look back and he made his way slowly to his own door.

Morgana hesitated only slightly as she stepped into the hall. She greeted Cripps as if nothing had happened, but inside she felt altered, as if Sloane had rearranged all her organs. He must have removed one of them, because she was aware of needing…something.

She sounded very normal when she spoke to Cripps about closing up the house for the night. She even calmly ascended the stairs.

But once out of her butler's sight, she ran to the door of her bedchamber. She felt like dancing—or weeping—she did not know which.

Amy waited in her bedchamber to help her undress.

'Did you have a nice evening, Miss Hart?' the maid asked as Morgana removed her gloves, resisting the impulse to stare at the fingers that had caressed his chest.

'Very nice,' she replied. She did not wish to talk. She did not want anything to break the spell of his touch, the nearness of his lips.

Morgana undressed as quickly as Amy's assistance would allow, but she was eager for the maid to leave so she could think about him holding her in his arms.

What did it mean that he'd held her so close? Why had he released her? Why, oh, why had he not kissed her?

Amy jabbered as usual, while removing Morgana's hairpins and loosening the plaits so her hair could be brushed. Morgana watched herself in the mirror, amazed that she still looked the same.

Soon enough she was tucked under her covers, and Amy had closed the door behind her. Morgana hugged a pillow, rubbing her cheek on the soft fabric, still feeling his hands gripping her arms, still filled with the clean masculine scent of him.

She squeezed her eyes closed as tightly as she could and rolled over.

He had pushed her away, after all. He did not want her. He wanted Hannah. Young, vibrant, beautiful Hannah.

Sloane melted into the darkness, standing in the shadows as she hurried through the doorway and out of sight. He stood in the darkness a long time, hoping the blood would stop surging through his veins.

He'd wanted her, wanted her like the very devil, like the rake he was. A second later and he would have tasted those lips, felt her soft body against his hard one—his much too hard one.

Instead of reaching for the doorknob, Sloane spun around and strode down the walk to the street. A brisk walk would cool his loins.

He made his way through Mayfair, in the general direction of Bond Street, caring not how far he walked. The night welcomed him like an old friend, and soon his step became lighter, quieter, smoother. He had almost forgotten this sensation, of moving through the darkness unseen, as if he were part of it. His agitation eased as the familiar role overtook him.

Slipping through the darkness, Sloane avoided St James's Street, where the gentlemen's clubs still spewed members on to the street. Sloane might, like them, pass some time at White's, even gamble a little, but he had no desire to break the spell the night had created.

St James's and streets nearby were nearly as busy as day, though most of the night people sought pleasures best hidden in darkness. Sloane thought about entering one of the gaming hells that attracted gambling of a more dangerous sort than the respectable White's Club, but the urge to test his skills in those deep waters had fled. Of course, there were establishments where he might slake the primal urges Morgana Hart had awoken, but Sloane, no matter what his reputation, had always avoided that sort of debauchery. If he wanted a woman, he could find a willing one without having to pay for her services.

The notion that it would be an easy matter to make Morgana willing quickened his step. He'd come very close to doing that very thing when he'd held her in his arms. No matter her birth and respectability, she had a wild nature underneath, one he could so easily exploit. It would be a simple matter indeed to ruin her, if she did not ruin herself first.

Sloane stopped in a shadow and shook his head. He must cease these rakish thoughts. Besides, far more likely than he ruining Miss Hart was that she would ruin him.

She was up to something. He needed to discover exactly what it was before she dragged him down with her when her fall came.

Sloane proceeded with new purpose. He made his way to Jermyn Street, concealing himself in the darkness, while he watched men come and go through the door of the glove shop. The front of the shop was unlit, but windows in the upper floors showed the peek of candlelight when the curtains stirred. Certain now that his suspicions of the establishment had been accurate, Sloane waited. He did not know what he hoped to discover, but the years he'd worked for the Crown had taught him to bide his time. Something useful always came his way.

His reward came when a man in a plain coat paused under the street lamp, giving Sloane a glimpse of his face. It was the man from the park. He entered the glove shop with the familiarity of a frequent visitor, but Sloane suspected his visit was for business, not pleasure.

Sloane left his place of concealment and crossed around the row of shops to the back. One light shone in a window on the ground floor of the glove shop. He crept closer.

The window was open, allowing the cool night breeze into the house. Sloane heard voices. He gripped the exterior sill of the window a couple of feet over his head and pulled himself up high enough to peek inside.

A woman's back was visible. The establishment's owner, he guessed. She shook her finger at a man facing her, the man from the park.

The woman's voice could be clearly heard. 'I do not want you to *try* to find my girls. I want you to *succeed* in finding them! And while you are at it, get me that pretty maid.'

'Never fear,' the man said in the rough voice Sloane remembered from the park. 'When I clamp my hands on that one again, she will not get away.'

'Hmmph.' The woman tossed her head. 'You could not hold her the first time. I wish I had held her when she turned up with that harridan.'

Morgana, Sloane thought.

The woman continued, 'Do you know where to find her?'

'I will discover her.'

Sloane's arms trembled with the strain of holding on to the window. He let himself slip to the ground.

He had heard enough. There was no doubt in his mind Morgana Hart was toying with a danger she could not imagine.

He meant to put a halt to this flirtation of hers with the Paphian world.

The next morning Sloane rose early. He'd slept little. Dawn had not been far off by the time he'd returned to the house and his brain was racing too fast to turn off.

Why had Morgana Hart gone to the glove shop that day? Why did she wish to contact Harriette Wilson, of all people? What mischief was she getting herself into?

He told Elliot he was going for a walk, not precisely a falsehood. He planned to walk around the row of houses to the back.

He'd retained enough of the previous night's mood to decide he would first watch her house, to learn what he could before confronting her.

As he stepped out of his door, a servant left Miss Hart's

house, hurrying down the street as if on an urgent errand. Sloane walked by Morgana's house at a slow pace, glancing into her window as he passed. A female he'd not seen before appeared briefly in the drawing-room window. There was something afoot in that house, all right.

He crossed the street and walked around to the backs of the houses. Stepping through the mews, he reached her gate. Through the gap in the gate, he peered into her property.

Finding it deserted, he tried the latch. It was locked, but Sloane made short work of picking the lock.

He slipped into the garden. Luckily it had bushes enough to conceal him. He inched his way along the wall, looking for a nice vantage point to watch the back of the house, and almost tripped over a pile of bricks. Catching himself, he saw a gap in the wall and laughed. He might have spared himself a great deal of trouble had he known he could step from his garden into hers.

It proved an excellent place to stand, providing him easy escape. So he settled in and, like the Peeping Tom of the Lady Godiva legend, and the English spy he'd been during the war, he fixed his attention on the back windows of Miss Hart's house, hoping to witness something he was not supposed to see.

He saw a great deal more activity than he would have expected. The sound of the pianoforte reached his ears, as well as a beautiful feminine voice singing to it. Either Miss Hart had exaggerated how badly she could play, or someone else had fingers on the keys. The voice did not sound like her either, too high and crystalline. A quite remarkable voice, none the less, but whose?

Sloane watched for over an hour, an inconsequential space of time compared to the long hours he'd put in for King and country. But instead of piecing the puzzle together, Sloane became more confused.

In the past hour, three women had walked out to the privy. One he recognised as Miss Hart's maid. The other two were dressed as maids, but somehow they did not fit the part. Another puzzling thing. They all seemed to be gathered in the back room. Why would a covey of maids spend so much time in one room?

Perhaps Mr Elliot would have a notion how many people Miss Hart employed. Elliot had a way of knowing such things.

Sloane slipped through the gap in the wall and entered his house from the back, causing one of his maids to shriek in surprise when he suddenly appeared in the passageway. He told the girl to find Elliot and send him to the library, a room mirroring the location of Morgana's busy back room.

When Elliot entered, Sloane was examining the books on the shelves.

'I have meant to rearrange the shelves, sir,' Elliot said. Sloane stepped back. 'Are they out of order?'

'Sadly out of order. Apparently no one has seen to their proper shelving in some time.' Elliot picked up a stack of books and placed them on this shelf or that.

Sloane watched, wondering what made it worth the effort. Very little on the shelf interested him. One or two titles caught his eye, but that was because they related to the political issues of the day, and the *Annual Registers* sometimes yielded useful information. The rest he would not miss.

'You wished to see me, sir?' Elliot said, having found the books their homes.

Sloane picked up the Register for 1816 and handed it to his secretary. 'How many servants do we employ?'

Elliot placed the *Register* right after that for 1815. 'There is Sparrow, your butler. Mrs Wells, the housekeeper. Cook.'

He counted on his fingers. 'Cook's assistant. A scullery maid. Two upstairs maids. Two footmen. And your valet, of course. That makes ten.'

'Ten?' Sloane almost laughed. There was a time when even one maid of all work would have been woefully out of reach.

'Unless you wish me to include your coachman and groom, and Tommy.'

He held up his palm. 'Ten,' he repeated. 'Tell me, do they employ so many next door?'

If Elliot thought this an odd question, he made no sign of it. He looked to be calculating in his head. 'I believe they have the same number. One more lady's maid, but no assistant to the cook.'

Sloane might marvel at how Elliot came by this information, but not much surprised him about the young man's ability.

'I see.' Sloane's brow furrowed. Either all the maids were gathered in the library at once, or there were more people in Morgana Hart's house than Elliot knew of.

Sloane contemplated a return to his hiding place near the mews. If he watched long enough, he suspected he would be able to count the different faces, but he would be no closer to knowing why so many were there.

'Did you wish to go through the invitations?' Elliot asked.

An impressive stack of invitations had arrived. Sloane received more each day, a measure of the increase in members of the *ton* who accepted him. Though Sloane was impatient to find a way to speak to Morgana, he dutifully sat down and discussed with Elliot which to accept and which to reject.

Another delay came that afternoon when Sloane received his first caller. His nephew David came to congratulate him on his purchase of the town house. Sloane received him in the drawing room, sending for some port.

He poured them each a glass. 'Your grandfather will not like you visiting me.'

David took a sip. 'Grandfather will most probably not ask, but, if he does, I shall admit to calling upon you.'

Foolish boy. It would be wiser to lie.

Sloane peered in his glass. 'You'd do better to cut me.'

David regarded him with a very serious expression. 'I know the circumstances of your birth, Uncle, but I cannot see why you have been made to suffer for it.'

David *knew*? This made the young man's friendliness even more remarkable.

But Sloane had no intention of discussing his place in the family—or lack of it. Instead, he asked David about his life. The boy's course had been similar to his own. Sent to Eton at age nine, then on to Oxford. David continued at Oxford, reading law, whereas Sloane had escaped at eighteen, using his meagre inheritance from his mother to lose himself on the Continent. The similarities ended there.

After another glass of port, David said, 'I thought it would be polite to call upon Miss Hart while I am in the neighbourhood, or at least leave my card if she is not receiving.'

Brilliant idea. Why had Sloane not thought of it?

Actually he had thought of it, but concluded it would cause talk if anyone saw him enter her house alone. With David it would not be remarked upon, however.

'Perhaps I will join you,' Sloane said.

'Look what Mary found, Miss Hart.' Rose handed her a small book. 'She wanted to put it away again, but I said you would want to see it.'

Morgana opened the book to the title page. *The Whore-*

monger's Guide to London. 'What is this?' She turned the pages.

'It has names and their direction as well.' Mary pointed on the page. 'I thought you might find your tutor in there.'

This was exciting indeed. Morgana glanced at the date of publication. 1803, the year she had been sent to school and her father had come to London. This must have been his book.

The idea that her father might have used this information gave Morgana a rather sick feeling. She firmly set aside that thought and made herself consider what use the book might be in her present endeavours. She quickly leafed through to see if Harriette Wilson was listed.

She was not.

'Thank you, Rose,' Morgana said.

Morgana had had the pianoforte moved to the library, and Rose sat down at it, playing softly. Mary sat with Katy, showing her a book, and Miss Moore put Lucy through an elocution exercise. Morgana's grandmother sat in a rocking chair where she could see everyone. She smiled and rocked and said everything was lovely to anyone who asked.

Cripps knocked on the door. 'Two gentlemen to see you, Miss Hart.' Morgana strained to see if there was any change in his manner towards her since the 'nieces' had arrived. She was unable to tell. 'Mr Cyprian Sloane and Mr David Sloane.'

Mr Sloane? Even though she had convinced herself he could never care for her, her heart leapt. 'Did you put them in the drawing room?'

'Yes, miss.'

'Oh, dear.' Her glance darted around the room. 'I suppose we should serve tea. Will you see to it, Mr Cripps.'

He bowed and left the room.

Morgana told herself she could see Sloane without him discovering her other guests. She walked over to her grandmother's chair. 'Grandmama, would you like to receive callers with me?'

Her grandmother smiled. 'That would be lovely, my dear.'

Morgana shoved *The Whoremonger's Guide* into the pocket of her dress and helped the frail old lady to her feet. They made their laborious way to the drawing room.

The two gentlemen turned at their entrance and waited to be presented. Morgana's eyes flew naturally to Sloane's.

'Grandmama, you recall our neighbour, Mr Cyprian Sloane?' Morgana said.

'Oh, yes,' said her grandmother agreeably. 'So lovely to see you, my dear.'

Morgana tried to ignore the knowing look in his eye as he took her grandmother's bony hand in his large one and brought it to his lips for a gentle kiss. 'It is my pleasure, Lady Hart.'

She presented David Sloane, and her grandmother responded to him in the same vague manner. He did not seem to notice anything amiss. Morgana prayed her grandmother would not say anything to reveal her infirmity of mind.

'Please sit, gentlemen,' Morgana said. 'Cripps is bringing tea.'

She felt Sloane's gaze boring into her as they chatted. He continued to examine her as she poured him tea and handed him the cup, and when they stood to leave fifteen correct minutes later. She left her grandmother in the drawing room and walked the gentlemen out.

When they had stepped into the hall, Sloane turned to her with a glint in his eye. 'Forgive my impertinence, Miss Hart, but I am desirous to know if your house has the same configuration of rooms as my own.'

To her alarm he headed for the door of the back parlour, where soft piano music could be heard.

'Is this the library?' He put his hand on the knob.

'Yes!' she cried. 'I mean, it is merely a small parlour my father used as a library.'

The voices of the girls inside the room were audible through the closed door. His brows rose.

'Is it configured as my own?' He turned the knob.

She put her hand on his, bare skin to bare skin. 'I think this not a good time. The…the maids are cleaning.'

He seemed to peer all the way into her lying soul. 'I see. They clean the pianoforte very melodiously. Perhaps some other time I shall beg a tour of your house.'

'I will arrange it with Cripps.' She turned sharply back towards the hall and the book fell from her pocket.

Sloane picked it up and read the spine. 'Miss Hart—' he whispered fiercely.

She merely extended her hand for the book.

'Are we leaving, Uncle?' called David from the hallway.

He was forced to give the book back to her, but his face looked like thunder. 'Directly,' he called to his nephew.

She led him back to the hall where Cripps waited with the gentlemen's hats. David said his goodbye and headed out of the door. Sloane held back.

'I will speak with you very soon.' He gave her a meaningful look that filled her with trepidation.

Morgana closed the door behind him and leaned against it. She glanced at Cripps.

He hesitated a moment before asking, 'Do you require anything further, miss?'

'Nothing.' She fled into the drawing room to collect her grandmother, knowing she'd not heard the last of this from Sloane.

David convinced Sloane they should also call upon Lady Hannah, and Lady Hannah begged the gentlemen to drive her through Hyde Park, where she waved happily to her friends, no doubt feeling triumphant at having two gentlemen to escort her. It was nearly two hours before Sloane could return to Culross Street. He drove the curricle to the stables himself and left the horses in the care of his tiger. Tommy would think it the most natural thing in the world for Sloane to cross the mews and enter from the back.

Once in his garden, Sloane crossed through the gap in the fence. Rain began to patter the stone of the garden with fat droplets, and he hurried to Morgana's rear entrance. Finding the door unlocked, he slipped inside her house. He would bet his fortune she was in her back parlour, from where he'd heard the other female voices.

Sloane experienced the same surge of excitement that he used to feel whenever he risked discovery. He hurried up the servants' stairs and stood in the shadows, but he was by no means hidden. Anyone who looked carefully would see him.

As he'd hoped, Morgana came out of the room.

He stepped out of the shadows. 'Miss Hart.'

'Oh!' She jumped in surprise.

He grabbed her arm and drew her away from the parlour door. 'Explain yourself,' he demanded.

Her back was against the wall. 'I, explain myself? You are the one invading my house!'

'I needed to speak with you privately.' He glared at her. 'Unless you wish me to discuss *The Whoremonger's Guide* with you at Almack's.'

'No.' Red spots appeared on her cheeks.

The colour only brightened her countenance, but he must not allow himself to think of how lovely she was. 'Now explain all. I will have no surprises.'

She expelled an angry breath. 'I do not see why I must. This is none of your affair, Mr Sloane.'

He gave a throaty laugh, appreciating her spirit more than he ought. 'Recall, Miss Hart, you manage to involve me at every turn.'

'Mere chance, sir,' she retorted. 'I did not plan to involve you.'

'Come now.' He gave her a level stare. 'You asked me about Harriette Wilson.'

'Merely her direction,' she said defensively.

'You involved me.' He gave her an emphatic shake. 'Now tell me what is going on.'

She twisted out of his grasp. 'Oh, very well! I shall tell you. Do not paw at me.'

He folded his arms across his chest. She looked everywhere but at his face. 'Now,' he demanded.

The words spilled from her mouth with hardly a breath in between. How her maid was bent on a life of prostitution, and how she was just as resolved to stop her. How she'd come upon her solution to the problem, and finally, the solution itself, complete with her reason for appearing in the glove shop and her desire to contact Harriette Wilson.

When she finally finished, he could only repeat in disbelief, 'You are training your maid to be a courtesan?'

She nodded.

He swung his arms in the air. 'What the devil has got into you? You cannot!'

'Well, I must.' She crossed her arms around her chest, a mimic of his previous gesture. 'And there are three other girls from Mrs Rice's shop. Well, two others. The third simply attached herself to them. I am going to train them as well.'

'Three girls?' His voice cracked.

'Four, if you count Lucy,' she corrected.

He swung away from her and whirled back to lean into her face. 'Are you mad?'

She shrugged. 'What else can I do? It is all I can think of to save these girls from that horrid Mrs Rice.'

'So you will be their procuress instead of Mrs Rice?' It was all he could do to keep from throttling her. 'This improves matters?'

'It is not like that!' She looked wounded. 'I am merely going to train them to be as agreeable as possible. To attract a better sort of man. If they attract many men, they shall have the freedom to select.'

He laughed again. 'You think it is that simple? Do you think Miss Wilson is any less at the whim of her patrons than a girl in a bawdy house?'

She gave him an exasperated look. 'Come now, Mr Sloane. You cannot convince me a girl in a bawdy house has an advantage over that woman I saw at the opera, in her fine clothes and jewels, all the men fawning over her?' She drew in a long breath. 'I have thought long about this. I cannot change what has happened to these girls. They are ruined. They have been tossed aside by everyone who once professed to love them. They cannot become housemaids or shopgirls or seamstresses. Once their past was revealed they would be turned out, and who then would hire them? I am merely giving them some advantage. If they behave wisely, they may create a secure life for themselves.'

'Morgana—' he gripped her arms again, unaware that he'd slipped into using her given name '—if even a whisper of this gets out, you will be as ruined as they.'

She averted her eyes. 'I know. But I cannot send them back to Mrs Rice. I simply cannot.'

She raised her eyes to his, their ginger colour intense with emotion. He felt excited and faintly sick, as if he'd twirled round and round like he'd done as a child, making the world spin when he stopped. Her scheme was as daring as it was foolish.

He tried another tactic to dissuade her. 'If you are discovered, the blame will fall on me.'

'On you?' She looked perplexed. 'Why should it?'

He shook his head in impatience. 'I am next door to you, Morgana. Someone is bound to think me the mastermind.' He released her. 'There are those in town who desire my ruin. They are eager to believe the worst of me. My family, for one. I can guarantee that if my father gets wind of this he will make sure I am banned from any respectable drawing room for the rest of my life.'

Her eyes softened. 'Your father hates you so much?'

'Yes,' he admitted gruffly, taken aback at how easily her sympathy opened his old wounds.

She leaned against the door, a frustrated expression on her lovely face.

Clutching at straws, he added, 'And you must think of your cousin as well. If you are ruined, the scandal will fall upon her too.'

Her eyes flashed at him. She did not speak for several seconds and then in a whisper. 'How am I to choose between ruining you, or ruining Hannah, or ruining those poor girls? Tell me how I am to do that?'

He responded in a soft voice. 'What of ruining yourself?'

She waved a dismissive hand.

He blew out a breath. He could not dispute the fact that those girls would be better off selling themselves for a high price than for a cheap one. They had all fallen from grace already; few who fell managed to climb up again. Some temptation always pulled at them, luring them back to the low life, as he well knew. He felt it. Felt it now. The lure of danger, excitement, relief from the crushing boredom of life as a gentleman.

He frowned. 'What did you intend to do with *The Whore-monger's Guide?*'

Her lip trembled. 'I need someone to tutor the girls in…in what I do not know about being a courtesan. I thought Harriette Wilson might do it.' She looked at him through her lashes. 'Because I do not know how to contact her, I am forced to use the book to find a tutor.'

Quite right, he thought. 'Harriette would not be a wise choice,' he said pensively. 'She has a loose tongue. Half the *ton* would know in no time.' He rubbed his chin. 'You need someone with more discretion.'

'I will find such a person, then.' Her voice became adamant.

'No, Morgana.' If she used that infernal book, she entered a different world, a world where the rules were not civilised. 'It will not do for you…' He paused. He suddenly felt seized with life and energy. Plans formed in his head in spite of his better judgement. He cleared his throat, and bit back a smile of anticipation. 'I will find your tutor.'

'You will?' she cried and flung her arms around him. 'Oh, thank you, Mr Sloane!'

Giddy and exhilarated, he lifted her off the ground and spun her about. When her feet again landed on the floor, she gazed into his eyes like a kindred spirit. He wanted to press her against him, taste her lips, show her how man might plunder a willing woman, a woman as wild as he was.

He caught himself and pulled away.

It was so easy to act the rake. So damned easy.

Chapter Nine

Morgana's cheeks burned with embarrassment. She had flung herself at him like some sort of hoyden. But more mortifying, he had pushed her away—again.

She held her breath a moment and promised herself to forget this…this attraction to him. It was enough he'd agreed to help her, no matter that he'd done so for Hannah's sake, for she was certain that that had been the deciding factor for him.

'Would…would you like to meet them? The girls, I mean,' she stammered.

He glanced away, then turned his warm eyes back on her and gave his lazy smile. 'Why the devil not?'

Her heart danced, completely ignoring her vow not to let him affect her so. She led him from the stairway, enlivened by his company, relieved that she was no longer alone in her enterprise. 'Come then.'

Morgana led him to the library, knocking before she slipped into the room alone. The girls looked up. Miss Moore smiled at her. Her grandmother chirped, 'How lovely to see you, my dear.'

'I have brought someone for you to meet. Someone who will help us.' Morgana stepped aside for Sloane to enter.

'Gracious,' cried Katy, jumping to her feet.

Miss Moore looked shocked, but Lady Hart smiled. 'How lovely of you to call, dear.'

'This is Mr Sloane,' Morgana announced. 'He is our neighbour…and…' she gave him a quick glance '…a man who can do many things. He has volunteered to find our tutor.'

Morgana made the introductions and, as if he'd met them in an elegant drawing room on Grosvenor Square, he greeted them with respect. She watched in wonder how his kind attentions to them made them sit up straighter and hold their heads higher, appearing more like ladies than otherwise.

'Do you honestly know a tutor, sir?' Rose asked, blinking her wide green eyes and speaking in her melodious brogue.

Sloane's voice had a catch in it when he answered, 'I have someone in mind.' He gave the girl a long look.

Morgana stiffened. She tried to tell herself it was good that he showed his attraction to Rose. It would help remind her that he was not attracted to her, but to her cousin.

He turned to her. 'I'd best take my leave.'

'I will see you out,' Morgana said, trying not to show her unexpected little surge of jealousy.

When he faced the assembly of women and bowed in a gentlemanly manner, Morgana felt like hugging him again for his kindness to them. She wished he would call upon them often so the girls could learn how a man ought to treat them.

Morgana gave herself a silent rebuke. It was she who wished his company for herself.

She led him out of the room and started for the front door.

He caught her arm. 'Through the back. You have a gap through our garden wall that I passed through.'

Understanding dawned. 'That is how you got in.'

He favoured her with a wicked wink in reply.

They descended the stairs and reached the door to the garden. Morgana did not wish him to leave.

'What do you think of them, Mr Sloane?,' she asked. Anything to detain him a moment longer.

He gave her a contemplative frown. 'Do you truly wish my opinion?'

A *frisson* of anxiety crept up her back. Was he about to scold her again? 'Yes, of course.'

'Rose O'Keefe will rise to the top, I suspect.' He spoke in a detached manner, and, in spite of herself, Morgana was pleased. He apparently had not been as captivated by Rose as she'd thought.

He went on. 'Katy Green is trouble, and I would watch out for her.'

Morgana knew that as well.

He shook his head in dismay. 'I confess, I cannot picture either Miss Phipps or your Lucy in the role at all.'

She sighed. 'I cannot either, but there you have it.'

He looked directly in her eyes. 'How have you explained the new girls' presence to the servants?'

She averted her eyes. 'We have told them they are Miss Moore's nieces.'

His stern look returned. 'They will not believe it. The girls have different accents and look nothing like each other.'

She cautiously faced him. 'I fear you are right. Miss Moore believes she has settled the matter by saying they are not sisters but cousins, but it sounds far-fetched to me. I fear Mr Cripps, the butler, is not fooled at all.'

His worried expression contained no censure this time. 'Let me think upon a solution. The servants must not talk or you will be discovered.'

She gazed at him in wonder. How good it felt not to be alone in managing this scheme.

'Another matter.' His grey eyes were intent. 'You must not allow the girls to appear on Bond Street or St James's or any other place where they might be recognised. And you must not be seen in their company.'

She had not thought at all on matters such as this. 'Why not?'

'Your Mrs Rice wants her girls back. That fellow from the park and others will be searching for them.'

'The man from the park?' He'd wanted Lucy. What did he have to do with Mrs Rice? 'How do you know this?'

He leaned closer, his eyes taking on a hard edge. 'I *know*. You will obey me in this, Morgana.'

The use of her given name made his demand seem even more sinister. 'As you wish, Mr Sloane.'

His expression softened. He lifted his hand and for a brief moment she thought he would caress her face. A foolish thought, because he drew it away again.

He gave her a raffish grin instead. 'Call me Sloane. If we are to be conspirators in your little venture, formality between us is hypocritical, is it not?'

Her own smile tickled the corner of her mouth. She presented her hand to shake. 'Then I give you *permission* to address me as Morgana.'

He did not miss her quip. Laughing, he accepted her hand. The contact of his warm, rough hand in hers, bare skin to bare skin, only intensified this new intimacy between them.

Breathless, she murmured, 'Thank you, Sloane.'

His laughter ceased and his expression turned serious again. He released her hand. 'You may not thank me in the end, Morgana. This is a foolhardy and dangerous business we are engaged in. Who knows what will come of it?'

With that he opened the door and left, but for quite a while afterwards Morgana stood still as a statue, gazing after him.

* * *

That evening's must-attend entertainment was a ball given to announce the latest *ton* engagement, a merger guaranteed to please the families, if not the young man and woman involved. Everyone was present, including Morgana.

Sloane spied her across the room, standing with her aunt. Her eyes caught his for a mere second, but he felt the exhilaration of intrigue. There were dangerous secrets between them and care must be taken that no one discover this change in their relationship. He held his breath that Morgana would do nothing to reveal it.

She did not fail him. After the brief contact with their eyes, she turned back to her aunt as if she'd not seen him at all.

Almost disappointed, he kept up his part of the pretence, but this secret between them, and the risk of discovery, heightened his enjoyment of the ball. It put his senses on alert.

He took care not to neglect Lady Hannah, engaging her in one early dance as she would expect of him. Suddenly his behaviour towards Hannah had become part of the subterfuge, making it easier to take part in the inconsequential chatter that passed as conversation between them. After the dance, he left her to her other suitors, whose number had increased of late. His nephew David joined the growing throng.

Sloane sauntered into the room where the refreshments were set out. Another gentleman joined him. The Marquess of Heronvale.

'You are Mr Sloane, are you not?' the tall, taciturn marquess asked.

'I am, sir.' He gave an inward groan.

A few months ago, because of a foolish wager, Sloane had threatened to expose the nefarious past of this powerful man's sister-in-law. She'd been the Mysterious Miss M. in the days Sloane had known her, the prize in a gaming hell. The threat had been nothing but a drunken bluff on his part, but no one knew he had never meant to carry it out. Certainly not the marquess.

Sloane braced himself. Heronvale looked at him intently.

Here it comes, Sloane thought, envisioning all his efforts to restore his reputation sinking into a cesspool.

Heronvale gave a slight nod. 'I hear you are a man of your word.'

Sloane released a relieved breath. He had given this man's brother his word that he would not disclose the damaging information. Sloane gave Heronvale a frank stare. 'I am many things, sir, among them a man of my word.'

The marquess smiled approvingly. 'I admire that. Tell me, are you carrying refreshment to anyone?'

'Merely seeing to my own thirst,' Sloane admitted.

'Excellent.' Heronvale nodded again. 'Sit with me for a moment and share a drink. I would value your company.'

Sloane sat with the Marquess of Heronvale, conversing over wine glasses, as if it were the most natural thing in the world. The marquess told Sloane duty had brought him to London that season. He came for Parliament, reluctantly leaving his wife and newborn son in the country. By the end of their conversation, Heronvale had invited Sloane to dine with him at White's the following evening, at which time they could discuss politics and what role Sloane might play in it.

After the men shook hands and parted, Sloane nearly danced a jig. The Marquess of Heronvale thought *he* might play a role in politics? By God, if Sloane had Heronvale's endorsement, what man would dare question his reputation? He felt triumphant!

He returned to the ballroom where a set was forming. Scanning the room, he found Morgana unattended. She was the one person in the room he wanted to be with at the moment. As casually as he could manage, he crossed the room and asked her to dance with him.

'You look happy,' she said when the country dance brought them together.

It was a simple observation, without any teasing flirtation attached. 'I am indeed.'

The figures separated them. When they came close again, she asked, 'Why so?'

He halfway considered giving her some bantering, evasive answer. It is what any other partner would expect. But this was Morgana with whom he shared many secrets. Why not share his good fortune with her as well?

'I have had a brief chat with Heronvale and I'm engaged to dine with him tomorrow.'

She looked perplexed. 'This is the source of your happiness?'

They had to complete the figures again before he could explain.

'Heronvale will make a powerful ally.'

'I see.' She glanced over to where Heronvale stood conversing with Castlereagh. She frowned. 'Will he make a good friend, though?'

A friend? Such a notion was unfamiliar indeed. It took him aback. 'Yes. I do believe I would like him for a friend.'

She smiled and the dance separated them once more.

At the end of the set, he was reluctant to leave her side, but he forced himself to circulate, even asking Hannah for a second set. Hannah's conversation was as gay as usual, but the set seemed unusually long.

Sloane declined her invitation to share the Cowdlin carriage for the trip home. He left the ball early, another errand to perform. Walking out into the night air, he became himself again, watchful and alert as he set off on foot to his destination, an innocuouslooking town house off of St James's Street.

He sounded the knocker and a huge bear of a man dressed in colourful livery opened the door.

'Good evening, Cummings,' Sloane greeted the man and handed him his hat.

Cummings made no sign of noticing that Sloane had not crossed this threshold for at least three months. 'G'd evening, sir,' Cummings responded in his deep monotone.

'Is Madame Bisou available?'

'In the card room.' Cummings disappeared into the back room where he stowed the various cloaks, hats and canes.

Madame Bisou owned this establishment, a gaming hell and brothel, as honest and clean as any gentleman could expect. She was also indebted to Sloane, who, right before he made his decision to abandon this sort of gaming, had broken her faro bank with one mad night of reckless play. He'd not had the heart to call in the debt. She was, therefore, much beholden to him.

He climbed the stairs to the gaming room where he'd once played whist with a woman in disguise. The Wagering Widow, they'd called her, and it had been wagers over her that drove him to make his empty threats about Heronvale's sister-in-law. Sloane had lost badly over the Widow. Twice. And he hadn't fancied being known for it.

When he entered the room, several men looked up from their cards. One older fellow called to him, 'Sloane! It has been an age! Come partner me.'

Sloane shook his head. 'I'm not playing tonight, Sir Reginald.'

Madame Bisou caught sight of him and came bustling over. 'Oh, Monsieur Sloane,' she cried in her atrocious French accent. 'How delightful to see you!' Her flaming red curls bounced as energetically as the flesh the low neckline of her bright purple dress failed to conceal.

She gave him exuberant kisses on both cheeks, but regarded him with some wariness. 'You have perhaps come to collect?'

He smiled. 'No, but there is something I wish to discuss with you.'

'You wish time with me?' She spoke so loudly everyone in the room could hear.

He glanced around, but everyone was too busy with their cards or dice to heed her very public invitation.

'To confer with you,' he clarified. 'But I will pay for your time.'

'Oh, no,' she protested as she led him out into the hall. 'We shall deduct it from what I owe you.'

She took him to the supper room and they seated themselves at the same out-of-the-way table where he'd got bloody drunk over the loss of his first wager over Lady Widow.

Madame Bisou lowered herself into a chair with a noisy rustle of satin skirts. 'What is it, *mon cher,* that you require of me?' She fluttered her lashes seductively.

'Ease off, Penny.' Sloane took the seat across from her.

She frowned at his use of her given name. 'Speak quietly, *Cyprian,* or I shall shout your name across the room.' Her French accent fled and she talked like the Chelsea girl she'd once been.

He laughed. 'As if everyone does not know it. My father has made certain of that.' He signalled to one of the serving girls, who brought them a bottle of brandy and two crystal glasses.

He poured for her. 'I am in need of a favour, Penny. An odd one, but I am persuaded you will be the perfect person for it.'

As methodically as he could, he described Morgana's plan, trying to make it sound as if it were not completely irrational. After he finished he downed a whole glass of brandy in one gulp.

Penny leaned towards him. 'Do you mean to say a baron's daughter has taken in some of Fortuna Rice's girls and she wants to train them to be high-flyers?'

Sloane poured himself more brandy. 'You have grasped it, Penny.'

'And you want me to teach them how to seduce men?'

He gave her a sly smile. 'If you know such things.'

She slapped him playfully on the arm. 'Of course I know such things! You know I do, darling. I am an expert!' She straightened in her chair and fussed with the lace on her bodice. 'I am to go to Mayfair, into this lady's house?'

Sloane's eyes narrowed. 'I suppose I could bring them here—'

'No!' she cried. 'I want to be invited to Mayfair. Now tell me, Cyprian. How much is she willing to pay?'

He wagged his finger at her. 'Do not rook her, Penny, or you will answer to me. If you tutor these girls, your debt to me is forgiven. That should be payment enough.'

She grinned and her eyes danced. She looked almost like the ambitious and beautiful young doxy he'd met ten years earlier. 'I declare I might have taken this on at no charge at all. It sounds a splendid lark.'

'But I warn you, you must speak of this to no one.' He leaned forward for emphasis. '*No one.* Or you will, indeed, answer to me.'

Early next morning Sloane sent a message to Morgana that he would bring her tutor to her at eleven o'clock.

Morgana and Miss Moore spent the morning drilling the

girls in how to walk, sit, stand and curtsy as a lady might do, but all Morgana could think of was that Sloane would be calling—with the tutor, of course.

Soon the clock struck eleven. Ten more excruciatingly slow minutes passed before the knocker sounded and Cripps came in to announce that Mr Sloane and 'a female person' were in the front drawing room.

'Very good, Cripps.' Morgana rushed out of the room. She left her grandmother and Miss Moore with the girls. With Sloane, the pretence of a chaperon was unnecessary.

When she entered the drawing room, he turned to face her. He was resplendent in dove grey pantaloons, shiny black boots, and a coat in a blue so dark it was almost black. He quite took her breath—and her speech—away.

'Miss Hart.' He stepped aside to reveal the woman he had brought with him. 'May I present Madame Bisou.'

The woman looked perfectly respectable in a plain brown walking dress and spencer. Only the flaming red hair peeking out from under her sedate matching bonnet gave hint to her profession.

'Madame Bisou.' Morgana offered her hand. 'I am grateful you have come.'

The woman appraised Morgana as she accepted the handshake. She gave Sloane a significant look. 'Cyprian, I begin to understand how you came to make this request.'

His face filled with colour, and Morgana rushed to speak. 'Mr Sloane is acting as my friend only because I have given him little choice, Madame.'

'Little choice indeed!' Madame Bisou exclaimed. 'As if Cyprian does anything he does not wish to do.' She put her hands on her hips. 'Now, what is it you require of me?'

Morgana begged them to sit while she explained.

When she finished Madame Bisou's eyes danced. 'I am

well able to teach your girls how to be pleasing to men. I have some experience in such matters, do I not, Cyprian?'

Sloane returned her glance with an ironic gleam in his eye. 'You do, indeed, *Penny.*'

Madame Bisou made a face at him, and Morgana realised with shock that the madam must have once been intimate with him. Was she still? Morgana felt the same sick feeling she experienced when realising her father must have used *The Whoremonger's Guide.*

No. Not the same feeling. This felt worse somehow.

She regarded Madame Bisou, her eyes narrowing. Surely the woman was older than Sloane, who must be in his thirties. There were faint lines around her eyes and at the corners of her mouth. Her skin had lost the tautness and clarity of youth. Still, she had an aura about her that made Morgana certain that if the two of them walked down the street, gentlemen would turn to look at Madame Bisou and not at her. But that was what she had desired in a tutor, was it not?

'Shall I do, Miss Hart?' Madame Bisou sounded amused.

Morgana shook herself. What business was it of hers with whom Sloane shared such…intimate behaviours? If anyone should be concerned it would be Hannah, but then Hannah would never know of this.

'I suspect you will do very well, Madame,' Morgana responded, avoiding a glance at Sloane. 'Shall I take you to your students?'

Madame Bisou clapped her hands. 'Oh, yes. The sooner, the better.'

Sloane stood. 'I doubt you require my presence. When shall I collect you, Madame?'

Madame Bisou looked to Morgana.

'In two hours, Sloane, if that would not be inconvenient?' Morgana still did not look straight at him.

He bowed, but stepped to the open door of the library to say a brief hello to Morgana's girls. Morgana hesitated a moment before ushering Madame Bisou into the room, pausing to watch Sloane head towards the hall.

Sloane walked out of Morgana's house at the same moment his secretary approached his own door.

Mr Elliot looked greatly surprised, no doubt wondering why his employer called upon a single lady before noon, alone at that.

'Good day, Elliot,' Sloane said in a deliberate tone.

Mr Elliot blinked rapidly. 'Good day, sir. I…I was just returning from town.'

'Seeing to my business, I suppose?' Sloane walked over to where Elliot stood.

Elliot still avoided his eye.

Sloane rather enjoyed the young man's discomfort. It belied his usual efficiency. But Sloane also realised that Elliot was not a fool. Even if Elliot concluded he was making a conquest of Morgana, what Sloane suspected anyone would conclude, he believed he could count on the young man's discretion. Still, it did not hurt to emphasise the point. 'Is there something you want to ask me, Mr Elliot?'

'Oh, no, sir.' Elliot sputtered. 'That is—it is none of my affair, I am sure.'

The two men walked together into Sloane's house. 'It is no *affair* of mine as well, but you will not speak of me visiting Miss Hart's house.'

His secretary looked wounded. 'Of course I will not, sir!'

Sloane nodded. 'Very good.'

He headed to his library, thinking a small glass of port might pass the time while he waited to collect Penny.

To his dismay, Elliot followed him into the room. 'There is something I ought to speak with you about.'

Sloane already had the bottle of port in hand. He gestured for the young man to sit and poured a glass for them both.

Elliot began, 'Sparrow, your butler, sir, informed me that one of the footmen informed him that Miss Hart's footman was talking of something havey-cavey next door. It seems there are some suspicious females present in the house.'

Sloane paused just as he was about to lift his glass to his lips. He tried to sound casual. 'Havey-cavey?'

Elliot shrugged. 'That is all I know. I shall discover more in time. I thought I ought to tell you of it, because you indicated reservations about moving next door to Miss Hart.' He stopped and gave Sloane a considering look. 'But perhaps you know of it...'

Because Elliot had seen him leave Morgana's house. Sloane stared at his secretary a long time. It had taken only a day for news of Morgana's strange guests to reach Elliot's ears, something he must deal with post-haste.

Elliot regarded him with a steady look. 'You do know of this,' he said simply. 'I beg you would instruct me how you wish me to proceed.'

Sloane appraised the young man. Elliot was alert and intelligent. Because the young man lived with him, it would be difficult to put much past him. Sloane was unaccustomed to trusting another person, but Elliot could be of great assistance. He could help keep an eye on Morgana when Sloane could not, an extra protection.

Elliot was beholden to Sloane, who, as a favour to a former smuggler, had taken on the man's son as secretary, providing him with a chance at a respectable profession. Even if Elliot was disposed to be loyal in return, was it fair to ask him to share the risk of Morgana's courtesan school being discovered?

Who was he fooling? If the courtesan school was discovered, Elliot would sink with the rest of them. Better for him to be warned.

'Drink your port, Elliot,' Sloane said. 'And I will endeavour to explain.'

A quarter of an hour later, Sloane had told Elliot the whole story. When he finished, he refilled Elliot's empty glass.

'That young maid wishes to be a courtesan?' Elliot asked incredulously.

Sloane sipped his own drink. 'She is bent on some sort of harlotry, Miss Hart insists. That is how this whole courtesan school came about.'

Elliot stared into his port. 'I wonder why she should wish to do such a thing.'

Sloane leaned back in his chair. 'Living with her father, I expect. He was one of the King's diplomats in Spain during the war. I suspect she pretty much did as she pleased in his house.'

Elliot looked baffled. It took several moments before comprehension dawned on his face. 'Oh, you meant Miss Hart. I was speaking of the maid.'

'The maid?' It was Sloane's turn to be bewildered. He took another sip. 'In any event, if this business reaches the ears of the *ton,* it shall be the downfall of us all. I may find your assistance useful from time to time. May I depend upon you?'

'Indeed, sir,' Elliot responded, but in a distracted manner.

Elliot proceeded to inform Sloane of the financial business he had transacted in town. The complexity of the investments Elliot had set up were a bore to Sloane, but the profits continued to be gratifying. He kept watch on the mantel clock.

He returned to Morgana's house early to collect Penny.

Miss Hart's butler admitted him. 'I shall announce you directly, sir.'

'In a moment.' Sloane handed him his hat and gloves. 'What is your name, man?'

'Cripps, sir.' The butler placed his hat and gloves on the marble-topped hall table and turned back to him.

Sloane gave the man a steely stare. 'It has come to my attention, Cripps, that the servants under you are passing tales about this household to my servants.'

Cripps returned his look impassively.

Sloane continued, 'This will not do. You have shirked your responsibility to protect this lady's privacy.'

A muscle in Cripps's cheek twitched, but he remained stiff and erect.

The man gave away little. Sloane decided to increase the stakes. 'I am a wealthy man, Cripps, but I can also be a dangerous man to cross. Treat this lady and her guests well and you and your staff will be rewarded. Bonuses to them all from me.' He leaned forward menacingly. 'Harm her with loose tongues or otherwise and you will incur my wrath.' He paused for Cripps's reaction.

The butler did not change expression.

'I assure you, you do not wish to displease me,' he emphasised.

Cripps finally responded in a low voice. 'I will do my duty, as I always do.' His face remained bland. 'Shall I announce you now, sir?'

Once with the students, Madame Bisou dropped her French accent and her flirtatious ways. Oddly, she reminded Morgana of one of the Spanish noblemen her father had entertained in Spain. The gentleman had been incredibly shrewd, extracting from her father exactly what he wanted, and exactly what her father had originally refused to give him. Morgana discovered later that the nobleman had manipulated the French just as effectively.

Madame Bisou had the same kind of cleverness and charm. She drew in the girls with a very friendly, motherly manner, and held them in her palm while she spoke of her origins.

'I was not always Madame Bisou,' she began in the spellbinding voice of a practised story-teller. 'I was born Penny Jones, and my mother died giving birth to me. As a child I walked at my father's side while he hawked dirty old clothes on Petticoat Lane. "Old clo," he'd cry over and over. "Old clo."' She looked heavenward. 'I can still remember it. Hearing the other street vendors' songs all day as well as my father's. I used to sing them myself and dance, and passers-by would throw me pennies. Pennies for Penny.' Her smile left her face. 'It was not long before men paid for more than my dancing.' She gave them all a significant look. 'By day I'd follow my father in the street and by night in the pubs, until one night he had no more coins for his gin.' Her voice got very low and Morgana could see each of the girls and Miss Moore, too, straining to hear. 'That night he sold me to a man in the pub for a few shillings. I never saw my father again.'

'That's dastardly,' cried Katy. 'What happened next?'

Madame Bisou gave a ghost of a smile. 'The man sold me at a profit to a bawdy house. After he had his way with me, that is. He sold me to a mean old abbess who beat her girls if they gave her any trouble. She kept all the money.'

There was a collective exclamation of outrage, and the madam went on to tell how she fooled the procuress and wound up with enough money and power to take over the house and drive the woman away.

Katy and Rose cheered with enthusiasm at this triumph.

Madame Bisou looked each of the girls in the eye. 'I know how to get gents willing to die for me,' she said dramatically.

'And that is what I will teach you. I'll show you how to make them beg to do what you want them to do. I'll teach you how to trick them into paying you much more than they thought they would. And how to have them stumble over each other to see who can buy you the biggest ring, the most expensive necklace or the most beautiful bracelet.'

Morgana was as mesmerised by the tale as the others, but she could not think of any gift she would want from a man, no dragon he could slay for her, no bauble he could purchase. Still, being such a temptress would be heady stuff indeed.

Cripps knocked on the door and announced Sloane, who entered the room to collect Madame Bisou. Katy and Rose begged her to stay longer. She laughed, saying she would return very soon. None the less, they detained her with more questions.

Sloane leaned over to Morgana. 'How did she do?'

Morgana looked into his smoky grey eyes. 'She told us the terrible story of how she came to be as she is today.'

'The terrible story?' The corners of his eyes crinkled. It so distracted her, she forgot what she'd just said to him.

'Oh—yes.' She swallowed. 'You know, how her father sold her for a pint of gin.'

His eyes shone. 'It is a hum, Morgana. Penny was an innkeeper's daughter who found life too tame and struck out on her own. I suspect her father still owns his pub somewhere in Chelsea and makes a fine living.'

Morgana burst out laughing, holding her hand over her mouth so the others would not heed her. 'Oh, she *is* splendid, Sloane. She had us all completely at her mercy. I think Mary had tears in her eyes. If she can fool us, then she must know how to fool men!'

His expression changed to a stern one. 'Is that what you desire, Miss Hart? To fool men?'

She was too happy to allow him to scowl at her. She mimicked the madam's low, attention-capturing cadence, as well as her accent. 'Yes, it is, Sloane. We must fool some very rich men into giving all their money, *n'est pas?* And then toss them away, keeping all their money in our pockets.'

Not only was he not amused, he looked thunderous. 'Do you wish to become a courtesan as well, Morgana?'

She responded to his grimace with a saucy smile.

Madame Bisou hurried to his side. 'Are you ready, Cyprian?' She batted her lashes at him. Morgana's eyes narrowed.

Sloane took Morgana's hand and leaned into her face. 'Do not jest with me, Morgana. Are you planning to become a courtesan?'

The clasp of his hand felt angry, but the contact was every bit as affecting as the day before.

She raised her eyes to his, suddenly serious. 'Do you jest, Sloane? What man would think me a courtesan?'

His eyes filled with heat and she felt his thumb caress her palm. He did not answer her. 'Good day, Miss Hart,' he said.

She did not immediately release his hand when he began to pull away. His expression turned quizzical.

She said, 'I hope your dinner goes well tonight, Sloane.'

'My dinner?' He looked startled. 'The dinner with Heronvale, do you mean?'

She nodded and opened her fingers so his hand slipped out of hers.

He lightly brushed her arm. 'Thank you for thinking of it.'

Madame Bisou, née Penny Jones, entwined her arm in his. 'Come, Cyprian.' She swept him out of the door.

Morgana lightly fingered her palm and her arm where the memory of his touch still lingered.

Chapter Ten

If Sloane had led a double life in the past, he now had tripled himself. He continued to play the gentleman for the *ton*, the possible suitor for Lady Hannah, the wealthy fellow who put in appearances at White's and talked politics with the Marquess of Heronvale. At night, after the *ton*'s elegant routs and balls, he slipped into the shadows, returning often to Mrs Rice's glove shop, keeping his eyes and ears open to possible danger from that quarter. To Mrs Rice's mounting rage, her lackeys had made no progress in finding her missing girls or in discovering the ladylike woman who had snatched the pretty maid from her grasp. Sloane would remain watchful, however, just in case.

During these past three weeks it had also become his practice to often look in on the courtesan school. He kept an eye on Penny, lest she be tempted to go back on her word not to exploit Morgana. He imposed his intimidating presence on the taciturn Cripps, to ensure the butler kept the servants in line. Sloane watched Morgana as well, in case he need rein her in from some risky exploit that might expose the whole affair.

It had become his habit to breakfast with Morgana and her girls, the most pleasant part of his day. The courtesan school, scandalous as it might be, was a relief from the crushing boredom that permeated the rest of his time. Sometimes Elliot joined him at Morgana's, as he did this day. Penny had requested they both assist the girls in her special dancing lessons. Both men slipped through the gap in the garden wall and entered Morgana's house unseen.

The formality of being announced long abandoned, they made their way straight to the dining parlour and entered to a chorus of good mornings. Morgana's grandmother's eyes lit up. 'How lovely of you to call.'

'Men at last,' exclaimed Katy, who nearly thrust her chest under Elliot's nose before Miss Moore pulled her into a chair.

Katy complained loudly. 'I'm tired of seeing only old Cripps. He's given the footmen such a lecture they run and hide when they see us!'

Sloane was greatly heartened that Cripps had been so cruel to poor Katy.

'You must remember, men are to throw themselves at you, not you at them,' Miss Moore told her. 'You are better than that, Miss Green.'

Sloane frowned as he and Elliot filled their plates. Morgana often said those words to the girls. *You are better than that.* For all Morgana's wide-eyed plans, he knew too well the world would not treat them so.

Elliot chose a chair at the far end of the table where Lucy, who still considered herself of the servant class, always retreated. Sloane sat next to Morgana.

She poured him a cup of tea, fixing it just as he liked. 'It is so good of you and Mr Elliot to volunteer to be dance partners.'

He smiled at her. 'I would not exactly say Elliot volunteered, but he is excellent at following orders.'

Her brow wrinkled. 'Is it against his scruples? I would not impose upon anyone who objected to it.'

He glanced at Elliot, who was engaged in a quiet conversation with Lucy. 'He is shy around women, I believe.'

Her expressive eyes glanced in the same direction. 'Katy must frighten the wits out of him, then. Lucy is shy, too, but they seem to get on together.'

'They talk of plants, I believe.'

Morgana asked his opinion of Naldi's performance as Figaro at the opera the previous evening. Lady Hannah had fished for an invitation and Sloane had obliged, including her parents and Morgana in the party.

He gave a dry laugh. 'Surely you know I find every opera a dead bore.'

She rolled her eyes at his comment, but went on, 'Well, *I* was not impressed. Naldi speaks as often as he sings, and often off key.'

Sloane had known without her saying so that she had not been impressed. While Lady Hannah spent the evening searching for her friends among the audience, he'd watched Morgana and had seen her opinion of the opera written on her face.

'I do wish I could have talked with Harriette Wilson,' she added. 'She could have answered so many questions.'

What a silent argument they'd had over the infamous courtesan. Morgana had given Sloane a hopeful glance when Harriette appeared in her opera box, and he'd returned it with a censorious grimace. She'd replied with a thinning of her lips and he'd countered with a pointed shrug.

'Do not act the fool, Morgana. You know you could not speak with her.'

She sighed. 'I know. I know. My reputation would be ruined.' She said this with exaggerated drama.

He put a stilling hand on her arm. 'You have no notion what ruin would mean, but, I assure you, I do.'

Her ginger eyes turned warm with sympathy.

Damnation. Such moments between them only complicated matters. He did not need her sympathy, nor her interest in his well-being. It only pulled at his baser urges. He'd thus far avoided playing the rake with her, but who knew how long he could last? He looked away and attacked his slice of ham.

A few minutes later Miss Moore announced it was time for the girls' lessons and helped Lady Hart to her feet. As Rose, Katy and Mary filed out of the room ahead of them, Miss Moore asked, 'Are you coming, Morgana?'

Morgana looked up at her. 'I shall be in shortly.'

Elliot left his half-eaten breakfast and followed Lucy, who paused uncertainly by Morgana.

'What is it, Lucy?' Morgana asked.

Lucy hesitated, and glanced shyly at Elliot. 'Mr Elliot and I were talking of how the primrose is in bloom, miss. May I show him in the garden?'

'Of course,' Morgana said gently.

Sloane peered at Elliot. Was his secretary attempting to make a conquest of Lucy? Lucy could do much worse than a liaison with a fine young man such as Elliot, so why did he feel he ought to cuff Elliot's ears?

Lucy curtsied more like a maid than a courtesan and she and Elliot hurried out.

Morgana turned to Sloane. 'Is that not remarkable?'

'What?'

'Lucy and Mr Elliot. She seems to blossom around him, like one of her flowers.' With a dreamy expression, she gazed at the door through which Elliot and Lucy had departed.

Sloane put down his fork. 'Do not make this into some Minerva Press novel, Morgana.'

She raised an indignant eyebrow. 'Whatever do you mean?'

He looked directly in her eyes. 'Those are not two innocents. It is not a flower bed they are in search of, but the other kind of bed.'

Her eyes flashed. 'Do not be vulgar, Sloane.'

'Then do not you be missish.' He made sure she listened. 'How much do you wish to wager on it? Elliot and Lucy are bound to engage in more than a waltz soon enough?'

'I do not wish to wager at all,' she said in a huff, but she glanced back at the door with a pensive expression. 'It is precisely what I am training her for, is it not? I dislike thinking on it.'

He made no effort to relieve her tension. 'You ought to think on it. You'd best realise what sort of life you are handing these young women.'

She gave him a withering look. 'I suspect you are about to tell me.'

Her sarcasm set him off. 'If they are lucky they will attract men of means. They will be selling themselves to the highest bidder. The man may be short or tall, fat or skinny. He may smell. He may be cruel. But one thing is for certain…' He paused so that she would be sure to pay him heed. 'To the man she will be a mere ornament and bed partner. That is all. And she will be at his mercy for the food she eats and the roof that shelters her.'

Her colour heightened. 'Will it be so different when you choose a wife, Sloane?' She took an angry breath, and Sloane did not miss the tantalising rise of her chest. 'Do you not seek a wife other men will consider beautiful? Will you not wish for the pleasure of her bed? I assure you, she will be at your mercy for her food and her shelter. At least my girls will not be tied to one man for life, if they do not wish to be.'

He'd be damned if he'd allow her to know she'd struck a truthful chord. 'Spare me this Wollstonecraft recitation. Next you will be penning *A Vindication of the Rights of Doxies and Harlots*.'

For a second he thought she would slap him across the face, which he surely deserved. Her eyes flamed and flashed with pain. She gripped the edge of the cloth on the table. But he suffered worse than the sting of her hand. He watched as she blinked, straightened her spine and erased all expression from her face.

How many times in front of his father had he done the very same thing?

He could barely make himself speak. 'Do not do that, Morgana. Please God, do not do that.'

'Do what?' she responded, eyes bland.

'Pretend I did not wound you.' His voice was a mere whisper. 'I wish to God I had not said that to you.'

She remained stiff and distant. 'It is of no consequence. My unguarded tongue…' She waved her hand dismissively.

He caught it in his. 'I fear I spoke like—in a manner I regret.' Like his father, he almost said.

She pulled her hand away, and he snatched it back again. 'You were correct, Morgana, about my marital desires. I do wish a beautiful wife and…the rest. It is the way of the respectable world, is it not?'

She darted a glance at their clasped hands. 'The way for you, perhaps.'

He rubbed her palm with the pad of his thumb. 'And for you?'

She again pulled loose of his grasp. 'If there exists a man who could consider me an ornament, with my outspoken nature, I am certain he would soon fail to find me decorative.' She let slip a fleeting glimpse of pain. 'So your assessment of me was not far off the mark.'

Did she not know her appeal partly lay in her outspokenness? No pretence, no coy flirtations. He put his fingers under her chin and turned her face towards him, forcing her to look at him.

Her eyes glittered like topaz, and their gazes held until he felt like walls were cracking inside him, walls that held back his own pain, the pain he'd fended off almost since birth.

He cupped her cheek in the palm of his hand, touching the corner of her mouth with the pad of his thumb. 'Morgana—' he murmured.

Katy's voice sounded outside the door and they broke apart just in time before she burst in.

'Make haste!' Katy cried. 'Madame Bisou has arrived and says you must come for the dance lessons.' She did not wait to see if they would follow her. Heading back out the door, she laughed. 'You ought to see the fribble she's brought with her.'

'Well.' Morgana stood. 'I suppose we ought to join them.'

Sloane's brow knit in worry. Who had Penny brought with her? There were already too many people who might leak information about Morgana's outrageous courtesan school.

He offered Morgana his arm and they walked to the library, where the lessons were to take place. When they neared the door, he stopped her. 'Forgive me?' He brushed her cheek lightly.

Her smile held a hint of sadness, but it heartened him that it was a smile none the less. 'Why the devil not?'

He squeezed her cheek playfully. 'Hoyden.'

She grinned this time. 'Rake.'

Katy came to the doorway. 'What keeps you? Come on. We are waiting.'

They obliged her, entering the room where all the furniture except the pianoforte and two chairs had been removed and the carpet rolled up. Miss Moore had settled Lady Hart in one of the chairs and she sat in the other that was placed at the keyboard of the pianoforte.

'Oh, lovely to see you!' exclaimed Lady Hart, catching sight of them.

Madame Bisou stood next to a young gentleman. 'Miss Hart, I have brought my friend Robert. Allow me to present him to you.' She used her French accent this morning. 'We need more gentlemen. Cyprian, you were to have brought your secretary.'

'I did bring him, *Penny*.'

Her eyes narrowed.

Katy gave a dramatic sigh. 'Lucy is pulling weeds with him, no doubt. I shall go after them again.'

But there was no need to do so, because Elliot and Lucy appeared.

'Excellent!' cried the madam. 'We shall have nearly enough gentlemen to go around.'

'I…I could sit out,' murmured Mary.

Madame Bisou poo-pooed the idea. 'Nonsense, my dear. We will take turns. One may learn by observing as well as by doing.'

Sloane watched as Madame Bisou more formally introduced her friend, Robert Duprey, to Morgana. Why the devil had she brought that fellow? Duprey was not only a very foolish dandy, he was also brother to the woman over whom Sloane lost his wagers at Bisou's gaming house. He had always been a favourite of Penny's, though it foxed Sloane why.

Madame Bisou raised her voice. 'Now, you will think you already know how to do the dances, but you will be wrong, ladies. I will teach you that the dance involves not only the feet, but also the eyes and the hands. I will teach you what to do with each.'

As she went on, Sloane sauntered up to Robert Duprey.

'G'day, Sloane.' Duprey's voice cracked. 'Didn't know you'd be here. Been an age. Not at Bisou's these days?'

Duprey not only wore the dandy's tight pantaloons, high collar points and elaborately tied neckcloth, but he also affected their irritating style of speech.

'I am not pleased to see you here, Duprey,' Sloane said fiercely.

The young man shifted from foot to foot.

Sloane glared at him. 'If I discover you have said one word about this lady's house and what happens here, I will personally come after you. You've heard rumours of how dangerous I can be, have you not?'

'Eep!' Duprey cried. 'Won't say a thing. Mum's the word. Swear it.'

'You had better swear it.' For good measure he gave the terrified fellow another menacing look before walking back to Morgana's side.

Miss Moore began to play, and Sloane was first paired with Katy. He could handle her. He knew her type, trying to act so self-assured, pushing herself forward lest she be forgotten entirely. He'd done likewise many a time.

Katy enthusiastically embraced Madame Bisou's lessons, fluttering her lashes at him, touching him wherever she could reach. She even added a few moves not in the lecture, such as making sure he could look straight down her dress. It was a relief to next be partnered with the beautiful Rose, who was more subtle and easier on the eye.

They completed the drill on country dancing. Sloane glanced at Elliot, who stood next to Lucy, talking quietly to her. Duprey had finished dancing with Mary, whose complexion was flushed rather prettily. Duprey pulled at his collar. Morgana stood near her grandmother, looking almost as if she were recovered from his hurtful words.

'Now what you have been waiting for. The waltz,' Madame Bisou announced.

'Gracious, I don't know that one,' cried Katy.

Lucy said quietly, 'I don't either.'

'Not know the waltz?' Madame Bisou trilled with laughter. 'We shall teach you then.' She pointed to Sloane. 'Cyprian, you must demonstrate with Miss Hart.'

He had waltzed with Morgana on several occasions at Almack's and other balls, but not in such a relaxed, friendly, *seductive* atmosphere.

He took her hand and led her out to the middle of the bare floor. He put his other hand to her waist and she put hers on his arm. Miss Moore began to play.

Their steps were awkward at first, perhaps from being observed, but soon the music caught hold.

'Look at each other!' commanded Madame Bisou.

Morgana lifted her eyes, like amber jewels, to his.

'Make him hold you closer!' Madame Bisou said, and Morgana moved towards him. He bent down, his face inches from hers, and gathered her to him. As they twirled around the room, he held her so close their bodies touched and their legs moved as one.

Too soon the music stopped. He forced himself to let go.

'That was excellent, Cyprian.' Penny's voice broke in. They started to move away from each other. 'Stay there,' Penny ordered. 'We are not done. Put your arms around each other again.' She made her voice louder. 'Everyone! Pretend the music has just stopped.'

Miss Moore replayed the final chord.

'Now, Miss Hart,' Penny instructed. 'What you must do now is stand on tiptoe and kiss him.'

'That's the thing!' cried Katy.

Morgana gave Bisou a startled look, but turned back to face Sloane. With her golden eyes wide, she rose on her toes while he lowered his head.

When her lips touched his, he felt his whole body flare with arousal and, all reserve gone, he put his arm around her, deepening the kiss, tasting her sweet, unschooled mouth at long last. His body craved more. Much more.

'That's enough,' called Penny as the room burst into applause and giggles. 'You did very well.'

He released Morgana, who looked as dazed as he felt.

Katy was his partner for the next waltz. She soon mastered the steps. At the end, her lips were more enthusiastic, more practised, and more frankly sexual, but it was Morgana's kiss that lingered.

Morgana rested her hand on the back of her grandmother's chair, pretending to watch the dancing. Instead she relived Sloane's kiss, the feel of his lips against hers. She resisted the urge to touch her mouth with her fingers.

When she'd been younger, before she realised no man would want to marry her, she used to dream of her first kiss. How glad she was that it had been with Sloane.

She shook herself, regretting what she had said about his intention to marry. She'd given in to her envy of her cousin, who would be Sloane's ornament and bed partner. That was not well done of her.

She glanced up and saw him smoothly guide Rose around the room. It was not Sloane who was out of step, but she. He was deftly making his place in society, with the same ease as he moved through the steps of the waltz. She was the one who did not fit.

After the dancing, they all went to the front drawing room for refreshment so that the footmen could return the library to its former state. Hungry and thirsty from the morning's exertion, they eagerly consumed the lemonade and biscuits Cripps served, the butler revealing nothing of his thoughts of the morning's activities. There was much laughter. Even Lucy laughed aloud at something Mr Elliot said to her.

Madame Bisou's carriage soon arrived and she had to drag her friend Robert away from the book he and Mary had their noses in. After they left, Morgana glanced over to where Katy and Rose practised flirting with Sloane. He looked up at the same time and caught her watching him.

It was almost as if she could feel his lips on hers once more.

Lucy appeared next to her, Mr Elliot standing behind. 'Beg pardon, Miss Hart, may Mr Elliot and I return to the garden? I had not finished showing him some of the plants.'

Morgana could not help but give the girl a quizzical look, but she said, 'Of course you may, Lucy.' Were they really sneaking away to bed?

The idea did not shock her at this moment. She touched her lips where Sloane had kissed and wondered what other thrills existed between men and women, matters Madame Bisou implied in every lesson. Until the feel of Sloane's arms around her and his achingly tender, then eager, kiss, Morgana had not quite grasped the madam's meaning.

Another carriage rumbled to a stop out in the street. Morgana wandered over to the window to see who it was. The blood drained from her face as she watched her aunt and cousin assisted from the carriage. 'It is Aunt Winnie and Hannah.'

'Oh, dear.' Miss Moore wrung her hands.

'How lovely,' her grandmother said.

Morgana heard the knock at the door and Cripps open it. 'It is too late to hide in the library.' They would be seen from the hall. She turned to the girls. 'You are Miss Moore's nieces, remember. You know precisely how to behave.'

Cripps came to announce the visitors. Miss Moore whispered, 'Katy, remember to be quiet and ladylike.'

Katy nodded, clamping her mouth shut.

Her aunt and cousin were the last people Morgana would wish to call upon her, especially with Sloane present, but she stood ready to face them. All the others rose from their chairs as well, standing like a line of soldiers behind their captain. Only her grandmother remained seated. Morgana patted her hair quickly and tried to tuck up the strands that had come loose during the waltz.

Her aunt and Hannah entered. Morgana smiled. 'Why, Aunt Winnie, Hannah, how lovely to see you.'

'Lovely to see you,' Lady Hart parroted.

Her aunt looked perplexed at the room full of women. Hannah's eyes landed directly on Sloane, though they narrowed considerably when she saw him standing between one pretty girl and one beautiful one.

'Come, meet Miss Moore's nieces.' Morgana kept her voice light. 'Remember, I told you they were visiting, and look who else has come to call—Mr Sloane.'

She made the introductions, but was not surprised when her aunt and cousin showed little curiosity. The nieces of a lady's companion would no doubt be almost beneath their notice.

Hannah looked daggers at Rose, but when Sloane sat in the chair next to her, she brightened a little.

'We decided we must call upon Morgana,' Hannah remarked to him, but for all to hear. 'We have been sadly remiss for not doing so before, but there are so many calls one must make. Today I insisted we must put her first on our list.'

Hannah regarded Sloane with her usual proprietary air, and

Morgana pushed away another wave of envy, felt more acutely so soon after experiencing his kiss. Hannah had recently confided that Sloane had not made an offer, but had asked Hannah's father if he would object to one. Uncle Cowdlin had not objected. According to Hannah it would be only a matter of time before her parents would be giving an engagement ball.

Morgana pressed a hand to her stomach.

Sloane had turned all his attention to Hannah. Katy sat very stiffly, her lips compressed into a tight line. Rose examined a piece of music that had been left on the table. Morgana sat between her grandmother and her aunt, trying to deflect any conversation that might cause her aunt to discover Lady Hart's infirmity of mind.

After about five minutes, Sloane stood. 'I have quite overstayed my welcome. It is time for me to take my leave.'

Morgana turned to him with a polite smile. 'Thank you so much for calling, Mr Sloane. It was kind of you.' She turned back to her aunt.

He said goodbye to the others and Hannah walked him to the drawing-room door. Sloane did not look at Morgana again.

After he left, Hannah and her mother prattled on for a few minutes about how Sloane was bound to offer for Hannah soon, information that had Rose, Katy and Mary passing surprised glances to each other. Then Hannah announced that she and her mother ought to depart to make their numerous other calls. Morgana saw them to the door and Cripps stood by to assist them.

'You do come to Almack's with us tonight, do you not, Morgana?' her aunt asked.

'Yes. Thank you so much for including me, Aunt Winnie.' In truth, Morgana had found the *ton*'s marriage mart a bit tedious of late.

Hannah gave Morgana a quick hug. 'Do not worry, Morgana. I will find some beaux to dance with you.'

'Thank you, Hannah,' Morgana responded tightly. 'You are too good.'

Sloane stepped out of White's after a dinner with Heronvale, during which the marquess had impressed upon him the necessity of a good marriage to succeed in politics. If that were not enough, Sloane's father had made an appearance, infuriated that Sloane shared Heronvale's table. The noise of carriages clattering by and the other street sounds were infinitely preferable to the Earl's grating voice. As was his habit, Sloane glanced around him.

His nephew stood a few steps from the bow window. 'Do you attend Almack's, Uncle?'

It was easy to read on David's countenance that he had something on his mind. 'I am headed there now.'

'May I walk with you?' David smiled tentatively.

'Certainly.'

'Does your grandfather know you waited for me?' Sloane asked as they crossed the street.

'Never,' exclaimed David. He glanced at Sloane. 'He has it in for you, you know.'

Sloane laughed. 'He always has had.'

'I think it irrational,' David said firmly. 'I disapprove heartily.'

'But not loudly, I hope.' The boy was still at the Earl's mercy, at least financially. Unless he wanted to take the hard road Sloane had taken, he'd best keep his opinions to himself.

His nephew flashed a quick smile and then they walked for a while in silence.

Finally David said, 'I have called again upon Lady Hannah. I thought you should know.'

'I've made no claim, David,' Sloane said. 'She is free to spend time with whom she pleases.'

'But I respect your interest in her. I—I just wanted you to know my reasons make no infringement on your interest. As I explained, I cannot even think of marrying, so my time spent calling on her and taking her for a turn in the park is mere friendship. If I called upon someone else, it might raise the girl's hopes unrealistically, but Lady Hannah has no expectation of me. It makes it a good arrangement between us.'

Sloane was glad Hannah had David's company. The busier she was, the less guilty he felt for avoiding any decision about her.

'Sounds fair,' he said.

They arrived at Almack's and soon entered the assembly room. Lady Hannah was already there. Her eyes lit up when she saw them approaching her.

But it was not Hannah who was on Sloane's mind. The band struck up a waltz, and he waited for David to engage Hannah for the set. He scanned the assembly room, finally spying Morgana sitting alone at the room's edge, a place for spinsters and dowagers.

He made his way to her. 'May I have the honour of this dance?'

She looked up at him, her eyes as warm and sultry and melancholic as when they had waltzed earlier that day. Without a word she accepted his hand and held his arm as they walked to the dance floor.

Sloane had all he could do to keep from holding her as close as he'd done in their more intimate waltz. That evening Heronvale had called Morgana unconventional. If he only knew how unconventional she could be, willing to dance seductively for the edification of her courtesan students.

Heronvale made it clear he thought Lady Hannah a good

choice for Sloane to marry—in spite of her unconventional cousin. Sloane had wrapped himself up so completely in Morgana's difficulties, he'd hardly given Hannah a thought. The Season was coming to an end. He must surely make his move soon.

How was Sloane to contemplate marriage to Lady Hannah when his senses were consumed with bedding her cousin?

He shook himself. He was thinking like a rake again. The direction of his thoughts needed turning. 'Why were you seated alone, Morgana?' he asked instead.

'Oh,' she responded vaguely, avoiding looking up at him. 'I have the headache, I suppose.'

'Fustian,' he said.

She did not reply.

'I insist you tell me.' He sounded demanding even to his own ears. Like his father.

She gave him a quick but defiant glance.

His tone softened. 'Forgive me again, Morgana. I am acting the brute. I meant to say, it is not your nature to sit in corners. You typically enjoy whatever tedious entertainment the *ton* offers.'

'Do I?' She met his eye. 'Or perhaps, like you, I merely pretend to enjoy myself.'

He nodded. *'Touché.'*

She increased the pressure on his hand, very slightly, but he did not miss it. 'I am quarrelling again,' she murmured. She wrinkled her forehead as if deep in thought. 'I confess I do not find Almack's to be *the seventh heaven of the fashionable world.* True, the intrigue of who dances with whom, which gentleman favours which young lady, who will next receive an offer of marriage, is all very interesting. And it does provide me an opportunity to dance.'

He pulled her in an infinitesimal bit closer. 'You sound as if you are trying to convince yourself to enjoy it.'

She gave him a frank expression. 'I suppose I am.'

They twirled around the floor, brushing near Hannah and David who were smiling and laughing together.

Morgana inclined her head in their direction. 'Hannah enjoys your nephew's company, I believe.'

He glanced back at the young couple. 'I believe she does.'

They circled half the floor, Sloane enjoying how she moved with him, the scent of her hair, the curve of her cheek. He wondered if he could get Hannah to invite him in the Cowdlin carriage again, if he could walk Morgana to the door and taste her lips again…

'Does it bother you?' Morgana broke his reverie.

'Does what bother me?'

'Hannah and your nephew.'

He had forgotten them. Besides, he disliked discussing Hannah with Morgana, especially when he was fantasising about seducing her. 'Should it?'

Her brows rose in response.

Sloane frowned. Hannah and David swept into view again. He need not concern himself with David's interest in Hannah. His nephew had explained how it was, but Sloane was reminded he must make his offer to Hannah soon. Lord Cowdlin might become desperate enough to select a suitor of smaller fortune, unlikely as that was.

A sick feeling settled in the pit of his stomach.

'Will you offer for her?' Morgana asked, as if reading his thoughts.

Her words were like a knife slicing into him. He wanted to offer for Lady Hannah, did he not? Why not simply tell Morgana he intended to do so?

He felt his face harden to stone. 'A gentleman would first inform the lady in question, not her cousin.'

She flinched as if a blow had been struck, and again Sloane regretted his churlish words.

The music stopped. The set was over. Morgana stepped out of his arms. He reached out to gather her back, to apologise again, but Hannah and David rushed to their side.

'Everyone is planning an evening at Vauxhall tomorrow,' Hannah said breathlessly. 'Does that not sound marvellous?'

He rose and his smile was all for Hannah. Morgana could not bear it.

'Marvellous indeed,' he said in an amused tone.

Hannah clutched his arm. 'We shall include Athenia, my brother Varney…well, everyone! Say you will go to Vauxhall, Mr Sloane?'

'I shall consider it,' he said, prevaricating, and wishing he could speak to Morgana alone.

Hannah pursed her lips like a petulant child. 'You must say yes.' She tossed him a pert smile. 'Athenia's parents will come so Mama and Papa will have company. They will pay little mind to me!' She fluttered her eyelashes at him. 'Say you will come with us, Mr Sloane.'

'Very well.' Anything to be rid of her.

'Will you act the host, Mr Sloane?' Hannah persisted.

This was an impertinence. If he had offered for her, she might have a right to ask. Sloane disliked being forced to be the gentleman.

'If your father permits,' he said tightly.

His tone went completely over Hannah's head. She clasped her hands together happily. 'That is splendid!'

Somewhat belatedly, she seemed to notice Morgana standing next to him. She touched Morgana's arm. 'You must come as well, Morgana. I insist upon it.'

Morgana gave her a pasty smile, which Hannah must have taken for assent. Hannah turned away from her cousin and back to Sloane, begging him to lead her out in the next dance. Again Hannah had trapped him.

He acquiesced politely, but when he turned to Morgana, she was walking away. She did not look back at him.

Chapter Eleven

Mrs Rice sat in the room behind her glove shop, sipping a glass of claret and mentally calculating the amount of money she could wring from her girls this night.

She frowned. She'd recruited one new girl, who was almost useless. Fit for nothing but streetwalking. Without Katy and Mary business had definitely slowed. Profits were down. At this rate, she might make more blunt with gloves than with harlots.

Trigg, the procurer who had let the maid slip through his hands, entered, wearing a smug look on his face.

'I hope this means you have girls for me,' Mrs Rice muttered.

'I have information.' He sauntered over to her table and leaned in close. She detested the odour of the man.

'Well, what is it?' She would love to get rid of Trigg, who was a bit too clever for her to control completely.

He grinned, showing yellow teeth. 'Word is out that a society lady has them.'

'A society lady.' She could guess which society lady. 'Her name?'

Trigg took a step back. 'I will discover the name soon.'

Mrs Rice drummed her fingers on the table. 'It is that *woman*.' She hissed. 'The one who charged in here big-as-you-please.'

Trigg's brows rose. 'Describe her.'

Mrs Rice huffed. 'I cannot. She obscured her face.'

'A Long Meg?'

'Why, yes, she was a bit tall.'

He frowned and rubbed his head. 'I know the one.'

A few minutes later Trigg stepped out into the street, pausing to take a swig from the bottle of gin he carried in his pocket. He headed for a pub he knew of, the place where an acquaintance had heard from another man that some footman spoke of females more like harlots who were guests in his lady's house. It was thin evidence, and the man said the next day the footman denied it all, but Trigg did not relish hearing Rice ring a peal over his head. Besides, he wanted to believe it was that lady in the park. He'd be pleased to consign her to the devil, quick.

He stepped into an alley, for another quick taste of gin. Suddenly hands grabbed him from behind, dragging him deeper into the dark and he felt a cold edge of steel against his throat.

A sinister voice said, 'I hear you've been asking questions about some missing doxies.'

Trigg nearly casting up his accounts, knew better than to show fear. 'What of it?' he growled.

The blade's edge pierced his skin and he felt his blood trickling warm down his neck. 'Stay out of it,' the voice—a familiar voice, he realised—snarled. 'If you want to keep your head.' The knife made another slice, not deep, but Trigg was afraid to move lest it sever more than his skin.

'What's it to you?' He tried to sound fierce, but his voice rose like a girl's.

The man laughed and it was enough to make Trigg taste his own vomit. 'I have them. The maid and that other one, too. The one who knocked you out. They are mine and the man who takes them from me will not live.'

Trigg tried to laugh, too, but succeeded only in making a gasping sound. 'Why should I listen to you? Who are you?'

The chilling laugh returned. 'I am the devil. Touch what is mine and I'll have my due.'

Trigg was pushed forward, and he fell to his knees into a puddle of filth. By the time he scrambled to his feet and turned around, the man—the man from the park—had disappeared.

Sloane watched Trigg from the depths of the alley, the man silhouetted against the lamplight coming from St James's Street. As he'd anticipated, Trigg broke into a run. Sloane figured he'd run all the way to whatever dirty hovel he called home.

He pulled out his handkerchief and wiped the blood from his knife. Tossing the handkerchief away, he put the knife back in its sheath in his coat pocket. He left the alley from the back and made his way to the street.

When he stepped on to the pavement of St James's Street, he looked like any other gentleman pursuing his nightly interests.

It was fortunate Sloane had refused Hannah's offer of a carriage ride home. The day's episodes with Morgana had left him disordered, restless, on edge. Having made his way to his post at Mrs Rice's window, what he'd overheard fuelled his already taut nerves with something more dangerous. The violence of the underworld had taken a step closer to Morgana, and Sloane needed to push it back hard. It was a good night for intimidation. He'd halfway wished for an all-out brawl.

His tactic was misdirection. Trigg would now abandon his search for the 'lady' and begin looking for a tougher customer. Sloane wagered the man would not guess it was a resident of proper Culross Street who, as easy as the roughest rookery thief, used a knife to draw blood.

Sloane would return to spy on Mrs Rice's place again, to make sure his trickery worked.

After thinking about it half the night, Morgana quite sorted it out in her mind that Sloane's familiarity towards her had been her own fault. He'd seen how unladylike she could be, and, therefore, felt less gentlemanly restraint in her presence. She could still enjoy his company, but she must never mistake it for something more, not when he was intent on marrying Hannah. Better Morgana throw her energies into her girls.

They were gathered in the library, Madame Bisou having just arrived. Morgana happened to mention her invitation to Vauxhall.

Katy flung herself down on the settee. 'Can we not all go to Vauxhall with you? I am sure I shall die if I spend one more day in this house.'

Morgana regarded Katy with sympathy. Her charges had indeed been trapped within the confines of this house, able to go no further than the tiny garden or the privy. Only Lucy had ventured beyond, but that was merely to the patch of land next door to assist Mr Elliot with his plantings.

'We cannot chance Mrs Rice seeing us, Katy.' Mary was at her most earnest. 'She would make us go back to her.'

Katy waved her hand dismissively. 'It is not as if Mrs Rice would go to Vauxhall. Besides, we could wear masks. They wear masks at Vauxhall Gardens, do they not?'

'They do indeed,' answered Madame Bisou, who gave Morgana a thoughtful look. 'As I think of it, our girls could do with a bit of practice. We ought not to launch them upon the world without a trial. Do you not agree, Miss Hart?'

How could Morgana agree when she really had no wish to launch her students at all? Sloane's words echoed in her mind—they would sell themselves to the highest bidder and still be at the mercy of a man's whims. What if they could not match the success Harriette Wilson had achieved? What happened to failed courtesans?

She feared they would wind up in shops like Mrs Rice's. Would all her hopes for the girls come to naught?

She had come too far to lose hope now.

'I do not know…' Morgana finally answered, her voice trailing off as Katy's mournful eyes bore into her.

She wished she'd never mentioned Vauxhall Gardens. She certainly did not want to go there and watch Hannah flirt with Sloane. Perhaps Hannah and Sloane might disappear down one of those dark walks that were so whispered about. She would sit in the box with Aunt Winnie and imagine what might take place between Sloane and Hannah.

She gave herself a mental shake and reminded herself again that Sloane had always been Hannah's, not hers.

'I have never been to Vauxhall Gardens,' Miss Moore piped up in a dreamy tone, merely adding to the growing pressure.

Morgana grasped at straws. 'We do not have clothes for you yet.'

She intended to ask Madame Emeraude to come to the house to measure the girls and make up some dresses for them, but had put this off. It was another task she must do before they could leave her.

Cripps knocked on the door. 'A trunk has been delivered,

miss.' He announced this as formally as if the Regent had come to call.

'A trunk?' Any delivery was unexpected. Morgana certainly did not expect her father to send her anything. He'd barely written to her.

'From Paris, miss,' Cripps added.

'Paris!' Morgana laughed. Her lost trunk!

'What is funny?' Katy grumbled.

Morgana walked over and tweaked Katy's chin. 'Your new wardrobe has arrived.'

'New wardrobe?' Katy asked cautiously. The other girls looked up in interest, even Lucy, who was beginning to lose some of her maid-like demeanour.

Morgana nodded, still astonished that her missing apparel should have come at this very moment. 'Unless I am mistaken, it is a trunk filled with the latest Paris fashions, and it has arrived exactly in time to dress you in style.'

'Paris!' shrieked Katy, reverting to less-than-ladylike behaviour. 'Give us a look at it.'

Fate, apparently, had decided to shove Morgana forward. Her girls would go to Vauxhall, after all, and would practice for the coming day when they would leave her house and go to some gentleman's bed.

Morgana told Cripps to have the trunk brought in to them. Barely had the two footmen set it down in the middle of the room than the girls begged to open it. They pulled out dress after dress of fine muslin and silk. Day dresses, evening gowns, walking dresses. Morgana had forgotten how many her new stepmother had insisted she purchase.

Katy squealed in delight as each one emerged from between layers of tissue paper. Rose took a deep wine-red gown and held it against herself. If such a thing were possible, her features shone even more beautifully with its rich colour.

Mary fingered a pale blue muslin, a shade as soft as her voice. Lucy held back, but Morgana handed her a pink confection and made her slip it over her plain grey dress, transforming her into as fresh and innocent a miss as had ever had her come-out.

'We have the dresses, Miss Hart. Do we go to Vauxhall or not?' Katy stood hands on hips, ready for battle.

Morgana glanced at Madame Bisou. 'Who would escort us? We cannot go unprotected.'

'Robert will come with us,' assured the madam.

Mary glanced up at the mention of his name.

'Perhaps Mr Elliot would come as well,' Lucy added. 'We could depend on him.'

'We can dance and have a high old time.' Katy pulled a paisley shawl from the trunk and wrapped it around herself. She danced around the room as if already at the pleasure gardens. Rose joined her, holding the red dress as if she were wearing it.

'Oh, very well!' Morgana smiled, resigned to seeing her fledglings spread their wings. 'But I will go with you, as will Miss Moore, and we shall all wear masks.'

'Hurrah!' cried Katy.

Rose ran to the pianoforte and began a rousing tune. Katy grabbed Morgana while Mary and Madame Bisou pulled Lucy and Miss Moore on to the floor as well. Even Morgana's grandmother rose to her feet and clapped her hands to the music. Rose began to sing: 'Come live with me and be my love, And we will all the pleasures prove...'

The others joined in: 'That hill and valley, dale and field, And all the craggy mountains yield...'

Sloane frowned as he stepped onto the pavement in front of his house. He could hear Morgana and her girls singing.

The shepherds' swains shall dance and sing;
For thy delight each May morning:
If these delights thy mind may move,
Then live with me and be my love.

Anyone passing by could hear it. In fact, people two streets away could hear it. Someone was bound to comment. Foolish Morgana. He'd told her to be more discreet.

Live with me and be my love echoed in his brain as he crossed the pavement and headed towards Bond Street. He had no particular errand, just a restlessness that he hoped to walk off. Perhaps he might look in at Lock's for a new hat or drop in at White's.

He gave a glance over his shoulder. Instead he might walk round to Morgana's rear door and join in their gaiety.

He was not sure why he suddenly thought he ought to avoid them. He lengthened his stride.

It was due to Morgana. His rakish interest in her was growing at an alarming rate. He could barely be in her company without exceeding the bounds of civility. Like kissing her as though he meant it. He *had* meant it, that was the rub—damn Penny for that little stunt. He wanted to dance with her again, not as he had at Almack's but as he'd danced with her in her parlour. He wanted to feel her body next to his.

This was hardly the way to think when he ought to be heading to Lady Hannah's to ask for her hand in marriage. Hannah would make a creditable wife. He had faith she would develop into a successful hostess and a pleasing bed partner. As Heronvale said, she would be an asset to any man with political plans.

So why did the idea of even spending a whole evening in her presence at Vauxhall make him want to head back to a smuggling den?

Sloane might have begged off, sent a note around that urgent business prevented him from keeping the Vauxhall engagement. Only one reason prevented him. He longed to see what Morgana thought of the place.

He shook his head in dismay at this thought, and crossed the street. A carriage, his father's crest on its side, rolled past him and came to a rather abrupt stop.

His father leaned out the window. 'Cyprian! I desire to speak with you. Get in, if you please.'

Sloane did not please. 'You may say what you will through the window, sir.'

The Earl of Dorton glared at him. 'I will not mince words, boy. I have come from Heronvale. The man wants to put your name forward for the Commons. Unheard of, and I told him so in no uncertain terms.'

Sloane gave him an unconcerned shrug. 'Then you need worry no further.'

His father sneered. 'I told Heronvale where you came from, boy. He knows it all.'

A muscle twitched in Sloane's cheek. His conception had always been a matter of conjecture in whispered conversations among the *ton*. Sloane always trusted his father's inflated pride to prevent him from confirming such rumours. Apparently the Earl's hatred of Sloane exceeded even that.

Sloane let his father's dagger plunge into his gut and twist, and then he mentally pulled it away, telling himself it did not matter. Heronvale must spurn him now. There would be no seat in parliament. It did not matter. Sloane still had wealth and that alone would give him power enough to plague his father to the end of the man's days.

Sloane leaned into the carriage. Giving his father a direct look, he lifted the corners of his mouth in the sardonic grin that always made the man hopping mad. 'Dash it,' he said with thick sarcasm. 'My political career is ruined.' He spun around and walked away.

'Stay!' the Earl ordered. 'Stay. I command you!'

Sloane continued on his way, but to his dismay the carriage caught up to him. As he walked, his father shouted from the window, 'And another thing! You'll not marry that Cowdlin chit. I'll see you do not.' The Earl's face turned an alarming shade of red. 'I will ruin you first. I swear I will. I'll send you back to the sewers or wherever you came by your ill-gotten wealth—'

Sloane stopped and the carriage continued on its way. He could hear his father pounding on the roof and shouting to the coachman to stop, but by the time the man did, Sloane had headed off in the other direction.

His destination was even more aimless than before. His cheeks flamed and he felt as sick to his stomach as if he'd again been nine years old. The streets had not been crowded and there was no indication that anyone had heeded the exchange, but Sloane felt as if he'd been laid bare in front of everyone.

By God, he'd thought he'd mastered this long ago, the humiliation of being pulled to pieces by the Earl in front of relatives, servants, schoolmasters—anyone. He'd perfected the appearance of not giving a deuce what his father said, or he once had. Why now? Why did his father's words wound him now? Because the Earl had spoken to Heronvale about his mother?

A memory of her flashed though his mind. A fragment, all he had left of her. A pretty lady, smiling at him, laughing, bouncing him on her lap and kissing his cheeks. He had no idea if the memory was truly of his mother, but many a childhood night he'd forced himself to believe so.

* * *

Sloane walked until the dinner hour. He had an impulse to beg a meal from Morgana, but they were probably sitting down at this very moment. He would wait to see her at Vauxhall. He had the odd notion that seeing her would mend the wound his father created. Of course, that was nonsense.

Elliot, efficient as usual, had made the arrangements for Vauxhall, engaging a supper box for the Cowdlin party and ordering the refreshments.

Elliot also had Sloane's dinner waiting for him. Afterwards his valet helped him dress for the evening, until all he need do was wait for the Cowdlin carriage.

He paced the Aubusson carpet of his drawing room, his footsteps so muffled by its nap he could hear the ticking of the mantel clock. His father's voice kept ringing in his head. To mask it, he started to hum a tune.

Come live with me and be my love…

His butler announced that the carriage had arrived, and Sloane gathered his hat and gloves. The night was warm, a harbinger of summer nights to come.

He walked up to the carriage and greeted Lord and Lady Cowdlin and Hannah through its open window. 'Would you like me to collect Miss Hart?'

'She is not coming,' said Lady Hannah.

Her mother added, 'She sent a note today, begging off.'

Sloane frowned as he climbed in, suddenly dreading the long night ahead. 'She is not ill, I hope?'

'Not at all,' Lady Cowdlin assured him.

He worried that something had happened with the courtesan school, while he was wandering the streets of Mayfair feeling sorry for himself. He frowned.

Hannah, who was in very high spirits, did not notice. She could barely sit still. 'Poor Morgana!' she said. 'I hope she did not feel she would be out of place among my friends. Indeed, she has little to say to them. You have been kind to engage her, Mr Sloane.'

'I find Miss Hart's company quite pleasant,' he said, tersely, offended at her characterisation of Morgana.

Hannah responded with a knowing expression, as if she understood he was merely being civil. Sloane gave it up. To say anything else might arouse suspicions that more went on than the Cowdlins should ever know about Morgana.

Hannah's giddiness wore very thin by the time the carriage rolled over the new Vauxhall bridge.

'I do wish we were to arrive by boat. It would be vastly more romantic,' sighed Hannah.

'Not good for my gout,' grumbled her father.

Hannah continued to prattle on about everything being 'exciting' or 'marvellous' and how she could not wait to tell Athenia Poltrop this or that. She barely took heed of the spectacle that greeted them when they crossed through the garden's entrance.

Thousands of lamps were strung throughout the tall elms and bushes, like stars come down to earth. Arches and colonnades and porticos made it appear as if ancient Greece had come alive in the stars, though the music of the orchestra sounded modern in their ears.

Sloane had always liked the fantasy that was Vauxhall. Nothing was as it seemed here, illusion was its only reality. Here a man could wear a mask and even the glittering lamps could not reveal whether he be a duke or the duke's coachman. Here rogues and pickpockets shared the walks with frolicking vicars and extravagant nabobs. Indeed, a lady might walk by her maid without knowing her. She might dance next to her footman or the man who delivered coal to her Mayfair townhouse. It was impossible to feel one did not belong in this place.

But Hannah hurried them down the Grand Walk, past the Prince's Pavilion and the theatre, past the colonnade, heading for the circle of supper boxes near the fountain.

Sloane wondered if Morgana would have rushed down the Grand Walk so quickly. Or would she have become distracted by the sights and all the people? Would she have tried to guess who the people were and to what sort of life they would return when the night was over?

'I declare, this place is filled with riff-raff,' Lady Cowdlin sniffed, apparently as oblivious to the splendour as her daughter.

'Pay them no mind, dear,' Lord Cowdlin advised. His lordship, however, paid particular mind to a group of women as pretty as flowers, all masked and escorted by two gentlemen. Sloane suspected Cowdlin would search out this very group as soon as the opportunity presented itself.

The supper box Elliot had arranged for them was in a spot with a view of the fountain, its water sparkling like tiny gold coins in the park's illumination. The music from the orchestra rose and fell, carried in and out on the wind.

Lord and Lady Poltrop were already seated in the box, sipping some of the good vintage wine Sloane—or rather Elliot—had ordered for the occasion. Athenia jumped up when she saw Hannah, and the two young ladies embraced each other as if it had been an age since they'd been together when it had probably been as recent as that very afternoon.

'No one else has arrived,' Athenia said to Hannah. 'Indeed, I feared to be the only one here. Can you think how humiliating? Your brother will come, will he not?'

'I wonder if he and the others were directed to the wrong box.' Hannah looked about her with a worried expression. She reached out a hand towards Sloane. 'Mr Sloane, do take us to search for the others! Perhaps they are on the other side. Oh, do take us.'

Lord Cowdlin was too busy whispering something to Poltrop to take heed of Hannah's request, but Lady Cowdlin magnanimously gave her permission. 'Do not venture into the Dark Walk, however,' she warned in a jocular voice.

As if Sloane would be so foolish as to take two silly girls into an area of the park more suited to the sort of rakish behaviour he had forsworn. He'd rather they quickly discover the missing members of their party so he could get some relief from the chatter.

The two young ladies walked arm in arm, keeping up an intense conversation and paying Sloane little mind. He walked a step behind them, close enough to prevent any mischief befalling them. They circled the area where men and women danced beneath the musicians' balcony. Though both girls craned their necks to search the crowd, they spent as much time whispering to each other. Sloane, out of a desperate need for respite from their company, looked around for Hannah's 'particular' friends, the ones who surrounded her at every society function.

He did not see them, but he spied the colourful group of ladies Lord Cowdlin had so admired. Not surprisingly, they had seated themselves in a box where they could be easily noticed.

He guided Hannah and Athenia past them, but one of the prettily dressed females cried, 'Well, now. Aren't you the handsome gent.'

Another giggled, but a third said a sharp, 'Hush.'

Sloane whirled around, but other strollers obscured his view. Lady Hannah and her friend kept walking, and Sloane had to push his way through the crowd to catch up to them.

He looked over his shoulder again and a gap in the crowd afforded him a good look at the group.

One of the young ladies was raven-haired, another a redhead, the others golden-haired and mousy brown. But it was not these his eyes were riveted upon. It was the tall, dark-haired woman who stood in the midst of them.

Morgana.

Chapter Twelve

How could he have not instantly known them at first glance? Before the crowd closed the gap again, he'd even recognised Penny and Miss Moore. He'd bet one of the gentlemen with them was Penny's favourite inamorato, that idiot Duprey. The identity of the other gentleman put a worried crease between his eyes. Few of Penny's masculine acquaintances would be men Sloane thought fit for Morgana's company.

He put his hand on Hannah's elbow. 'Ladies, let us go back to the supper box. Your friends may have arrived in our absence.'

'Oh, let us do that,' Hannah replied enthusiastically.

They all walked at a brisker pace: Hannah, to find her friends; Sloane, to find a way to get back to Morgana.

Several young people could be seen in the supper box. Hannah and Athenia broke away and hurried to greet them. Hannah's brother Varney saw them, rushing forward to escort them into the box.

Sloane's nephew appeared to be the only one to notice Sloane's arrival. 'Good evening, Uncle,' David said. 'Is this not a beautiful night for the Gardens?'

Sloane agreed that it was, but could say little more, because the supper arrived and soon everyone was piling plates full of paper-thin slices of ham and tiny chickens. A fruit girl filled dishes with fresh strawberries and cherries, and a sideboard offered a selection of wines and arrack, the heady punch always served at Vauxhall. His nephew dipped into the arrack more than once.

Soon a bell signalled the start of Madame Saqui's daring rope dancing, and the young people poured out of the box in a hurry not to miss a moment of it. Lady Cowdlin and Lady Poltrop begged off, assuring Sloane they would be very comfortable in the supper box with each other for company and certain their husbands would return at any moment.

Sloane did not follow the young people to view Saqui's performance, but rather strode across to the South Walk's supper boxes to find Morgana.

Penny and Miss Moore were the only ones of the party seated in the box. Sloane's eyes narrowed. Sir Reginald, one of Penny's gaming-hell regulars, was there as well, not exactly the sort of company Morgana should keep.

She and the girls were likely watching Madame Saqui. Sloane threaded through the crowd exactly like the pickpockets were doing. He looked for Morgana, finally finding her, standing with Rose at the edge of the crowd, chatting with a grey-haired man. Just as he'd feared, they had attracted an admirer.

He pushed his way through.

'Morgana!' he cried, seizing her arm.

Morgana jumped, pulling away, before she realised the man who had accosted her was Sloane. She felt flushed with excitement to see him, even though she had not wished him to know they were there. Vexed at Katy for her impudent gibe as he passed them, Morgana saw the precise moment he'd recognised them. She should have realised he would come after her.

'You have found us.' She gave a defiant toss of her head. 'I am going to box Katy's ears.'

'What the devil do you think you are doing?' he said in a fierce whisper as he squeezed her arm.

She pointedly stared at the hand grasping her. 'I am watching Madame Saqui,' she said in patient tones. 'And I do wish you would not always come rushing up to me, screeching my name.'

He released her.

'I beg your pardon,' he muttered.

She turned back to the spectacle, but her heart beat wildly, not at Madame Saqui's daring exploits, but that she could be in this magical place with Sloane even for a few minutes. Perhaps for the time being she could pretend he was her beau, pretend he was not about to scold her again.

Madame Saqui faltered on the rope and teetered for several seconds before regaining her balance. The crowd gasped a collective 'Ohhh!' Perhaps Madame experienced the same sensation Morgana felt, as if she could tumble through the air.

Morgana had forgotten Rose was by her side until the girl touched Sloane's sleeve. 'Mr Sloane, may I introduce my father to you?'

'Of course.' He sounded as surprised as Morgana had been.

'Mr Brian O'Keefe, one of the musicians here.'

Morgana had nearly fallen to the ground when the man came up to Rose. She'd made the girls promise they would not engage in any liaisons this first outing. Morgana had been about to send the man packing when Rose told her who he was.

Sloane shook the man's hand. 'Indeed?'

Madame Saqui was joined by her husband and son and the

crowd applauded with approval. Morgana was more interested in watching how easily Sloane conversed with the musician, as at ease as if he were talking with a gentleman at Almack's. It was a quality she greatly admired in him.

Rose and her father stepped away to watch the rest of the performance, and Sloane leaned in to whisper in Morgana's ear, 'What possessed you to bring those girls here? Do you not know what happens in this place? You are noticed, believe me. You look like a group of harlots.'

She knew this scold was forthcoming. 'We *are* a group of harlots,' she replied, her voice unapologetic. He must reconcile himself to the life they were training these young women to lead. So must she. 'Madame Bisou said some practice would be beneficial.'

The performance ended to another burst of applause and cheers and the crowd began to disperse.

Rose came up to her again. 'May I spend some more time with my father, Miss Hart? He will bring me back to the box.'

'I think that would be very nice for you.' Morgana smiled. She watched Mr O'Brien escort his daughter to the two-storey gazebo, from where the orchestra played high above the crowd. 'Rose's father. Imagine that.'

'Gainfully employed, as well,' Sloane added. 'What the devil is she doing in your courtesan school?'

His scold seemed to be over, and he seemed more her friend again. It made her want to dance the night away with him.

'I was wondering the very same thing.' She took a breath to steady herself. 'I should go back to the supper box.'

He took her arm more cordially than before. 'That puts me of a mind to tell you that the gentleman cosying up to Penny is no man you should know.'

That puffy man with the exaggerated manners? Morgana

could see no harm in him. She gave Sloane a saucy glance. 'Oh, is he scandalous? As scandalous as you?'

He dipped down to her ear. 'You have no idea how scandalous I can be.' His voice was low and his breath on her skin warm.

She swallowed.

They passed under the arch near the supper box. Mary rushed up to them, Robert Duprey at her side. 'Miss Hart! Miss Hart!'

Morgana was about to beg her to stop calling out her name, when Mary cried, 'Lucy has run off!'

'What?' Morgana stopped.

Mary saw Sloane and gave a quick curtsy. 'Good evening, sir.'

Duprey nodded. 'Oddest thing. Standing happy as you please. Calls out, "He's here!", then takes off.'

Mary added, 'Mr Elliot ran after her, but we thought we should find you right away. Or at least that is the advice Mr Duprey gave, which I thought was excellent.'

'Elliot?' exclaimed Sloane. 'What the devil is he doing here?'

Morgana held up her hand to silence him. 'Where did she go?'

'Ran down the Dark Walk. Worst place. Dangerous,' Duprey responded.

Lucy had been doing so well. She'd even seemed happy sometimes, blossoming, like her garden. Morgana could not bear it if someone had frightened her.

She turned to Sloane. 'Will you take me to look for them? I dare not go alone.'

Sloane hesitated only a moment. 'Come along.'

The Dark Walk was not totally without light, but the lamps were fewer and dark alcoves and small private rooms were dotted along the path. Some sounds of revelry could be heard from the shadows, and Morgana was glad Sloane was at her side.

'I wonder if she saw the man from Hyde Park,' Morgana said. 'I cannot think anyone else would frighten her so. She wore a mask, for goodness' sake. He would not have known her.'

'I recognised you,' Sloane reminded her.

'Yes,' she admitted. 'But only after Katy made her silly comment.'

He stopped her for a moment and made her face him. 'Morgana, when will you realise that you cannot truly hide behind a mask or a hat with netting? If you are where you should not be, it is always possible for someone to discover it.'

She averted her eyes. She knew he spoke the truth. She had come to accept the likelihood of ruining herself over the courtesan school.

He took her chin in his fingers and turned her face back to his. 'You greatly risk your reputation with activities such as this. Already your name has been called out.'

'By you, as well,' she protested.

He nodded, but it only brought his face closer. 'I am sorry for it,' he murmured, his voice as soft as the orchestra's music drifting in from the distance. 'Forgive me.'

She lifted her face to his, remembering how easy it had been to stretch just a little farther and taste his lips.

The sound of giggles reached them, and Sloane pulled her aside so that they were shuttered by the bushes. A young couple walked by laughing and kissing. Morgana was shocked to see the lady was Athenia Poltrop and her companion Morgana's cousin Varney.

Sloane recognised them as well. 'Well, at least now I know what she and Hannah were whispering about.'

Recalling Hannah always returned Morgana to her senses. 'You must need to return to your party.'

He wrapped his arm around her back and squeezed her against his side. 'Let us find Lucy first.'

They walked all the way to the hermitage before they found her. Lucy, racked with sobs, sat on a bench with Mr Elliot holding and rocking her.

'Lucy.' Morgana wanted to rush to her, but Mr Elliot shook his head. 'What is it, Mr Elliot? What has happened to her? Has someone hurt her?'

She felt Sloane stiffen beside her, felt him as ready as she to fly to Lucy's defence.

Elliot's expression was pained. He turned to Lucy. 'Shall I tell them?'

Lucy gave them a miserable glance and nodded to Elliot, who did not release her from the circle of his arms.

'She's been hurt, all right, but it was a long time ago…'

In his precise, methodical voice, Elliot explained what Lucy had shared with him a little at a time in their quiet talks together pulling weeds and planting seeds. Lucy had been seduced at the shocking age of fourteen. The man next door, a family friend, seduced her and gave her to think it was her fault, that she'd been the one to entice him. The man found time for her often, Elliot went on, and Lucy in her naïveté came to believe it meant he loved her. He gave her money and other presents.

'But right before you hired her, Miss Hart, something else happened.' Lucy buried her face against Elliot's chest. 'This man took her to a place with two other men. They all had their way with her, and the men paid her for it. A few days later, the man took her to be with other men. She protested this time and he laughed at her, telling her to simply enjoy herself. He told her she was nothing but a common harlot. So Lucy believed that was what she must be.'

'Oh, Lucy!' Morgana felt tears sting her eyes. She knelt beside the girl, who fell into her arms. 'How very awful for you.'

'I was startin' to think maybe I wasn't all bad.' Lucy managed between shuddering sobs. 'Your lessons—Madame Bisou's and Miss Moore's—you tell us all the time that we are worth somethin' no matter what, that we deserve nice things. I was startin' to believe it, but I saw him, and I remembered…' Her voice trailed off.

'Who was it?' Sloane's voice cut through the night like sharpened steel.

Lucy looked up at him, and her sobbing stopped. 'His name is Mr Castle. He has the button shop next to my father's hosiery.'

'Where?' Sloane said in the same honed voice.

'Cheapside,' she answered. 'Milk Street.'

He nodded, still thin-lipped.

Morgana rose to her feet, her eyes on Sloane, sensing the danger rising in him. It filled her with dread.

Elliot spoke up. 'I'll bring her back in a bit, when she's a little calmer.' He gave Morgana a direct gaze. 'You can trust her to me.'

Morgana had no doubt she could. Lucy was in very good hands indeed. 'Well, we shall go then. I'll tell the others she was scared for a moment, but you talked her out of it, reminding her of the mask.'

He nodded agreement.

As soon as she and Sloane were out of earshot, Morgana asked, 'What are you going to do?'

'Do?' He stared straight ahead, but his voice still held that timbre of violence.

'About the man who molested Lucy.'

He did not answer.

'Are you going to kill him?'

He met her eye. 'You think me capable of such a thing?'

She did not look away. 'Yes.' She could easily imagine him able to kill a man.

His eyes narrowed. 'It does not shock you?'

'No.' A wild part of her wanted to kill the man herself for the wrong he'd done to Lucy. She dared not examine that part too closely. 'Will you do it?' Her voice came out all breathless.

He stared at her a long time 'No.' He took her arm suddenly and said, 'Come with me.'

Instead of returning her to the supper box, he led her to one of the small restaurants along the colonnade, selecting a small table in the corner where they were relatively private. He ordered them both a glass of wine. She felt unreasonably happy to be in his company.

'I must speak with you, Morgana.' Sloane's tone of voice did not mirror Morgana's gaiety, however. 'Does this not prove to you the dangerousness of this escapade? Suppose that man had recognised Lucy? What might have happened then?'

She avoided his eyes. 'But he did not see her, any more than Miss Poltrop or Varney saw us.'

He waved aside her comment. 'What if I had not been with you? Would you have run down the Dark Walk yourself, searching for Lucy?'

The server brought the wine and Morgana waited until the man left. 'I would have made Mary and Mr Duprey come with me.'

'No, you would not. You would have gone by yourself. You are reckless, Morgana.' He took a sip of wine before saying more. 'You do not perceive how easily one's reputation can be ruined. This business of yours already risks too much.'

She flashed her eyes. 'It is too late to scold me for this! It is done and I will not fail those girls now.' Morgana fought a wave of nausea. Was teaching Lucy, Katy, Rose and Mary to pander themselves so different than that man pandering Lucy?

'Give it up,' Sloane commanded.

She gazed at him, hoping he could not see the pain in her eyes. 'How can I?'

He did not answer but looked away, drinking his wine. Morgana felt the bitter sting of failure, the loss of his friendship, the shattering of her secret dreams. The only thing worse would be for him to realise that she herself knew how thoroughly she'd mismanaged everything.

She placed her glass on the table and made herself look defiant. 'Do you know that I envy them? I envy those girls. They will not be constrained by conventional behaviour. They will be able to do as they wish!'

She captured his attention, because his eyes flashed at her. 'They will have constraints of a different kind.'

She secretly agreed, but could not stop herself from going on. 'You are one to talk, Sloane. You have known the freedom of doing whatever you wish. My cousin Varney told me of it. It seems to me your choice to re-enter society is more mystifying than my desire to break its chains.'

A muscle in his cheek flexed. 'Being on the outside is not necessarily being free, Morgana.'

She took another sip of her wine, her brief effort at defiance merely leading her to inadvertently wound him. Her misery returned.

He plucked another sensitive nerve. 'Do you not wish to be married, Morgana?'

She gave him a pained expression. 'Do you?'

He averted his gaze. 'I do. It is a respectable thing to do.'

With effort, she refrained from rolling her eyes. Though

he would not look at her, she stared at him, deciding to answer his question truthfully.

'I have long accepted that no man would want a woman such as me. And I dare say I would chafe at the binds a husband would place on me.' His eyes darted back to her. 'But what I cannot understand is why anyone would give up their freedom so readily. I fail to see why respectability has such value to you.'

He reached over and took her hand, the tenderness in the gesture startling her. 'It is because I have been on the other side. It is why I worry for you, Morgana.'

Nothing was resolved between them, not really, but the warmth in his expression was enough to push her misery aside. She smiled at him. 'Oh, let us not quarrel, Sloane! Not in this place. The night is so fine.'

The music from the orchestra sounded in her ears, mixing with shouts of revelry. The lights twinkled and the scent of food, spirits, and people filled the air. The orchestra began a new tune and a high, crystalline voice carried in the crisp night air:

> Stay not till I learn the way;
> How to fib and how betray,
> E'er I can my thoughts disguise…

'Listen,' Morgana cried.
The voice went on.

> Force a blush or roll my eyes.
> Take me, take me, some of you,
> While I yet am young and true.

'It is Rose!' She jumped up from the chair, still holding his hand. 'Hurry.'

They pushed their way through to where the orchestra

played. Rose, without her mask, stood in front of the musicians, as if she had been their featured songstress. Her voice carried in the air distinct, sweet and sultry at turns.

> Could I find a blooming youth,
> Full of love and full of truth,
> Of honest mind and noble mien…

'Is she not lovely!' Morgana felt a surge of pride, as if she had created this beautiful creature whose wonderful voice cast its spell over the now quiet crowd.

'You did not know she would do this?' Sloane did not sound as pleased as she.

'No, indeed.' She smiled.

> Take me, take me, some of you,
> While I yet am young and true.

Rose finished the last refrain, and the audience burst into applause and cheers.

Morgana clapped as enthusiastically as the rest. 'Well done!'

Sloane muttered, 'She selected the right song.'

Morgana's smile faded at his grim expression. 'Can you not enjoy it, Sloane? What a lovely moment for her!'

'She places you in jeopardy, Morgana. If you are associated with her, questions will be asked.'

The orchestra started playing a waltz, and several couples in the crowd started to dance.

Morgana glanced around her, savouring the gaiety. 'Oh, do not be cross any more, Sloane.' She gazed up at him and her voice turned low. 'Dance with me.'

His eyes held hers for a moment, then he suddenly gathered her to him and swung her into the dance. The lamps above them blurred as they whirled round and round, and Morgana felt as if she were indeed soaring in the stars, with Sloane's arms around her. His chiselled features softened as he gazed down at her. He held her as close as he had when they'd danced in her parlour. Morgana thought she knew how heaven might feel.

The orchestra segued from the waltz into a more rousing, lively piece, and the dancing became more boisterous. Sloane guided Morgana away from the carousing. They were about to enter the path when they saw Katy walking with two gentlemen, one on each arm.

'What is she up to?' Morgana said with irritation.

Katy came closer, and Sloane pulled Morgana halfway into the bushes, hiding them both by putting his arms around her.

'You see her companions?' he whispered.

Katy was flanked by none other than Morgana's uncle and Lord Poltrop. Like Rose, she had shed her mask. Even worse, she was gaily allowing the gentlemen to place their hands upon her, one of them squeezing her *derrière*.

Sloane held Morgana out of view as they passed.

'She promised…' she began, but, when she lifted her head, he was so close, she forgot what she was about to say.

He did not release her, and her arms had nowhere to go but around his neck. His eyes darkened, and he pressed her against him so firmly she could feel his arousal from beneath his clothing. From Madame Bisou's lessons, she knew what it was—and what it meant. Sparks of pleasure glittered through her like the lamps strung through the trees. She laughed and pulled his head down to her eager lips.

His hand slid down to her hips and ground her against him.

His tongue played in her mouth. She met his kiss eagerly, daring to let her tongue frolic with his, feeling her whole body come alive with need. His lips slid to her neck and she heard herself whimper at the ache of pleasure created as he tasted her tender skin. His hand moved to her breast and Morgana covered it with her own, urging him to not move it away, but to fondle her more.

'Sloane,' she moaned, her voice husky. It started to make sense to her, all of Madame Bisou's lessons. She wanted more of him, could imagine the sensation of feeling his bare skin against hers, of feeling his hands upon her. This was desire, she realised, and it frightened as much as it thrilled her. How easy it would be to become carried away, to allow him to lead her down the Dark Walk with him.

Still, she did not wish him to stop. She found his lips and tasted him again. She pressed herself against him, unable to stop herself, unable to allow this moment to end.

He broke away. 'This is madness.' He held her at arm's length, panting, every fibre of his being on fire for her. By damn, he *wanted* to make love to her, wanted to discover how that depth of emotion that swung her from weeping for Lucy to cheering for Rose, that passion would play out in bed. The same recklessness he chided her for, he'd been willing to exploit. And her enthusiastic response showed him she wanted him to be the rake, not the reputable gentleman.

'That was not well done, Morgana,' he said.

She looked at him with a puzzled and wounded expression.

He had to impress upon her, convince her that this path she was bent upon would only bring her pain and eventual loneliness. If she did not exercise some restraint, how could he? 'Were you practising Bisou's lessons, Morgana? Practising at being the harlot?'

Even in the dim light, he saw the shock in her eyes. She

swung her hand back to strike him, but he caught her wrist before her palm connected to his face. 'You are making a spectacle. Someone will see.'

Under her mask, her eyes blazed. 'What will they see? They will see the very reputable Mr Sloane cavorting with a *harlot*. Take care, Sloane. Your hard-won respectability may be ruined by me.'

'Indeed it may.' He still gripped her wrist and held her so close he could feel the angry rise of her breast against his chest. 'You are not acting the lady, Morgana.'

Her arm flexed again, but the movement only rammed her full against him. 'You are not acting the gentleman.'

Her words struck the blow her hand had missed.

She hissed, 'Perhaps you ought to return to your very silly, respectable *Lady* Hannah. A gentleman would not keep her waiting.'

Hannah? He had forgotten about her while he held Morgana in his arms. Even now, while they exchanged angry words, his body came alive with the feel of her. He wished more than anything to be the rake he once had been.

He pushed her away before he could kiss her again and act on that nearly irresistible impulse.

'I will return to her.' He spoke more to himself than to Morgana, trying to convince himself that he wished to return to the task of acting the host.

'Yes.' Her voice was so low he could almost not hear her. 'Of course you will return to her.'

Before he could speak another word, she spun around and ran to her supper box, skirts flying. She did not look back.

Sloane followed, sickened by his own behaviour, but more by his words. He'd blamed her for that kiss, for his own arousal, for his own desire to risk her ruin in the gardens at Vauxhall.

He watched to see that she reached the box without mishap. Katy had returned and was now busily flirting with Sir Reginald. Lucy, Elliot, Mary and Duprey were there as well. He wanted to order Morgana to take them all home now, before something worse happened. But, damn him, even more, he ached to grab her hand and run with her down the Dark Walk.

Some gentleman he was. If anyone cared to examine him in the light of day, they could undoubtedly see he was as shabby as Vauxhall's plaster columns and painted walls.

He quickly backed away before the others of Morgana's party saw him. He made his way through the revellers to the other side of the park, and slipped into his own party's supper box. After him came Hannah and David, the other young people good-naturedly teasing them about being together. Cowdlin and Poltrop now sat with their wives in domestic harmony, and behind their backs Athenia held hands with Varney. Hannah looked unusually subdued. David fetched her a glass of wine and returned to fill his own glass with some more of the arrack punch.

Sloane joined him.

'Have you missed us, Uncle?' David asked, slurring his words. The young man must have dipped into more than his share of the arrack.

'I confess I wondered where everyone went off to,' Sloane lied.

'Just looking at the sights,' said David, his eyes drifting over to Hannah.

Athenia whispered something in Hannah's ear. Hannah whispered back. Sloane felt relieved of the obligation to join her.

His mind and senses were still filled with Morgana, not the thoughts of a man intent upon offering for a society miss. At the moment, any thought of marrying Hannah was unbearable.

The signal sounded for the illuminations to begin, and everyone in the party hurried out of the box to get a good view. Sloane looked through the crowd and found Morgana, standing with her girls, all looking like the high-flyers they would become. The sight of Morgana roused him all over again. Instead of the illuminations, he watched her, the flashes of light catching her mask. The sparkle and crackle and boom were nothing to the explosions ricocheting inside him.

He'd be damned if he did not find in Morgana a kindred spirit, but one who would cause him to lose the game he'd bid so high to win.

Later that night, after a very subdued Hannah and her dozing parents delivered him back to his town house, Sloane donned dark clothes, grabbed his swordstick and his knife, and slipped back out into the night, bound for Milk Street and the living quarters above the shop of a certain button seller.

As he blended with the night on his way to Cheapside, he formulated his plan, glad he had a target for the pent-up emotion inside him. Murder might be justified, but he would settle for frightening the fellow. He gripped his swordstick tighter as he hurried to avenge the man's evil deeds.

Sloane knew exactly what would keep the man's breeches buttoned when the next pretty girl came into view.

Chapter Thirteen

Over the last month of the Season, Morgana saw little of Sloane, though he was often at the same balls and routs she attended. He continued to show some attention to her cousin, but never to her. Worst of all, he no longer slipped through her garden wall to share breakfast or dinner or to assist with Madame Bisou's lessons.

Mr Elliot, who, like Mr Duprey, visited more frequently than before, disclaimed any knowledge of why Sloane avoided Morgana's company. He said Sloane spent a great deal of time secluded in his library, adding that Sloane seemed irritable at times, snapping at Elliot but apologising afterwards.

Morgana knew precisely why he avoided her. He thought her no more than a harlot, a threat to his desire to be accepted into the *beau monde,* to marry her cousin.

Still, she could not help gazing out of windows, hoping to catch sight of him leaving his house, to see his tall figure striding down the road. Her heart ached for missing him.

She realised the loss of his company had been her fault. He had scolded her for her wildness, but then she'd kissed him as wantonly as any harlot might do. He had lost respect for her, and that was painful indeed.

Why could she not have merely employed the pretty flirtations that gave Hannah such success? Hannah, though her manners were lively, never strayed too far from what was proper. Unlike Morgana.

Even Hannah's spirits had altered lately, her gaiety forced. Morgana could only suppose that Hannah worried that Sloane would not make an offer after all, although she long had been convinced that Hannah loved the idea of marrying a rich man more than the man himself. Indeed, Hannah seemed to prefer David Sloane to his uncle.

Partly to keep her mind off Sloane, Morgana allowed her girls more outings, all of them wearing hats that obscured their faces. They shopped at the Soho bazaar with money Morgana had given them to buy trinkets. They attended a performance at Astley's Amphitheatre. Daring indeed, because five lovely young ladies together, even though chaperoned by Miss Moore and escorted by Mr Elliot and Mr Duprey, attracted nearly as much attention as the arena's spectacular feats of horsemanship. Robert Duprey had also taken them each for rides in Hyde Park.

This morning's breakfast conversation was all about Mr Duprey.

'I shall never ride with him again,' Katy said dramatically. 'He near enough turned the curricle on its side—'

'*Nearly* turned the curricle on its side,' Miss Moore corrected.

Katy stared at her. '*Nearly* turned the curricle—'

'Do stop!' cried Mary. 'I think Mr Duprey is quite good at handling the ribbons. I am sure *I* never worried for one minute about it.'

'He is a menace!' Katy shouted. 'Rose, you must agree.'

Rose, who was chewing a piece of toasted bread, could not respond right away.

Katy did not pause. 'He near enough—*nearly*—ran into some fellow in a phaeton—'

'A gentleman, dear,' said Miss Moore. 'Not a fellow.'

'I tell you, I *nearly* got my neck broke.'

Mary sprang to her feet. 'I will not hear Mr Duprey so maligned. He has been nothing but kindness and generosity and all that is proper.'

'How proper can he be spendin' all his days with a pack of dolly mops!' Katy demanded, a bit too loudly to be ladylike.

Morgana massaged her temples. The headache that roused her before dawn still pained her, and the discussion at hand was not helping. 'Do not call yourself a dolly mop, Katy. You are better than that.'

Katy laughed. 'Gracious, Miss Hart. We ain't nothin' more than fancy dolly mops.'

Morgana sighed. There was no use arguing with Katy. It would only egg her on and make the headache worse. Finishing her now tepid cup of tea, Morgana bade them good morning as an example of ladylike manners, and went in search of Lucy.

It did not take long to find her. She was in the garden pulling weeds. Mr Elliot stood nearby, chatting with her.

'Good morning, Miss Hart,' Lucy said, rising to her feet. Mr Elliot nodded.

Lucy smiled at Morgana. Either the morning air or a blush had put colour in her cheeks. Or had she and Mr Elliot found a private place to be together?

'I was just telling Mr Elliot the news my mum sent to Amy and me. Did she tell you of it?'

'No.' Amy had lately chattered more about her sister, how

she feared for Lucy in her new life, how she wished Lucy would content herself with being a maid and forget this notion of being a courtesan.

Morgana shared Amy's sentiments. As the days went on, she dreaded more and more the moment she would have to release them into the life she had created for them. Two months ago Morgana had been convinced that she would be providing them with a better life. Now she feared she would only cause them more unhappiness, like the unhappiness she now felt.

'What was the news, Lucy? No one is ill, I hope.'

'Nothing like that, miss.' Lucy glanced to Elliot, who nodded encouragingly. 'It is the shop next door to my father's. The button seller. Do you remember about him?'

Morgana was not likely to ever forget. 'I remember.'

'Well, my mum said he moved away. Just up and moved. He's gone.'

Morgana could barely speak. 'Indeed.'

'And I was asking Mr Elliot if he thought it could be Mr Sloane's doing. Do you think so? Mr Elliot says he does not know, but I think Mr Sloane made him go away. Mr Castle has run the shop for ever and his father before him and now it is empty and he's gone.'

Morgana felt her senses, so dormant of late, come to life. Of course Sloane had been responsible. Like a secret champion, he'd avenged Lucy. Sloane had driven the man off.

'It does seem odd,' Morgana managed.

Lucy and Mr Elliot shared smiles, and Morgana felt a wave of envy. Lucy and Elliot had found a steadfast friendship, perhaps more than a friendship, though Morgana dared not ask. Morgana was happy for her even if, at this moment, it made her own loneliness seem more acute.

A voice sounded from the other side of the garden wall. 'Elliot, where the devil are you?'

Sloane.

He stepped through the gap in the garden wall and caught sight of Morgana. 'Oh.'

Elliot sprang to attention. 'Did you have need of me, sir?'

Sloane looked as if he were about to retreat back to his own property. 'No, just wondered where you were.'

Morgana remained riveted to the spot, but Lucy skipped over to Sloane.

'Thank you, sir,' she said with meaning in her voice.

He backed up a step. 'What for?'

She gave him a worshipful look. 'For whatever you did to Mr Castle, because he is gone and his shop is closed.'

Morgana watched a muscle in Sloane's cheek flex. He paused before responding. 'I am glad of it, Lucy. But do not assume I had anything to do with it.'

'I know you did, sir,' Lucy seized his hand and kissed it. 'And I am grateful to you.'

Sloane glanced over to Morgana, but glanced away as quickly.

'Perhaps Mr Sloane is busy, Lucy.' Morgana knew Sloane wished to escape her company.

Cripps stepped out of the doorway. 'Madame Bisou wishes me to inform you that she has brought you a visitor.' He looked unusually stern. 'Miss Harriette Wilson.'

'Harriette?' barked Sloane, with a searing glare at Morgana. 'What the devil is she doing here?'

Morgana was every bit as shocked as he. 'I have no idea.'

Elliot excused himself, saying he must return to his duties, but Sloane followed Morgana and Lucy into the house.

Miss Wilson sat in the front drawing room wearing a stylish white India muslin gown trimmed in blue satin, with embroidered flounces at the hem and neckline. Her cap, complete with blue and white feathers, matched perfectly. Look-

ing at her, one could only conclude that the life of a courtesan was very lucrative indeed. Mary, Katy and Rose sat gaping at her.

Madame Bisou presented Miss Wilson to Morgana. Her introduction ended with, '…and you know Cyprian, I believe.'

'Yes, indeed,' Miss Wilson responded, giving Sloane a
frank look of admiration that made Morgana feel faintly ill.
'But it has been much too long since you have called upon
me, sir.'

Sloane's expression remained stormy. 'What are you doing
here, Harriette?'

'I insisted Penny bring me to see this courtesan school.'

Sloane shot Penny a scathing glance.

'Do not look at me that way, Cyprian. I did not tell her of
it.'

He turned his glare to Morgana. 'If Harriette knows, your
activities are no longer a secret.'

'Not everyone knows, Cyprian, my love!' Harriette chirped.
'That odious Fortuna Rice offers a great deal of money to dis-
cover this place. But she believes some man runs the school.'
Harriette laughed as if such a notion was ridiculous.

Morgana's breath caught to hear Mrs Rice's name. She'd
not imagined the girls were still in danger from the woman.
It had been weeks since they'd left her.

'Sir Reginald!' cried Madame Bisou. 'It must be he who
told you, Harriette. He must have pieced the story together
after meeting us at Vauxhall.'

Harriette did not deny this. Morgana glanced at Katy. The
girl returned a defiant look, and Morgana could imagine Katy
prattling on while she practised her wiles at Vauxhall.

Sloane glowered at Morgana, then marched over to her.
'Morgana, I need a word with you. Excuse us.' He gripped
her arm so that she had little choice but to follow him.

He propelled her into the library and still kept hold of her, holding her so close she could feel the heat from his body. She could also see the fire in his eyes.

'Let me speak plain, Morgana. If that woman knows of you, in minutes the rest of the world will know. You cannot trust her.' He gave her a little shake. 'You must end this now.'

She lifted her chin and stared directly into his face, even though it was only inches away. 'How do I end it, Sloane? Toss them out? Will that make them safer? Or am I suddenly not to care if Mrs Rice punishes them for leaving her?'

He acted as if he'd not even heard her. 'You have become too reckless. Taking them to Vauxhall. And even that wasn't enough for you. You had to take them to Soho and Astley's. Where were your wits? Have you gone totally mad? You have no notion what you risk.'

Who could have told him such things? She glared at him. 'I thought Mr Elliot more discreet.'

He huffed. 'Elliot is the model of discretion. Did you assume he was my only source of information about your doings?'

She had not imagined he cared a fig about her doings since the night at Vauxhall, when he held her much less painfully than he did now.

She addressed him in a haughty tone. 'Do take your hands off me, Sloane. I do not fancy having bruised arms.'

He released her so quickly she almost fell against him. He caught her again and only stepped back after she regained her balance. She rubbed where his hands had gripped her.

It suddenly felt as if walls were falling in on her, but she could not allow him to realise that. 'I should like to know your source of information, if it was not Mr Elliot.'

'Take your pick,' he shot back. 'The circle of those who know of you is widening rapidly. The floodgates are open, Morgana. It is time to cut and run.'

'I have no notion of what that means,' she snapped.

He glowered at her. 'It means that your activities are in imminent danger of being revealed—'

'And my reputation ruined?' she finished for him. 'Did I not tell you, Sloane, that I do not care?'

This was a lie. Her ruin and banishment from a society that heretofore had only grudgingly accepted her truly terrified her. Her father would disown her. How could he do otherwise when her shame might reflect on his new wife? The part of her fortune her father did not control was modest. What would happen to her?

She almost laughed. She knew too well what happened to young women with no money and no friends.

'*I* care,' he shouted. 'I told you from the beginning I would not allow you to bring me down with you. Not after I have worked so hard to earn my good name. I'll be damned if I allow you to ruin it.'

She crossed her arms over her chest. 'Then you must prevent my discovery, must you not?'

He swung away and paced in front of her. 'It is not only that, Morgana. This is a dangerous business. Deadly dangerous. Your altercation in the park was nothing compared to what could happen. That glove-shop proprietor is nipping at your heels, and, believe me, she will not stop until she is revenged upon you.'

Morgana's eyes widened in surprise. 'How do you know this?'

He stopped pacing but did not answer right away. He finally turned to her and the look on his face made her shiver. 'I have my means.'

They stood no more than three feet from each other, staring like two cats daring the other to pounce. The pause merely reminded Morgana of the weight of the responsibility she carried on her shoulders. She ought to have figured out another way to help the girls. She ought to have protected them all instead of bringing danger and ruin.

But she must not weaken now. She straightened her spine and gave Sloane a steady look. 'I will see this through to the end, Sloane. I have no other choice.'

His angry expression changed to one more vulnerable, until he covered that over with no expression at all. It was like a cleaver chopping her in two. To save the girls she risked ruining him. And he had wanted nothing more than a good name.

He gave her a curt nod and, without another word, turned away from her and walked out the door.

Morgana dropped her face into her hands, giving in to the grief of knowing how she had wounded him. She could no longer pretend she did not love him. Even if she did not count the physical desires he aroused in her, she loved the man. Loved his strength. Loved the rakish side of him that mocked the very world for which he pined. She could weep for the pain of his family's rejection and for his longing for friends such as the Marquess of Heronvale. She knew that sort of loneliness.

The agony was, she had put all he desired at risk. His association with her, the mere fact of living next to her, would most probably be his ruin.

Laughter came from the drawing room. She raised her head and squared her shoulders. She must make certain her plans succeeded, no matter how abhorrent they had become to her. She must successfully launch her girls into the world of the demi-rep and hope that they found protectors and ultimate wealth. She would lose them, too, as she'd lost Sloane.

Morgana set her chin. She still must deal with Harriette Wilson.

She returned to the drawing room, where Miss Wilson had the group enthralled.

'First, always value yourselves very highly—'

'That is what Miss Hart says, as well,' Katy broke in.

'And you must always remember that you choose the gentleman; the gentleman does not choose you…'

Madame Bisou saw Morgana enter and hurried over to her. 'Miss Hart, Harriette has thought of the very thing to launch the girls. It is a splendid opportunity!'

Harriette interrupted her lecture. 'It is indeed. Tomorrow night there is to be a masquerade ball at the Argyle Rooms to mark the end of the Season. It promises to be very merry. Your girls will attend. It will be the perfect place to show them off and tantalise potential clientele.'

'Is it not brilliant?' cried Madame Bisou.

Katy looked at Morgana as if daring her to refuse. Mary glanced around with frightened eyes. Lucy sat thin-lipped with resignation, and Rose, who was silently fingering the keys of the pianoforte, gave no indication of having heard the discussion at all.

'I am not certain—' Morgana began.

Madame Bisou cut her off again. 'It is time, Miss Hart.'

She sounded so much like Sloane, Morgana thought she would laugh—or weep. As much as Morgana wanted to clutch them all to her bosom and never let them go, this provided her the best chance of making matters right for Sloane. She had no better alternative.

Perhaps they could all move to the country in a little cottage or something of which her father would approve. If she withdrew from society before the scandal hit—

No. What sort of life would that offer them all? The sheer boredom of it would drive Morgana mad, if not the rest of them with her. Except perhaps for Mary. She could offer Mary a chance not to be a courtesan.

'Well, Morgana?' asked Miss Moore. She seemed to be as excited about the prospect as Katy.

A masquerade? It seemed a safe enough place to begin. Like at Vauxhall, they could hide behind masks. No one need know who they were, unless they desired it.

'We will attend.' Morgana would go with them, she resolved. She would look out for them one last time.

After leaving Morgana's house in a towering rage, Sloane paused in his hall long enough to pick up his hat, gloves and swordstick before rushing out again. Elliot, who'd heard his noisy entry, had dared try to ask him a question. Sloane had bellowed, 'I am going out!'

He knew precisely where he was bound.

If Morgana would not end this foolishness, he must do his best to keep the leaking information from engulfing her. He had not needed Harriette Wilson to tell him that Mrs Rice was becoming more and more obsessed about discovering the courtesan school. He knew it from his own surveillance.

There was one leak he could plug and plug it he would.

Sloane strode off to Fenton's Hotel, where he asked to be announced to Sir Reginald.

When Sloane was admitted into Sir Reginald's rooms, the older man was still dressed in his dressing gown, although it was nearly noon. Sir Reginald put down the copy of the *Morning Post* that he'd held in his hand.

'Good morning, Sloane.' Sir Reginald gave a cordial smile and gestured for him to sit. 'A bit early, eh? To what do I owe the pleasure?'

Sloane sat and a servant appeared to pour tea. He waited until the servant scurried away into another room. 'I'll not mince words.' He leaned towards the older man, who was just about to take a swallow. 'You told Harriette Wilson about the courtesan school, did you not?'

Sir Reginald gulped and went into a spasm of coughing

before replying. 'I—I suppose I did. Saw her the other day at Covent Garden—some play or some such. Don't rightly recall…'

Sloane gave Sir Reginald a menacing look. 'No one must know of this. No one, do you understand?'

Sir Reginald gave a snort. 'Cannot see why not. Capital idea, *training* young women. Imagine a lady doing so!'

'What do you know of the lady?' Sloane demanded.

The man sputtered. 'A Miss Hart—'

Sloane seized him by the front of the robe and lifted him out of the chair. 'You are *never* to speak her name to anyone.'

Sir Reginald's eyes bulged. 'I won't. I won't.'

'Your word on it,' Sloane demanded, shaking him.

Sir Reginald stuttered. 'I…I…I give my word.'

Sloane released him and Sir Reginald landed back in his chair, breathing as hard as if he'd run the full length of Hyde Park.

Sloane rose from his chair.

Sir Reginald cowered as Sloane advanced on him one more time. 'I shall take my leave. But, mind this, if you loose your tongue again, I will discover it. You will not wish to see what I will do to you.'

Sir Reginald nodded so vigorously the loose skin on his neck shook.

Sloane strode out of the room.

When the door shut behind him, Sir Reginald reached for his tea, the cup clattering in its saucer from his shaking hands.

His manservant crept out from behind the bedchamber door. 'Are you injured, sir?'

'No, of course I am not injured,' Sir Reginald snapped.

'What a terrifying man!' His servant picked up Sloane's tea cup.

'He is indeed,' agreed Sir Reginald.

As his man tidied the room, Sir Reginald stared at the *Morning Post* without seeing a word.

All he could hope was that Sloane never found out he had mentioned the courtesan school at the dolly shop where he tarried after leaving Covent Garden. Just in passing, mind. A harmless comment, no names mentioned. Except Madame Bisou's.

He rubbed his face and lowered his forehead on to the tabletop with a groan.

That evening Madame Bisou walked through the game room of her establishment, checking that the tables were stocked with cards and other necessities.

She sighed and flung herself into a chair. Toying with a stack of counters, she recalled the look upon Robert's face when he came to call upon Miss Hart and her girls that afternoon after Harriette Wilson had finished her interminable lesson. Robert acted like a besotted suitor. Was she to lose him? He was such a dear…so…so predictable.

She rued the day she brought him to Morgana Hart's house so the girls could learn how to be with a man, if one could call Robert a man—a boy-man perhaps, a sweet, harmless thing. She supposed he would take his business to that Mary Phipps as soon as she was established. Some thanks that would be.

Cummings entered the room. 'You have a caller, Madame.'

He always made everything sound like doom. 'You know we are not open, Cummings.' She had no wish to see anyone, even if they were open.

'It is Mrs Rice,' he intoned. 'And she insists upon seeing you.'

'Oh, that odious Fortuna Rice.' Madame Bisou waved her hand. 'Have her meet me in the supper room.'

She followed him out of the door and crossed the hall to the supper room, stepping into the back to bring out a bottle of Madeira wine. If she had to endure Fortuna Rice, it would be with liquid spirits.

She sat and downed one glass before the woman entered the room.

'Come join me, Fortuna,' she said, pouring two more glasses. 'Have some wine.'

'A choice bottle, I hope. You would not be serving me your cheap wine, would you, Penny?' Mrs Rice sat across from her.

Madame Bisou bristled, but decided to let the catty comment pass. 'Only the best for us, Fortuna. We have earned it.'

'Which is why I am here.'

Leave it to Fortuna Rice to waste no time on niceties. 'I have heard you are involved in a courtesan school. Is that so?'

Madame Bisou delayed answering, covering up the time it took to contrive an answer by taking a long sip of her wine. She decided the best tactic was avoidance. 'Why do you ask, my dear?'

Mrs Rice frowned. 'I have had two girls stolen from me and a third I was about to bring into the house. I want them back.'

Madame Bisou lifted her brows. 'Careless of you to lose them, Fortuna. I treat my girls well and they stay of their own accord.'

'I treat mine well, too,' snapped Mrs Rice. 'But I have been ill used and I want them back.'

'I am certain you do.' Madame Bisou took another sip.

'Well, what do you know of it?'

Fortuna Rice was an unpleasant woman, the madam decided, and not too smart to have shown all her cards at once. Penny lounged in her chair. 'I know nothing of it. I am sure I do not know why you supposed I would.'

'Sir Reginald let something slip about it. Said you were showing off the girls at Vauxhall last night.'

Madame Bisou made herself laugh with great heartiness. 'Oh, that is famous! What a buffoon!' She pretended to wrest control of herself again and dabbed at her eyes with the handkerchief she pulled from between her ample bosoms. 'I was at Vauxhall with some of my girls, all masked! We told him a story and he believed it.'

Mrs Rice put both her palms flat on the table and glared at her. 'This is not the first I've heard of a courtesan school. It was talked of in one of the pubs as well. It is said a man and a lady run it and they teach the girls to think themselves better than they ought.'

It was fortunate that Madame Bisou had nearly a lifetime of telling whatever she wished others to hear, gentlemen especially. She prided herself on sounding earnest and believable, whatever she said. 'Why, I have heard the rumours myself, Fortuna. Now Sir Reginald thinks the courtesan school is mine. Is that not fun?'

Mrs Rice swallowed the contents of her glass and stood. 'I do not believe you, Penny, but I make you a promise. I will find where my girls are and I will take them back and no one—I repeat, no one—will stop me.'

She flounced out of the room.

Madame Bisou poured another glass of wine and again downed it in one long, nervous swallow.

Chapter Fourteen

Morgana stared at the note once again.

Dear Niece,
At my particular request, your neighbour, Mr Sloane, has agreed to escort you to our dinner party tonight. Mr Sloane has been gracious enough to offer the use of his own carriage. Do not neglect to bring your maid with you for propriety's sake.
Yours, etc. W.C.

She let her hand fall into her lap, wondering if there was still time to pretend a headache and beg off. In truth, her head had been pounding all day, especially after she and Sloane had crossed swords.

Amy entered the drawing room. 'I have your shawl, Miss Hart. We are quite prepared now.'

Morgana set the note aside on the table and picked up her gloves. 'I hope this will not be too tedious for you, Amy, since you are obliged to accompany me.'

'I expect to have a jolly time, miss. My mother's cousin is

housekeeper there, you know, and it will be a treat to visit her.' Amy carefully draped the shawl, the same deep green silk as Morgana's evening dress, over her arm.

Morgana pushed her fingers one by one into her glove before smoothing the rest of the white kid up to her elbow. 'Remember, not a word about the courtesan school, and do not let slip that you have been helping fashion costumes for the masquerade.'

'I will be very careful, miss. There is enough news from home to keep us talking.' Amy then looked critically at Morgana, as one would a vase of flowers to arrange. She fussed with the long curled feather that she'd fashioned to frame Morgana's face, another clever means she employed to disguise her lady's stick-straight hair. This night, Amy had twisted strands of Morgana's hair into loops artfully cascading from the crown of her head. 'It is good of Mr Sloane to drive you, is it not, Miss Hart? What a gentleman. We have seen so little of him of late.'

It had not been so long ago that Amy described him as a pirate. Indeed, much had happened since their first encounter, not the least of which was Morgana falling quite despairingly in love with him.

With Harriette Wilson's unexpected arrival and then a flurry to plan costumes for the masquerade, Morgana barely had time to think of Sloane and how he'd stalked out after they quarrelled. Then the note had come from her aunt, unnecessarily managing the transportation. Cripps could have procured a hack for her easily enough. Now she and Sloane would be trapped together.

The knocker sounded and Morgana jumped, her heart pounding against her chest. Sloane had arrived and she would sit with him in the confines of the carriage for perhaps ten full minutes.

'Mr Sloane, miss,' Cripps announced.

Morgana clasped her hand to her throat. 'We are ready.'

She and Amy followed Cripps to the hall, where Sloane waited, his hat in his hand, his white breeches gleaming against the deep blue of his coat.

He did not smile, but bowed formally. 'Good evening, Miss Hart.'

'Mr Sloane.' She dropped into a graceful curtsy.

Amy hurried to hand her the shawl, but Sloane took it from her and draped it over Morgana's shoulders. But even though his strong hands brushed against her, he paid more attention to her maid.

'I hope you are well, Miss Jenkins,' he said.

Amy also bobbed into a curtsy. 'Very well, indeed, thank you, sir.'

At the carriage, Amy allowed Sloane only a mere touch of her hand as she scrambled inside. For Morgana, however, he held her elbow and guided her with a hand to her back. After she sat down, she still felt his touch upon her, though he sat as far from her as possible.

The silence in the carriage made it difficult for Morgana to breathe. She resisted taking big gulps of air. Instead, she forced herself to converse with him.

'It is kind of you to transport me, Mr Sloane. I expect you would have simply walked the distance otherwise.'

He turned his eyes on her. 'That is so.'

She glanced out of the carriage window. It was still light out. 'It is a fine evening.'

He did not respond, but when she turned back to him, he still watched her. She felt the impulse to squirm under his scrutiny.

Morgana lifted her eyes and stared directly into Sloane's. He did not look away. It was as if each of them were loathe to be first to break the contact. As a little girl, she'd played a similar game with her cat. This seemed so different.

They arrived at her aunt's house just a few minutes later. Sloane put his hand to her waist to assist her from the carriage. She held his arm while they walked the few steps to the front door. Once inside she supposed he would avoid her.

Amy hurried off in search of the housekeeper, and Morgana and Sloane entered the hall. The Cowdlin town house was a bit grander than Morgana's and furnished in the very latest bright colours and varied designs. From the Prussian blue hall where they were announced, to the primrose yellow drawing room with its stencilled wallpaper and Brussels-weave carpet.

Her aunt bustled up to them. 'Dear Mr Sloane, how good of you to escort my niece. Do come in. Cowdlin will see you have some nice claret before dinner.' She spared Morgana a quick glance. 'Morgana, dear, so good of you to come.'

While Lady Cowdlin took charge of Sloane, Morgana greeted some of the other guests, whom she had met many times during the Season. She made her way to the corner of the room where David Sloane and Hannah were looking into a small tube aimed directly at the nearby lamp.

'Is it some sort of telescope?' Morgana asked.

David Sloane leapt to his feet and Hannah looked up at her. 'Oh, Morgana! It is the most wonderful contraption. Come, look in it!'

Morgana sat and peered into the glass optic. Sparkles of colour appeared in symmetrical shapes on the inside. 'Oh, it is lovely!'

'Here, turn it,' David instructed, and the colours changed shape before her very eyes. 'It is called a kaleidoscope.'

'It is quite new,' said Hannah. 'Mr Sloane—Mr David Sloane—brought it to me.'

Morgana marvelled as the colours formed a new pattern.

'What is this?' a familiar voice said.

Morgana did not stop looking into the device, but suddenly the changing shapes and colours garnered less of her attention.

'Good evening, Uncle,' David said.

'Hello, David.' Sloane added, 'Lady Hannah, I hope you are well.'

'Very well, sir,' Hannah replied.

Morgana moved away from the kaleidoscope and rose from the chair.

'You must look, Mr Sloane,' insisted Hannah. 'It is called a kaleidoscope and your nephew has brought it to show me.'

Sloane took the chair Morgana had vacated and Morgana backed away, nodding politely to other guests and exchanging a few words with them. She was not certain what she said to them, however. All her senses were attuned to one man, his voice, his scent, every move he made. She strolled to the other side of the room, hoping more distance from him would help, making herself look anywhere but at him. She watched Athenia Poltrop and her parents greet her aunt and uncle. Athenia's gaze riveted upon her cousin Varney and his upon her.

Morgana settled in a chair at the corner farthest away from where Sloane had ceded his place at the kaleidoscope. Hannah called to Athenia to come and look at her new curiosity. Lord Cowdlin signalled Sloane over and handed him a glass of claret.

Morgana forced herself to watch Hannah and Athenia. Athenia glanced towards Varney and quickly looked away. She glanced at him again and twirled a lock of her hair in her finger. Varney excused himself from the gentleman with whom he had been conversing and quickly came to Athenia's side.

That morning, Harriette Wilson had taught those exact techniques—how to manipulate a man's interest by mere glances and the simplest of gestures. Athenia performed the exact steps just as if she'd been present at the lesson, summoning Varney to her side as effectively as if she'd shouted his name. Morgana stifled a laugh. Harriette's tactics had worked! Where had Athenia learned them? Was snaring a man's attention really so easily achieved? Could even Morgana make a gentleman approach her side merely by employing a few coquettish tricks?

Morgana glanced at Sloane, the only man she wished to draw to her side. If she could make Sloane come to her, Sloane, who wanted nothing to do with her, it would indeed prove the power of Harriette's techniques. She strained to remember them.

Sloane happened to glance in her direction. Morgana gazed at him pointedly, then quickly averted her gaze. She glanced back. He was looking at her! Her heart skipped a beat. She felt for the lock of hair that escaped Amy's efforts and now tickled the nape of her neck. She twisted it in her fingers and quickly averted her gaze. A second later she dared peek through her lowered lashes.

Sloane found his gaze naturally wandering to where Morgana sat, even though he'd resolved to avoid her. She was tinder to his senses. One little spark and they'd both go up in flames.

Still, catching sight of her was vastly preferable to enduring the sudden hospitality of Lord Cowdlin. There was not enough the toadying hypocrite could do to see to his comfort. A glance at Morgana had become like a rope tossed to a drowning man.

Finally another guest arrived to snare Cowdlin's attention, and Sloane scanned the room for a place to hide, his eyes lighting on Morgana. She sat alone in a corner of the room, her lively ginger eyes taking in everything, even taking in him. Her eyes were particularly captivating this evening, set off by the dark green of her dress and the feather in her hair.

Damn him. He craved her company. They were two of a kind, he and Morgana. Both too ready to cross the bounds of correct behaviour, just the reason he should stay away.

He forced his gaze elsewhere and Lady Cowdlin caught his eye, giving him a meaningful smile and inclining her head ever so deliberately towards her daughter.

Sloane inwardly groaned. He let his gaze travel past the woman, as if he had not noticed her blatant signal to dance attendance on Hannah. Coming to this dinner party only put him in deeper with the Cowdlins—as well as bringing him back in close company with Morgana.

He looked over to her again. Her eyes met his, looked away again, and very slowly glanced back. She again fingered that lock of loose hair that had been driving him to madness with how it caressed the soft ivory skin of her neck.

He might as well go mad in her company as by staring at her across the room. He walked over to her and sat in the chair next to hers.

'Are you enjoying yourself, Morgana?' *Enjoying your torture of me,* he meant.

She turned her magical eyes upon him. 'Shall I be honest, Sloane, or do you wish me to say what is proper?'

The thought of how improper Morgana Hart could be put his senses on high alert, the very sort of reaction he needed to avoid. 'I do not expect what is proper from you.'

Her smile froze on her face and he kicked himself for his illchosen words.

'I will be proper, then, to spite you. I am having a delightful time. And you?' Her eyes glittered with anger, which merely caused the blood to race faster through his veins.

He met her gaze. 'I think it is a dead bore.'

She laughed, an unaffected sound that caused one or two of the company to look over at them. 'Me, too,' she whispered.

More guests were announced. 'Lord and Lady Rawley.'

'Deuce,' muttered Sloane, as his brother and sister-in-law entered the room. He glanced at Morgana, ready to apologise for his profanity, but was taken aback by the sympathy in her eyes.

'Tell me, Sloane,' she said quickly. 'What did you think of the kaleidoscope? Was it not remarkable?'

He peered at her, then realised she was trying to distract him and give him a reason to avoid his brother's pointed glare of dislike. Such kindness surprised him in light of their hot words that morning.

'Very remarkable, Miss Hart. I've rarely seen such beauty.' But he spoke of her beauty, not the bits of coloured glass.

She fingered that stray lock of hair, and he longed to feel its silky texture between his own fingers. Putting her hands in her lap, she gave him an intent look. 'Some day, Sloane, if you should ever need a friend's ear, I would listen.'

There was no curiosity lurking in her offer. He examined her face and found only concern. When had anyone last been *concerned* about him, especially someone he'd so pointedly hurt with his sharp words?

'Good evening, Sloane.' His brother stood before him.

Sloane stood. 'Rawley.' He turned to Morgana. 'Miss Hart, may I present Lord Rawley.'

Morgana offered her hand with a gracious expression. 'We met at the *musicale*, Lord Rawley.'

Rawley shook her hand, barely grasping her fingers. He gave her a knowing leer. 'You live next door to Cyprian.'

Sloane's hand curled into a fist at the use of his given name and the insinuation towards Morgana in Rawley's expression.

'Yes.' She managed to sound admirably ingenuous. 'I do indeed. And where do you live, sir?'

Well done, Morgana, Sloane thought.

Dinner was announced and protocol separated them. Sloane wound up seated next to Lady Hannah, his nephew on Hannah's other side. Rawley and his wife were above them, and Morgana was on the other side of the table, not quite across from him. Sometimes when he glanced at her, she quickly looked away. Sometimes she engaged in conversation with the gentlemen on either side of her, both husbands of Lady Cowdlin's friends and not the best dinner companions for an eligible young lady. Lady Cowdlin ought to stand in place of Morgana's mother, see her well situated, instead of neglecting her.

But the idea of Morgana with a serious suitor did not quite please Sloane. He stabbed at a piece of meat and glanced around the table at the two dozen guests as he chewed. His nephew and Morgana were the only two whose presence he could tolerate for more than half an hour. He ought to admit to himself that he found society a dead bore. Why the devil had he made that infernal bet with himself?

He caught his brother watching him. Rawley quickly averted his eyes, but Sloane had not missed the contemptuous expression on his face. It must rankle with Rawley indeed that this bastard brother was seated at the same table. And rankle with his father as well.

By God, that was reason enough to persist in his plans to make a place for himself among these tedious people.

'Do you like the potatoes?' Lady Hannah asked, bringing him back to the present.

'Delicious,' he muttered.

Hannah smiled. 'My mother shall be so pleased.'

She turned back to her plate. Hannah was a sweet girl. The

perfect bride, he thought, as he studied her profile for a moment.

But not for him.

He'd been bored with her after a fortnight, he realised. Think what would happen after years together. All her promise of becoming a warm and responsive woman would wither like a rosebud in early frost. She deserved better.

Heronvale might advocate the connection between them, but ruining Hannah's life was too high a price to pay for a career in politics. Sloane would be better off marrying a woman like Morgana.

He dropped his fork and it clattered against his plate as it fell, causing a few heads to turn. He stared at Morgana. By God, why had he not realised it before? He did not have to act the rake towards her; he could be her husband. He could marry wild, unpredictable Morgana. Who cared if she leaped over the bounds of propriety? He'd jump with her and have a vastly better time than he'd had these past few months. He *wanted* her.

She looked over at him as well, her eyes lingering as she again fingered her hair. He wanted to tuck that lock up where it belonged before it drove him to complete distraction. She looked back down at her glass of wine and slowly brought it to her lips. Taking a sip, she glanced at him again, her pink tongue peeking out to lick a droplet of wine from her full, kissable lips. He would go mad indeed.

The footmen came to remove the dishes and the cloth. Sloane forced himself to chat with Hannah until the cakes, fruit and ices were served. He joined Lady Hannah in taking a glass of champagne, all the while on fire for the moment he could be alone with Morgana.

Soon dessert was over, and the ladies left the room. As Morgana passed his chair, he felt her hand graze his shoulder, a touch so light it was almost indiscernible. It acted upon him as if she'd raked her fingernails along his naked flesh.

He endured the dull conversation of the men while the Madeira, port and claret were circulated around the table. Lord Cowdlin pointedly included Sloane in the discussion. It was definitely time to make it clear he would not offer for Hannah. Whatever might happen to Cowdlin's debts was none of his concern. There were other, more eligible young men for Hannah; one of them ought to be rich enough to suit her father.

Cowdlin announced it was time to rejoin the ladies, and Sloane lagged behind, hoping to contrive some time with Morgana. As the other gentlemen entered the drawing room, Lady Hannah appeared in the doorway of the room next to it.

'Psst!' She waved her hand for him to come to her.

Damn. He had no wish to be with Hannah, especially not alone. He walked over to her.

'Mr Sloane, may I speak with you for a moment?' She looked upset.

'Alone, Hannah? I do not think so.' He certainly did not want to be trapped in a compromising situation with her.

'For a moment, please,' she persisted. 'We may leave the door open a crack.'

He stepped just inside the doorway of the Cowdlin library, leaving the door open wide enough for his back to be visible to anyone passing by. He hoped that would prevent any accusation that he was engaged in a private meeting. 'What is it, Lady Hannah?'

The room was dimly lit by only one branch of candles, but the distress on her face was easily visible. 'My mother has had words with me…a moment ago, but my father earlier today…' She broke off.

'And?' He crossed his arms over his chest.

She picked at her fingers like a distressed child. 'Will you offer for me, Mr Sloane? My father is in desperate need of money and he has so counted on you offering for me. I…I know you like me and we…we got along famously at first. So, will you?'

He gazed down at her, so sorry he had led her and her family to count on his suit. He'd selected Hannah primarily because her father was friends with his father, he now realised. Merely to vex his father, he had toyed with this young lady's hopes and expectations. It had been very wrong of him.

He tried to make his voice sound as gentle as he could. 'No, Lady Hannah. I will not offer for you.'

Her face crumbled and she grabbed at his arm. 'But you must, Mr Sloane! My father—'

He put his hand over hers and slowly removed it. 'Your father is wrong to solve his problems by saddling you with a man such as me.'

'I am certain we will suit,' she cried.

'And I am certain we will not.' He tried to sound sympathetic.

'Then what am I to do?' She began to shake and take quick breaths. 'What am I to do?'

He steadied her with a hand on her arm. 'You are to marry a man who would give you the regard you deserve, Hannah.'

She collapsed against him, sobbing. 'If only I could! It is impossible, though. He thinks of you, for one thing. And his fortune, it is not his to offer.' She sniffled loudly.

He set her away from him, holding her at arm's length. 'Of whom do you speak?'

She gave him a miserable look. 'Of your nephew, sir!'

He nearly laughed. David and Hannah in the tortures of young love, impeded only by the wealthy uncle who was expected to marry her? It was a villain role he'd never expected to play.

He controlled his smile. 'Do you wish to marry David?'

She straightened, suddenly in control of all the passion of youth. 'What I wish is of no consequence. I must do my duty.'

He did laugh then. 'Rubbish!'

She glared at him. 'It is not a joke, sir! My father requires money and David, thanks to his grandfather—your father—has none until he is twenty-five.'

'I repeat, Lady Hannah, your father's problems are not yours to solve. Does David return your affection?'

'He will not declare himself out of loyalty to you,' she said, her face dreamy and, oh, so young.

He smiled again, feeling like Methuselah. But perhaps a new hand had been dealt him, one he might win by losing. 'My dear Lady Hannah, you may tell David that I am no longer a suitor, and he has my full permission to court you. You may also tell him not to worry over his lack of funds, for I shall attend that as well.'

She gazed up at him, with hope dawning on her face. 'You can do this for him?'

He smiled. It would give him great pleasure to manipulate his father into giving David his fortune early. 'I will be delighted to accommodate you both.'

'Oh, thank you, Mr Sloane!' She flung her arms around his neck. 'Wait until I tell David!'

'Only David,' he cautioned, extricating himself from her grasp. 'Do not tell anyone else or I might not be able to manage the affair.'

She nodded, smiling brightly, and ran past him out of the room.

Sloane wandered into the library. He walked over to the

globe and spun it absently, waiting a few discreet minutes so it would not be so apparent that he had been with Hannah. He spun the globe again, feeling as if he were Atlas relieved of its weight. Lord Cowdlin would be almost as delighted as Hannah that her marriage—and the rescue of his finances— would be with David Sloane rather than Cyprian.

Sloane turned his thoughts more happily to the golden-eyed woman who would share his carriage on the ride home. How might he contrive some time alone with Morgana? He had much to discuss with her.

He smiled in anticipation of holding her in his arms again.

Morgana happened to be standing by the drawing room door when Hannah walked in, her colour high and eyes bright.

'Oh, Morgana!' She gave her cousin's hand a squeeze. 'I am so happy. I cannot tell you, for it is a secret, but you shall know soon enough!'

Morgana smiled dutifully, but she could guess what had brought such excitement to her cousin's face. It had not escaped her that Sloane and Hannah had been absent from the room at the same time. Sloane had caught Hannah alone, undoubtedly, and had finally made his offer.

Hannah skipped over to where Athenia stood with David Sloane sipping tea, but the others did not seem to notice that her usual liveliness was heightened. In contrast, Morgana's spirits plummeted, though it was nonsensical for them to do so. She had always known he would offer for Hannah.

Still, it seemed as if a door had slammed in her face. All hope was gone that she and Sloane could recapture that intimacy they'd so briefly shared, the one that had led to her coming alive to her passion for him. How was she to bear it?

By the time Sloane walked in the room, Morgana had taken over the pouring of tea from her aunt. It helped for her to have a task to perform. When he walked over to her and she poured for him, knowing precisely how he desired his tea, she sensed the same pent-up excitement in him so evident in Hannah. She dared glance at his face as she handed him his cup. His grey eyes were as warm and soft as smoke.

Would that they could be that warm for her.

Chapter Fifteen

By the time she entered Sloane's carriage, Morgana felt quite in control of herself. Tears no longer threatened to embarrass her, nor did his lighthearted mood make her heart ache—very much.

Amy had already seated herself in the backward-facing seat, and Sloane took his place beside Morgana, tapping on the roof for the coachman to be off. He sat too close, it seemed, taking away all of Morgana's air.

'Did you have a nice visit, Amy?' she asked. Better to converse with her maid than endure Sloane's cheerful silence.

'Oh, yes, miss, a lovely visit,' Amy responded. 'And I did not say one word about the masquerade.'

'The what?' Sloane's voice boomed in the small confines of the carriage.

Amy's hand flew to her mouth and she glanced in alarm at Morgana, who was not in any mood to hear Sloane upbraid her one more time.

She lifted her chin defiantly. 'The masquerade at the Argyle Rooms tomorrow night. We are to attend. It is to be how we launch the girls.'

She could feel his eyes burn into her, though she could not clearly see them in the dim light of the carriage lamp. 'Surely you are not seriously considering this?'

She could not explain to him that she agreed to this plan in part for his sake, to extricate him from the courtesan school. If it no longer existed, it could not threaten his happiness—or Hannah's.

'They must be set on their way sometime.' She sounded exactly like Madame Bisou, but she did not care. 'This masquerade is the perfect opportunity. Harriette Wilson says so.'

'Harriette Wilson,' spat Sloane. 'Damn her for coming to your door.'

Amy gaped at them both.

'I thought her very charming.' Morgana's voice was impudent. 'In a way, she started the whole idea of the courtesan school. She was the inspiration, you might say. To me, it is fitting we use her idea of attending the masquerade.'

He snatched her hand. 'Morgana, do not tell me you will attend this masquerade. I forbid it.'

She pulled it out of his grasp.

Forbid it? He had no right to tell her what she should and should not do. She was nothing to him. *Nothing.* Merely the cousin of his fiancée. 'Of course I will attend. I am quite looking forward to it.'

He leaned towards her in the darkness, so close she could feel his breath on her face. 'Morgana, it is bad enough that you allow those young women to become courtesans, but you must not attend this masquerade. You have no idea what happens at such events.'

She shrank back from him, but it was his proximity that disturbed her more than his warning. She knew enough of the world to realise the masquerade would be a raucous affair. She intended to be there to make sure her girls remained safe, that was all. He ought to understand her need to do so. But he could not understand the other emotions swirling inside her, the arousal of her senses caused by just sitting next to him.

'This is not well done of you at all,' he went on.

No, it was not well done to fall in love with the man affianced to her cousin. Nor was it well done of her to wish she could do with him all the things that Harriette Wilson and Madame Bisou hinted a woman might do to please a gentlemen.

'I think it is very well done of me, sir.' She faced him, anger rising inside her, piling on top of emotions that were no more than a jumble of pain twisting inside her. Loss, desire, loneliness—emotions that drove her to shock him further. 'In fact, I think you are wrong about my girls becoming courtesans. I am quite convinced that this is exactly the life a woman should lead. Think of the independence. The excitement.'

He shook his head, looking contemptuous. 'Be sensible, Morgana.'

Sensible? That was the last thing she could be right now. She could taste tears in the back of her throat. 'Do you wish to hear more, Sloane? I have decided to join my girls. I will set up a business for myself. I am quite convinced it is the sort of life I would desire.'

Amy gasped.

Sloane grabbed Morgana's arm. 'You are not serious!'

Of course she was not serious. She was merely broken-hearted and trying so desperately not to reveal it.

'I assure you, I am quite serious.' This time his grasp was so firm she could not pull away.

The carriage came to a stop and Sloane turned to Amy. 'Go on, Miss Jenkins. Miss Hart will be along directly.'

Amy scurried out of the carriage.

He turned back to Morgana and shook her. 'I do not believe you, Morgana.'

'I do not care what you believe, Sloane.' Morgana was near hysteria now. 'Do you think I wish to lead a life as dull as my cousin Hannah's?' She made herself laugh. 'Oh, no. I desire excitement. I want to attract as many men as Harriette Wilson. I can do it, too.'

'Do not be foolish.' He was so close that her nostrils filled with the scent of him. She could almost taste his lips upon hers.

'Do you not think I am able?' Her voice wobbled.

'I think you are being absurd.' His face was inches away.

'Harriette taught us well. I made you come to me, even though you have barely spoken to me for a month.' Her breath quickened.

'You did not.'

'I can make you kiss me, too,' she added.

He gaped at her. She lifted her eyes to his and slowly circled her mouth with her tongue. Then she parted her lips and closed her eyes.

She felt him crush her against him and press his lips to hers, tasting her as hungrily as if he were a man starved of food. She returned the kiss, every bit as ravenous, ignoring Harriette's admonition about withholding her tongue. She wanted to fully savour him. One final time.

He abruptly drew her away from him. 'Leave me, Morgana. Leave me now, before I do something we both will regret.'

'I won't regret it,' she murmured, lost in the sensation of him. She kissed him again.

His hand rubbed up and down her back and circled around to her breast. She sighed, relishing the touch, wanting him to reach inside her dress, wanting to feel his hand upon her bare skin.

Instead, he pulled away. 'No, Morgana.' He opened the carriage door. He climbed out and extended his hand to her. She quickly straightened her dress and wrapped her shawl around her shoulders. She took his hand, but only for as long as it took to climb out of the vehicle. Without waiting to see what he would do next, she ran to her door and took refuge inside her house.

Sloane signalled the coachman to stable the horses, then slowly walked to his own door. How could something he wanted so desperately go so far awry? He barely refrained from jerking the door open and slamming it behind him. His footman jumped to his feet at his abrupt entrance. With only a nod to the man, Sloane tore up the stairs, still on fire for Morgana and furious at her for playing the coquette. If she acted like that with another man—a thought that made him see red—she'd indeed ruin herself. Did she not know that, once lost, she would never get her reputation back? A man might be forgiven his passionate indulgences, but never a woman.

His valet shot out of his chair nearly as high as had the footman. 'Go!' shouted Sloane.

As the man nearly tripped in his hurry to get out the door, Sloane scoured the drawers and cabinets, finally finding where his man had put his brandy. Not bothering with a glass, he drank directly from the bottle.

The next day proved that Morgana, Amy and Miss Moore were excellent costumers. With fabric hurriedly purchased at the linen drapers, the older woman and the young maid had fashioned each girl an alluring outfit according to Morgana's design, complete with identity-disguising masks. The costumes were simple, draped gowns, all in classical white and fashioned with fabric attached to their arms so as to resemble wings. Their masks were created from white silk trimmed with feathers. The girls were garbed as the Sirens of Greek myth, winged creatures whose singing lured sailors to their doom. For their début into the world of courtesans, Harriette Wilson had arranged for them to enter the Argyle ballroom as a group, singing a song, with Rose as the soloist. It would be a grand entrance.

Morgana planned a quieter entrance for herself in the Argyle Rooms. She would dress in a voluminous gold domino she had found in an attic trunk. It came with a matching gold mask to further disguise her identity. No matter what she had declared to Sloane, she meant to attend the ball merely as a spectator, to watch her fledglings take their first flight. After this night she would see them set up in rooms of their own. She would pay the expenses, of course, until enough money came in from gentlemen. But whenever she thought that far in advance, a sick feeling settled in the pit of her stomach.

It was time to leave for the masquerade. She joined the girls in the hall, where a thin-lipped Cripps stood to assist them.

Katy's spirits were so high, it was a surprise that her feet touched the floor. Miss Moore, who never in her life expected to be dressed in a grey domino bound for a masquerade, was nearly as excited as Katy. Mary, Rose, and Lucy were more subdued. They waited for Robert Duprey and Madame Bisou to collect them in one hackney coach and Mr Elliot in another.

'Remember,' Morgana whispered to the girls out of Cripps's hearing. 'You are not to give yourselves to any gentleman this night. You are a far more valuable commodity than to sell yourself to the first bidder. Recall what Miss Wilson said. Let the gentlemen pine for you.'

Her words turned sour in her mouth. Her girls were not

objects to be sold at auction, but young women as dear to her as sisters would be. But everything had gone too far to turn back now.

Mary, Rose and Lucy gave solemn nods. Katy laughed.

Morgana tapped her on the shoulder. 'Katy, did you hear what I said?'

The girl made a valiant attempt to look sober. 'Yes, Miss Hart. I am too valuable to be sold this first night!'

Morgana winced.

'The coaches are outside!' Amy called from the drawing-room window. She rushed over to give her sister a tearful goodbye. Lucy clung to her, looking anything but gay at the parting.

Mr Duprey and Mr Elliot soon were admitted into the hall and the girls sorted themselves into some order. As they left the house, Morgana refused to consider what the neighbours might think if they spied them all leaving at this hour of the night. By plan none of them had donned their masks yet, but anyone might guess they were off to a masquerade, *the* masquerade everyone knew about.

Morgana only truly cared what Sloane thought, if he gave it any thought at all. She'd seen him go out earlier in the day and had not seen him return. He must have gone to the *musicale* where Hannah and her parents would be. Morgana had refused her aunt's obligatory invitation to go with them. It was late, though, and the *musicale* might already be breaking up.

Morgana rode in the hackney with Lucy, Mr Elliot and Rose. Mr Elliot would know what Sloane's plans were for the evening, but she would not dare to ask him.

They arrived at the Argyle Rooms with all speed and were admitted without delay. By the time they had tied their masks into place, Harriette Wilson herself came out to greet them.

'You look splendid, ladies.' She gave them all a charming

smile. 'Everything is arranged. We need only wait for the music.'

She led them to the ballroom door, cautioning them to be very quiet. When the music began, the doors opened and Harriette led them in as they sang:

Sweet is the budding spring of love,
Next blooming hopes all fears remove...

Morgana, Miss Moore, Elliot and Duprey slipped in behind them as Rose's crystalline voice dominated their chorus. A hum of excitement spread through the crowd.

When the song came to an end and the shouts of 'bravo' had ceased, Harriette announced, 'Gentlemen and ladies, these are the Sirens. Beware of their delights!'

The Sirens, clearly a sensation, were surrounded as the orchestra again started to play and a quadrille was formed. Each of the girls had several gentlemen begging for the dance. Katy looked as if she were a cat dropped in a vat of cream. Rose backed away, and Mary seemed to have a smile frozen on her face. Lucy, on a happy gentleman's arm, walked with a determined step to take her place in the set.

Several rather gaily and daringly dressed women glared at these newcomers who had captured the men's attention so thoroughly. Morgana, uneasy as well about the gentlemen's enthusiastic response, glanced towards Miss Moore, who beamed with pride. Madame Bisou strode proudly through the crowd, assuring all the gentlemen that the Sirens were every bit as entrancing as those of the Greek legends. Both Mr Elliot and Mr Duprey melted into the crowd, to enjoy themselves, Morgana supposed.

More people entered the ballroom, and Morgana became separated from Miss Moore. Through the sea of carousers she glimpsed the older lady heading towards chairs at the side of the room. The walls of the ballroom were adorned with a collection of classical statues in various poses, set high above the crowd. On the dance floor, the Sirens, in their white dresses, looked like the statues come magically to life, a perfect complement to the décor. The women dressed as medieval maidens, voluptuous milkmaids or lithe pages looked sadly out of place. Morgana circled the edge of the crowd to find a good vantage point to keep watch over her girls.

Suddenly an arm circled her waist and a man with brandy on his breath squeezed the flesh of her buttocks. 'Well, well, and who might you be, m'dear?' The man's voice was thick with drink. 'Have we met, by any chance? If not, I'd fancy knowing you.'

Morgana tried to pull away, but, though the gentleman was shorter than herself and much older, his hold on her was firm. The hood of his black domino fell away from his face as he tried to kiss her, and she realised with alarm that this was her uncle. Lord Cowdlin wore a mask, but there was no mistaking him.

'Release me this instant,' she cried, pushing at his chest.

He laughed. 'Playing it coy, eh? Come. Come. I can make it worth your while.'

'No!' She brought her heel down hard on his foot.

With a cry of pain, his grip loosened and she wrenched herself from his grasp. She pushed her way through the throng of people to get as far away from him as she could. He had not recognised her, thank goodness.

Her arm was caught by another gentleman in a black domino. Without a thought, she swung a fisted hand towards the man's face. He blocked it easily, grabbing her wrist.

'Easy, Morgana,' he said, leaning to her ear.

She glanced up and recognised her captor even through his mask. Relief mixed with exhilaration. 'Sloane!'

He guided her to where the wine was flowing, and handed her a glass. 'I told you this was no place for a lady.'

A lecture was not what she wished from him. 'I thought I told you, I have no intention of being a lady.' To prove it, she downed the glass of wine.

His brows rose. He took the glass from her hand. 'Another?'

She shook her head, glancing around the room.

How many of these black dominoes concealed the very same gentlemen who graced the dance floors of a society ball? Men like her uncle who were married, who led *respectable* lives? How many of these men kept mistresses in some fine little house off St James's Street? Would Sloane tire of marriage to Hannah and seek a mistress instead?

Of course he would. He might desire marriage to Hannah, but it was her respectability that attracted him, just as his money attracted her. How long before they both looked elsewhere for something more?

If Morgana did become a courtesan some day, as she'd threatened him she would, perhaps she would meet him again at a ball like this. Perhaps he would dance with her. Perhaps he would even take her to bed and she would discover the delights his kisses promised.

She would never be a courtesan or a mistress. Or a wife, for that matter. And soon she would even be without Lucy, Katy, Rose and Mary. She would be without Sloane.

A man and a woman, arm in arm, nearly careened into her. Sloane grabbed her and pulled her out of the way. The man and woman smiled at each other beneath their masks, happy and unapologetic in their enjoyment. She envied them.

Sloane continued to hold her even as they passed. Morgana faced him and tilted her head to him. He gazed down at her with his smoky grey eyes.

Why could she not be the courtesan for one night? What harm would it do? She would be doing nothing with Sloane that he would not do with another after his marriage. It was not so very bad, was it, to want one single night?

The orchestra began a waltz. She lifted her arms to circle his neck. 'Dance with me, Sloane.'

Sloane gazed down into her face, still lovely even under a mask. He felt like a man suddenly seized by a fit of insanity. He pressed her to him, ignoring for the moment the crowds of people around them.

She led him on to the dance floor, and he took her into his arms again. Here in the Argyle Rooms there was no need to maintain the decorum of Almack's. He held her flush against him, and they moved to the music as one, spinning and turning. His senses filled with her. He reached inside the gold domino that matched her eyes, and she reached inside his. The folds of their garments hid the play of their hands on each other, the intimacy of their bodies.

How had he ever considered being with any other woman but Morgana? No other possessed the same wild, untamed nature as he himself possessed, that sense of searching for something just beyond reach. She was what he searched for, and she was in his arms now. He was not about to release her.

At the end of the dance, he forgot the crowd, leaning down to taste her lips, lips she generously offered him. She tasted, not like the forbidden fruit a rake might grab for his own, but like a homecoming.

The sounds around him faded as he deepened the kiss. She entwined her fingers in his hair, and he gave himself to the moment. But there was a shout and a scuffle not far from where they stood. Sloane reluctantly released Morgana and pushed her behind him. Through the crowd he saw Elliot, of all people, swinging punches at a burly gentleman who tumbled on to the floor. Lucy looked on in alarm as the man rose and charged at Elliot. Sloane dived into the fray, Morgana at his heels. He grabbed the man by the collar of his coat and used the man's own momentum to send him crashing into the crowd.

He caught Elliot by the front of his domino. 'Get Lucy,' he yelled to Morgana. 'Find the others and be out of here.'

'He put his hands on her!' Elliot cried as Sloane dragged him to the door.

'What the devil did you expect?' Sloane muttered.

An alarmed Robert Duprey caught up to them, with Mary dragging a protesting Katy.

'Do we have to leave now?' Katy cried, looking back at two disappointed gentlemen. Rose hurriedly took a card from a grey-haired gentleman and followed them. Madame Bisou and Miss Moore pushed through the crowd.

When they were all outside the door, Sloane removed his mask. 'It is time to leave,' he said.

They could hear angry shouts from inside the ballroom. 'I'm going after her!' a man shouted.

'Leave now!' ordered Sloane. He seized Morgana's arm and led them to the street. Elliot and Duprey quickly helped the other women into the waiting hackneys. Sloane closed the door of one, saying, 'Miss Hart will come with me.'

The burly gentleman, two of his friends trying to hold him back, ran into the street as the cabs pulled away. He spied Sloane. 'You interfering—' He barrelled straight for him.

Sloane pushed Morgana out of the way and swung his fist hard, hitting the man in the stomach. The punch barely slowed the man. He knocked Sloane to the ground and fell on top of him. The man had his fingers around Sloane's throat before Sloane could get his own grip on the fellow.

Just as he was about to knee the fellow hard in the groin,

a flurry of gold silk covered them and the man cried out in pain. Morgana's fingers gouged at the man's eyes. He released Sloane and turned on her, but Sloane knocked him off and sent him rolling into the side of the building.

Morgana scrambled to her feet.

'Hurry!' Sloane urged as he led her to his carriage.

The coachman jumped on to his perch. 'Be off,' Sloane shouted, nearly tossing Morgana inside. When he fell in after her, the carriage was already moving.

She laughed, pulling off her mask. 'You are a prime scrapper, Morgana,' Sloane said as he brought his mouth to hers.

He untied the ribbons of her domino and removed the pins from her hair, which was already half-tumbling around her shoulders. He let his fingers slip through the silky dark locks.

She smiled at him. 'Make love to me, Sloane. Please. Just this once?'

He looked into her eyes, but did not answer.

She grabbed at the front of his domino and pulled him closer to her. 'I want to be with you,' she insisted. 'Just once. Please. Just this once.'

He had no intention of being satisfied with just once, but he need not tell her that. She'd discover soon enough. He captured her lips once more and let his actions speak for him.

Chapter Sixteen

Mrs Rice hurried to the door of the Argyle Rooms as the burly man staggered in from the street. 'Who was that?' she demanded.

'Cyprian Sloane,' the man's friend said. 'But you do not wish an altercation with him. He's a dangerous man.'

'Heard he's gone respectable,' another man said.

Mrs Rice cared nothing about that. 'What does he have to do with those girls?'

'The Sirens?' the same man asked. 'I would not wish to find out.'

Cyprian Sloane, Mrs Rice thought. Finally a clue as to who had stolen her girls. She'd send Trigg to discover his location. Signalling for her cloak, she hurried out of the building and made her way back to her glove shop, smiling at this lucky break. She'd get her girls back now, for certain.

And she'd make certain they would be punished for daring to leave.

When the coach stopped in front of Sloane's house, Morgana feared he would send her home. She did not want to leave his arms, not even for an instant.

'Come in with me,' he said.

She smiled in delight. He wrapped her domino around her and led her to the door.

'I told the servants not to stay up for me.' Sloane fumbled for the door key.

He opened the door and brought her inside, gathering her into his arms for a long, breathtaking kiss. She'd shed her gloves in the carriage and now pressed her bare palms to his cheeks, gazing into his eyes in the dim light of the candles left burning in the hall.

'Are you certain about this, Morgana? I will take you home at once if you are not.' His voice rasped with need, but also with restraint.

She looked directly into his eyes. 'I am entirely certain, Sloane. I want this more than anything I have ever desired.'

His smile flashed white in the near darkness, but it just as quickly disappeared again into a frown. 'You could conceive a child.'

Secretly she thought that would be the most marvellous thing in the world. To have Sloane's child growing inside her. To feel his baby suckling at her breast. 'It is unlikely,' she said instead. 'Besides, Madame Bisou taught us how to prevent it.'

But she would take no steps to avoid pregnancy. She might even pray for it to happen.

He stared at her a long time, then whisked her into his arms and carried her up the stairs, as if she were some petite miss weighing no more than half a dozen stone. She nestled her face against his neck and tasted the skin, now rough with a growth of beard. He carried her into his bedchamber and kicked the door shut behind him. A lamp burned in the room, and a small fire in the fireplace warded off the chill of the night. He marched directly to the bed and placed her upon it.

As she flung her domino on to the floor, he tore his off and shrugged out of his coat. She kneeled on the bed and reached up to unbutton his waistcoat. He went very still as she did so. She wanted nothing more than to laugh with joy.

Amazing herself with her boldness, yet proud at the same time, she pulled his shirt from where it was tucked into his breeches and reached underneath it to pull it over his head. His bare chest glistened in the lamplight, and Morgana paused, her breath momentarily forced from her lungs at the definition of his muscles, the peppering of dark hair on his chest. Just when she thought her eyes could take in no more, he unbuttoned and removed his breeches and drawers, and for the first time in her life her eyes feasted upon the body of a naked man.

What a glorious, exciting sight. She let her gaze drop to that most private male part of him and her pulse raced so fast she thought she would explode. He was large and erect, exactly the way the courtesan instructors intimated would bring delight. She lifted her eyes to his, her mouth open.

His gaze burned down on her. 'Your turn,' he said, climbing on to the bed and reaching around her to the buttons on the back of her dress. He handled the unfastening of her dress with surprisingly gentle hands, but having him so close and so bare was enough to drive her into a frenzy she did not understand. Once her buttons were free, he lifted the dress over her head and tossed it aside. She felt her breasts suddenly straining against her corset. 'Turn around,' he said and he untied her laces quickly so she was soon free of its constraint. Nothing was left between them except her shift. His hands were hot against her skin as he reached under the thin fabric and slid it off, inch by tantalising inch.

She gasped as he threw her shift aside and it fluttered to the floor. It was his turn for his eyes to feast upon her, and she felt his gaze as acutely as she'd just felt his hands.

'Oh, Sloane,' she breathed, her voice as thin as air. She trembled in need for him, a need she did not entirely understand, but one she was both frightened of and eager to slake.

He gently eased her down on the bed, kneeling over her. His fingers skimmed her flesh, causing her to feel she might come apart when he touched her breasts ever so lightly.

His eyes were reverent when he cupped her face and stared at her. 'Beautiful,' he murmured.

She rose up and placed her lips on his, winding her arms around his neck and burying her fingers in his thick, dark hair. Finally she felt his naked chest press against her, but still the need was not satisfied. Her heart pounded faster.

Nothing had ever felt as right as this. She'd never felt before as if she were in the right place at the right time and belonged there. Tears stung her eyes. How could finally feeling she was no longer alone make her realise the ache of loneliness she'd lived with her whole life? And would return to again?

While his lips continued to feast on hers, his hand cupped her breast and squeezed, sending a shaft of pleasure through her. She writhed beneath him and his male organ pressed against her, increasing the thrill. This was lovely, but not enough. She wanted more of him. She wanted all of him.

He broke off the kiss and stared down at her again, from her face to her breasts to her abdomen to the thatch of hair between her legs. He filled his hands with her breasts, rubbing her nipples against his palms. A strangled cry escaped her lips. His hands travelled lower and lower, until one hand slipped between her legs. Common sense told her to clamp them closed, but other senses had taken over. She opened herself to him.

'I need to touch you,' he whispered. 'It will lessen the pain for you.'

'You will not hurt me, Sloane.' She gasped as he fingered the most private part of her, feeling joyous that it was Sloane's fingers entering her, feeling eager for his body to join hers.

The sensations became more and more intense, stronger than she could have ever conceived. 'Sloane!' she cried.

'Am I hurting you?' He withdrew his hand, but she grabbed it, placing it back to where she ached with a new sort of need.

'No,' he said, rising over her instead.

Her legs parted and she felt him pressing against her, felt him enter her and begin to fill her. 'Morgana,' he rasped as he thrust into her.

The pain was sharp, but she rode it out without uttering a sound. She did not want anything to make him stop, not now, when she was so close to…to something she did not yet understand. 'Please, do not stop, Sloane,' she murmured.

'Morgana,' he repeated.

Slowly he moved inside her, in and out. It felt like heaven, like nothing she would have imagined. She rejoiced that Sloane created these sensations in her. She would never desire another man to do so. Only Sloane, even if for only this one night.

Her body responded to him, moving with him, the rhythm as intoxicating as the sensations it created. Inside, her need increased. She'd not known it was possible to desire something with such intensity and she still did not know what it was she desired.

His thrusts increased, harder and faster, and she matched him stroke for stroke. Harder. Faster as both the need and the pleasure grew.

Suddenly she felt as if she'd come apart in shining sparks, as bright and jubilant as the illuminations at Vauxhall. She cried out in joy and clung to him and he convulsed inside her, his gasps filling her ears. She held on to him tighter while wave after wave of pleasure washed over her.

Finally they collapsed in one heap against the bed linens. He was heavy upon her, but it felt glorious. He began to kiss her again. Her forehead, her temple, her nose, lips, neck. He rolled off of her, but continued to hold her in his arms.

Morgana seemed to have liquid where her bones ought to be, and he tasted of her with such relish as to have her suspect she'd perhaps turned to syrup. He, in contrast, was as firm to the touch as if he'd been sculpted, except there was nothing of cold stone about him. His skin was warm and smooth with a sheen of perspiration that bespoke of the energy of their lovemaking.

He was planting light kisses on the ticklish skin of her stomach. She played with his hair.

'Can it happen again?' she asked, her voice coming out light and breathy.

He peered at her, dark sultry eyes gazing from between her naked breasts. His slow grin grew, and suddenly she provided her own answer to the question. Her body told her it would happen again.

He answered her. 'I am counting on it.'

A gasp escaped her lips and she dug her fingers into his shoulders. He rose above her, the wicked smile still on his face, 'Do you want me, Morgana?'

'You know I want you, Sloane.' She tried to return the smile, but he mounted her once more and gently pushed inside her. Their initial joining had been at an eager pace, but this time he moved with a languorous leisure.

'Are you teasing me, Sloane?' she whispered when his ear came near her lips.

He moved back and forth before he answered, grabbing a taste of her ear as he did so. 'I'm loving you, Morgana.'

If his body created sensations so deep inside her she could not even imagine them, then his words touched something even deeper. She was joined to him. She was not alone.

Tears briefly stung her eyes before she allowed herself to feel the elation of it. His lovemaking was a glorious gift she would never, ever forget.

Morgana let herself be carried along thrill by repeated thrill. This culmination was different than the first, reached in unison with him, a quieter, stronger pleasure that rolled through her, making her unsure where she ended and he began.

He eased himself off of her and nestled her against him.

'Can it happen again?' she murmured.

She felt his voice rumble in his chest. 'Not without making you sore. Sleep now, Morgana.'

She was determined to stay awake and savour every second of being with him. To hear the rhythm of his breathing. To feel his warm skin against her cheek. To inhale his scent, a mix of manliness and spice.

But soon enough she did what he commanded. She fell deeply into a satisfying, restful sleep.

Sloane barely heard the scratching at his door. He opened one eye. Morning had come much too soon but, now reluctantly awake, the soft, sensual woman nestled against him roused his senses as well.

The scratching continued.

Had Elliot not seen fit to train these servants when to give their employer privacy? Sloane gazed at Morgana so peacefully asleep and carefully eased away from her. She sighed and he froze, fearing he'd awoken her, but she rolled to her other side and curled up, looking like an innocent child.

He slipped out of bed and searched for something to wrap around himself. He grabbed his shirt, tying it on his hips like a loincloth as he padded to the door in his bare feet. He opened the door a crack and peeked at who dared interrupt him at this time.

'Elliot!' He almost forgot to whisper.

The young man was fully dressed and looking very upset. Sloane stepped out into the hall, closing the bedchamber door behind him.

'What the devil are you doing, Elliot?' he said.

Elliot held a paper in his hand and a worried frown on his face. 'I beg your pardon, Sloane, but there is an urgent message for you.'

'An urgent message?' Sloane reached for the paper. 'From whom?'

'Your nephew, sir. The man who delivered the missive was instructed to see that it was placed in your hands immediately.'

Sloane broke the seal with his thumb.

The letter read,

Dear Uncle,

It is imperative you come immediately. I have learned that Grandfather and my father are planning to ruin your marriage plans to Lady Hannah by spreading a rumour of an affair between you and Miss Hart. They are composing an item for the newspapers at this very moment. Needless to say I am appalled at their behaviour. Come quickly. They will not listen to me.

    Your nephew, D.S.

Morgana. By God, what irony. It would not be her courtesan school that would ruin her, but the incredible bad luck of having him move next door to her. Did his father know she had spent the night in his bed? Did he stoop to sending spies to watch the house?

Elliot gazed at him intently. 'Is there anything I might do to assist?'

Sloane glanced up at him. 'No—yes. Have my horse saddled immediately. I must get dressed.'

Elliot nodded and hurried off without once questioning what news the letter contained. An estimable young man. A man to count upon.

Sloane hurried back in the bedchamber and began rummaging around for clothes. The difficulty with having a valet was that he did not have any notion where things were put. He gave up on clothes and decided to shave instead. If he showed up at the Earl's residence unshaven, it would merely make an unnecessary distraction. He intended to go looking like a gentleman.

There was a pitcher of water, some soap and his razor on the chest with the mirror, and he made quick work of the job. As he returned to rummaging for clothes, he closed the door of the wardrobe with a bang. The rustle of bed linens made him twist around.

Morgana sat up, holding the blanket across her lovely naked breasts. 'Sloane?'

'I am here, Morgana.'

She smiled when she located him in the room, a smile soft with sleep and gratification. 'Good morning.'

He took three long steps to reach her side, put one knee on the bed and took her face in his hands, giving her a kiss with the sort of promise he had no time to fulfil. She flung her arms around his neck and tried to pull him down on top of her. His arousal came swiftly, hard and insistent. What would a few minutes hurt?

He obliged her, covering her with kisses, rubbing his hands over her smooth creamy skin. He felt like laughing out loud, an odd impulse in the midst of this crisis, but he did not care. She made him feel joyous. As if he deserved all the passion she had so innocently and wholeheartedly bestowed upon him.

He took her quickly, entering her with a force that made her gasp, but not with pain this time. His Morgana never did anything by halves. She joined his fierce pace, making intoxicating mewing sounds as her need escalated. When coupled with her like this, Sloane felt nothing like a gentleman, but everything like a man. So fast they reached the pinnacle. Together they plunged into an ecstasy of pleasure. Sloane's landing brought him collapsing on her now damp skin.

'Ah, Morgana, I was too rough. I am sorry.' Surely he must have hurt her.

She reached up and caressed his cheek. 'Not too rough,' she murmured, making him want to take her again, right here, right now.

But he remembered his nephew's letter. 'I must go.' He climbed off the bed and started to dress. 'Do you wish me to see you home? Or you may stay in my bed as long as you like.'

She glanced towards the daylight streaming through the window. 'I suppose I ought to go home. I cannot imagine what they will think.'

He came back to her and swiped his hand through the disarray of her hair. 'They will think you spent the night in my bed.'

She gave a wan smile. 'Yes, I suppose that is so.'

He stared at her, wanting her all over again, wanting to hold her spirit, so untamed and unafraid, inside him. She was the woman created for him. He had no doubt of that now.

As he pulled on a pair of trousers, he watched her climb off the bed and search the floor for her clothes. She donned her shift and positioned her corset. He walked over to tie it. When he finished he put his hands on her shoulders and leaned her against him.

He wanted more mornings like this, with lovemaking and

easy talk between them, casual touching, ordinary life. She turned and smiled at him, picking up the neckcloth that he'd found folded in a drawer. She put it around his neck and tied it.

'Morgana, I have been summoned to my father's house.'

She looked up into his eyes. 'He sent for you?'

'No,' he admitted, the despicable plan of his father filling him with anger and pain. 'My nephew warned me.'

Her expression turned questioning.

He slid his hands down her arms, clasping her fingers. 'Morgana, my father intends to ruin me by sending out a tale that you and I are lovers.'

Her fingers flexed tightly in his. 'They have seen me come here?'

'I do not know. It would not be beneath my father's scruples to hire someone to do such a thing.' He looked directly into her eyes. 'I will convince him to remain quiet, but he is bent on seeing me disgraced. It will all come to naught, however, if you marry me.'

She went very still, the pupils of her eyes growing large. 'What about Hannah?'

'I have not offered for Hannah—' he began.

She interrupted him. 'She was to be your means of gaining respectability.'

'Hang respectability. You and I will do very well together.'

Morgana slowly pulled her fingers from his grasp and took a step back. She looked at him long and hard, loving him enough to give him whatever he desired.

What he desired was respectability. He'd worked diligently to earn it, and now his father was about to snatch it away again. Through her. If the Earl was so bent on ruining Sloane he would have the house watched, how long before her secrets were known to the man? Even marriage could not erase the scandal of a wife who trained women to be courtesans.

She took a deep breath, like a dying person gasping for one last breath. 'But I do not wish to marry you, Sloane.'

He flinched. It was almost imperceptible, but she caught it. 'You…do not wish to marry me?'

Morgana made herself smile, trying to remember how Harriette Wilson looked when she turned on her charm. 'Oh, no. I thought I told you I did not.'

His brows dropped and his voice became very low. 'After last night, do you expect me to believe you would not desire the marriage bed?'

It was Morgana's turn to flinch. She only hoped she hid it as effectively as he. To belong to Sloane, to make love to him, until death parted them was everything she desired. It was why she'd begged him for this past night. He must not pay by giving up everything he desired, merely because he had obliged her.

Morgana's mind whirled with ways to convince him that she did not want him, though her soul ached for him even now. 'Oh, I desire the lovemaking.' She aped the light flirtatious voice of Miss Wilson. 'Thank you so much for showing me that I would enjoy it. It quite informs me that I should like that part of a courtesan's life.'

'Morgana,' he cried in a fierce groan.

She fluttered her eyelashes and went about collecting her dress. 'Now do not lecture me, please do not.' She put the dress on over her head and placed her back to him so he could fasten the buttons. 'My mind is quite made up.'

'You will not marry me?' Another man might make this sound like a plea, but in Sloane's voice it sounded like a pirate about to attack. He fastened her buttons with lightning speed.

She made her voice light. 'Do not be absurd. You've no wish to marry me! Goodness! To think you would propose out of some obligation. You need not play the gentleman with me, Sloane.'

Her words wounded him. She saw it in his eyes. For a moment she wished he would strike her. The pain might distract from the wrenching ache inside her. But she knew he was too much a true gentleman to do so.

She picked up her stockings and balled them in her hands, putting her bare feet into her dancing slippers. He shrugged into his coat and ran a brush through his hair. Morgana put hers in a quick plait.

'I will see you to the back entrance of your house. If we are careful, no one outside will notice you.'

It was a gentlemanly thing to do. He could have just opened the door and pushed her out.

'Thank you,' she said, failing to maintain her bright-sounding speech.

He did not appear to notice. He opened the bedchamber door and walked her down the stairs. She managed to put one foot in front of the other, although all she truly wanted to do was sink into a puddle of despair. On a table in the hall was her gold domino, folded neatly. He put it around her shoulders and pulled the hood up over her head. His touch was like a smithy's tongs hot from the forge.

When they walked out of the door and through the gap in the garden wall, they did not speak. The silence spread through her like some wasting disease.

She had given him the means of retaining his hard-won respectability. She had given him a clear path to offer for a respectable wife—her cousin. But she'd hurt him. Not with her refusal of marriage. A man soon got over such a blow to pride. No, she'd treated him as if he were not a gentleman.

That made her no better than his father. And it made her feel sick inside.

The door to her house was unlocked. He opened it for her and she stepped inside. She turned quickly to bid him good-bye, but he had already withdrawn. He did not look back.

The man wore a vendor's apparel and carried a sack of brushes on his shoulder. He'd wandered around Culross Street since dawn, finally discovering a way to slip through the mews to a shrouded place where he could spy on Cyprian Sloane's townhouse. Instinct told him to watch the back of the house. Instinct, and lack of success witnessing anything of consequence from the front.

It was too bad he could not watch the house next to Sloane's where he'd briefly spied the pretty girls through the window. Sloane's place was as quiet as a church cemetery.

Just as he was about to leave, Sloane's door opened. There was the man himself, a woman with him. He walked her over to the other house and she entered it.

What an arrangement, thought the man with envy. *Some men have all the luck.*

Morgana paused when reaching the door to the library. It was open a crack, and she could hear the girls' voices and the reedy laughter of her grandmother, who undoubtedly found everything to be very lovely. Oh, to have her grandmother's forgetfulness, to live in a present that was perpetually lovely. How much easier life would be. How much less painful.

The voices were not sounding happy, however. Katy's shrill tones rose above the others. 'We need Miss Hart! She will know what to do.'

Morgana glanced down at her hand, still holding her stockings. She stuffed them into a pocket inside her domino and stuffed her numbing despair along with them.

She opened the door. 'I am here.'

Katy leapt up from her chair. 'Gracious, Miss Hart!' She looked her up and down. 'Did you have a nice night?'

Lucy and Rose stared at her, and Miss Moore, seated near her grandmother, gave her a kind, knowing smile.

It felt as if someone had ripped off all her clothes in a public square, but she realised it was not making love to Sloane that made her feel exposed. It was the ache in her heart.

She tried for a vague smile. 'A lady does not speak of such matters, Katy.'

Katy laughed. 'Harriette Wilson had no trouble speaking about it.'

Morgana gave her a candid look. 'But Miss Wilson is not a lady.'

Was it too late to convince them that they could be ladies? Oh, not ladies of the *ton,* perhaps, but respectable women who deserved men who loved them and who would never walk away?

Lucy stood up. Her face looked drawn. 'Miss Hart, we must tell you about Mary.'

If something had happened to Mary while she was making love to Sloane… 'What of Mary?'

'It is nothing bad,' assured Rose.

Lucy gave an imploring glance to Miss Moore.

Miss Moore beamed at Morgana. 'It seems our Mary has run off to Gretna Green with Mr Duprey.'

'That cowhanded sapskull…' Katy shook her head '…how could she?'

Tears sprang to Morgana's eyes. She walked over to Miss Moore. 'Is it really so?'

Miss Moore handed her a letter. Mary wrote that she was

sorry to disappoint Morgana, but Mr Duprey had proposed to her at the masquerade, promising to save her from such unpleasantness and give her a good home. He did not have a big fortune, she added, but Mary looked forward to making little economies to make his life pleasant. The letter then went on for a whole page, heaping praises upon Mr Duprey.

When Morgana finished she clasped the letter to her chest.

'That slow-top could have purchased a special license here in London.' Katy shook her head in disgust.

'Gretna Green is romantic, is it not, Miss Hart?' Rose directed her beautiful green eyes on Morgana. 'It is good that she marries, is it not?'

Morgana smiled through her tears. 'It is wonderful for her!' She would miss the shy, gentle girl. Her loss was Mr Duprey's gain—and Mary's salvation.

Morgana thought of Sloane. 'It is wonderful for her,' she repeated. 'Well done, Mary.'

Chapter Seventeen

Sloane's horse was waiting for him when he tore back into the house. Elliot stood in the hall and the butler hovered in a doorway.

It was Elliot who handed him his hat and gloves. The look of compassion on the young man's face nearly jolted him out of the towering rage that consumed him.

Morgana.

He grabbed his hat and gloves and thundered out the door, snatching the reins of his horse from the groom, and mounting in one easy motion. He fleetingly considered detouring into Hyde Park to ride off the storm inside him, but even a hell-for-leather gallop down Rotten Row would not suffice. He must simply wrest control back, push down the pain that kept shooting up through the anger.

Morgana.

He could not think straight. He felt as if she'd pushed him off a very high cliff. Hitting the ground, he had met with pain too intense to bear. She had refused him. Said she'd toyed with him. Accused him of being no gentleman.

His head told him not to believe a word of it. Morgana, a courtesan? Nonsense.

Did she concoct that story as an excuse to refuse his offer of marriage? She had wanted their lovemaking as much as he, but only when he'd mentioned marriage did she repeat her outrageous story. Sloane's insides felt as if a dozen sabres had slashed him to ribbons and his head whirled with the suspicion that she wanted him to be the rake, not the gentleman. She craved the excitement, not the man. Sloane had gone through plenty of women like that, who'd made love to him so they could say they'd been seduced by the dark and dangerous Cyprian Sloane.

Sloane thought Morgana different. He could not have so thoroughly misjudged her when his skill at judging character had always been razor-sharp.

He turned a corner and, nearly colliding with a slow-moving coal wagon, reined in his steed and tried to pull himself together.

He had one thing clear is his head. If she carried his child, she *would* marry him, even if he had to drag her to the altar to do it. No child of his would ever be burdened by questions of paternity.

Sloane kept his horse apace with the curricles, carriages and wagons in the streets while he tried to push Morgana out of his mind. The immediate task was to confront his father. Ironic that the job at hand was defending the good name of the woman who merely craved his bad one.

He finally turned down the Mayfair street where his father resided, not precisely calm but at least resolved. Sloane pulled his horse to a halt in front of his father's townhouse. Calling for a footman to see to the horse, he waited in the hall while another servant fetched David. His nephew did not keep him waiting and quickly drew him aside.

'I am glad you are here.' David wrung his hands. 'They have not yet sent the message to the papers. There is still time to change their minds, though I am not sure what you can do to convince them.'

Sloane frowned. 'Do you know when the Earl and your father conceived this plan?'

'I do not know when the idea first occurred to them.' David gave him an earnest glance. 'I think it was right after Lady Cowdlin's dinner party—'

Where Rawley had seen them both, Sloane thought.

'—but they discussed it last night after our evening meal. I looked for you at the *musicale,* but you were not there. So I sent the message first thing this morning.'

Last night? Before the masquerade. No spy saw Morgana enter his house. Sloane expelled a relieved breath.

David's expression suddenly changed into one of ill-disguised pain. 'My father heard your offer for Lady Hannah's hand would be imminent. Grandfather had words with Lord Cowdlin yesterday. You must know the Cowdlin family and our own have been close for many years—years you were absent. Grandfather does not wish you to marry into the family—'

A muscle contracted in Sloane's cheek. Sloane had been ready to ruin Hannah's life, just as his father now aspired to ruin Morgana's. The similarity between himself and the Earl of Dorton sickened him.

David paced back and forth. 'Grandfather ought not stand in the way of your happiness. I...I cannot fathom it.'

Sloane gazed at his nephew, who suddenly looked as young as the much-beloved toddler he'd envied so many years ago. He had nearly forgotten David and Hannah's tragic love affair.

'David, I am not making Lady Hannah an offer. I will not marry her.'

Instead of looking joyous, David's face flashed with panic.

'You cannot mean…' His face turned white. 'But what will happen to her? I confess, I could at least rest easy knowing she would be under your protection. Who will Cowdlin try to sell her to next?'

Sloane put a firm hand on his nephew's shoulder to still these dramatics. 'To you, nephew.'

David's mouth dropped open.

Sloane almost smiled. 'But you and I must play a careful game, if we are to win this hand. We have little time to plan…'

A few minutes later Sloane and David were admitted to his father's library, where both the Earl and Rawley gloated.

'What brings you to this house, Cyprian?' the Earl asked with a smirk.

Sloane advanced upon him as if a man possessed. 'I will brook no interference from you in my plans, sir. You have no control over me or who I marry.'

The Earl tossed Rawley, the *real* son, a smug expression. 'You, Cyprian, are nothing to me; therefore, you have no say in what I do.'

The barb, so predictable, did not even sting. Sloane shot back at him. 'Come now. You have some lunatic plan to send lies to the newspapers, to spread gossip about me throughout the *ton*. I will stop you. I will not be deterred from marrying Lady Hannah. You have met your match in me, sir. I have money enough to destroy you, and the skill to succeed. Think what a public suit for defamation would cost you, both in reputation and in fortune.'

'But I would ruin you first,' cried his father, rising to his feet. 'A clandestine affair will do the trick, I think. Rawley's brilliant idea! Cowdlin would refuse you his daughter in a minute, if he thought you were rooting with his wife's niece.'

Sloane's fingers curled into fists at this coarse reference to Morgana.

David interceded. 'Grandfather, you must think of Miss Hart. This would ruin her, too. And I think it unlikely that Cowdlin can refuse Uncle Cyprian, no matter what gossip prevails. He needs the money. He needs a rich husband for his daughter.'

The Earl swung around to his grandson. 'Are you speaking to me, boy? Do you dare?' He pointed his cane at David. 'You brought this—this person here? You informed him of my plans? You betray your own flesh and blood. Do not think I will forget it.'

Rawley jumped to his feet. 'Father, I beg you. David is my son—'

But David, Sloane noticed with pride, did not waver. He remained steadfast in the face of his grandfather's anger. He addressed his grandfather in a low, calm tone. 'Did you expect me to stand by and watch a lady's reputation ruined? Honour prevents me from allowing you to use her so shabbily. It is very poorly done, Grandfather. You make me ashamed.'

'Oh, bravo, nephew.' Sloane made his voice drip with sarcasm, but in his heart he meant every word. 'Gentlemanly sentiments, I am sure. Too bad *you* have no fortune or you might wed the Lady Hannah yourself. What chivalry that would be.'

David, still making Sloane proud, twisted around to him in admirable fury. 'I *would* marry her, too, sir, if I could save her from being sold to you. Do not mistake me, I sent for you only to preserve Miss Hart's reputation, to convince my father and grandfather that there is no affair between you and the lady.'

'Ha!' Sloane laughed. 'The only sin she is guilty of is living in the house next to mine, but that is none of my concern. Oh, I could have her if I wanted, I am sure. Remember, I have enough wealth to get whatever I want.' He turned back to his father. 'What I most desire is to rub your nose in my success, *dear Father*. At every *ton* event, I will be there. When you stand in the House of Lords, I will be in the Commons. When you meet your cronies at White's, I will be in the midst of them. You cannot ignore me, sir. I intend to be wherever you turn.'

The Earl's face flushed with rage. The hand clutching the knob of his cane turned white and the man trembled all over.

'Father?' Rawley said worriedly.

David stood his ground bravely, still looking defiantly righteous.

Sloane took it all in and suddenly realised how little what his father did mattered to him.

At the gaming table, Sloane often threw in his cards when there was no other way to come out ahead. Now he mentally tossed in his cards. The wager he made with himself, to gain back respectability and throw it in his father's face, no longer mattered. Nothing mattered but Morgana.

He dealt himself a new hand, one he would win at all costs. He would see Morgana safe—safe as his wife.

He turned his gaze on David, so young and valiant. David also wagered his future on a chance to win the woman he loved.

In a moment they both would win.

The Earl slowly eased his grip on his cane. His complexion returned to its normal sallow colour. A malevolent grin creased his wrinkled cheeks. He used his cane to point to Sloane.

'You will not win this one, Cyprian. No respectable wife for you.' He leaned on his stick again and turned to his grandson. 'I will release your fortune, boy. I can do with it as I choose. Do you want your money?'

David inclined his head, as if reluctant to admit it.

The Earl grinned. 'You may have it on one condition. Marry the Cowdlin chit and your fortune is yours.'

David levelled his grandfather a steely look. 'No, sir. Another condition must prevail. Agree not to defame Miss Hart's name, and I will do as you request.'

Well done, David. Sloane applauded inside.

The Earl gave a trifling wave of the hand. 'As you wish. There is no need as long as Cyprian is cut out.'

Rawley finally caught up. 'You'll give David his fortune?' He broke into a happy grin. 'I cannot complain of that.'

Sloane could barely keep from laughing, but, instead, he pretended to protest. 'See here, you cannot do this,'

His father bared his teeth. 'I can and I will!'

Sloane swore at his father and made other protests and threats just to convince his father he'd been severely injured. For his exit, he picked up a decanter of brandy from one of the tables and sent it crashing into the cold fireplace, then he stalked out of the room.

When he reached the outside and was about to remount his horse, David caught up to him.

'How can I thank you, Uncle?' The young man extended his hand.

Fearing his father or brother might be watching from a window, Sloane did not accept the handshake. 'It is I who must thank you, David. You prevented the dishonour of a lady I admire very much. I am proud to know you.'

'And I you, sir,' David said.

They stared at each other a long time before Sloane swung himself into the saddle and rode away.

Sloane felt as if he'd been navigating a ship in stormy seas. Rising high on the wave, only to plummet, only to rise again. He felt buoyant now, as if nothing could ever sink him again.

He planned to grab Morgana and drag her to some room with him—his bedchamber, preferably—and keep her there until he finally convinced her to marry him. Re-experiencing his father's hatred gave an ironic contrast to his feelings towards Morgana. He loved her.

He returned his horse directly to the stables and crossed the mews into his garden, now a fairly respectable showcase of flowers and plants, thanks to Elliot and Lucy. But when he entered Morgana's garden, flowerbeds were trampled and torn up. Her back door was wide open. The hairs on the back of his neck stood on end as he edged his way to the door.

As stealthily as a cat, Sloane slipped into Morgana's house. He heard a woman crying in the library. He hurried to the doorway and peered through the crack of the door.

Elliot sat on a chair, Morgana's butler holding a cloth against his head. Blood stained his face.

Sloane nearly leapt into the room. 'Good God. What happened?'

On the sofa, Morgana's maid shrieked. Miss Moore held the weeping girl in her arms. Other servants were scattered around the room.

Cripps looked up. 'We have been attacked, sir.'

Elliot waved the butler away and held the cloth against his own head. 'Ruffians broke into the house and abducted the women. I—I tried to stop them, but there were too many—' He took a ragged breath.

Sloane advanced on him. 'Who was taken?' No one answered him at first. 'Who was taken?' he demanded, his voice rising.

Cripps responded. 'Miss Hart, and Misses Jenkins, O'Keefe and Green.'

'Lucy,' her sister cried. 'Lucy and Rose and Katy and Miss Hart.'

Morgana. 'Who took them?' Good God, he must find her. 'Who was it?'

Elliot shook his head. 'Some ruffians. No one I know.'

Sloane ran a ragged hand through his hair. He swung around to the footmen. 'Where the devil were you when this happened? Are you not supposed to protect them?'

One of the footmen met his challenge. 'We were doin' the work of the house, sir. None of us were around the drawing room. I chased after them, but they were too far ahead. I saw the carriage, but I could not catch up to it.'

Sloane said, 'Would you recognise the vehicle?'

'The type at least, sir. It were a landaulet I saw, sir. Shabby it was. Might have been a second one as well. I cannot say.'

'Would you recognise the one you saw?' Sloane asked.

The footman nodded vigorously. 'Indeed I would, sir.'

'Excellent,' Sloane said. 'I need you to change out of your livery into clothes that will not get you noticed. We are going to search for that landaulet.'

'Yes, sir!' The man hurried out.

Putting his hands on his hips, Sloane looked at the others in the room. 'Who else knows anything?'

Miss Moore released the maid. 'I was in the room. Five men rushed in and just grabbed them. They were looking for four girls. "Four, she said", I heard one of them say.'

'She?' Sloane repeated.

'Yes, I am sure he said "she".' Miss Moore gave a vague shake of her head. 'I wonder if it was Mary they wanted. Not Morgana.'

'Where is Mary?' Sloane looked around the room.

'Mary eloped with Mr Duprey,' Miss Moore explained, a hint of a smile flashing across her worried face.

With Duprey? Sloane thought. Bravo for her, but who would have guessed Robert Duprey capable of such a thing?

Sloane pressed a hand to his forehead. 'It must be the glove maker.'

'Oh, yes, new gloves. Very nice. Very nice indeed,' said Morgana's grandmother, rocking in her chair and smiling.

Sloane frowned. 'We must plan carefully.'

It was a cellar room, a room to store Mrs Rice's wine—cool, dark, and with walls so thick no one above them could hear a thing. It also had a door with a very big lock on the outside. They had been imprisoned there for hours.

Rose rubbed her arms against the chill. 'Where are Lucy and Katy, do you suppose?'

Morgana paced the small area back and forth. 'In the upper rooms, I imagine. I suspect Mrs Rice will be putting them to work tonight. If she put enough fear into both of them, that is.'

Rose wiped a tear from her eye. 'It sounded like they got a beating.'

Before they'd been locked in the cellar, they'd heard Lucy's cries and Katy's string of obscenities. Morgana's stomach clenched with the memory and with hunger. She and Rose had not been given any food since being dragged through a nearly hidden door underneath the glove shop.

'Why did they not make us do the work, too?' asked Rose. 'I do not understand it.'

'I convinced them you are a virgin.' Morgana kept pacing. 'They knew better of Lucy and Katy.'

Rose looked over at her. 'But why should that matter? They don't want me to stay a virgin, not if I am to be made to do what Lucy and Katy are going to do.'

'There are gentlemen who would pay much to bed a virgin, especially one as pretty as you. I suspect Mrs Rice will be taking bids for you.'

'Bids?' Rose shivered. 'It is too awful.'

Morgana ignored the pain from the bruises on her legs and arms. She touched her cheek. One of the men had hit her hard before Mrs Rice yelled at him for spoiling the merchandise. The spot still stung when she touched it. The pain would not prevent her from putting up another fight. She would not quietly do Mrs Rice's bidding.

'I am, you know,' Rose said.

'You are what?' Morgana continued pacing.

'A virgin.'

She stopped. 'You are?' Morgana had always thought Rose came to the courtesan school already ruined, like the others.

Rose nodded.

Morgana was mystified. 'But why desire to be a courtesan unless you…?'

'I didn't,' Rose said. 'I never desired to be one of those types of ladies.'

Morgana gaped at her. 'Why did you come to me, then?'

Rose gave a wan smile. 'I overheard Katy and Mary talking in the street. I knew they were talking about lessons from a lady, as you are a lady, to be sure. So I thought you would teach me some pretty behaviour, like ladies have, and that is what you have done.'

Morgana still stared. 'But pretty behaviour for what? Why did you want to learn such things?'

'Some of the things I did not wish t'learn.' Rose shook her head. Then her eyes filled with tears. 'More than anything, I want to be a songstress. The kind who has posters all over town to advertise her singing. The kind Vauxhall or Covent Garden or some such place will pay a lot of money and the newspapers will write pretty things about.'

'A songstress?'

A tear trickled down her flawlessly perfect cheek. 'I—I

would have had employment, too. I met Mr Hook at Vaux-hall and again at the masquerade. He wanted to hire me.'

Morgana was too taken aback to address the girl's tears. 'Who is Mr Hook?'

Rose gave a loud sniffle. 'He is the composer of songs and organist at Vauxhall. Surely everyone knows of Mr Hook.'

Morgana almost smiled. Everyone who had a musician for a father and an aspiration to sing, perhaps. 'Was he the bald-ing man who attended you at the masquerade?'

Rose nodded again and swiped at her eyes with her fingers.

'You did not wish to become a courtesan,' Morgana said it again.

'No.' She looked at Morgana with her huge, glistening green eyes. 'Miss Hart, what will happen to me now?'

Nothing, Morgana thought. 'We must escape this place.'

'I—I hoped Mr Sloane or Mr Elliot would come save us,' Rose said with a shuddering breath.

Sloane. Would he even discover they were taken until it was too late—too late for Rose, and until Lucy and Katy were forced to degrade themselves? And Mr Elliot had been hit so hard. Was he even alive? Sloane would come for them when he could, she believed with all her heart. He would charge in like a one-man avenging army and wipe out all these horrible people, but Morgana could not wait for him. They needed to escape now.

Morgana began pacing again.

She grabbed one of the wine bottles and sat next to Rose on the barrel that lay on its side. 'I have an idea…'

A few minutes later the sound of crashing glass reached the ears of the man sitting outside the locked door, and screams of 'Oh, help! Help! Stop her. You must stop her!'

When the locked door opened, Rose was huddled in the

corner surrounded by broken glass and spilled wine. She scraped at her wrist with a jagged piece and blood covered her arms.

'You must stop her!' Morgana begged the man. 'Hurry.'

He rushed over to the beautiful girl, squatting down to both reach her and try to pull her up. Morgana followed him. Rose struggled and moaned that she would rather be dead. Such a lovely creature in so much distress would be difficult for any man to resist.

He was no different. While he was distracted by Rose, Morgana came up behind him and hit him hard on the head with one of the bottles of wine.

He fumbled, but did not fall. Instead, he came at her. She swung the bottle as hard as she could and hit him in the stomach, as Sloane had done to the man in the park so long ago. This man doubled over and staggered backwards.

'I have the key,' shouted Rose, holding it up in the air.

Morgana grabbed her and pulled her towards the door. She slammed the door shut and leaned on it while Rose turned the key in the lock.

A roar of outrage came from the inside of their cellar prison. Their captor banged loudly on the door, but would not be heard any better than they had been.

'Are you all right, Morgana?' Rose asked. She caught Morgana's hand and looked at the cut Morgana had made to smear blood on Rose's arms.

Morgana's hand throbbed, but she said, 'It is nothing. We must hurry.'

They made their way down the cellar corridor until they came to a staircase. Creeping up each step as softly as they could, they heard the sounds of voices above them.

'Let us try the other way.'

Morgana led Rose past the wine cellar door where their

captor still pounded and swore at the top of his lungs. At the other end they discovered the wooden door leading to the outside. It had a heavy metal bolt. Morgana's cut hand shot with pain as she forced the bolt sideways and pushed on the door.

They were met by a crisp breeze and freedom. It was night, but the new gas lamps on nearby St James's Street gave a faint illumination. Rose turned to her.

'Go,' Morgana said. 'Return home. Find Sloane. Tell him to come.'

'What about you?' Rose asked.

'I must go after Lucy and Katy. Please, Rose. Hurry. Bring Sloane.'

Rose gave her a quick hug and, after a look to see if anyone was watching, slipped out of the door into the night.

Morgana hurried back through the cellar to the stairway they'd found before. She heard voices, but she crept up the stairs and into a dark room. A sliver of light shone from under its door. Morgana groped around the room, making her way to the door. She felt something soft on a shelf against the wall.

Gloves.

She picked one up and put it on the hand she had cut with the piece of glass. It helped relieve the sting and the soft kid kept her hand supple. Shrugging, Morgana put on the glove's mate.

Morgana inched her way to the door. She hoped to find a way to the upper floors where she supposed Lucy and Katy were kept. She opened the door a crack and peered through it. It led to a hallway at the end of which was the stairway to the upper floors. To the left was another room separated by a curtain. Morgana took a deep breath and started to cross towards the stairs.

She heard Mrs Rice's voice coming from behind the curtain.

'I do not care how you do it. Dispose of her. She is trouble. Have her put on a ship or something—that would serve her right—or toss her in the Thames. It is of no consequence to me as long as I am rid of her.'

Chapter Eighteen

Morgana stifled a gasp. Mrs Rice was speaking of her! Morgana had fought her captivity, and Mrs Rice had not been pleased. Morgana shuddered. The woman wanted her killed.

Even if it came to her death, she could not leave Lucy and Katy. She would see them safe or die trying.

The voices faded and Morgana rushed to the stairway, taking the stairs as quickly as she could. When she reached the top she again heard Mrs Rice's voice, but sounding suddenly very congenial. Morgana carefully peeked around the corner. She could just catch a glimpse of Mrs Rice talking to a well-dressed gentleman.

Mr Cripps!

Her emotions flashed from elation to anxiety. What was her butler doing in such a place?

'I should like a young lady,' he said, sounding exactly as he did when announcing dinner. 'Fair or red-haired would be my preference and I also like them young.' He pulled a book from his pocket and tapped on its cover with his finger. 'It says in this book that you provide clean, pretty girls.'

The Whoremonger's Guide. Morgana bit her lip. And all along she had worried about his disapproval.

She shook her head. It defied logic that he would visit such a place like this the day his employer and guests were kidnapped. And Cripps was too old a man to be a rescuer. He would get himself killed.

Mrs Rice gave him a sideways glance. 'I am certain we can accommodate you, sir. Show me some coin.'

Morgana heard the clink of coins. Lots of them.

'I've not seen you here before.' Mrs Rice spoke conversationally.

Morgana held her breath. Did Mrs Rice suspect he was not a genuine customer?

'Indeed. This is my first time.' He pointed to the book. 'But it says here—'

'Yes, yes,' Mrs Rice broke in. 'We shall accommodate you very well.'

Morgana dared to peek out again, but ducked back quickly when Mrs Rice turned to escort Cripps up the stairs. Wildly looking for a place to hide, all she saw were closed doors. She didn't dare enter them. Mrs Rice and Cripps came closer. Morgana ducked into a dark corner and hoped the woman would not look too carefully into the shadows.

Mrs Rice led Cripps to one of the doors at the other end of the hall. 'This one is a very lively girl. If she gives you trouble you tell me. I'll teach her to behave.'

'I enjoy a spirited young lady.'

Cripps said this very convincingly. He followed Mrs Rice into the room.

A moment later Mrs Rice came out again, saying, 'I shall return when your time is up.'

When Morgana was certain Mrs Rice had reached the bottom of the stairs, she crept from her hiding place and tiptoed towards the room into which Cripps had disappeared.

She had just passed the stairway when a door behind her opened. 'You there!' a man yelled.

She swerved around and came face to face with one of the men who had abducted them. She made a mad dash for the stairs, but he caught up to her.

'Oh, no, you don't, missy.' She could smell his foul breath as his hands grabbed for her.

She caught hold of the banister and tried to pull herself from his grasp, but he held on. From behind her, she heard Lucy cry, 'Let her go!' But other footsteps sounded and Lucy's cries were muffled. The man dragged Morgana down the stairs, the fingers of her gloves tearing from her efforts to hang on to the wrought-iron spindles of the banister.

'What is this?' Mrs Rice rushed out of the curtained room. She spied Morgana. 'Not you! Get her out of the hallway.'

'She's a devil, she is,' the man said, dragging Morgana through the curtained door into a room decorated like a fine drawing room, but with a desk at one end.

Morgana could not free herself so she opened her mouth and screamed as loud as she could. The man clamped his dirty hand over her lips. She bit it.

'Ow!' Letting go with one hand, he hit her so hard in the face she saw stars.

'Take her out of this house!' cried Mrs Rice. 'I want rid of her!'

Out in the darkness, Sloane heard the scream and could wait no longer. He turned to where Elliot and Morgana's footman stood with a still-trembling Rose. 'I must go in. Be ready to follow me at the signal.' He glanced at Rose. 'If we do not come out, you get yourself home.'

Rose nodded.

Sloane slipped through the shadows, nearly invisible in his dark clothing. He headed for the wooden door where they had seen Rose emerge. He opened it carefully and went inside, climbing down the stone steps into the cellar where sounds of pounding could be heard.

A man yelled, 'Let me out!' from behind a locked door.

Sloane did not oblige him. He smiled, guessing it had been Morgana's work that put the man there. He ran down the cellar's corridor and up the stairs. Crossing the dark room to the door on the other side, he opened it a crack and heard the voices.

'You cannot get rid of me.' It was Morgana, speaking with bravado. 'I will escape again. This fool cannot hold me!'

'Shut your clapper!' a man shouted, and Sloane heard the sound of a fist connecting with skin.

'Kill her now, Trigg!' Mrs Rice commanded.

Sloane rushed towards the voices, charging through a curtain into a room and straight towards a man who held Morgana by the throat.

Shocked at the surprise attack, Trigg released Morgana.

'Sloane!' she rasped.

Sloane knocked Trigg against a table, which shattered, spilling them both to the floor. Trigg grabbed a candlestick that had fallen to the floor. He swung it towards Sloane's head. Morgana grasped the candlestick in both hands and held on, while Sloane regained his footing.

'Come! Come! We need help,' Mrs Rice screeched.

Footsteps pounded from above them. Trigg pulled out a knife and charged at Sloane, who whipped out a long dagger from his boot. The two men slashed at each other and their knives connected like swords. From behind him Sloane heard the loud report of a pistol. Instinctively he ducked and swerved to see Morgana holding Rice's wrist, the pistol smoking in her hand.

Screeching like a banshee, Trigg came at Sloane again, so close he slashed the fabric of Sloane's coat. Another man ran into the room and grabbed Sloane's arms. Trigg started to jab with his knife.

'No!' Morgana pulled at Trigg's arm.

'Run, Morgana,' Sloane commanded. 'Get out of here!'

She flashed him a determined look. 'No.'

From above came a loud boom, freezing everyone in their places. 'Fire!' someone yelled, and the scent of smoke hit Sloane's nostrils. People could be heard coughing and running down the stairs.

Mrs Rice quickly went to her desk and unlocked a drawer. She removed a metal box. Clutching it in her arms, she cried, 'Make way!'

As she ran out of the room, Trigg and the other man looked at each other and pelted after her. Morgana scrambled over to Sloane.

He threw his arms around her, holding her tight. 'Morgana.' Though the air was becoming thick with smoke, he kissed her. 'Morgana, my love.'

She took his face in her hands. 'I knew you would come.'

Above the din of fleeing bodies, Elliot's voice could be heard. 'Lucy! Lucy!'

'Oh, my goodness! The fire! We must find them!' Morgana pulled away. 'They were abovestairs. Cripps, too!'

Sloane held on to her. 'You do not have to save them, Morgana. Cripps created the diversion. Elliot and your footman will save them.'

She looked at him with a puzzled expression.

'Come.' He kept one arm around her and led her to the door.

When they made it to the outside, a crowd had gathered and the bell of a fire brigade could be heard.

'Oh, I hope no one is hurt!' Morgana looked up at smoke pouring from the high windows. 'Lucy! Katy!'

'Make haste, Morgana. You do not want to be seen here.' Through the nearby alley, he took her to the back of the house. 'No one will be hurt, love. It is smoke, not fire. Cripps set it off.'

'Cripps?' She gaped at him and suddenly laughed. 'You are very clever, are you not?'

He gave her a very hard, very relieved kiss. 'Damned clever!' He grabbed her arm and the two of them hurried away.

'Gracious, look what we got!' Katy ran up to them, the footman at her side, carrying Mrs Rice's metal box. 'I saw her coming and tripped her. She let go of the box and I grabbed it!'

'Oh, Katy!' Morgana enfolded the girl in her arms.

'Well done, Katy,' Sloane said.

They walked to the area behind a storage shed where Rose anxiously waited. 'Miss Hart, oh, are you all right?'

Morgana, Rose and Katy hugged each other.

Cripps stood nearby, looking very smug. 'Had the devil of a time finding a way to set a candle under the bag, but Miss Katy and I worked it out.'

'You did very well.' Sloane shook the man's hand. 'Where is Elliot? Did he find Lucy?'

Morgana broke away. 'Lucy?'

Cripps gestured to the side of the shed where Elliot and Lucy clung to each other. Elliot held her face in his hands and was raining kisses on it.

'Oh, my!' Morgana said.

'Looks pleasant enough.' Sloane grabbed Morgana and

gave her a kiss that heated her from top to toe. She was breathless when he released her.

'We have to leave.' He called to Elliot. 'Come on! This way.'

Their homecoming in Morgana's drawing room was full of joyful tears. Miss Moore clasped Morgana against her bosom, tears streaming down her cheeks. Morgana's grandmother smiled and said, 'Lovely to see you, my dear.' Amy had an equally tearful reunion with her sister and then insisted Morgana come with her to be tidied up.

Morgana had no wish to be separated from Sloane for even a flick of an eye, but knew she must look a fright. Besides, she quite longed to feel clean again.

As Amy helped her wash and chattered on about how surprising it was that Lucy and Mr Elliot had fallen in love and how grateful she was to Sloane for saving her sister, all Morgana could think of was wanting to return to Sloane's side.

He came to save them all. As much as she'd hurt him that morning, he still came to rescue them. Morgana's hands went to her throat, remembering the moment she'd thought she'd taken her last breath. Sloane had saved her.

'You are bruised all over, Miss Hart,' Amy said, though it was no news to Morgana, who felt each and every one.

She glanced in the mirror. Even by candlelight, she could see the ugly black circle around her eye. She shook her head. It did not matter. Nothing mattered except that everyone was safe. Sloane had seen to it.

'Oh, do hurry, Amy,' Morgana said.

When they finally walked into the library, Sloane's eyes followed her. Morgana went directly to him, seating herself next to him. He took her hand in his, then lifted it and looked at the bandage Amy had wrapped around it.

'What is this?' he asked.

'A trifle,' she replied. 'A mere nothing.'

Rose piped up. 'A nothing, she says. She cut herself so it would look like I was bleedin' and then she hit the man over the head so we could escape.'

Sloane glanced at her hand again, then slowly lifted it to his lips. Morgana felt the kiss flash through her, surprised that even in this room full of people and after all they'd been through, a simple kiss from Sloane could inflame such desire. She wished they would all go away—all but Sloane.

The other servants were also gathered in the room, everyone enjoying the second or third retelling of the tale. Mrs Cripps listened adoringly to her husband's share of the tale, blushing and laughing when one of the footmen teased her about him knowing just how to act in a brothel. The other footman poured wine for everyone. It was like being in the bosom of a close, warm family.

Morgana watched Lucy slip out of the room with Mr Elliot. Her brow wrinkled. Lucy could do worse for a protector, but the life of a mistress was still not a respectable life. Sloane handed her a glass of wine. Katy's laughter filled the room.

Sloane stood.

'I would like to propose a toast!' he said.

'Hear, hear,' someone responded.

Sloane lifted his glass towards Morgana. 'To Morgana Hart,' he said in loud clear tones. 'Who saved everyone.'

'To Miss Hart!' one of the footmen piped up. 'To Miss Hart!' The others joined in.

Sloane clinked his glass with Morgana's and gazed into her eyes. Her heart felt about twice the size of her chest. She did love him so.

Rose sat down at the pianoforte and began to play and sing

a lively tune. The others gaily joined in. Sloane took Morgana's hand in his again and turned it over, lightly kissing her bandage.

'I must take my leave,' he said. 'Walk out with me?'

Morgana stood and took his arm. When they were outside the room, he gathered her in his arms and pressed his lips against hers.

'Oh, Sloane.' Her bruises were nothing to the ache he created inside her.

'Goodnight, my fearless girl.' He smiled down at her, the force of his eyes almost as potent as his lips.

'Let me go with you,' she pleaded. 'For tonight. Let me share your bed again, Sloane. Even for the last time.'

His eyes narrowed. 'The last time?'

Her words tumbled out in as much disarray as her emotions. 'I know it is wrong of me, but I want to love you, Sloane. I want to!' She pulled him towards the door leading out to the garden. 'I know we cannot repeat this, not with you betrothed to Hannah, but—'

He stopped her. 'I am not betrothed to Hannah.'

Her heart pounded. 'Oh, I know you may not have settled the whole matter, but I saw her, how happy she was. At the dinner.'

His brow remained wrinkled for a moment. Then it cleared and he gave a deep laugh. He grabbed her by the shoulders and put his face to within an inch of hers. 'You are mistaken, love. I made no offer to Hannah. By now she is betrothed to someone else.'

'Who?' Morgana asked, stunned.

'To my nephew David. They are in love.'

Her mouth flew open. 'I do not believe it.'

He laughed. 'It is true. My word on it.'

She stared into his eyes and took a breath. 'Then take me

to your bed, Sloane. There is no impediment.' She pulled his arm, but he did not budge.

'No, love.' She could not read his expression. 'I will not bed you tonight.'

Morgana felt like he'd punched her as hard as that wretched Trigg. 'Why not?'

He returned her gaze. 'You must marry me.'

'Marry you?' Morgana cried. Shaking her head in disbelief, she carefully examined his face. It finally registered with her what he meant. 'I told you this morning that you were under no obligation to marry me, Sloane. I quite know what I am doing. All I ask is for one more night, then I promise I will do nothing to keep you from a respectable marriage to some other lady. There will be no courtesan school. It is over.'

He took his finger and let it outline her bruised eye. His gaze bore into her, so intensely, it made even her toes go warm. 'The only lady I want is you, Morgana. If we are not respectable enough for the *ton,* they can all go to the devil.'

She gasped.

He went on, 'My behaviour has been worse than rakish. I nearly destroyed the lives of others, merely to get back at a man who can no longer hurt me. It makes me ashamed.'

'No,' she cried. 'I will not allow you to speak of yourself in that manner. You are the best of gentlemen. That is the truth. I did not mean what I said this morning—'

He put his fingers on her lips. 'I know that, Morgana.'

He leaned back against the wall and crossed his arms over his chest. One corner of his mouth lifted in a smile, the smile of a practised rake. 'If I am the best of gentlemen, you have no reason to refuse my offer of marriage, you know.'

She countered with a sober look. 'Except that I cannot promise to always be right and proper. I am not a proper lady, Sloane.'

His eyes twinkled as he leaned forward. 'Did you not know that a rake craves a bit of danger?'

She lifted her face to his. 'Then the rake will certainly agree to take me to bed.'

He grinned. 'He will. After we are wed.'

'How long?'

'A week or two, no more. After I procure a special license.'

His expression turned pensive. 'As a matter of fact, if I know my secretary at all, it may be two special licenses.'

'Mr Elliot—?'

'And Lucy,' he finished for her.

Elliot would *marry* Lucy? Morgana blinked in wonder of it all. Would that not be a happy ending for the girl?

'So, you see, you cannot refuse me.' His tone was still bantering.

She gave him a serious look. 'Are you certain of this, Sloane?'

He laughed and gathered her into his arms. 'Very certain. I love you, Morgana.'

Morgana wrapped her arms tightly around his neck. 'I love you, too, Sloane. I love you.' Joy burst inside her. 'Let us go to bed—'

He unwrapped himself from her embrace. 'After we wed. I am determined on this.'

She pursed her lips in disappointment. 'I think I preferred the rakish Sloane to this stuffy, reputable one.'

He took her in his arms again. 'Just a few more days, Morgana, and I will show you just how rakish I can be.'

Morgana could not reply because his lips crushed hers in one more toe-melting, passion enflaming, happiness-promising kiss.

Epilogue

The June breeze was warm and caressing as Sloane escorted his wife through the entrance of Vauxhall Gardens. She paused as he'd known she would, gazing at the lamps strung through the trees, at the arches and porticos.

'It is more beautiful than I remembered!' she exclaimed.

He smiled. It had not been even two months since their last excursion to the pleasure garden, so very different from this night. Now the magic of his life outshone the garden's spell. He'd been married only three weeks. Three glorious weeks.

The rest of their party crowded behind them, and he urged Morgana to move. 'We are blocking the way.'

She laughed, glancing back at the others, a motley mix of the people Morgana cared most about. The other newly wedded couples gathered around them. Elliot and Lucy, married the same day in the same church as he and Morgana. Robert and Mary Duprey, returned from Gretna Green, just in time for this outing. Miss Moore attended, as did Mr and Mrs Cripps, the maid Amy and the footman who had so bravely assisted in Morgana's rescue. Mr Cripps had insisted the servants remain in their place, so they hung back a little, though

Sloane and Morgana knew they were as much a part of this celebration as the others.

Morgana took his arm and walked close. Her eyes were busy taking in the sights. 'I can see so much better without the mask,' she said.

'Me, too,' he said. She did not much heed him, but it did not matter. The mask he spoke of was the one he'd worn since embarking on his foolhardy quest for respectability. There was still much of his past to conceal, but presently he felt more himself than any other time in his life.

They made their way to the supper box Elliot had arranged, the same one with the view of the fountain that he'd taken before. This group did not look askance at the less reputable Vauxhall visitors this night. They were too full of high spirits and anticipation. They were all present to witness the début of Vauxhall's newest songstress, Rose O'Keefe.

Mary said, 'It is so fortunate Robert and I returned when we did. I would have been greatly disappointed if I'd missed this.'

'Imagine. Our little Rose.' Miss Moore sighed with all the pride of a mother whose child had just taken its first steps.

'I wish Katy were with us.' Mary sighed.

Sloane glanced at Morgana and caught the fleeting sadness on her face, though her smile remained fixed. 'So do I,' she said.

Katy had left two days after he and Morgana married. With the moneybox she'd pilfered from Mrs Rice, she slipped away during the night. When Morgana read the note, in Katy's primitive hand, her face paled. Morgana blamed herself for a fate Katy had always embraced as her own choice.

It had taken Sloane no time at all to discover that Penny had taken Katy under her wing and was acting the procuress for her, but he merely told Morgana that Madame Bisou was looking out for the girl.

'When does Rose sing?' Lucy asked.

'Not for an hour or more,' Sloane answered.

Elliot attended to the last-minute details of the refreshments, which were brought to them almost immediately. Before Mr Cripps and the footman began serving the food, Sloane had them pour champagne for everyone, servants alike.

He raised his glass. 'To Rose's success!'

'Hear, hear,' they chorused.

As they clinked glasses, a familiar party walked by and caught sight of them.

Lady Hannah skipped over, dragging her fiancé with her. 'Morgana! Mr Sloane! We did not know you would be here, did we, David?' She rushed over to her cousin, nearly jumping up and down.

Sloane said a silent prayer of thanks that it was David squiring Hannah and not himself.

David Sloane leaned over to shake Sloane's hand. 'I am glad to see you, Uncle.' The young man gave Sloane's hand an extra squeeze.

'Is all well?' Sloane asked him.

David smiled and glanced over at Hannah. 'Very well.' He looked back at Sloane. 'Grandfather is gloating about how he got the better of you. I never know whether to laugh or to be sick.'

Hannah's voice reached Sloane's ears. 'Who would have thought you would marry before me!'

Lord and Lady Cowdlin, clearly wishing they could pass by, reluctantly joined Hannah. Lord Cowdlin gave Sloane a curt nod. Lady Cowdlin cast a disapproving eye over Morgana and Sloane's guests. 'Morgana, how do you do.'

Morgana darted an amused glance towards Sloane. 'I assure you, Aunt Winnie, I do splendidly.'

Her aunt leaned forward and whispered something to her. Morgana shook her head.

After they had walked on, Sloane asked, 'What did your aunt whisper to you?'

She gave a grin. 'She asked me if I were increasing.'

His brows shot up. 'Are you?'

She put her hand on his arm. 'It is too soon to know such things. My aunt thought it the reason for our hasty marriage.'

He glared at Lady Cowdlin's receding back. 'The devil she did!'

Morgana squeezed his arm. 'It is a lark, is it not? I'm quite flattered she thought me worthy of seduction by a rake.'

He laughed and planted a light kiss. 'She did not know the half. Last time we were here I almost dragged you down the Dark Walk.'

Her eyes widened. 'But you scolded me. You thought me a harlot!'

'I did not,' he said in all seriousness. 'I thought myself a rake.'

They all sat down to the light meal, and Sloane thought it the most enjoyable dinner party he'd attended since the Season began. It was a fitting end to the Season. Within the next few weeks, the *ton* would flee London for the pleasures of Brighton or the quiet of their country houses. He and Morgana were to travel to Italy to call upon her father, a very different sort of Italian trip from the one he'd made as a much younger man.

But all was different since Morgana had come into his life.

The bell rang to announce the performance, and they excitedly rushed to stand below the orchestra's balcony. Sloane wrapped his arm around Morgana as the crowd around them grew thicker. He saw Hannah and David walk through the

crowd, hand in hand. Elliot had his arm around Lucy, as did
Duprey around Mary.

'I am so happy, Sloane,' Morgana said excitedly.

'About Rose?' he asked.

She gave him a quick hug. 'About everything.'

The orchestra played a brief piece of music and Rose
walked to the front of the balcony. Morgana burst into applause, as did the others. Rose looked down and saw them and
gave them all a special smile.

She began to sing:

> Abroad as I was walking
> Down by the river side,
> I gazed all around me,
> An Irish girl I spied…

Sloane held Morgana tighter and she gazed up at him.
When he thought how easily he might have let her slip though
his fingers, he re-experienced the emptiness he used to carry
around inside him. But now, for the first time in his life, he
was not alone.

He lowered his head and touched his lips to Morgana's, a
light kiss of gratitude for being in his life.

Rose's remarkable voice continued:

> …I wish I was a butterfly,
> I'd fly to my love's breast;
> I wish I was a linnet,
> I'd sing my love to rest;
> I wish I was a nightingale,
> I'd sing till morning clear,
> I'd sit and sing to you, Pollie,
> The girl I love so dear.

The audience burst into applause and Morgana laughed, tears in her eyes. Shouts of 'Bravo' rang through the crowd.

A woman called out, 'Rose! Rose!'

The flame-haired woman wore an expensive-looking green gown that showed plenty of skin. She waved enthusiastically, still crying, 'Rose!'

'It is Katy!' Morgana gasped, and started towards her, but stopped abruptly. 'She…she has men around her.'

Indeed, Katy was surrounded by a flock of men, whose eyes were on her, not the songstress.

Morgana's face fell. 'Oh, Sloane, she has done it. She has become a courtesan.'

'It appears so, my love.' He kept his arm firmly around her waist.

'I had hoped she would not. She had Mrs Rice's money, enough to live on if she were careful.' She whispered, 'What have I done?'

Sloane took her face in his hands and made her look at him. 'It was her choice, Morgana. It was what Katy wanted.'

She shook her head. 'Still, I ought—'

'*You* gave her the opportunity to choose. You are not responsible for her choice.'

She leaned against him. 'I wish she had not chosen that life. Sloane, by the end, I was sick at what I had done—'

His arms encircled her. 'By the end, love, you gave each of those girls what they otherwise would never have dreamed to have. Even though you disagree with her choice, Katy looks happy. We all are happy, Morgana, because of you.'

She nuzzled against his chest for a long satisfying moment. 'Sloane?'

He enjoyed the feel of her in his arms, the scent of her hair, the warmth of her body. 'Hmm?'

'Take me down the Dark Walk.'

He looked down at her in surprise. She entwined her arm in his and gave him a smile so seductive it would have made any courtesan proud. But she was more, much more. She was his *wife,* his love, the piece that completed him and made him whole.

He grinned back at her with the knowing smile of a rake. They pushed themselves through the crowd, under the archway, heading towards the path.

Rose's voice followed them, clear as a mountain stream after winter's thaw:

Over the mountains
And over the waves,
Under the fountains
And under the graves,
Under floods that are deepest,
Which Neptune obey
Over rocks which are the steepest,
Love will find out the way…

The Heart's Wager

by

Gayle Wilson

Gayle Wilson taught English and world history before turning to writing full time. A winner of a number of prestigious writing awards, she is also the author of over ten contemporary romantic suspense novels. Gayle Wilson is married, with one son, and lives in Alabama, USA.

Don't miss Gayle Wilson's next glorious Regency romance! Look for *The Gambler's Heart*.
Coming soon from M&B™

Prologue

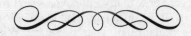

"Gentlemen, you may now place your wagers."

The pleasantly pitched and very feminine voice carried clearly above the din to the gamesters who clustered eagerly around the table. Juliette de Valmé's slim fingers, with their shockingly tinted nails, hovered over the faro bank, allowing them time to lay down their stakes.

"My dear, can you offer an explanation for this phenomenon? Why do we come each night to lose our money to a dealer with such prodigious good luck?" one of her patrons teased.

"Perhaps if you were wiser in placing your bets," another answered, laughing, "you'd not bother Juliette with ridiculous questions. I, personally, can think of no one to whom I'd rather lose a wager. Julie, my beloved, my heart and my money are yours," he finished, sketching the lovely banker a courtly bow.

"I believe you're right," she said smiling, indicating with a graceful movement of her hand the winning pair she had just drawn from the bank. Laughter circled the table at her comment and at the evidence of her continuing good fortune.

"Apparently we are all in that same predicament—so en
amored that we endure our losses in the hopes of winning
a smile, a kind word, and less importantly, of course, the
occasional wager," said the Baron du Deffand.

"But how ungallant, Deffand," argued another of the
young aristocrats who languidly jockeyed each evening for
the positions at this particular table. "I, my dear, have no
interest in winning any money from your father's establish
ment. I don't care how many Louis you wrest from my quite
willing fingers. It is sufficient that I am allowed to bask
nightly in the radiance of your presence. With that I am
content."

Julie's dark eyes smiled up at him from under a sweep
of impossibly long lashes, and she asked lightly, "Ah, but
the question is, when you have tallied your losses, will you
still love me tomorrow?"

"My heart is yours through eternity," he answered, put
ting his hand over his breast to signify the sincerity of that
pledge.

"Then I can only hope, my dear comte, that your bankers
are as faithful and that your accounts with them are as deep
as your devotion," she answered, her delicate fingers ex
pertly gathering his stake from the table. Laughter at the
nobleman's expense echoed again through the vast room,
and more than one jealous gambler, unlucky enough to be
relegated to play at another table, wondered what sally the
"Divine Juliette" had made to cause such merriment.

The blaze from the Austrian chandeliers and the noise
that swelled and ebbed from the densely packed throng who
crowded the rooms of this elegant house in the Marais dis
trict of Paris were as familiar to Juliette de Valmé as was
the beating of her own heart. She had spent most of her life
in one gambling den or another, and she understood very
well why the English called them hells. Souls were bartered
on the turn of a card, the spin of the wheel. She had seen
more than one loser leave the table where his fellow sports
men had avidly watched the death of his hopes, to go out

to end his life in some Parisian alleyway when he realized the enormity of what he had done.

At least her father's house was honest. The odds, of course, were still heavily in favor of the establishment, but there were no Johnny Sharps or shaved decks here, and the roulette tables had not been tampered with. Her father had insisted on fair play, and in these last years, as she had taken from his increasingly frail hands the reins of this business, she had respected his rules. Satisfyingly, the profit margin had remained healthy, especially now, after the defeat of Napoleon. Since then an influx of English gamblers had swelled the select group that sought admittance each night to what had become the most popular club in the city.

She knew that its popularity, to a large extent, was due to her presence here each evening. She considered it part of her professional duties to display both wit and unfailing good humor; to charm recalcitrant drunks out of whatever retaliation they threatened for their losses; and to deal baccarat, vingt-et-un and faro with a skilled line of patter that she could, and indeed believed she often did, deliver in her sleep.

She was well aware that the gentlemen who gathered around her table seldom watched her skillful fingers, uncaring if this particular dealer employed some sleight-of-hand in arranging the cards. Their fascinated eyes were more apt to dwell on the gloss of the blue-black, upswept curls, or on the artfully enhanced lashes that alternately hid and then revealed the laughing, expressive sparkle of her dark eyes, or on the revealing décolletage of whichever expensive dress had been delivered that week from LeRoy, the most fashionable dressmaker in the most fashionable city in the world.

Tonight the gown was bloodred, and she had highlighted her cheeks and lips to complement the glow that vivid color gave her ivory skin. She knew that every man here realized that the beauty nature had generously bestowed by virtue of her Anglo-Gallic heritage had been supplemented with her carefully applied cosmetics, but she knew also that none of them cared. They enjoyed in Julie what they would vehemently decry in the women who graced their drawing rooms.

She casually watched the action at the dozen tables without seeming to neglect in the slightest the entertainment of those crowded around her own. She had become aware some minutes ago of the heightened excitement that whispered around the rooms and centered on the heavy betting of a handsome and extremely drunk young English aristocrat who was being urged on by a group of his fellow Corinthians.

She had also caught Jean's warning, so she unhurriedly finished the game and, to the accompaniment of disappointed groans and lighthearted rebukes, she gracefully moved to the table she had been watching.

The Englishman was rather cheerfully disclaiming his bad luck, which he didn't seem to blame on the house. But drunk he certainly was, and her father's policies forbade taking the last ecu from those who did not, even if they should, know what they were doing.

She moved closely enough that by the costly scent she wore, if by nothing else, he was made aware of her presence. She smiled at his surprise in finding such a charming *mademoiselle* under his elbow, and she saw clearly the flush the unaccustomed alcohol had given to the downiness of his cheeks. A lamb ripe for the taking, but if he stupidly desired to lose his entire fortune at the tables, he would have to do it somewhere else.

She placed her small, carefully manicured hand lightly on his arm and watched in the unfocused eyes his interest in the table die a quick death, to be replaced by interest in a far more entertaining activity his body was trying to suggest to his brain.

"I know a quiet place where we can be alone," she whispered in unaccented English, softly enough that only he could hear through the swirling noise.

His sweating palm came up to cover her fingers, and with a minimum of fumbling, he managed to convey them to his lips with a rather charming ineptitude.

Certainly not a rake, she thought with amusement, turning to thread her way through the tables.

She knew from experience, knew without looking, that he would follow her. She was aware also of the dark figure that moved parallel to her own path, separated from the ongoing drama by the width of the room. The man, through whose efforts she had succeeded at taking control of this business in what had been exclusively a man's world, was again supporting her decision.

They were already out the rear door and into the bite of the evening air before the boy had realized their destination. "Do you remember the address of your lodging?" she asked quickly, hearing Jean move behind her in the darkness.

"Of course," the Englishman answered in surprise, wondering if she intended to go home with him. Even in his befuddled state, he could imagine how his hostess, a friend of his mother and father, would feel about his bringing a demimondaine, no matter how beautiful, into her house.

"Then tell him," she said, and, taking his right hand, she pressed into it a small, heavy purse that clinked full of coins. "And tell your friends that neither they nor you will be admitted to this house again during your stay. If you intend to lose every centime you have, it won't be here. *Bonsoir, monsieur,* and welcome to Paris, where one seldom gets a second chance to make a fool of himself."

She turned quickly, leaving him in Jean's very capable hands. She could hear his soothing, persuasive voice quieting the boy's questioning protests, and then she forgot the incident in her professional assessment of every corner of her kingdom. She had hardly known any other way of life, except during the years after her mother's death, unhappily spent in one of the convent schools.

When her father had realized how little, other than etiquette, she really knew, he had brought her to live with him and had engaged the first of a series of tutors. And so it was in his Paris casino that she had been educated by her teachers in the classic texts and, perhaps regretfully, by her life in the various depravities and dishonesties of which the human soul is capable. She had, in her twenty-three years, literally seen it all.

"I put him in a hired coach and sent him home." Jean's deep voice spoke softly against her ear.

She turned and smiled up into the scarred face of the man who had been like an older brother for the last three years. Her father had found Jean, and she would never know what argument had been used to convince him to take over the physical aspects of the running of the casino. But only Jean's intimidating presence, his quick eye and even quicker intelligence kept the kind of tight control necessary to manage a successful gambling operation in these uncertain times. He received a generous salary, of course, but not nearly what she knew he was worth, and she often wondered why he stayed.

Her father had always maintained that there was some mystery about the gambler's past. He was far too well-traveled, too knowledgeable and sophisticated, too sure of his abilities, to fit the personal history he'd offered when he'd applied for the job. But through the years, Jean had given no other explanation. And they both knew that his past, like the scars he bore, were forbidden territory.

She supposed that Jean, like so many of those who inhabited her world, was running from something, although she had yet to see anything or anyone frighten the Frenchman. He was as tall and as dark as Satan, and as handsome, too, she thought, in spite of the marred right profile and the black patch securely held in place by the ribbon that lost itself in the matching midnight of his hair. She became aware suddenly that his hazel eye was lazily watching her, and that he knew she was thinking about him in a way that was unusual for their relationship.

To her, he had always been simply Jean, a part of her family almost as much now as her father. And so the smile he bestowed in response to her scrutiny did nothing to quicken her heartbeat, as it would have that of almost any other female in the city. She no longer even thought about the rather endearing crookedness of his smile, the damaged corner of his lips scarcely moving in response to any emotion revealed in those dark features.

"I thought he was a little old for rescuing," he said softly.

"He was a child," she said, knowing she was being chided about her determination to follow her father's strictures.

"He was older than you," Jean said in amusement. His smile faded, however, at the flash of pain his unthinking comment had caused in the depths of her dark eyes.

"I'm older than he by a thousand years, and you know it."

He heard the surety in her voice, but he said gently, his thumb touching under her chin, "Not so old, little one, as all that. Young enough, I promise."

His smile this time coaxed an answering one from her lightly rouged lips.

"And what do you promise I'm young enough for, my friend?" she questioned lightly.

"For all the things you want," he responded immediately.

"Better wines at cheaper prices, a house run to rival that we had in October, for the coal merchant to forget to present his bill," she listed, laughing.

"No," he said softly. "For a time when you don't have to worry about all those responsibilities. For someone who will take care of you, for a change."

"I'm a little old for fairy tales," she mocked. "Go tell the boy you just deposited in that coach those fantasies. That's not what lies ahead for me. And to be truthful, I'm not sure anymore that I would be happy doing anything other than what I have done for so long. Somehow, I can no longer envision myself married to the coal merchant and dutifully producing a child a year. I think I'll be satisfied with the evils I know."

"And are you so sure that marriage is an evil? I have it on the best authority that some people even manage to enjoy the state of wedded bliss. And I didn't have the coal merchant in mind," he denied.

"Then who?" she said, laughing again as he had intended. "The only men I know are the merchants who come to this house to collect their bills. And our noble customers. Are you suggesting..."

"I'm suggesting that there are other men than those. And that you'll eventually discover that interesting fact."

"And, of course, those men would be interested in me?" she questioned sarcastically. "The proposals I've had have not been marriage proposals, I assure you. Nor are they ever likely to be."

She had never thought of Jean himself in the light of a lover. She needed him in a different way, and so she read nothing into his remarks beyond the gentle camaraderie they always shared.

More aware of her dependence on his friendship than she realized, Jean smiled and reached to tweak a dark curl between his long fingers. "Then if you're determined not to trade your expertise at running a hell for the running of a household, I suggest you return to your courtiers, who eagerly await your majesty's return."

He bowed deeply, every movement of his body smoothly controlled. His slimness belied a strength that had been tested only occasionally when he was new to the house. By now his reputation had eliminated any need to prove there was steel underlying the velvet.

Julie kissed her fingertips and blew a swift kiss in his direction, but he was already forgotten as she turned and began to make her way back to the endless watch over the busy tables, unaware that he tracked her graceful movement through the crowd. Then there was a slight disturbance at one of the roulette wheels, and Jean, too, returned to the demands of the small world they shared.

It was after three when Jean deftly slipped into Julie's place at the faro table, conveying her father's message, and in almost the same breath, piquing the interest of those who might protest the change in dealers by offering new odds that seemed to put the house at a disadvantage. Her father's summons in the midst of a successful evening was unusual enough that she found herself hurrying toward the office in which he presided now only over the accounts of the business he had begun many years ago.

He was seated at his desk, his frail shoulders draped with a heavy woolen shawl against the night air that he felt so painfully. His thin, long-fingered hands, the hands of the English aristocrat he had been born, rested on the surface of his desk. He and Julie both knew, and had known for several months, how ill he was, but the careful facade of normality had been strictly maintained between them. Tonight, however, she could sense his unaccustomed agitation as soon as she entered the room.

"Lock the door," he ordered quickly and waited until she had completed that task. "You know that I would never ask you to do anything that was not for your own good."

"Of course," she began, but he quieted her with a gesture and continued to speak rapidly, holding her eyes.

"I'm afraid, my dear, that I've endangered you by my activities on behalf of my country. I know that you must be aware that this establishment has provided a cover for those activities through the years, and now it seems that the French authorities are also aware of my role in the downfall of the Emperor. They see it as a betrayal, as spying on my adopted country, but England—"

His voice broke suddenly. They both knew that he would never see his beloved homeland again. She put her hand comfortingly over the fragile bones of his shoulder, but he cleared those memories and began again, speaking with a sense of urgency that was so foreign to his usual tranquillity.

"But now...because of me, because of my espionage for England, you must disappear. Take the money from the safe and run. Bury yourself as deeply as you can in the countryside, as far from Paris as it will take you. There are those who will want you in their power because they will believe, since you're my daughter..." He hesitated again, shaking his head. "They're capable of anything to secure information about my contacts in England. Torture, Julie, or even worse. You cannot imagine the depths of depravity to which you would be subjected if you fall into their hands."

"But I have no information. I know nothing," she began and stopped as her father's eyes shifted suddenly toward the front rooms where there seemed to be a slight difference in the normal flow of talk and laughter, and then they came back to focus on her face.

His trembling finger pointed to the safe behind him, and she quickly removed the small, heavy pouch that was resting alone on the shelf, as if prepared for this moment, for these bizarre instructions. But she noticed that the papers her father had always kept locked in that strongbox were no longer there.

"We have even less time than I thought. Remember, my dear, how much I love you, how much I have always loved you."

She was bewildered by what was happening, but she, too, heard clearly now the disturbance that was moving through the casino as a tear, once begun, runs through fabric.

"Jean," she whispered, turning unthinkingly toward the door to the main salon. The gambler had taken her place at the table, perhaps putting himself in danger. She knew that she had to warn him.

"No," her father said, frantically catching her arm. "My God, don't you understand? Jean is delaying them, giving me time to get you away. And you're wasting those precious minutes."

"Do you think I'll let Jean be the sacrifice here?" she argued, pulling against that frail white hand that held her prisoner with its death grip. "Do you believe that I'll accept my freedom at the cost of his?"

"They're not interested in Jean. As far as they're concerned, he's a loyal Frenchman. And besides..." Her father hesitated, and then hurriedly continued his reassurance. "There is nothing to taint Jean with what I've done. But they won't believe *you're* innocent. They'll think, because you're my flesh and blood, that you'll know something they can use," he said urgently. "Don't throw away the opportunity Jean's providing. You know he's far more capable of taking care of himself in this situation than you would be. If you fall into their hands... There is nothing, or no one, that can protect you in a French prison, Julie. Nothing..."

Again the sounds of raised voices from beyond the closed door clearly gave evidence of an altercation of some kind, and her father opened the drawer of his desk. She saw the gambler's sleeve gun and wondered how he intended to stop anyone with that toy.

"Don't be a fool," she said, putting her hand over the small pistol and trying to push it back into the drawer. "You can't fight them with that."

"I don't intend to fight them," he said quietly, but he raised his eyes and held hers unwaveringly. Finally the pressure of her fingers against his eased as she understood what he intended.

"I've always hated the thought of this lingering death. What more could you wish for me, my love, than to die for England? What better end? But not in their hands. Not tortured to death to reveal the names of those I've served so long. As *I* choose, Julie. *My* choice."

There was no fear and no regret in his dark eyes as they held hers.

Slowly she released the skeletal hand that gripped the weapon and put her arms around her father, pulling him close against her trembling body. She buried her face in the sparse white hair and fought the burn of tears behind her lids. Finally she bent to place her lips against the crepelike skin of his cheek, speaking, without words, her last good-bye.

"Be brave, my dear heart," he said.

"As brave as my father," she whispered. His hand lifted to push her away, and she stepped back in obedience to his command.

"Go," he said as before, and she nodded, against all her own instincts, giving in to his wishes, because, as he had reminded her, he would ask her to do nothing that was not right.

Pulling a cloak from the peg, she cautiously opened the door to the alley that backed the house. There was no one there, and she had already begun to cross the threshold when she heard her father's urgent whisper behind her. "The Limping Man, Julie. Look for the Limping Man. When I realized they knew, I shut down his network, but I sent him word, and he'll come…"

Then the crash of a heavy body resounded against the locked door of his office, and at his frantic gesture she pulled the street door closed and ran out into the pitch blackness. None of this made any sense. What had he said about a limping man?

She heard behind her the single crack of the tiny pistol, and after it, the inevitable splintering of the wooden door, and with those sounds, whose sequence she agonizingly understood, she acknowledged that whatever was now happening in that small room was no longer of any concern to her.

And so she ran from sheltering darkness into deeper shadow, but always into streets that led away from the only home she had known for over half her life.

Chapter One

London—March 1815

No one in the Horse Guards would be surprised to find the lamps burning late in this particular office. Considering the news that was slowly filtering like wisps of smoke from the Continent, the light in the office where Colonel Devon Burke pored over the stack of encoded dispatches was certainly not the only one still lit in Whitehall this particular spring midnight.

But the man who sat at this cluttered desk had, in the course of these last months, too often watched dawn touch the sky through the tall mullioned windows that now stretched blackly behind him. For him, work had become a refuge, and an escape, from the emptiness.

Finally the tightness in his neck and the numbness that in the last hour had begun to radiate unpleasantly from between his shoulders signaled that tonight he had gone beyond his body's limits. Placing both hands on his desk, Colonel Burke pushed himself up, feeling the price he would pay for this night's vigil in the cramping tightness of his back and in the unresponsiveness of his right leg. He walked to the windows, limping slightly, flexing his shoulders and trying to stretch out the aching muscles along his spine.

He paused before the divided glass that mockingly threw back his reflection. The gleam of the short chestnut hair, the intensity of the dark blue eyes, all the subtle marks etched on the ruggedly handsome face by his experiences were, of course, hidden in the blackness that stretched beyond the panes. The breadth of his shoulders and the muscled chest covered by the elegant coat, the narrow waist and the strong length of leg revealed by skintight pantaloons and gleaming Hessians were, however, clearly mirrored and appeared, remarkably, exactly the same as when he had been commissioned.

The changes that had been wrought in Devon Burke by the last two years were no longer outwardly visible. Invalided out of the army after Salamanca, he had been brought home from the Peninsula to die. Instead, he had surprised everyone by surviving, despite the massive damage inflicted by the explosion of a French shell directly behind him.

He had lived, but for months his confined existence had been governed by the threat of some movement of one deadly sliver of metal that had rested precariously against his spine. Those were months that he no longer allowed himself to remember.

One of many things he tried not to remember.

And that was why, of course, he was here, surrounded by an environment that was totally masculine. He was always surprised by the minor stimuli capable of setting off the memories that he sought to block—a breath of lavender or even the gracefully erect posture of some woman on the street. And with that admission, they were there again, running fleetingly through his mind.

Elizabeth, he thought, and against his will felt the cold, clenching sickness of her rejection in his gut. For he knew that these images of the woman who had haunted his dreams, both waking and sleeping, for the last five years would inevitably be followed by the darker ones he also fought.

Only the knowledge that Elizabeth was waiting for him had kept him sane in the hell of countless battles, and— with the possibility of recovery provided by the French surgeon his brother-in-law had miraculously found—even through the agonizing months he had spent attempting to become the man he had been before the injury. Only for her had the grinding pain of rebuilding his shattered body been worth it, only for her was the endless effort justified.

And then…

God, he'd been such a fool. He had never realized that Elizabeth's life would not, of course, have remained as static as his during those long months. And so, as soon as he had deemed himself fit to ask, he had gone to beg again for her hand.

He found her already married to the Earl of March, a man old enough to be her father, and heavily pregnant with his heir. Devon suddenly closed his eyes, to force out of his brain the picture of Elizabeth with March, an unspeakable vision engendered by the whispered reputation of the aging roué she had chosen over him.

In these intervening months, he had moved beyond anger, even beyond the sense of betrayal, but the bitterness of disillusionment still had the power to threaten his hard-won acceptance. Fighting against emotions he had long ago rejected as self-pitying, he leaned forward, his forehead resting against the cold glass and the knuckles of both hands pressed too hard into the unyielding sill of the window. And unbelievably, he heard behind him, sharp and unmistakable, the opening of the door to his office.

Bloody hell, he thought, steeling himself to face whoever was invading this refuge, an intrusion that demanded a control he was far from feeling.

Devon removed his hands from the sill and allowed his fingers to tighten over the pen he'd unthinkingly carried with him from the desk, deliberately bending it until he felt

it snap. He turned and threw the ruined instrument against
the papers scattered over the desk.

"Damned nuisance," he began, but the words died in his
throat as he raised his eyes to the figure by the door.

"You need to get out of this office more, and then the
paperwork wouldn't become such a chore. Even his grace
knew that," the quiet, familiar voice offered.

"Moss?" Devon said incredulously, recognizing the
small gray-haired man who stood before him. At first he
could imagine no reason his brother-in-law's very unusual
and highly trusted valet might be calling on him in the pre-
dawn hours. But then his mind began to formulate the kind
of message that would send this particular agent of the Duke
of Avon to seek him out.

"What are you doing here?" Devon whispered, dreading
the answer. He knew very well that Moss was always under
the direction of Avon, that his every action was dedicated
to the service of that brilliant and enigmatic man who was
married to Devon's only sister. "What's wrong with Emily?
Or is it Will?"

"There's nothing wrong with your sister or with your
nephew. Not that you'd know, of course. Your not having
been to your sister's home in some weeks now. But it's not
her grace I've come about. I need your help, Colonel."

"Of course. You know you have only to—" Devon began, and Avon's valet cut him short.

"I want you to understand that the decision to seek you
out was not lightly made. But considering how you feel
about Dominic…" Moss hesitated for the first time, and
Devon recognized that he was weighing his words carefully.
"And also considering what you owe him," the valet suggested softly. They both knew that suggestion would never
have been allowed by the man they were discussing. The
Duke of Avon called due no debts from those he loved.

Two years ago it had been his grace, the Duke of Avon,
who had offered Devon a job in intelligence, an opportunity
to perform valuable work for the war effort despite the use-

lessness of his body. And it had also been Avon who had persisted until he had found a surgeon willing to risk the removal of that fragment of metal that had held Devon captive in an imprisonment that was, for him, far worse than death.

"And I remembered what you told him the day he left. So I thought you might be willing..."

"I owe Dominic more than my life, Moss. And he is my friend. Whatever you think—"

"I think," Moss interrupted again, "that you're the brother he never had. And I'm probably the only man alive who knows what that relationship means to him."

"And to me," Devon affirmed softly. "So why don't you tell me what Avon wants me to do."

"It's not exactly— You see, the duke didn't send me." Again Moss paused, and Devon waited, knowing that what the valet had come to ask must be something he knew his master would disapprove of. And obeying Avon had been Moss's habit for twenty-five years. But Devon could never have anticipated the valet's next words. "I need you to find the duke."

"Find the duke?" Devon repeated, his voice unconsciously rising as he grasped the import of what had been said. "What the hell do you mean, find the duke?"

"Dominic's disappeared. And I can't contact anyone in France. None of his agents responds. It's as if they've all vanished from the face of the earth. And the duke with them. But I can't go. I gave him my word I wouldn't leave the babe and the duchess. He told me he was no longer my concern. That they were. I've never broken my word to him, and so that leaves you."

"Disappeared. My God, Moss, do you know..." Devon began the unthinking question, and then realized that the valet couldn't possibly know what was happening in France. Only yesterday had the dispatch marked "Most Secret" crossed his desk. Napoleon had escaped from Elba and was even now marching toward Paris.

"How long since you've heard from him?" Devon asked, his mind already considering the intelligence aspects of the disappearance of the man who had been so vital to the Emperor's defeat. Not only was Avon his friend, the husband of his sister, but he was also England's master spy. And his disappearance in these circumstances could not be coincidental.

"Almost three months," Moss answered, and Devon felt shock wash through his body.

"Three months," he repeated. "But that's impossible. Emily's had letters—"

"That he wrote before he left. He knew he'd have no way to write her from France, and he didn't want her to worry. So he left them for me to give her. But I've run out, and she's sure to suspect something's wrong. He never intended to be gone this long. I'm certain of that. I would have come to you earlier, but he's more than capable of looking after himself. I know that. He'd call me an old woman," Moss said, and they both remembered the mocking tone with which Avon greeted any expression of concern over his very dangerous activities. "But *three* months, Colonel. Something's very wrong, and I knew it before he left. I tried to tell him—" The valet deliberately cut off the almost frantic desperation.

"Three months," Devon repeated, remembering his own forebodings as he had stood in the shadowed hall of the duke's town house that December morning, listening to Dominic's quiet explanation of this mission. Avon's chief agent in Paris had sent a brief warning through the espionage network, which had once stretched across France, but the duke had been unable to reestablish contact with him after that communication. And so he had gone himself, disguised, to investigate the breakdown in the system that had provided invaluable information during the war.

Someone's taken a hand in the game the diplomats think is being played out in the Congress at Vienna, the duke had said, *and the stakes are too high to chance how a new player might affect the outcome.*

And remembering that cold dawn, Devon remembered, too, his own whispered vow to the man to whom he owed so much.

If you need me, Dominic, he had promised, responding to the dark presentiment that had brushed icelike along the brutal scars that marred his back, *you have only to send word. You know I'll come,* he had pledged grimly, meeting the calm silver eyes of his brother-in-law, *if I have to climb out of the very pits of hell.*

Devon Burke's comrades-at-arms would have said that he had never known what it was to be afraid, even in the most desperate charge, the most furiously fought battle; but standing in the quiet foyer of Avon's elegant town house, he had known that they were wrong. He had been very much afraid, inexplicably terrified, for the man to whom he was saying goodbye.

Then, in his own selfish concerns, he had lost the troubled conviction, which Moss apparently had shared, that Dominic's mission to France was more dangerous than anything he had undertaken before.

Three months, he thought again, wondering if the trail were too cold to follow. And with the news from the Continent, he also wondered if it would now be possible to even make the attempt.

France—A week later

To the amusement of the watching crowd, the boy who twisted futilely in the hold of the burly farmer was protesting his innocence with a blustering combination of excuses and profanities. Since the evidence of his crime bulged in the pockets of his stained, tattered smock, it seemed a ridiculous performance. Although the child was clearly outnumbered and outmatched, none of the good French villagers had felt the urge to go to his aid. The man who held the writhing figure was dragging him relentlessly to the wagon he had driven into these quiet, sun-dappled streets only a short time before. He had been bringing the winter apples to market and had naturally resented the urchin's theft of even so small a part of his crop.

The boy's fists beat ineffectually against the massive forearm wrapped tightly about his thin body as the farmer prepared to toss him up into the bed of the wagon where a helpful villager waited. The apples had been shifted to the front of the wooden conveyance, their sale apparently forgotten, at least temporarily, in the much more satisfying endeavor of bringing such a dangerous criminal to justice.

"You won't go stealing no one else's apples," the peasant promised, as he added his other arm around the struggling body and locked his hamlike hands together over the front of the heaving chest. The child kicked back with the wooden sabots he wore on bare and very dirty feet, but the farmer stepped nimbly out of the way. As the only reward for his valiant attempt, the boy lost one of his shoes. The crowd laughed appreciatively, and he cursed again and tried to bring his shod foot down on the toes of the man who was still holding him quite securely, in spite of his efforts.

The child was undoubtedly helpless against the forces determined to control him. Perhaps it was that very helplessness and his rather gallant resistance that stirred the pity of the blue-eyed stranger who quietly surveyed the unfolding scene. He had stopped to ask about accommodations at whatever inn might be nearby, and his attention had been attracted by the crowd's laughter and the boy's shrill, angry protests.

For several minutes now he had been sitting on the roan gelding, unnoticed by the mob. Had this lively entertainment not been provided, they would certainly have been aware of the outsider in their midst. The gleaming Hessians and the doeskin breeches, both covered now with the dust of the road, would have clearly marked for the crowd his class, in spite of the simple lawn shirt and the leather waistcoat that covered his upper body. In response to the bright winter sun of the March afternoon, he had put away in his saddlebag the woolen cloak he had worn against the morning's chill.

Helpless, he thought again as he watched the uneven battle, and compelled by his memories, he urged the well-trained mount into the middle of the melee.

The crowd parted reluctantly before the horse, and the rider stopped in front of the farmer who held the struggling urchin.

"Let him go," the stranger said softly, and at the quiet tone of command in that slightly accented voice, all activity stopped, even the frenetic struggles of the child, whose dark eyes gazed with sudden hope out of a small and remarkably dirty face.

His savior sat militarily straight on the back of the huge horse. As he watched, the man reached into the pocket of his waistcoat and flipped a coin worth more than the entire cargo of apples to the feet of the man who held him.

The peasant stood frozen, not responding to the generous offer. The villagers started to mumble their disbelief, wondering at his hesitation in accepting such a gift from Providence.

"Let him go," he said again, as quietly as before. "Your apples are more than paid for."

The brute who held the child studied the calm face of the man above him. The straight nose was slightly sunburned, the chin square and resolute, but it was whatever he read in the depths of the dark blue eyes that finally caused his sausage-shaped fingers to reluctantly free their prisoner and pick up the gold that gleamed temptingly from the dust of the street.

At the release, the child shot like a shaft from a crossbow to stand against the dusty boots that rested in the stirrups of the worn but obviously expensive saddle. Looking up into her hero's face, Julie watched the quickly concealed amusement push at the corners of the well-shaped lips.

Then the stranger turned the horse in the direction of the inn. Julie jumped when she realized she was alone again in the middle of the uncaring crowd and hurried to resume her place at the side of the ambling thoroughbred. It seemed the rider was in no hurry to reach his destination, and she had no trouble keeping pace.

She was aware that the blue eyes had flicked over to her stumbling figure. She hopped on one foot until she could pull off the remaining clog, in spite of the cold ground, and offered helpfully, "*Monsieur* desires a guide?"

The man looked down to study the eager, upturned face. "Do you know the White Horse?" he asked consideringly.

"But of course," she assured him and moved to the front of the slowly moving animal.

The rider didn't approach the entrance of the inn, which was nestled snugly under the trees that shaded its doorway from the afternoon light. He turned the gelding instead into the dimness of its stables.

Julie stopped on the threshold and raised her nose like a scenting puppy. The smells of hay and oiled leather and the sharp, friendly odors of horses and manure colored the air. She breathed deeply and looked up to find the stranger's blue eyes focused on her face with the same intensity with which they had stared down the bully. She again watched the man's hand find and toss a coin, which her quick fingers caught spinning in midair.

It was not as large as the bribe the stranger had offered her tormentor, but it was a more than generous reward for the small service rendered.

The stranger's lips slanted into a smile at the skillful, one-handed catch.

"Thank you," the man said simply and turned the gelding into the interior of the long dim aisle that stretched between the stalls.

Julie looked at the coin and then again at the stranger who had begun to dismount. She watched the quick grimace distort that handsome face and heard the softly spoken English expletive. English, she thought in sudden understanding. That explained so much. The stranger rolled his shoulders and then stretched the long muscles of his back, the sighing breath Devon released as he moved clearly indicating the unpleasantness of the entire operation.

Julie's mouth twitched upward, her smile hidden, she hoped, in the gloom of the entryway.

"*Monsieur* does not ride?" she asked ingenuously, recognizing, she thought, the muscle fatigue of an inept or inexperienced rider who has just spent too many hours in the saddle.

She watched as the blue eyes, wide with shock at the unexpected question, swung to her face.

And then the Englishman, a man who had literally ridden before he had walked, laughed with genuine and ironic amusement.

"Apparently not," he agreed softly, almost to himself, "at least not anymore." Still smiling, he spoke again. "What are you waiting for? The adventure's over. Go home and ask your mother to say a prayer for all fools," he laughingly commanded.

Julie nodded reluctantly, and although her eyes remained locked on the stranger's face, she bit professionally into the metal of the coin to test its value. Then, apparently satisfied with the genuineness of the gift, she turned and began to move out of the dark shadows of the barn and into the pleasant afternoon shade.

English, she thought again, smiling. No wonder the stranger had come to her aid. The English—forever slaying dragons and rescuing fair damsels. *Especially* fair damsels. Her lips quirked again in amusement.

Julie moved into the coolness of the approaching twilight and, her mind still occupied by her savior, she was totally unaware of the man who waited beyond the inn yard. She pushed her cold hands into the deep pockets of the smock and found with surprise one of the apples that the farmer had stuffed there to justify his attempt. She bit into it and made a face and spat the offending morsel onto the ground.

She had raised a slim arm to toss the rest of the rotten apple away when her hand was instead pulled behind her, and she was again locked in her pursuer's grip.

"You're clever," the man whispered into the disordered cap of short black curls that covered the girl's well-shaped head, "but not so clever as to outsmart me."

His laugh turned into a pained yelp as Julie's even white teeth bit down hard on the palm that blocked her mouth.

As soon as the offending fingers were removed, Julie filled her lungs and released a remarkable scream for so small a body, and kept on screaming until she was slapped hard across the face and then backhanded with equal force. The tears started unbidden in the furious brown eyes, but determinedly the mouth opened again, only to be filled with a gag, hastily contrived from a sweat-stained kerchief.

Julie's hands were twisted behind her, and she was thrown onto the back of the farm wagon to roll hard against the wooden side. She lay stunned by the force of her landing a few precious moments, and then realized her predicament was more serious than this afternoon's as the horses pulling the wagon began to gather speed.

The horses were, however, merely hired hacks and certainly no match for the well-bred muscles and boundless stamina of the stranger's gelding that had already carried his master so many miles today.

The roan raced behind the flying wagon, its long legs eating the distance between. The rider was stretched out along the reaching neck, and it was only as he raised himself and shouted to Julie that it became obvious he was riding bareback.

Monsieur does not ride, indeed, she thought in quick amazement as she removed the gag, and then, realizing the intent of the rapidly approaching rescuer, she scrambled to the rear of the wagon.

The command was given, a command seen more clearly

in the shape of the firm lips than heard, one word shouted above the noise of the drumming hooves and the creak of the rocking wagon bed.

"Jump," he ordered, and the slim figure launched unhesitatingly into the rapidly closing space between the back of the wagon and the galloping steed. Jumped and was caught too low, so that all the weight of the small body, light though it was, rested for long, agonizing seconds in one corded arm and against the straining pull of the damaged muscles of the rider's back.

Dark eyes locked with blue, and both were aware of the scope of that struggle. Neither spoke, knowing that words could not change the outcome nor alter the terrifying consequences should his strength fail. The brutality of the effort that finally lifted the length of the slim body securely into the saddle in front of his own had blackened the air around the rider's head, and he had to fight to remain conscious, to stay upright, to hold on as two feminine arms twined trustingly around his neck.

Finally he was in control enough, despite whatever he had just done to the recently healed muscles of his back, to put his left arm around the slim waist.

"Not the apples, then?" Devon questioned softly, attempting to hide what the rescue had cost.

He watched the brown velvet of the girl's eyes come up to answer the ironic amusement in his own.

"No, not the apples," she agreed with matching mock-seriousness.

He gripped the reins, turning the horse in a direction that would take them away from the bouncing tail of the wagon. But the fight to pull her into the saddle had taken too many long, dangerous seconds.

Julie felt his body jerk as the shots she had expected from the beginning rang out clearly now from behind them. Devon dug his heels again into the sweating flanks of his horse, sheltering the fragile form that he now knew, with absolute certainty, did not belong to a child, as they outrode the determined pursuit.

The exhausted horse had slowed to a stumble. The body that held Julie had begun to tremble several long minutes before, and the shirt crushed against her ragged smock was drenched with cold sweat.

"I know a place," she said finally, recognizing their surroundings. "It's not far," she continued reassuringly.

"Wherever," he said, "it had better…"

The muscled arms that had held securely during the wild ride suddenly relaxed, and without warning, the tall figure that had been wavering slipped off the horse's back to lie sprawled in the dust of the road. She jumped down from the gelding and knelt beside the fallen man.

Her slender hand felt his forehead and then gently and unthinkingly caressed the stubbled cheek. His head turned restlessly, and a low moan escaped. Even in the darkness she could see the blood that covered the white shirt. So much blood, and there was no way, without light, to ascertain even the location of his injury, much less to treat it. She had realized, finally, that he'd been hit, but their pursuer had been too tenacious and at times too close for them to do anything about the wound. Even now…

Julie looked up from the fallen man to examine the road that stretched behind them in the moonlight. There was no sound. So perhaps it was safe. And she really had no choice. The Gypsy's camp was tantalizingly close, but she hated to leave him even the short time it would take to get help. She sighed, unaccustomed to uncertainty about any course of action. But then she had seldom been responsible for the welfare of someone else. And she wasn't sure she liked that responsibility.

Finally making the decision that was inevitable, given the situation, she pulled the weary animal to a nearby stump and struggled to mount. Both bare heels bounced against the heaving, foam-flecked flanks, and the courageous heart again answered the demand. The gelding turned to look once more, questioningly, at the figure lying in the moonlight, and then gave himself up to the guidance of the small fingers that now controlled his reins.

Much later those same cool fingers rested again against Devon's forehead, edging his mind into an unwanted consciousness. He listened to the muffled sounds around him, but since there were none he could identify, he gave up that attempt and opened his eyes.

The glint of silver danced in the light of an oil lantern, and he wondered idly what she was going to do with the knife. Then he focused clearly enough to realize that the tip of the blade was moving dangerously close to his body. His hard fingers latched onto a fragile wrist, and he looked up into the dirty face of his afternoon's companion. He twisted his hand slightly, and the knife dropped onto the wooden floor on which he was sitting, his aching back propped against something hard and unyielding.

"What are you doing?" he asked hoarsely, barely recognizing his own voice.

"Shh," her low voice soothed. "I'm just going to cut up your sleeve."

"Why?" he asked, trying to remember where he was. His eyes closed, exhausted by the loss of blood that had left him drifting in and out of consciousness as they had loaded him into the pony cart and brought him here. Wherever here was. He remembered other hands and voices. Masculine voices. And the girl's. But nothing clearly, and nothing that made much sense.

He finally forced his eyes open again and found dark velvet eyes studying his face, the same eyes that had this afternoon met his so bravely when he had almost let her fall beneath the deadly, flashing hooves of the gelding. And their beauty, framed by the dirty face and disheveled black curls, was as incongruous as he had found it then.

"Why are you dressed like a boy?" he asked, the question he had wanted to ask her during their escape.

"How did you know?" she asked softly and picked up the knife. He watched it disappear under the smock and into the waistband of the grimy, shapeless trousers. "No one else..."

"Maybe no one else has ridden for miles holding you against his chest. Your body may be boyish—"

"Boyish?" the undisputed toast of the Parisian underworld interrupted. Her eyes narrowed slightly, and then she smiled. She realized with some surprise that the man who had rescued her was totally unaffected by the practiced lowering of lashes and the provocative smile.

"A very believable boy," he said, but his eyes closed again with the effort of explaining.

Julie wondered at the spurt of anger she felt at his assessment. It was, of course, what she had intended. She had entered into the role with all the considerable acting talent she possessed and had been pleased with its success. So she couldn't understand why she was disconcerted by his compliment on the success of her disguise.

"Let me," Devon heard another voice say, remembering it as the authority that had directed the men who'd moved him.

The Gypsy leader, impatient with the conversation, pushed the girl aside and gripped Devon's sleeve in one gnarled brown hand. He inserted the point of his own knife, ripping up the fabric without hesitation.

He grasped the edges of the slit and pulled them apart until the hole the apple farmer's ball had made was exposed. He turned the arm slightly, so that the light of the dim lamp better illuminated the wound. An involuntary gasp was wrenched from Devon's suddenly colorless lips at that movement, but he locked his teeth into the bottom one, determined not to react any further to the examination.

"Move your fingers," the old man ordered, and Devon found that he was able to obey.

"And the wrist."

Again the order was carried out.

"Nothing broken," the old man said with satisfaction, turning to reach behind him for something on the table. The gold earring glinted though the silver strands of his hair, and Devon's fascinated eyes lowered to take in also the gaily embroidered shirt he wore. He glanced at the girl, who was now kneeling beside him holding the lantern for the Romany. She was certainly dark enough, Devon thought, but there was something about the heart-shaped face that...

"Here," the Gypsy said, holding out a stone bottle.

At Devon's hesitation, he gestured again with the container. "Whiskey. Drink it," he ordered. "You'll need it."

"Why," Devon asked, but given his experience, he was afraid he knew.

"Because I'm going to clean the wound. It's only a flesh wound, and the ball went through. Inflammation's the greatest danger, so if we can prevent that..."

"How?" Devon asked softly, his eyes resting on the old man's face.

The stone bottle lifted again, the glaze on its brown surface glinting softly. "Even the Romans used wine to speed healing," the Rom explained.

Devon took a deep breath and reached for the whiskey. He drank as long and as deeply as he could, the burn as unpleasant as that which was beginning to throb like flame through his arm. He head swam suddenly, the effects of the alcohol on top of the loss of blood.

He lowered the bottle and wiped his mouth on his left sleeve. And then he handed the whiskey back to the old man.

"Hold his arm," he ordered the girl. Her dark eyes, wide with shock, raised to the walnut brown, lined face of the Gypsy. He laughed suddenly.

"If you're going to faint," he said derisively, seeing the blanched features, "I'll get one of my men."

But having had an opportunity to assess the character of

this girl during the weeks she had lived among his people, he wasn't surprised when the long lashes fell, hiding the glaze of her eyes. And when she raised them again to his face, they were as calm and as steady as the blue ones of the watching Englishman who lay propped against the wall of the caravan where they had laid him.

"I don't faint," she said deliberately and took Devon's right hand in her left. She put her right palm under his elbow and held the arm out for the old man's ministrations. And the small fingers that gripped Devon's didn't tremble.

The burn of the alcohol was as terrible as he had imagined it would be. He thought he could feel it tracing the path the ball had taken through his arm, cauterizing with its agony. He was unaware that his fingers had tightened unbearably over the small ones that held his, held still without trembling. He had made no sound beyond the first gasping inhalation as the whiskey bit into the damaged flesh.

And finally it was over. The old man's fingers were surprisingly gentle and reassuringly competent as he mopped up the liquid, pink-tinted with the freely flowing blood, and then almost professionally bound the wound tightly with strips of cotton.

At last, Devon found he was cradling the injured arm against his stomach. He opened his eyes, and the Gypsy handed him the whiskey bottle. He realized, as he drank, trying to hold the container steady in his left hand, which seemed determined to shake, that the girl was gone. Grateful for her absence, he lowered the bottle and tried to hand it back.

"Keep it," the old man said. "You'll need it."

Devon closed his eyes, allowing his head to fall back against the hard wall behind him. And he thought that the Rom was probably right.

Julie had stopped at the corner of the caravan she had just left. She stood, gulping long breaths of the cold night air, her head swimming, still smelling the fumes of the liquor the old man had used.

''I don't faint,'' she had said within the caravan. But now she lowered her head, comfortingly hidden by the darkness, and thought how close to being a lie that particular claim had just come.

Chapter Two

The next morning the curtain that barred entry to the caravan where Devon lay was pushed aside by the old man. Because he had no choice, Devon accepted the Gypsy's help in accomplishing the morning's necessities. The arm, too, was examined and rebandaged, and he was grateful beyond words when, in spite of a definite tender swelling around the wound and the slight fever, the Gypsy didn't suggest a repetition of last night's treatment.

After the old man left, Devon lay back down on the narrow cot and thought how worthless a rescuer for Avon he was turning out to be. All because of an ill-conceived feat of quixotic derring-do to save a Gypsy girl who, for whatever reasons, had been masquerading in boy's clothing. Possibly his mission to France had been the fool's errand he had feared from the beginning, but it had been one he was more than willing to undertake for the debt he owed the duke. And instead of success, he had only proven himself to be the fool he'd suspected from the start.

He didn't even open his eyes when the weight on the steps leading up to the caravan indicated his privacy was again about to be invaded. He hoped whoever it was would believe he was asleep and leave him alone.

It wasn't until she had moved so close to the low bed he

could smell the aroma of the stew she carried in the chipped bowl that he gave up his pretense of sleep.

She was dressed as a girl today, the shining dark hair combed into a riot of loose curls all over her head and threaded through with a scarlet ribbon. The beautiful heart-shaped face was clean, and the smooth cream of her bare shoulders was only a shade or two darker than the low-necked peasant blouse that also left most of her slender arms exposed. The long, patterned skirt swirled around trim ankles and slender, slippered feet.

Julie waited for the expected impact of her careful toilette to appear on the features of the man who lay watching her. She had been frequently and lavishly assured of her beauty most of her life, but for some reason, his dismissal of her face and figure last night as "believably boyish" had rankled. And so she watched for the accustomed admiration and was again disappointed in the unwavering assessment of the dark blue eyes.

No wonder she'd made a believable child, Devon was thinking. She was tiny, probably less than five feet tall, and perfectly proportioned for her height. There was no denying her rather exotic beauty, but since that beauty was the opposite of everything he had ever admired in a woman, he wondered at the sudden lurch in his stomach at the sight of this startling transformation.

He allowed himself to briefly picture Elizabeth's blond perfection, which he knew, for him at least, was the epitome of womanly attractiveness. Her cool, poised elegance had always left him breathless, and he wondered how he could find in the slightest way appealing someone so different from that old ideal. The response he had felt was obviously for the enticing aroma of the food she had brought, and not, of course, for the dark, slim beauty of the girl herself.

"I thought you might be hungry," she offered, taking her own inventory. The fine lips she had admired as he'd struggled yesterday not to reveal his amusement at her supposed hero-worship were today tightly set. The lines around his mouth were too distinct for his age, but she found that she liked the multitude of laugh lines that fanned richly around his eyes. And his lashes, dark brown and shading to gold at the tips, were as long and as thick as her own.

"No," he said, but she knew by the pause, a pause that had stretched long enough to allow her to consider what she had found so appealing about his face yesterday, that he had at least thought about the food. Which meant he was probably as hungry as she suspected, in spite of what she was beginning to recognize as the same stiff-necked English pride her father had always displayed.

"I'm not suggesting that you let me feed you," she said and held out the slim hand that had supported his arm so firmly last night.

The debate between pride and hunger was brief, and Devon put his left hand in hers and let her help in the awkward struggle to sit up. She made no comment about the stiffness of his wrenched back. Instead, as soon as he was upright on the edge of the bed, she placed the bowl of stew on the small table that crowded the central aisle of the caravan. She swept a few scattered items that had rested there out of the way and then removed from the pocket of her skirt a small loaf of bread wrapped in a clean napkin and laid it down beside the bowl. She poured a cup of water from the pitcher that had been left for him on the table last night. He hadn't noticed the water, but then he'd gone to sleep almost as soon as his head had touched the narrow mattress, drugged by the old man's whiskey, blood loss and the exertions from the first days he'd spent in the saddle in over two years.

He realized suddenly that she had completed her preparations for his meal and was waiting for him.

With his left hand he grasped the post of the bed, using it to pull himself to his feet. It wasn't a particularly smooth ascent, but he was up and moving fairly normally toward the table before he realized that the girl's dark eyes had watched and evaluated the entire operation. And he knew sitting down would be just as awkward.

What the hell, he thought suddenly. Given his condition six months ago, he found himself grateful that yesterday's activities hadn't resulted in more serious impairment today. Just strained muscles, and he knew that the soreness would work out.

He put his left hand flat on the surface of the small table, hoping it was stronger than it looked, and then lowered his body by careful stages onto the chair.

This time he didn't even glance at her face. Whatever her reaction, he'd seen it before. He'd seen them all. And since this particular injury was a result of his efforts on her behalf, it certainly was not cause for embarrassment in front of her.

He picked up the spoon with his left hand and began to eat. In spite of his real hunger and the awkwardness of having to use the wrong hand, there was no lapse in his innate good manners.

Julie was well aware of what that revealed about this man. His speech, his dress, even the equipment and the valuable horse he rode, all had marked him as a member of the class Julie had learned long ago only tolerated people like her on its own terms. Only for the ''services'' they could render. And now his manners confirmed the suspicions she'd had yesterday about his place in the world. Intent on his meal, Devon wasn't aware of the cynical smile that touched her lips.

He reached for the small loaf of bread, realizing as soon as he touched it that there was no way, one-handed, he could break it apart. And he refused to add trying to manage the damaged arm to the show he'd already presented. Since he was as incapable of tearing chunks off the whole with his teeth as he would have been of beating his horse or of cheating at cards, he simply gave up the thought of the bread and turned his attention back to the stew. Considering the primitive nature of the meals he'd eaten on the Peninsula, the stew alone was a feast for kings.

Having seen that decision reached and, having now firmly fixed his position on the rigid social scale that governed society, Julie took the loaf and began to tear it into small pieces.

Devon noticed the slight swelling and discoloration of her left hand as she worked, and he wondered if that had happened yesterday in her battle with the apple farmer, whoever he really was.

"Thank you," he said automatically when she had reduced the bread to manageable portions.

"What happened to your back?" she asked softly. He had known the question was inevitable, but he'd hoped. He always hoped.

His head remained down, eyes locked on the flavorful meat for a few seconds. His close-cut chestnut hair caught the light from the open curtain. That and the hand holding the spoon were all that she could see of her rescuer.

His eyes, when they were raised to her face, revealed only amusement.

"Well," he began, in the time-honored fashion of storytellers, "there once was a boy who was caught stealing apples…"

"No," she interrupted. "I saw you before. In the stables. That's why I thought you couldn't ride. Before—"

At the sudden break in that sentence, Devon realized that her insult to his horsemanship had just been acknowledged. And he judged rightly that this was the only apology he was likely to get. But the question she had asked still lay between them.

"Shrapnel," he said concisely and turned back to the stew. It was, after all, the complete explanation.

"Shrapnel?" she repeated with surprise. "Then…you were a soldier."

He didn't interrupt his eating to agree to the obvious. And the loss of his profession was not a topic that he was able to discuss dispassionately. Not that he'd ever tried. Not with anyone other than his father.

"Somehow..." she began, and when she laughed instead of finishing that thought, he glanced up. "Somehow," she started again, studying those tired blue eyes, "I'd decided you were something quite different."

His question was asked with raised brows and a slight tilt of his head.

"An aristocrat," she suggested. "A very proper English *milord*," she said, her low voice rich with sarcasm.

"And you don't like milords?" he repeated, retaining her mocking inflection. "Then you'll be glad to learn that I'm not one."

"No fancy English title?" she asked.

"Not even a minor one," he said, and his lips moved into the upward slant she was learning to anticipate, the smile she had enjoyed yesterday.

"Perhaps growing up with the Revolution's lack of respect for titles is to blame for how I feel about the nobility," she said, knowing that the real reason was her treatment by the men of that class. The sexual innuendos, the offers, the speculative gleam in leering, amorous, oh-so-noble eyes. She had found nothing to admire in the blue bloods who had crowded her father's casino. "And Bonaparte's new aristocracy hasn't managed to change my opinion," she acknowledged truthfully. "Have you ever known an aristocrat who deserved the titles he bore?" she challenged.

"Spoken like a true revolutionary," Devon said, smiling gently at the understandable class rebellion of the Gypsy girl. "No wonder royal families all over Europe dreaded the spread of those doctrines. And yes, I *have* known noblemen who lived up to their titles and positions," Devon said, thinking of the man he had come to France to find. "Not only those born to wealth and power abuse them. I should have thought that Robespierre's bloodbath would have convinced everyone of that."

"I wasn't in Paris then," she said and quickly stopped that revelation. She could trust no one, not even someone who had risked his own life to save hers. Coming back here had been dangerous enough. If they had been able to track her to the village where she'd lived after she'd left the Gypsy's camp, then they might be aware of where she'd spent her time before she'd so successfully become the orphaned urchin. And if so...

"Do you think you might find me a razor somewhere?" Devon asked, and her mind came back to the present. He had finished the stew and the bread she'd broken. "I'd like to try to get rid of these," he said, running long, tanned fingers over the stubbled cheeks.

Following that movement with her eyes, she wondered irrationally if his beard would be blond if he let it grow. The morning sun was touching it now with the same gold that tipped his lashes. She realized suddenly that the direction of her thoughts was too personal, too intimate. She was intrigued with his beard. Thinking about its color and texture. As she had thought about his smile. And the thick lashes that surrounded the blue eyes. The laugh lines. God, she thought, her self-discovery catching her by surprise, I'm attracted to him.

The emotion was so foreign to her usual wary reaction to men that she was unsure at first of the validity of her surmise. But a quick assessment of the attractiveness of the strong, angular planes of his face, of those tiny lines around his eyes, of his mouth... My God, she thought again. She wondered why he was looking at her so strangely, and then she realized that she hadn't answered his question. What had he asked? she thought, trying desperately to remember. A razor. Something about a razor.

"And you're going to try to shave left-handed?" she managed.

"Unless... I had wondered if you might be willing..." His voice faded at her expression, trying to analyze what it meant.

"I've never shaved a man before," she said. Her usually decisive voice was almost a whisper. She cleared her throat nervously, and forced her eyes away from that beautifully masculine face.

"Well, you certainly can't do any worse than I'd do left-handed," he said, laughing.

The pleasantness of that sound drew her eyes back, and she found herself confronting the full, unleashed force of his smile. Her knees were suddenly water.

What's the matter with me, she thought angrily. But she knew. Even the thought of touching him, of holding his face, of standing close enough to him to accomplish what seemed to her now the much too intimate act of shaving him was disturbing.

"I'd ask the old man, but somehow the thought of a razor in his one hand and my throat in the other..." He let his voice trail off with that suggestion, and smiled at her again, inviting her to join his amusement.

But there was no answering smile. Her eyes were as wide and dark as they had been last night. He wondered what was wrong, and then he realized that he'd just insulted the Gypsy. His irreverent sense of humor had made him a popular member of Wellington's staff, but it had also gotten him into trouble on more than one occasion. And now, when the old man had been good enough to take him in, he'd offered only insults in return. Maybe they were even related, he thought suddenly. Maybe...

"Your father," he said, putting it all together. "He's your father. I'm sorry. I didn't mean to insult him. I just—"

"My father!" Julie repeated incredulously, thinking about the gentle, dignified English aristocrat who had pampered and spoiled his only daughter, such a contrast to the brutal, despotic old Rom. "He's *not* my father," she denied vehemently, as if the suggestion were too ridiculous for discussion. "But you were right. He'd cut your throat for a centime, and without a second thought. And he's *not* my father," she said again.

She turned and, angrily pushing the partially opened curtain out of her way, she left him alone.

Behind her in the silence of the caravan, Devon looked at the curtain that moved, swinging, for several moments in the violence of her departure.

Not my father, she had said. And he wondered at the strength of that denial. Why would she be so adamant about the impossibility of that?

The thought, when it came, was as repulsive as the images of Elizabeth and March. The old man and the beautiful, dark-eyed girl. He remembered the touch of her slender fingers on his arm, and somewhere in the back of his mind came the sudden, sure remembrance of their gentle tracing over the stubble he had just asked her to help him remove. And unbidden and unwanted, the image of those slender fingers moving, caressing and enticing, through the long silver locks of the Rom. In the sudden bile that filled his throat he knew that, in spite of its contrast to Elizabeth's cool perfection, the girl's beauty had *not* left him indifferent.

He fought the pull back to the comfort of the narrow cot and was still sitting at the table, methodically flexing and unflexing the swollen fingers of his right hand. He was just as methodically avoiding any thoughts of the girl when a dip in the steadiness of the caravan toward the curtained doorway announced his next visitor. He took a deep breath and looked up from his self-appointed task to find the Romany watching him with amusement.

"Sore?" he questioned rhetorically. "You think that will help the soreness?"

"It can't hurt," Devon said simply, having no desire now to talk to the Gypsy. He hadn't been as successful as he'd hoped in convincing himself that whatever was happening between the Romany leader and the girl was none of his affair. It had nothing to do with him or the reason he was in France. And that mission was all he intended to think about from now on.

"It won't matter," the old man said, his high good humor apparent. He was very satisfied about something. "The girl's fingers are nimble enough for you both," he finished, thinking of the very lucrative proposition she had just made.

The old man didn't understand the sudden sharp movement that locked those slowly flexing fingers into a fist. But the English were a strange breed. Besides, discussing the girl's newly revealed talents was not the purpose of this visit.

"I brought you a shirt," he said, dropping the indigo garment on the table in front of the Englishman.

The long fingers eventually unclenched and touched the smooth softness of the material.

"I can't pay you," Devon said, controlling the anger that had surged through his body at what he viewed as a confirmation of his earlier suspicions. "All the money I had was in my saddlebags. When I rode after the child...after the girl," he amended, and then knew there was no point in explaining his foolish, unthinking gallantry. "I left them in the stable at the inn. I can—"

"It's all right," the old man said dismissingly as he turned to leave. "The girl will more than compensate me for the shirt."

The crash of the chair in the confines of the small wagon drew his dark eyes to stare in amazement at the man standing across the table from him. Despite the strained muscles, there had been no hesitation in the surge of movement that had this time brought Devon to his feet.

"No," he said bitterly. "I don't know what your previous arrangement has involved, but she won't pay for *this* that way." He grabbed the shirt from the table and, balling it angrily in his fist, he threw it suddenly at the old man. It hit him squarely in the chest but, bewildered by the Englishman's actions, the Gypsy made no effort to catch it. The cotton slithered to the floor, its fall unwatched by either pair of eyes.

In the dark ones of the old man there was only astonishment. And briefly, complete puzzlement. But something in the rigid jaw and furiously blazing blue eyes must have given him a clue as to the source of Devon's anger.

"You think..." he began, and then the ludicrous suggestion was dismissed by a universal and contemptuous gesture of his liver-spotted hand. "You think I would sleep with children," he mocked.

And with that taunting ridicule, the tight disgust that had knotted in Devon's stomach since the inception of that thought loosened.

"I have grandchildren older than she," the Gypsy said derisively, his distaste apparent. "My wife would cut her throat. And probably mine," he finished, his good humor and his vanity making the Englishman's suggestion now a source of enjoyment. His accusation would make a good story.

"Then how—" Devon began, only to be cut off.

"You ask her. Like you, she's my guest. In her case, a paying guest. And her secrets are her own. I haven't asked what an English aristocrat's doing in France in these... unusual times," he said, choosing his words cautiously.

But in the very carefulness of that phrasing Devon recognized that the Rom knew about Napoleon's slow yet inexorable march to the capital. And he wondered at the old man's sources of information.

"And I haven't asked the girl why she's here," the Gypsy continued.

"Then she's not a member of your..." Devon stopped, unsure of correct wording of the question he needed answered.

"Harem?" the old man suggested sardonically, one thick white brow raised. "Family," he supplied at Devon's embarrassed head shake. "I don't believe in asking questions of people who obviously don't want to answer them. It's a practice you might consider."

He turned again to leave, almost stepping on the crumpled shirt. He bent to pick it up and tossed it accurately to land in the center of Devon's chest. Although he hadn't been expecting it, Devon's reflexes were still well-honed enough to make a quick left-handed grab at the material, preventing its fall.

"And you may consider the shirt a gift," the Romany said, pushing aside the curtain and descending the three short steps from the caravan to the ground.

The man who stood in the slightly rocking wagon wasn't thinking about the Gypsy's displeasure, as dangerous as he knew it probably was. He was thinking again about the girl. A guest, the old man had said. If she didn't belong here, then who was she? He knew he wouldn't get the answer from the Gypsy. The Rom had made that clear.

Devon looked down at the dark shirt he held. A touch of red that gleamed brightly against the indigo caused him to take a closer look at the old man's gift. Forcing himself to awkwardly use the aching right arm, he held up the shirt until the embroidered flowers that decorated the collar and wide cuffs were plainly revealed.

An involuntary smile at the thought of the picture he'd present in this grew into a broad grin. Never in his life, he thought, shaking his head, had he ever worn anything so exotic. The array of picturesque uniforms he'd donned through the years never entered his mind, because, of course, he'd never seen anything even remotely unusual about those. They were simply the very honorable garb of his profession.

And then he turned his attention to the Herculean task of getting out of the bloody, mutilated shirt he'd worn for the last two days and into this. But the entire time he was undressing, the small self-derisory smile quirked the corners of his lips.

He managed a rough bath using his ruined shirt and the cold water remaining in the pitcher. He combed dampened fingers through his hair, leaving it curling over his forehead. And he was wearing the shirt. At least he felt clean and more in control. He had learned in Portugal the almost mi-

raculous boost in spirits that a bath and a shave could provide. He ran his fingers over his face, feeling the two days'
growth with disgust. But it seemed there was nothing he
could do about that.

The shifting dip that announced visitors to his small room
could be clearly felt again. As popular as the punch bowl
at Almack's, he thought in amusement, mocking one of the
more ridiculous rituals of that artificial society he'd long ago
come to view with disdain. The Marriage Mart, the bachelors had nick-named the popular club, and at the remembrance of the hopeful mamas and their dressed-up charges,
he smiled again.

He hadn't stopped to analyze the upswing in mood he'd
experienced since the confrontation with the Romany leader.
If he'd thought about it at all, he'd have put the near-elation
down to the effects of clean clothes and a relatively clean
body.

He turned to the door, expecting to greet the old man
again, and instead found the girl, carefully balancing a brim-
ming basin of steaming water, a razor and piece of white
flannel.

Julie met the shock in his eyes with a practiced smile, her
emotions very much under control now that she'd had time
to assimilate his effect on her senses and to rationalize those
feelings as a very understandable gratitude. He had, after
all, saved her freedom, if not her life. And at a not incon-
siderable cost to himself.

My hero, she had mocked herself as she prepared the
necessary equipment to provide the shave he'd asked for.
She had accepted the task almost as a challenge. She was
certainly sophisticated enough to shave a man without
swooning over the length of his lashes or the shape of his
nose. Or the blue of his eyes. The almost navy blue of his
eyes, she found herself thinking now.

For the first time she became aware of the indigo shirt he
wore. The embroidered collar and cuffs and wide, flowing
sleeves looked so exotically out of place with the skintight

English doeskins that molded the long length of muscular legs and disappeared into the tops of the now-shining boots. It was the deep blue of the shirt that enhanced the color of his eyes and warmed the pallor yesterday's ordeal had given his face. The short chestnut hair was still damp from his ablutions, which she suspected had been accomplished from that same pitcher from which she'd poured the water that had earlier accompanied his meal.

"That's a very attractive shirt," she said, trying to command her twitching lips into obedience.

"It's ridiculous, I know, but at least it's clean," he said, smiling easily at her amusement.

And in spite of the determined admonitions she'd given herself, in spite of her careful mental enumeration of all the despicable characteristics of the men of his class, she felt a fluttering warmth in the center of her heart. A heart that had always remained remarkably untouched until she'd met this Englishman who knew how to laugh at himself.

"Are you still interested in a shave?" she forced herself to ask calmly and registered the surprise in his eyes.

"Of course," he said. "I'd be very grateful. I had just thought that a shave would complete…"

"The transformation," she suggested when he hesitated.

"The recovery," he said, almost on top of her words.

"You *do* look better."

"I'm fine. I need only a shave to be a new man," he said.

"I didn't find much wrong with the old one," she admitted carefully. "I haven't told you how grateful I am for yesterday. I really—"

"A shave, and we're even," he broke into her expression of gratitude. He'd never wanted that. He was always uncomfortable with thanks, especially for those actions that anyone would have undertaken. The idea that a child could be abducted without anyone lifting a hand to prevent it had demanded his automatic response, unthinking and unquestioning. Although one heard stories of stolen children sold to sweeps or Gypsies... He smiled at the irony of his thoughts of the previous day as he had struggled to mount the gelding he'd just unsaddled.

"I think you'd better sit down," she suggested, wondering what had caused that smile. "You're too tall."

He lowered himself into the chair, and she was pleased to note that the movement this time was far less careful than it had been before.

She put the objects she'd carried into the caravan on the table and took the soap she'd begged from one of the women from the pocket of her skirt. She efficiently coaxed a slightly soapy foam from the harsh, lye-based lump. Eventually her hands were covered with the watery mixture. But when she realized it was time to transfer the soap to his face, she hesitated. He glanced up as water dripped onto his thigh and saw her standing, still as a statue, with soapy hands extended.

"What's wrong?" he asked.

She shook her head, breaking the spell she'd created by thinking about touching him. She resolutely put her palms against his cheeks and wondered if he could feel the almost physical jolt of reaction that moved through her body at the pleasantly rough warmth of his skin. She rubbed his face determinedly, and then, resorting again to the soap, transferred more onto his chin and the narrow area between the strong, nearly Roman nose and the molded lips. He had turned his head accommodatingly as she'd worked, and she struggled to keep her reaction to touching him from being communicated through her fingertips.

When she had finished soaping his face, she unconsciously released her building tension in a soft sigh. The sound caused the blue eyes to open, and Devon realized that he had shut them almost with the first stroke of her fingers against his cheeks.

There had been something strongly sensuous in the caress of those slender fingers against his face, and there had also been an immediate response to the soft, very womanly breasts, which had been exactly on the level of his eyes. As her body had shifted slightly, moving with the stroking movements of her hands, the clean, pleasant aroma of that small, perfect body had wafted under his nose. He had closed his eyes to fight the response he'd felt to both her touch and to that fragrance.

He forced himself to picture the icy mountain streams in the Pyrenees, imagined himself wading knee deep in their frigid waters. And then deeper. Allowing the ice to cover his thighs. But nothing was interfering with his awareness of those fingers playing over his cheeks, of her breasts moving just in front of his face. He shifted uncomfortably in the chair and carefully crossed his legs.

"Are you all right?" she asked suddenly, wondering about his back. There had been something in that sudden movement that had communicated his discomfort quite clearly.

"Of course," he said, his voice slightly unsteady. He unnecessarily eased the injured arm into his lap. That movement served more than one purpose, and apparently it was convincing, for she picked up the razor and tilted his face to allow her better access to his cheek.

The pressure of the moving blade was better than her hands, but wielding it had required that she move her body closer to his. She was leaning now, almost touching him, her knee resting against his thigh and her breasts again in too-close proximity to his face. He had only to move the fingers of his hand, or to lower his head to give his lips access to that dark, fragrant valley…

She stepped back suddenly, and he wondered if she could know what he'd been thinking. He opened his eyes and found her critically assessing the area she'd just finished. Her tongue was protruding slightly between small, even teeth, and when she became aware that he was watching her, she smiled at his expression.

"Not very professional, I'm afraid," she began to apologize.

"It's fine," he said. "It's bound to be better than before."
Just get it over with, he thought, before I embarrass us both.

He wondered suddenly if, because she was not one of the
elegantly poised women of his circle, he was more inclined
to think about... The realization of exactly what he had been
thinking surprised him. It was so against the rigid code that
had always governed his actions where women were concerned. Because, he was forced to admit, he had been thinking about making love to her. A woman alone and apparently unprotected beyond the purchased sanctuary of the
Romany camp.

"This way," she said softly, directing his chin with those
slender fingers. He'd been unconsciously resisting her placement of his face, lost in his thoughts.

Too long without a woman, he mocked himself ruefully.
And she was very beautiful. And perhaps... He deliberately
blocked that idle fantasy.

He wasn't aware of the bitterness of his slight smile at
even the thought of exposing himself to the kind of pain
Elizabeth's rejection had inflicted.

And so until he knew the secrets this woman was hiding,
he decided grimly, whatever emotions she was able to evoke
would be very carefully controlled.

Chapter Three

It was almost dusk when Devon descended the three steps of the caravan for his first look around the camp. After the girl had left today, he had taken advantage of his solitude to rest. And in the peaceful lull of the spring afternoon, that rest had, due to the continuing low fever, turned into sleep.

One of the Gypsy women woke him when she brought his dinner—bread and a small cheese—and he'd forced himself to eat it all. The quicker he got his strength back, the quicker he could continue his search for his brother-in-law. It was that which had brought him to France and not whatever was going on with the girl.

As if in response to that thought, his eyes drifted across the circled camp to find her sitting under the shelter of a tall oak, a small table in front of her stool. She appeared to be manipulating something on its surface. He looked around at the scattered caravans and found that, in the growing twilight, no one was paying the least attention to the girl or to himself. Driven by an emotion that certainly wasn't logic, he walked across the dusty compound and stood watching her swiftly moving fingers.

Julie glanced up, smiling, and then her eyes returned to the flashing hands and the shells they were directing.

This morning she had been forced to consider the pitiful hoard of coins she carried. She knew that the old man's hospitality was based strictly on a guest's ability to pay. He had taken her in when her father's money had paid the way, but her remaining treasury would not have covered the cost of her own food, and this time she had brought another mouth to be fed.

So she had made the dangerous, but necessary, offer and had watched the shrewd Romany mind assess her value. She had not been surprised when he had demanded a demonstration, and although he had hidden his elation well, she knew he had been pleased.

But even if the Gypsy hadn't noticed, she had known that she was out of practice after three months away from the casino's tables. Not that this was, of course, a game her father had ever countenanced there. It depended on deception more than skill or strategy, and he would never have approved of what she was doing for the old man. But she had no other choice. Not if she wanted his protection, both for herself and for the man who now stood watching her.

Her left hand betrayed her suddenly, the ball dropping from between her fingers to roll across the table and into the grass at her feet.

"Damn," she said under her breath, knowing that if that happened at the fair tomorrow, she'd end up in the village gaol or with a knife in her back. Unthinkingly, she flexed the slightly swollen hand.

Suddenly long masculine fingers were resting under her small ones. Devon turned her hand in the fading light, seeing again the slight discoloration he'd noticed earlier.

"What happened to your fingers?" he asked.

She found that she had no answer, the sight or the sensation of his hand supporting hers robbing her of her usual ready wit. And so she sat, silent as the village idiot, while he held her hand. His thumb caressed her knuckles, and her mouth went dry.

"It looks like…" he began, and then he remembered crushing fragile bones last night when the old man had poured the whiskey into the rawness of his wound.

"My God," he said softly. "I did that."

He waited, hoping for her denial, but once again her eyes were simply locked on his face. He had never in his life hurt a woman. Except, apparently, this one. And the small bruised fingers rested still so trustingly in his.

"I'm sorry," he said softly. "I never meant…"

The soft palm was lifted from his, and she smiled, shaking her head.

"It's nothing. I probably hurt it when he threw me into the wagon." The lie easily made, she changed the subject by gesturing to the shells on the table. "But it makes this a little challenging."

"This?" he questioned, uncertainly.

"Le jeu des gobelets."

"Le jeu…" he began to repeat without comprehension and saw her quick smile at his obvious puzzlement.

"Thimblerig," she said in English, and he realized suddenly that she had spoken English all along, from the time she had answered his question about the apples until her unexpected reply just now in French. Surprisingly, her English was as pure, as educated and cultured and as unaccented as his own. He could have carried her into any ballroom in London, and no one would have had the least suspicion that she was anything other than another attractive debutante come to the capital for her season.

"My father was English," she said simply, as if that alone would explain the enigma of her identity. She watched the thoughts chase across his face.

"Thimblerig," she said again, closing the door to the questions she could see forming by bending to pick up the ball she'd dropped. "Do you know it? It's all the rage. The Gypsy's willing to accept our addition to his band in exchange for my expertise at the game. The crowds we'll attract at the fair tomorrow and their wagers will more than cover whatever our food and lodging costs him. He'll be more than compensated for his kindnesses."

"Thank you for taking care of me last night, for bringing

me here," he said, thinking back with somewhat ironic amusement on all the Gypsy's "kindnesses." She smiled away his gratitude.

"We're even. Remember?" she said, but the reminder of his words in the small caravan this morning brought back too strongly the memory of that pleasant intimacy. She wondered why, with him, she couldn't seem to keep the distance she usually had no trouble maintaining in her dealings with men.

"Would you like to watch me practice?" she asked, again deliberately moving away from the personal.

"Of course," he agreed, and her quick fingers began to manipulate the shells in ever-faster circles.

When she looked up at him and arched her brows in question, he said with a great deal of assurance, "The middle one."

And she lifted the shell to expose to his disbelieving eye the nothing that rested beneath it.

"How…" he began, and she laughed.

"One doesn't ask a magician to explain his magic. And the shells can't lie. You must not be watching closely enough. Try again," she offered generously.

It hadn't seemed possible to him that her fingers could move any faster than they had before, but when she stopped and questioned his choice with her eyes, he wasn't as sure as before. And, of course, he was just as wrong.

"At least you aren't betting any money," she said, laughing. "Again?" she suggested and, without waiting for his reply, began the slow, preliminary movements that so convinced the unwary they were, this time, going to succeed in following the ball's course.

She looked up to find his eyes, not on her hands as she had expected, but watching her face. Her fingers hesitated in their practiced motion, and the air was thick with some element she couldn't identify.

"Who are you?" he asked softly, his eyes still intent on hers.

She placed her palms over the shells and sat too still for a moment.

"For now, a Gypsy girl," she said finally. "Only a girl who has a skill the old man can use." The dark eyes flashed, her smile carefully maintained. "Deception," she said, her tone almost challenging. She turned her hand palm up, and he could see the ball he thought she had placed under one of the shells held snugly hidden in the space between two of her fingers.

She watched the faint crease form between his brows, and she swept the shells and the ball into one small hand and rose smoothly.

But she was still smiling when she warned, "The only skill I have is the ability to make people believe they see one thing, when in reality…" She stopped because of what was in his eyes.

"You cheat," he said, surprised at how pained that accusation sounded. He was no innocent, given the years he had spent in the brutal conditions of Iberia, but the thought that she would deliberately set out to deceive those who would play tomorrow was abhorrent.

"And if you make the enemy believe that your forces are stronger than they are, or that you intend to attack from one direction and then charge from another…" she began to argue and saw him shake his head.

"That's not—"

"Deception?" she questioned softly, mockingly.

"That's not cheating," he finished doggedly.

"You're such a child," she jeered. "The English and their damned rules. And if you break one—" She stopped, knowing that in her bitterness at his judgment she had given away too much.

"And if you break one?" he repeated quietly.

"Then you're never forgiven. You become no one," she finished, her voice a whisper.

"What's wrong?" he asked, watching the struggle for

control, the dark eyes glaze quickly with unshed tears. "Why are you crying?"

"Crying," she said, laughing suddenly, her tone derisive, and the long dark lashes quickly veiled whatever had been in her eyes. "I'm not crying. I don't cry. I never cry," she said more strongly. The eyes she raised to his were angry and mocking, but the moisture was gone, so he was forced to doubt what he'd seen. Maybe he *had* been mistaken.

"Who are you?" he asked again, but she turned away, unable to look at the condemnation in his eyes. Now she knew what her father had faced, some small part of what had driven him from his country and from the judgment of men like this.

She heard him say something else, but she didn't turn back.

"No one," she whispered bitterly to herself, repeating the only possible answer to his question. But she moved across the compound with the deliberately swaying walk that made the colorful skirt swing enticingly around her bare ankles, knowing that he was watching her.

The afternoon had been long and successful. The ancient crossroads bustled with people who had come to take advantage of the presence of the merchants and entertainers.

The ache that had begun to gnaw between Julie's shoulder blades attested to the hours she had enthralled the succession of yokels who begged to be taken in by her nimble fingers and distracting spiel. She had been watched over by the hawklike eyes of the old man, guarding his investment, as the members of his band exhorted the wagers of the crowd.

It was unusual enough to have a woman, especially one so beautiful, openly engaged in the games of chance that her patrons had far outnumbered those of her numerous competitors.

One of those patrons was a drunk who had crowded close to the table where she entertained. Since this particular customer had been betting with increasing frequency and with a total disregard for his losses, the old man had indicated with a small upward movement of his chin that he desired her to milk his inebriation for all the profit possible. So she had laughingly endured the drunk's occasional fondling touch on her arm. His fingers had even once trailed across the bare skin of her exposed shoulder. With the Romany daggers so readily at hand, she knew she was in no danger, other than to her sensibilities. She blocked her distaste and began again to invite the crowd's fascinated attention.

Halfway through the practiced performance, she felt the drunk's moist hands rest heavily on her shoulders and then begin the caressing descent downward. Her quick twist from his hold and the grimace of disgust were reflexive. She shivered convulsively at the thought of those hands against her breasts.

She heard the muttering complaint of the crowd at the interruption in the swift movement of her hands. She looked up to offer some laughing reassurance and met instead the coldly furious eyes of the Englishman who stood before her table like some medieval warrior.

"Don't touch her again," he said softly, his gaze locked on the drunk's flushed face, locked without any trace of fear. He was as calmly in control now as when he'd compelled her captor to release her in the village.

The man lurched belligerently around the table and toward the Englishman. Devon braced himself, knees bent and legs slightly apart, preparing to meet the wild charge everyone was aware was coming.

The drunk's fist swung with more control than his drunkenness should have allowed, but a small, carefully timed twist of Devon's upper body caused the blow to pass harmlessly by his left ear. Then his circling movements mirrored the aggressor's, whose staggering steps and upraised fists made it clear he intended to try again to land a fist on that calm and watchful face. Instead, Julie slipped her small body under the drunkard's elbow and stood between his raised arms. She leaned back, pushing strongly against the malodorous body, and at the same time she spoke to Devon, who stood, still in that almost relaxed fighter's stance, watching her.

"Stop it," she hissed, outraged by his intervention. "Go away. My God, what do you think you're doing?"

Something flared hotly in the narrowed blue of his eyes, and then they moved away from her face to his attacker's.

"You belong to him?" the drunk questioned, reading more in her defender's face, perhaps, than she had.

He moved from behind the barrier of her slender body and swept Devon a low and clumsily mocking bow. "My apologies. I didn't know she was your whore. I thought she was fair game. After all," he continued unwisely and looked up just as Devon's well-placed left exploded against his nose, and the rest of whatever insult he had intended remained unspoken.

The crowd had not particularly liked the interference of the drunk in their entertainment, but he was one of their own. Seeing him so suddenly defeated, they began a threatening surge against the lone figure who stood over his downed and forgotten foe, his eyes riveted now on the features of the furious girl.

"How dare you?" she said. "Do you have any idea, damn you, what you've done?"

Disbelief moved into his face, and his hand closed suddenly on her elbow, but she jerked from his grasp far more violently than she had from the drunk's. She watched his lips tighten, but she was too angry to care. She knew very well what the Gypsy's reaction to the loss of such a ripe pigeon for plucking would be. And now the watchers were hostile, wary. All her hard work to develop a rapport had been for naught.

Then the Rom was there, pulling her away in a grip far harder than that she had just broken. A grip she knew better than to fight against.

"Tomorrow," he said to the disgruntled crowd. "Come back tomorrow. The game's closed for the day."

"What about our money?" a voice questioned and, in the sudden remembrance of bets that had already been fixed and then forgotten in the ensuing excitement of the fight, the question was picked up to be repeated in a multitude of demanding tones. The Gypsy signaled his men, who began to repay the wagers as he pulled her from the middle of the mob and pushed her angrily before him down the road to the encampment. And his touch was not gentle.

"You control your man," he said harshly, as soon as they were out of earshot of the crowd, "or you leave. That," he said, with a quick twist of his head in the direction of the jeering comments that followed their retreat, "will not happen again. I swear I'll put a knife between his ribs myself."

"He's not my man," she answered hotly, "and I can't control him."

"Then get rid of him. Or I'll do it for you. You didn't tell me he was a fool. What did he think he was doing?" he asked in disbelief.

At the sudden realization of exactly what he had been doing, her anger evaporated.

"He thought he was protecting me," she said softly, knowing that was the sum of his reasons. And if they made no sense to her or to the old man, that didn't mean in his world they were invalid. Protecting me, she thought again. A small feeling of wonder began to grow.

"From what? You were never in danger. You knew that," the Gypsy said, still furious over the rich prize the Englishman had driven away, over the profitable afternoon's loss.

The girl looked up suddenly, her expression unreadable. "Not from that," she said. "From what he did. From touching me."

"He wasn't hurting you." The girl's explanation was ridiculous, quickly rejected by his practicality.

"He put his hands—" she said, and then stopped. She knew she'd never make the Gypsy understand how outrageous that touch was in the Englishman's world. Not in theirs perhaps, but in his. And to have been protected in that way, as he believed women should be, was surprisingly pleasant. Jean would have laughingly lured the drunk away, taking care never to anger the customer. But Devon had chosen instead to defend her.

"No more. You tell him. You make him understand or by God..." the old man threatened, his eyes brooking no defiance. She knew her position was such that she couldn't afford to question his authority here where his word was literally the law.

Perhaps she was valuable to him, but the Englishman was not. He was nothing more than a burden that the Rom, thus far, had put up with for the ample payment her skills were providing. But if the Englishman persisted in interfering in that contribution, she knew the old man would do exactly what he had indicated. He would swiftly and without the least compunction destroy what he saw as a hazard to the success of his ventures.

She took a breath to control her emotions and promised grimly, "It won't happen again. You have my word."

The ancient eyes looked deeply into hers for a moment and then he nodded and strode on, leaving her standing alone on the dirt road.

Near twilight, directed by one of the men who had helped placate the afternoon's angry mob, she found Devon at the stream where the horses had been tethered. She had ignored the admiring gleam in the young man's dark eyes and had thanked him for the information without making any explanation.

The Englishman was standing quietly by the water's edge, the gelding contentedly nibbling grass nearby. He held a stick in his long fingers, and she watched as he idly broke pieces from it and threw them to swirl aimlessly in the water that rushed through the small stream at his feet.

Although Julie's slippers had made no noise on the mossy slope, he turned and watched her approach. She thought he might make some comment about what had happened today, but instead he simply waited for her to speak.

"If you ever interfere again, the old man will kill you," she warned. She would have expected disbelief or even anger from most men at the blunt message, but instead amusement replaced the patient wariness that had been in his eyes.

"My God," she exploded, her fear for him fueling her words, "do you think that's a joke? He means exactly what he said. And here—" her hand swept to encompass the grazing horses and the wagons circled in the gathering dusk "—he's king, judge and executioner. There's no law to prevent him if he wants to murder you in your bed. This isn't London."

"Believe me, people have been trying to kill me for a number of years," Devon said, smiling at her. "And the law has seemed remarkably unconcerned about those attempts. I don't suppose he'll succeed any better than the others have." The amusement lurked still in his eyes as well as in the calm voice. There was no arrogance in that statement, but rather a smiling resignation.

"Excuse me," she mocked bitterly. "I see I was wrong. I thought you were merely foolish. Now I can see that you're stupid, as well. At least you've been warned."

His continued calmness in the face of the warning infuriated her as much as her fear for him had earlier.

"Don't you understand," she began, but his quiet voice stopped her, and there was now no humor in its tone.

"I don't understand why you were angry today. I should have thought—"

"I was angry because you interfered in something that wasn't your affair. I had made a commitment to the old man. And your heroics lost him a very profitable customer. Over nothing. There was no reason…" she stopped as she suddenly remembered she knew his reason.

She had found, even in the hours she'd spent thinking about what she should say to convince him of the danger the old man represented, that his action, although ridiculous, was also, somehow, very pleasant. As soon as she'd convinced him that the old man would stand for no more meddling in his enterprises, she might allow herself to savor that pleasantness. But for now...

"It's no wonder he was furious, and he still is. You don't know how dangerous he is."

"And what his profitable 'customer' did? And said? It didn't bother you to be pawed? It didn't bother you to be called a whore?" he questioned softly.

"Your whore," she reminded him bitingly. "And your interference alone was responsible for what he said."

He said nothing in response to that accusation, and although she knew she was being unjust, she continued her attack. "Why should I take offense at what an amorous drunkard says? Believe me, I've been called much worse," she said, smiling defiantly, but he heard the bitterness that underlay her claim.

"Worse than my whore?" His voice was still quiet, but it probed too deeply the pain she was trying to hide.

"I'm nothing to you. Don't defend me. I don't want you to. I don't need or want a knight-errant. And I certainly don't need your *valorous* protection," she lashed out, hating Devon's soft repetition of the insult. It hadn't bothered her from the man at the fair, but, somehow, to hear herself characterized as a whore by this man...

"Then you're satisfied with the Gypsy's 'protection'?" he mocked softly. "Somehow, in what happened this afternoon, I wasn't aware that anyone was concerned with protecting you."

"Because I wasn't in any danger."

"Not physically, I suppose. But—" he paused, seeming for the first time to be uncertain. "But your reputation, your honor—"

Her laughter was derisive. "My reputation," she repeated and laughed again. "And my honor." She shook her head, but the smile with which she mocked him was almost twisted. "I don't have any honor. And my reputation? Per-

haps you should have listened to the drunk today. He
seemed to have a much better idea—''

Her words stopped with painful suddenness, cut off by
the belief that whatever had been in his eyes when she had
shown him the ball hidden under her palm was there again.
And against her will, she hated it. So she set out to destroy
any possibility that she might ever have to face its censure
again.

''I lie. I deceive. I even *cheat,*'' she said with mock horror, deliberately ridiculing his rigid code of behavior.

''And you whore?'' he asked softly into her defiance and
saw the question take her breath, stop the jeering words.

She swallowed hard, the sudden movement running the
slender length of her throat. His eyes followed that reaction,
coming to rest again on the shadowed warmth of the darkness between her breasts, café au lait against the ivory.

''How much?'' he asked, forcing his eyes back to her
face. She could read nothing in his voice beyond the calm
seriousness of his question.

''What?'' she whispered, not understanding.

''If you're a whore, then how much?'' he said again. And
he touched her as the drunk had today, bringing both hands
to rest lightly on the bare skin of her shoulders, exposed by
the low neck of the peasant blouse. His lips smiled at her,
but whatever was in his eyes hadn't changed.

''No,'' she denied, wanting to erase what was happening
between them. This was what she had wanted him to think,
but the reality was far more painful than anything she could
have imagined. He had treated her before with a gallantry
her world mocked. And now that he was trying to move
into the lie she had created, she hungered for what had been
between them before.

His hands moved caressingly down her arms, and she
could feel the broken, blistered skin of his palms, caused by
their prolonged and unaccustomed contact with the gelding's reins. Their roughness moving over her skin was the
most seductive sensation she'd ever felt in her life.

Devon had intended to use his mouth to punish her. For her anger, perhaps, or for being what he didn't want her to be. But the fragility of the collarbone that he had touched, the silk of her arms...something had changed that harsh intent.

Her eyes closed when he tightened his grip, pulling her to him by his hold on her upper arms. And so she didn't see the sudden tenderness of the smile that recognized the involuntary nature of that reaction to his touch.

And then his mouth was over hers, turning to caress, fitting against her lips that answered, instinctively welcoming. He kissed her twice, softly, his lips tracing over hers, gentle and undemanding. When he lifted his mouth away, hers followed, wanting more than the touch of his. Experienced far beyond what she might have guessed, he accurately read that desire and lowered his head again, using his tongue to command entrance. Teasing and probing, until her lips opened, the breath shivering out, warm and sweet, to meet his. And then inside, moving, hard and demanding. Coaxing a response from the small body that he was holding almost totally off the ground.

Julie swayed against him, unconscious of what she was communicating to him as surely as if she had put her feelings into words. Words that she would never say because she had no right. Because she knew the barriers that were between them. As her body apparently did not.

She had no idea how long the kiss went on, his mouth softly ravaging, robbing her of any ability to deny whatever he wanted. But finally his hands put her from him, holding her steady as the strength his touch had stolen slowly flowed back into her legs.

She opened her eyes to find him watching the wonder in them that she was not enough in control to even try to hide.

"Whatever else you are—" he began softly, savoring the unpracticed and spontaneous reactions he had just elicited from her. But when fear moved into the velvet brown of her eyes, he smiled at her before he finished. "You are *certainly* a liar."

"What's your name?" she asked without thinking, a question she hadn't intended, for it opened the possibility of his corresponding one. But she wanted a name. It and this memory might be all she'd have.

He briefly considered the wisdom of telling her the truth, then rejected arbitrarily all the arguments that could be made for not revealing this small part of who and what he was.

"Devon," he said simply. "Devon Burke."

"Devon," she repeated, thinking that its unusualness was right because he was, of course, unique. In her experience, at least.

"I'm not a whore," she said, unable now to maintain the pretense, unable to let him leave, believing that.

"I know," he said, as softly as the question he'd asked before.

"But," she began, unsure of what she could tell him, the old man's threat ever present in the back of her mind. She owed it to this man to protect him from the Gypsy's code that was as foreign to him as his chivalry had been to her. And from her other enemies. She had sought to create bitterness and enmity between them. But now that wouldn't answer. And so she settled for the truth. At least part of the truth.

"I really don't need your protection. I'm grateful for what you did in the village, no matter how this sounds, but I'm the last person to need someone to look after me. I've been looking after myself for a long time now. I'm well able to defend myself from the attentions of men like those today. I'm accustomed to doing it. I don't need—I don't *want*—your help."

"You seemed to need my help before, in the village."

"I would have thought of something," she said. "And besides—"

"Besides?"

"You'll only get hurt. Like you did then. I don't want that."

"Don't you think," he said, smiling, "that I'm capable of taking care of myself?" She could hear his amusement at the thought that *he* needed *her* protection.

"Why? You don't think I'm capable of taking care of myself."

His lips lifted suddenly into the smile she liked, the lines around his eyes creasing slightly.

"That's a little different, I think."

"Why?"

"I'm not the one with the enemies," he reminded her.

"Everyone has enemies," she said. "And I'm afraid that you made a very dangerous one today."

"I'm not even afraid of the Gypsy," he said, still smiling.

"Then you're the fool I called you before. He'll kill you. And I don't want your blood on my hands. I think you need to leave. In the morning. I think you'll be safe tonight."

"And you? Will you be safe tonight?" The husky tenderness in his voice matched that which she had not seen in his eyes. But she couldn't allow herself to react to that. He didn't belong to this dangerous world she understood so well. And so to protect him from its harsh realities, she rejected his concern.

"I told you," she said strongly. "I don't need you. I don't want you."

And despite what her body and eyes had just told him, Devon reacted to that repeated denial, unconsciously remembering the rejection of the last woman he'd allowed himself to care about.

He turned away, gazing over the swift stream into the woods that stretched on the other side. She waited a long time in the gathering dusk, but he didn't look at her again. Finally, recognizing that she had destroyed, as she'd intended, the strange bond she'd felt with this man from the first, she turned and left him. And she knew that this time he didn't watch as she walked away.

Chapter Four

Julie had been deeply asleep on her pallet when the old woman's words pulled her back into wakefulness.

"The Englishman," she'd whispered, and Julie's immediate and unquestioning response had been to rise and put on the skirt she'd discarded before she'd lain down. There was little moonlight as she hurriedly descended the narrow steps and found the Gypsy leader waiting for her.

"Follow me," he said simply. She drew the ends of the heavy shawl more tightly around her shoulders against the night's cold. She was trying to think what could have happened that would make Devon send for her and walked without suspicion behind her host. It was not until she was face to face with her nemesis of the apples that she realized what a fool she had been.

Although she knew it was useless, she couldn't resist asking the Gypsy, "Why? Wasn't I worth more to you here, alive? Working the crowd for you? No more golden eggs if you sell the goose."

"Perhaps." There was no guilt in the black eyes that met hers unwaveringly.

"You told him where to find me the first time," she accused, recognizing his treachery. The old man was the only one who could have sent her father's enemies to the village. "Why? I've done nothing to you."

"Because you have powerful enemies and dangerous friends. And I do what's best for my people."

"And my 'dangerous' friend?" she asked, thinking of Devon. Was the same fate in store for him, the same betrayal? "What are you going to do with him?"

"He's still asleep. I don't know who his enemies are, but they haven't yet made me an offer."

"How fortunate for him," she said mockingly and was aware that her helpless anger amused him.

"Fate," he said, smiling. "My daughter, you must learn to accept your fate."

"A fate arranged by your greed," she said bitterly.

"That's enough," the apple farmer ordered impatiently. He was no longer dressed for that role. His cheap clothing marked him clearly as a city dweller, as did his accent. Paris, she recognized at once, and knew that in spite of all she had done to carry out her father's instructions, she had failed. They will do anything, he had told her, because they will believe you have information. The irony, and also the danger, was, of course, that she had none.

With the old man's help, the Parisian subdued her quickly. She fought, but this time she didn't cry out. She knew that if she called, Devon would come, but after what she had said this afternoon, she had forfeited any right to seek his help, and so she said nothing, even as she struggled futilely against the restraints.

It was the old man who removed the knife she carried and who laid the shawl with a curious gentleness over her bruised shoulders after he had helped put her, hands bound, on the gelding. She wondered if he had sold the horse with as little emotion as he felt over selling her.

"I thought you said he wasn't your man," the Rom mocked softly, for her ears alone. He, too, apparently, had known that Devon would come if she screamed and that, because she cared about him, she had chosen to protect him. The old man stepped back, waiting for the buyer to mount, then handed him the roan's lead.

She thought about what the Gypsy meant as the man he'd sold her to led her horse out of the clearing and into the stream. She wished she could honestly deny what his words implied. She wished also that she had at least said goodbye. And then she forced herself to concentrate only on the difficult task of balancing as the gelding picked his way carefully over the slick rocks.

The old man sat hunched over the fire as dawn fingered faint pink-and-yellow streaks onto the horizon. The coffee he cupped between his palms had been dosed with brandy against the night's chill and perhaps even against something he was forced to acknowledge might be the stirrings of regret. That unaccustomed emotion was almost as disturbing to him as the visions of what might now, as he sat by the secure warmth of his campfire, be happening to the girl.

He found himself remembering the mute and futile struggle she had waged against the casual brutality of the man to whom he had sold her. But times were increasingly dangerous, and as he had truthfully told her, he knew the quality of her enemies.

He suddenly became aware of the figure standing before him against whose set face the flickering flames cast light and shadow. He didn't allow himself to react even when the fingers of the Englishman dropped to grasp talonlike into the colorful kerchief around his neck. They twisted into the cloth and then pulled it upward. The Gypsy controlled the fear that clutched instinctively at his gut as the band tightened painfully.

The sentry's knife was at his assailant's throat almost before the final twist was completed. Only the Romany leader's guttural command, occasioned by his guilt over what he had done to the girl, halted the plunge of the blade into the strong column of Devon's neck. As the tip bit into the skin, a drop of blood swelled and hovered, gleaming in the firelight like some obscene jewel, until it rolled smoothly down the blade, to be followed by the slow welling of another.

The old man's eyes looked up into the deadly gaze that had locked unflinchingly on his as the blade had pierced the skin. There was no fear reflected even now in the lucid midnight blue.

"Where is she?" Devon asked softly. Despite the ridiculousness of the emotion, given the vulnerable position of his questioner, the Gypsy felt a shiver of fear again ice down his spine. And he was a man who had spit in death's eye more times than he cared to remember.

"It's difficult to be afraid of a man when I've helped him…" he began, with a bravado he didn't feel.

"Don't." The threat in the whisper was as convincing as the drunk had found it. As convincing as the farmer had believed it to be in the peaceful, sun-dappled streets of the village.

"What have you done with the girl?" he repeated.

"I sold her to the highest bidder," the Gypsy admitted defiantly, but he felt again a brief remorse for that action move through his eastern-European pragmatism.

"But you didn't give any other bidder a chance," the Englishman's voice taunted. Devon's fingers tightened their grip imperceptibly, tightened so skillfully that the man holding the knife to his throat was unaware of the increased pressure against his commander's.

"And do you have a bid?" The old man struggled to produce the question, interested in spite of himself.

He knew now that he had underestimated this man who had lived so quietly among his people these few days. It seemed that there might be more to his resources than had been apparent at the beginning. And there had also been, of course, the sacrifice the girl had gallantly made for him with her silence. Perhaps there was more to this man altogether than he had imagined.

"I want the directions—correct directions—to wherever the bidder has taken her and enough money and provisions to get me there.'' The Englishman listed his demands concisely.

"And a horse," the Gypsy added with dangerous mockery and was rewarded with another reactive tightening of the impromptu noose.

The struggle became one to pull enough air into his lungs past the constriction on his throat. But for some reason, he didn't want to give the signal that would result in the quick death of this interesting new player in what was, to him, an old game. He watched the flow of blood increase sluggishly down the knife's edge, glad to see that his sentry had at least been aware enough to recognize the last movement.

"Where's my horse?" Devon asked. His voice had become even softer, but he loosened his hold enough to allow the old man to answer.

"I sold him with the girl. She needed a mount," he said, as if that were the only consideration. "What do you intend to offer in exchange for these very expensive commodities I'm to provide you?"

The Romany's pause was mockingly expectant, and then the body of the man holding him straightened. In one fluid motion, he released the kerchief and reached over the arm that had held it to fasten his hand on the wrist of the man pushing the knife against his throat. The sentry was suddenly on his knees, his arm twisted and held high behind his neck. The knife dropped from his nerveless fingers. Using his booted foot to push the kneeling figure aside, Devon bent to pick the dagger out of the dirt. Then the Englishman rose to face the two men who had just observed a sleight-of-hand as practiced as any the girl's slender fingers had performed before the fair-goers.

"Tell your boy to go to bed," Devon suggested. "This is between the two of us."

"My 'boy' is older than you," the old man said, trying to identify what he had seen in his guest's eyes as he'd handled the sentry. The look was gone now, faded into the same blue serenity as before.

"No," Devon said easily. He spoke with conviction. "He's much too young to associate with the likes of us, and you know it."

The Rom finally gave the required command, and the sentry rose from his knees to stumble out of the clearing, still clutching his injured wrist.

Devon's fingers fumbled against the blood-soaked neck of the shirt, lifting the gold chain and Avon's seal from its position against his heart. Moss had provided this talisman because he had insisted that if Devon were to succeed, he would need the help of the men most familiar with the dark world of espionage in France. The seal, used on all secret communications from the duke, was something whose authenticity would be easily recognized by Avon's primary agents in France. But it was, of course, its intrinsic value that Devon was counting on now.

He slipped the chain over his head and placed the glittering links and their precious burden into the horny hand of the Gypsy, the hand in which now rested the fate of the girl, as well.

A variety of emotions churned in his stomach as he watched the old man study the gold holder with the secret seal carved into the emerald it held. It was, perhaps, the key to finding Avon, and he had just offered to trade it for the dubious assistance of a greedy, treacherous old bastard who would put a knife into him as soon as he'd spit a hare for his dinner. Trade it for a girl whose name he had never learned. But the seal was all he had of value, and in spite of his success with the sentry, Devon knew he was far from holding the winning hand at this table. And so he waited.

The dark eyes, when they finally rose from their contemplation of the emerald to meet his, gleamed in the light of the dying fire with some emotion Devon could have sworn was humor.

"I told the girl she had powerful enemies, and that was true," the Gypsy said. "But it seems that you, my friend, have even more powerful friends. Why have you waited so long to show me this?''

Hope flared, and Devon said, lying to give himself time to think what the recognition of Avon's seal by this old bandit might mean, ''Because I didn't need your help until now.''

And the old man laughed with the first genuine amusement Devon had heard him express.

''Three days ago you needed my help to piss,'' the Romany king cackled. In the face of the man's continued delight in his own joke, a slow smile finally slanted Devon's lips, and then, incredibly, they were laughing together. Neither was aware of the questioning eyes that watched from the curtained doorways of the encamped caravans. And they watched wonderingly because it had been years since anyone could remember hearing the old man laugh that hard.

The chain and the emerald seal had been restored to their hiding place around Devon's neck. The saddlebag on the horse had been packed with provisions and a small pouch of gold coins. The bloodlines of the mare the Romany had provided were not as obviously aristocratic as the gelding's, but he believed the old man's promise that she would carry him without fatigue and without faltering to the end of whatever journey he set for her.

The Gypsy had talked the whole time the preparations were being carried out, and Devon believed the information he had provided was the sum of what he knew. The problem was that, by design, Avon's agents operated almost independently of one another. Their dealings with Avon were carried out by an intricate system of reporting procedures that left them unaware of the identity of those above them in the chain of command.

''Except for the Spider in Paris and, of course, the Limping Man,'' the old man had explained. The Spider everyone in the network knew by reputation. He was the hub of the web Avon had woven across France. It was from him that the order had come some months ago for Avon's agents in France to disappear. But the descriptive nickname was all the information the old man had. And Paris.

In the other sobriquet Devon recognized his brother-in-law. Whatever disguise Avon might undertake, he would always be the Limping Man, marked by nature with a twisted knee, a dangerously distinctive characteristic in the avocation he had chosen.

The sharing of information was not reciprocal, and the Romany didn't seem to expect a return for any of the things he had provided. Seeing Avon's seal was apparently sufficient in itself to obtain his cooperation.

When Devon was ready to leave, the Gypsy dismissed his followers who had, at his command, rushed to accommodate their departing guest. Now he alone stood by the mare as Devon unnecessarily checked the girth again.

Because he could still feel the results of the last day he'd spent in the saddle, Devon had unconsciously been delaying this moment. His unwillingness to mount finally communicated itself to the watcher, who asked bluntly, "Do you need a hand into the saddle?"

The amused blue eyes lifted from the cinch to rest briefly on the seamed face.

"Only if I come off the other side. Otherwise, whatever happens, just put it down to poor horsemanship," he answered, smiling as he had at the girl's question.

He put out his hand to the old man, and the black eyes moved down to it and then back up to his face.

"That's not our way," he said. A jeweled dagger lay suddenly on the Gypsy's palm. "We swear our loyalty in blood. A primitive custom to you perhaps, but I've never betrayed a man whose blood I've shared." He waited while the Englishman considered the offer.

"I should think you'd spilled enough of my blood to-night," Devon said with grim humor, but he took the proffered dagger and, without hesitation, sliced into the fleshy mound at the base of his thumb. He allowed the blood to flow around and under his own outstretched hand to drip slowly into the absorbing dirt as he held the knife out to the Romany.

The old man made the same cut and then moved his palm to rest above Devon's, his fingers locking the handclasp.

"What makes a man unafraid to die?" he asked softly as their blood mingled. "I've never before met anyone whose eyes betrayed no fear of a knife at his throat."

The pause was so long he thought the Englishman was not going to respond, but then he answered simply, "Maybe knowing there are many things worse than dying for something you believe in."

"And what do you still believe in, my son?" the Gypsy questioned, watching the darkness he had seen before stir in the blue depths. Again the silence stretched thinly between them.

"I believe in my country, in family and friendship," he said quietly, "and in honor."

"And in nothing else?" the old man persisted.

"There *is* nothing else," Devon said. He pulled his hand away and put it to his lips to suck at the edges of the cut. He was aware of the jet eyes still studying his face in the growing light of dawn.

"And into which of those does your quest for the girl fit?" the old man asked, smiling at the sudden blue flame of reaction in Devon's eyes.

Finally the Englishman shook his head and, setting his foot into the stirrup, lifted his long body into the saddle. His hands gathered the reins, his horseman's thighs communicating his surety to the animal who acknowledged his command. He never looked back, because they both knew he had no answer for the old man's question.

The girl's captor had stopped at twilight in a clearing beside a stream whose current ran with bloodred glints in the last rays of the dying sun. He had pulled her unceremoniously off the gelding and had shoved her to sit with her back against the rough bark of one of the slender trees that shaded the water. He had tied her bound hands to the tree, knotting the rope well above her head.

She had no choice but to watch as he cared for the horses and built a small fire from carefully selected deadfall. In spite of his city background, the resulting flame hardly smoked at all. He didn't intend to be interrupted by unwanted visitors.

As she watched him eat his cold supper of bread and cheese, she became aware that his small, porcine eyes slid frequently over her breasts, which, with her arms stretched above her head, were outlined too obviously against the thin cotton of her blouse. She thought she could not have been more sickened had his hands been caressing her. His gaze skimmed hotly over the smooth hollow and the delicate column of her throat and touched on the dark cleavage. Her nipples tightened with the cold fear that clenched her stomach, and she knew that he watched their tautness grow because she felt the oily touch of his eyes there, too.

But when he finally approached her, she decided that she wouldn't give him the satisfaction of knowing how terrified she was. And she was determined to fight, despite her bonds. She didn't intend to make it easy for him. Her pupils were dilated with fear, but her face was controlled, studying him as he moved closer, waiting for any opening that would allow even the slightest chance...

Then he used the tip of the knife to cut through the cord that gathered the low neckline of her blouse and to slit the material, exposing her body. Pushing aside one edge with the cold blade, he allowed its tip to score lightly down an ivory globe and circle the rose areola. She realized she was holding her breath, and if she released it, if she moved at all, the blade would cut the delicate skin.

"You bastard," she said softly and forced her eyes to meet his. "You damned coward. Is this the only way you can get a woman? To tie her up and take her by force?" Knowing there was nothing she could do to protect herself, she decided she had nothing to lose by defying him. And her brave words helped control her fear.

When he looked up from his contemplation of the knife point against her skin, she spat in his face, her eyes full of contempt.

But instead of angering him, her puny rebellion seemed to amuse him. He used his sleeve to wipe away the spittle, and then he smiled at her, revealing broken teeth. She could smell on his breath the fetid ripeness of the cheese.

"Why shouldn't I have a taste of what half of Paris has already enjoyed? I'm not as rich as the *aristos* that swarm around that fancy club, but that won't matter once I've had you."

In his eager anticipation of that thought, he allowed the tip of the knife to move slightly away from her breast, and knowing this might be the only opportunity she would have, she kicked upward suddenly. But he had read her intent, signaled too clearly by her eyes. He turned his body to avoid the kick and used his fist to stop any further attempt at resistance. The girl's head lolled back against the tree in unconsciousness. But in striking her, the Frenchman had shifted the knife away from her body.

The long form that launched itself from the gathering darkness had been silently and patiently awaiting any such opening. There was no hesitation in Devon's attack. He had lost none of the decisiveness that had served his troops so brilliantly on the Peninsula. As he had intended, the force of his body pushed the man with the knife well past the girl's unconscious body.

While they were still being carried by the momentum of his leap, Devon's fingers had fastened around the wrist that held the blade. He was aware suddenly of the slight weakness in the injured right arm, but he forced the pain from his mind, blocking it from consideration. After all, he had a lot of practice in exercising that control.

The man twisted under him, trying to bend his knees to get his legs up enough to throw him off. Devon pressed his body down over the larger one beneath him, fighting to hold him still while his left hand sought a grip on his opponent's throat.

The knife jabbed upward suddenly, seeking Devon's face, and he was forced to pull his head out of the way. The resulting shift of his body gave the Frenchman a chance to twist away from his reaching fingers. But Devon's reflexes were too good, and in the flurry of movement, he managed a quick, short punch into the man's Adam's apple. The resulting choked gag was reassurance that he hadn't lost his touch.

Dealing with that unexpected agony, the Frenchman's hold on his weapon loosened slightly, and with Devon's sudden jerk against his wrist, the knife fell, lost somewhere on the dark turf. Realizing that the blade no longer offered any danger, Devon grasped for the man's throat. Now that he had control, his fingers closed around the muscular neck, methodically squeezing, until he felt the windpipe collapse, crushed under the pressure of his thumbs. He kept his fingers tight a long time after the struggling body under him had stilled. There was no chivalry in the business of killing. And killing had been Devon's profession for a long time.

With the knife of the man he had just fought, he cut the cords that had bound the girl's wrists, then chafed them to restore circulation to the cold fingers. As they rested still unmoving in his hands, he began to be afraid that she had some wound, afraid that the Frenchman had already inflicted some injury with the knife he hadn't been aware of in the gathering darkness. He examined her carefully, pulling the ruined blouse gently back over the small, perfectly shaped breasts.

His throat tightened when his fingers brushed unintentionally against their ivory softness. And then, because he could find no marks other than the abrasion caused by the Frenchman's fist on her chin and the raw wrists, he sat down against the tree to which she had been tied and held her against his chest, cradling her in his lap. He folded the icy hands so that they rested caught between the warmth created by their bodies.

He found himself imagining what would have happened had he reached the clearing only minutes later, if he had stopped to rest or had missed the faint indications that the pair he followed had left the road to make camp. With the vision of what had been about to take place here in this peaceful spot, his arms tightened protectively. He wondered at the force of his reaction to her danger, a reaction he could allow only now, when that danger had passed.

The shivers that eventually began to shake her frame made him aware that she was returning to consciousness. He held her securely, but without restricting the first stirring movements. Her palm turned to lie flat against the hard muscles of his chest, and then he felt her head move. He smiled down into the open eyes that knew, now, his face.

Her fingers were warmer, and they lifted to trace lightly over his cheek, stubbled again with this day's growth of beard. Her thumb moved to caress the lines that fanned from the corner of his eye.

"Devon?" she whispered in disbelief.

"It's all right," he said, answering what her eyes had asked.

"How…" she began. He watched her tongue moisten dry lips and felt the shuddering breath vibrate through the body he still sheltered against his strength.

"He's dead," he said. He didn't explain how it had been accomplished. "You're safe. I promise," he finished softly.

She swallowed and nodded once, trusting him, as she had from the beginning. She laid her head back against the warmth of his chest, hearing the even rhythm of the slow, steady heartbeat. She eventually became aware of the stiffness of the cloth under her cheek, and her hand lifted again to touch the bloodstained shirt.

"You're hurt," she said. She pushed away from the comfort of his body to look for the source of the blood.

"No." He laughed suddenly, shaking his head. He read

puzzlement in the anxious brown eyes. "A souvenir of your friend the Rom. We're blood brothers, in more ways than one," he explained, and felt her relax as she heard the amusement in his voice.

"I don't understand," she whispered, but her cheek nestled again into the curve of his shoulder. She took a deep breath, the masculine aromas of his body soothing. The evening noises in the woods around them had resumed, and the campfire was fading to a dim glow.

"How did you know where to find me?" she asked. In the peaceful security of his arms, her mind was beginning to function again.

"The old man," he said. Unthinking, he brushed the dark curls away from her temple, and his fingers remained, tangled in their softness.

"But he's the one... That doesn't make sense. Why would he sell me and then tell you where to find me? He must have known that you'd—" She stopped, wondering how she could explain her conviction that everyone had known he would come. She didn't understand how she herself had been so sure, sure enough that she hadn't dared cry out, hadn't wanted to put him into danger again, even when the Frenchman was taking her away.

"He sold you because he's afraid of the man who's hunting you."

"The man—"

"Fouché. Even the Gypsy respects Fouché's power," Devon said softly, wondering if she'd tell him why one of the most powerful men in France had, according to the Gypsy, literally put a price on her head.

"Fouché?" She echoed the name of Napoleon's former minister of police, who was much more than that simple title implied. Fouché had held a position in France under the Emperor that corresponded very closely to that which Avon occupied in the British government.

"You didn't know?" he asked.

"But why would Fouché—?" she began and then took a

small, shivering breath as she realized the head of French espionage had obviously been the one who had discovered her father's activities, and that Fouché was now seeking her for whatever information she could provide about them.

"The old man said he told you that you have powerful enemies," Devon said, again inviting her confidence but trying not to probe into whatever secrets she guarded. He hadn't revealed all that had brought him to France, and so, he supposed, she still had a right to her privacy as well.

They didn't speak for a long time. The pleasant night sounds increased subtly around them as the last light faded from the western sky. He wasn't even aware that his hand was now moving in slow, caressing patterns across her shoulders. He felt her inhale, and her whisper was barely audible, even as close as she lay to his heart.

"Why would he tell you how to find me?"

"One of the women told me that you were gone, that he'd sold you. I think she felt sorry for you, for what he'd done." His voice was almost as quiet as hers. "And then I convinced the Rom to tell me where Fouché's agent was taking you."

"Did you kill him, too?" she asked, but there was no remorse for the Gypsy in the question.

Devon laughed at the contrast between the image created by her question and the reality of their encounter.

"We parted on the best of terms. I told you. We're blood brothers."

"I don't understand," she said again. "How could you convince him to help you?"

"I reminded him of someone he fears, or respects, more than Fouché. I wish I'd done it sooner. It would have saved us all a lot of trouble," he said. She could see the corners of his mouth lift into the smile she had thought she would never see again.

She put her thumb over his lips, brushing lightly across, and was surprised to feel them part. They touched her finger in what was almost, she decided, a kiss. He turned his head slightly until his chin lifted, unconsciously nuzzling the roughness of his beard against the knuckle of her thumb.

"Devon," she whispered and watched his gaze come back to her face.

"Hmm?" he said, smiling down into her eyes.

"I'm sorry."

He waited, and when she didn't explain, shook his head.

"Sorry? For what?" he whispered. "What do you have to be sorry for?"

"For saying that I didn't need you. That I didn't..." She stopped, realizing what she had been about to admit. If she was sorry she'd said she didn't want him, then that implied, of course, that she did. And although that was certainly true, she couldn't tell him.

He laughed and pulled her tighter against the warmth of corded muscle and solid bone.

"Don't," he said, his chin resting against the fragrance of her dusky curls. "It doesn't matter. I know you were only trying to protect me."

She could hear again his amusement that she would think that necessary. But because she didn't know his hard-earned fighting skills, she didn't understand.

"But *I* need you now," he said lightly, knowing she would have to realize any danger from this henchman of Fouché's, who had so relentlessly hunted her across France, was over. "You're going to help me dispose of that body. A winch couldn't get me back on a horse again tonight, but that doesn't mean I intend to sleep next to that bastard's corpse."

Together they rolled the stiffening body into the stream's flow. Even in the near-moonless night, Devon was aware that she clutched the remnants of her torn blouse over her breasts with one hand as they worked. And aware, also, that she was sometimes unsuccessful in her efforts at concealment.

Finally he pulled the bloodstained shirt over his head and held it out to her. He doubted he'd sleep anyway, and he'd be awake early enough to slit one of the blankets to wear as the peasants in Spain did. Until then, the darkness would cover his back, would hide what he knew was a shockingly unpleasant sight.

"I'm sorry, too," he said, smiling, when she hesitated over taking the shirt he offered.

"Sorry for what?" she asked, answering his smile, knowing from his voice that she was about to be teased, but unable to anticipate his target. "For again saving me from Fouché's clutches. For coming after me, in spite of what I said. Sorry for—"

"No," he said, interrupting her litany of thanks. "I'm not sorry for any of those. But I am very sorry that I called you boyish. That, my dear, was an unforgivable error in judgment."

In the darkness he couldn't see the slow blush, and he couldn't know that she was unable to remember the last time a man's words had provoked that reaction. But he saw the white hand reach finally and take the shirt from his.

"Thank you," she said softly and was rewarded once more with his smile.

While he saw to the horses, she replaced the ruined blouse with the shirt the Gypsy had given him. The fall of indigo reached almost to her knees. She removed her skirt and spread it over a low branch and wrapped one of the blankets the Gypsy had provided around her body. And waited.

She watched him walk back across the clearing, the pale doeskins lighter than the exposed skin of his chest.

"You're limping," she said, noticing a slight hesitation in his long stride, the result of too many long hours spent in the saddle.

"If only I'd known you were watching, I assure you I would have tried much harder not to," he said, smiling at her. "Forgive me, but sometimes I limp." He paused, feeling no obligation, after his success tonight, to explain his injuries. And so he finished, teasing her with what she'd suggested about his abilities as an equestrian. "Especially, incompetent horseman that I am, if I've ridden all day."

"The Limping Man," she interrupted. She saw shock wipe the smile from his face. "That's what my father said. I'd forgotten until just now. He said he'd sent for the Limping Man. He told me to look for him. Are you— Is that why...?"

"No," he said sharply. "No, you're wrong. I'm not the man you're looking for. But I have to know exactly what you know about him and the circumstances under which your father told you. I asked you once before, and you wouldn't answer me. But now I think you must, whether you trust me or not. Who are you?" he asked again, as he had in the Gypsy camp.

This time, she knew, that in spite of her father's warning, she would tell him.

Chapter Five

Dawn touched the sleepers in the clearing, its light rimming the muscles of a hard masculine arm stretched protectively over breasts that rose and fell with each breath sighing through the girl's parted lips.

Julie had told him her story last night. She omitted nothing, from her flight after her father's instructions in the office of his Paris casino until the time when Devon had found her in the arms of Fouché's agent. He realized her father had been the Spider, Avon's chief operative, driven to his death by the French authorities because of his valuable work for the British Crown. And his daughter had been left with a vague reference to the Limping Man and ordered to disappear.

Her odyssey had led her fortuitously to the Gypsy's camp, where she had bought obscurity with her father's gold. But eventually she had ventured, well disguised as one of the homeless orphans who roamed the countryside, to the village where Devon had found her. She had remembered its name on more than one of the documents her father kept locked in his office safe. She had hoped for some connection there to the people her father had worked for, and her conjecture had been shrewdly accurate.

The name of the agent who had lived in the village was one of the few Moss had been able to provide Devon. But, following the Spider's orders when the French had begun to unravel the network, he had already disappeared, long before Devon had arrived. And so he and Julie had met.

Devon spoke little, an occasional question to clarify some point in her narrative until it had become his turn to explain his reasons for coming to France, to tell her about the man he sought, whose code name her father had whispered that night.

She had listened to all that was revealed by his tone, if not by his words. She wondered at the quality of this friend whom he clearly admired above all others. What kind of person must the Limping Man, this mysterious Duke of Avon, be, she wondered, to attract the loyalty of men of Devon's caliber? And of her father's?

When they had finally exhausted most of their questions, they had lain down on opposite sides of the campfire he'd rebuilt against the late March chill. But in the unfamiliar noises of the rural night, she had heard too many echoes of what had almost happened today and had remembered the cold threat of the knife blade tracing with provocative slowness over her breast.

Finally she had come to stand over the long form covered by the blanket. Surely, by now, he must be asleep, but as she stood there, wondering if she dared to lie down nearer the safety of his body, he spoke to her.

"What is it?" he asked softly. "Are you cold?"

"I can't sleep," she answered and watched him sit up, the blanket falling away from his shoulders.

"What's wrong?" he asked, his hand reaching to take hers.

"Let me sleep…" she began. He felt her fingers tremble in his as she realized what she was asking.

"I'm sorry, Dev," she whispered, "but I can't forget— I can still feel that knife. And his eyes. Please, just let me sleep beside you. I know…"

The attempt to explain her need for human comfort faded in recognition of what he must be thinking.

"My sister calls me Dev," he said, pulling her down to cradle her against the long, hard warmth of his body. "Go to sleep, little one. No one's going to hurt you tonight."

"Julie," she reminded him softly, wanting to hear him say her name.

"Julie," he repeated obediently, his breath stirring the dark tendrils. "I promise, Julie, tonight you're safe."

Except from what I have begun to feel for you, she thought. Except from the dangers that those feelings represent to what my life has always been.

She lay awake a long time, held securely in his arms, and finally when she felt his breathing even into a slow rhythm and knew that he slept, she turned slightly to face him. Unable to resist, her fingers moved to touch the softness of his hair. Then they returned to curl under her chin, and she watched him in the dying light of the fire until she, too, slept at last.

She woke first and decided to slip from under the pleasantly confining weight of his arm to take care of her morning needs. She carefully inched upward, to sit finally with Devon's left arm lying loosely across her thighs. She looked down at the glaze of soft, light hair that glinted over his forearm. A smile touched her lips at the memory of the intimate position they had shared last night, and while he still slept, she decided to allow herself a brief, private moment to admire the long, muscled body stretched out beside her. He was lying almost on his stomach with his head resting on the shoulder of the right arm that bent above it.

The smile froze and then faded at the sight of the grotesque network of scars that marred the whole of his back. Some were wide, irregular circles, their colors ranging nearly to purple, pitting the skin like craters on a battlefield. Others were deeply furrowed and elongated. And over several were thin, precise lines of neatly stitched surgeries, some redder and more recent than the fading paleness of earlier ones.

The blue eyes of the waking man watched her face a moment, and then reacting to what he thought was revealed there, Devon sat up. He rejected his inclination to reach for the protective covering of the blanket that lay over his legs. Instead, he turned so that his back, and the damage he had never fully seen and could only imagine by the reactions of those who did, was hidden.

Her gaze lifted slowly to his face, and the emotions, evoked both by the thought of what he must have endured and by the realization of the extent of the injuries he had hidden, were still exposed, raw in the brown eyes.

Shrapnel, he'd said, the understated simplicity of that explanation made ridiculous by what she had just seen.

"God, Dev..." she began and knew by his closed features that any of the comments her brain was formulating would be construed as pity or horror or disgust.

And so she forced her frozen lips to say instead, "What a very expensive doctor's charge you must have had."

She rose, using his broad shoulder to help her stand. She could feel one of the thick, ridged marks under her fingers, and because of that, she let her hand rest there a moment longer than she required to find her balance.

Her shapely calves and ankles were now on the level of his lowered eyes, and he thought irrelevantly how small her feet were, pink toes gripping in the grass like a child's.

She left him sitting on the blanket they had shared and deliberately spent a long time several yards downstream. Hidden from the camp by the thick undergrowth, she removed the shirt and stepped into the frigid water. She scrubbed her skin and washed her dark hair, shivering but refreshed by the sense of having removed the filth of yesterday's captivity from her body.

She used the blue shirt as a towel, and when she had finished drying off, she rubbed at the stain at the neck, rinsing it with the cold water of the stream, until she had removed most of the blood. In spite of its dampness, she put the shirt on, and on her way back to the campsite took her skirt from the branch and stepped into it and into her slippers.

Devon was feeding the fire, dressed as he had been on the day she'd met him in the neatly mended and freshly laundered lawn shirt and the leather waistcoat. He had found them carefully folded in the saddlebag the Romany had had his women pack.

He straightened, but he didn't speak as he watched her from across the clearing. He was remembering his physical response last night to the very feminine body that had fitted so perfectly into his. And when he had first awakened this morning, long before the sun had moved above the horizon, he had been forced to ease his growing arousal away from the soft buttocks that were resting trustingly against his thighs. Because no matter how much his body desired to carry their relationship into a different path, he knew he couldn't. Her story last night had placed restrictions on the emotional response that had been growing between them. Avon was not here to provide the protection she was entitled to. Therefore, because of her father's service to the country both he and the duke loved, that obligation now rested in Devon's hands. And it didn't include making love to her, especially as vulnerable as her father's death and his enemies' search had made her.

When she had asked to share his blanket last night, he had known there was nothing sexual in that request. She had wanted the thing she had so adamantly denied before— simply his protection. And when he had taken her hand, he had undertaken to provide *only* protection. Even if it meant protecting her against himself. Especially if it meant that. As she gracefully crossed the remaining distance that separated them, he could feel the pressure of his body's response even now to her unconsciously sensual appeal. Despite the horror he had seen in her eyes when she'd become aware of the scars. But her comment had robbed that look of its ability to hurt. No pity. No emotional expression of concern. Well done, Julie, he saluted silently. Far better than most.

She couldn't know that he was mentally commending her reaction. Especially from his face. His features were still as set as when she had left. She glanced down at the open bag at his feet and dropped easily to her knees beside it.

"What did the old man send for breakfast? 'Fillet of a fenny snake? Eye of newt and toe of frog'?" she quoted Shakespeare's witches lightly, her fingers busy among the carefully wrapped packages that included simple medical supplies and even fishing hooks and a line. "Or perhaps something less literate and more deadly—toadstools boiled in bats' blood? No, nothing so exciting, I'm afraid. A cheese and winter apples. Why do I find those so familiar, I wonder? And so unappetizing."

She finally looked up to meet his blue eyes, calmly resting on her face. She held out one of the apples to him, but he didn't move to take it.

"Actually," he said softly, "you handled that better than most people. Even Dominic looked away."

Her hand with the offered apple dropped to rest in her lap. She swallowed the lump that had grown in the back of her throat, but she held his eyes.

"It wasn't because..." she began to explain and then stopped. "It was just so unexpected. You acted as if whatever had happened to your back was nothing. An inconvenient soreness."

"That's all it is," he said. *Now,* his mind finished the thought, but he didn't intend to ever remember what it had been before.

"I'm going to Paris," he said, changing the subject. "I think your father's casino is where my search will have to continue. But I'll take you back to the Gypsy first. I promise you'll be safe with him now."

"No," she said, rising smoothly to stand before him. "I know you trust him, but I'm afraid my memories of his treachery are all too current. And I'm *not* his blood brother.''

The corners of his mouth lifted slightly, and he said, ''Then wherever you want me to take you. You have only to say.''

She hesitated, wondering about her motives, and told him what she wanted to do.

''In spite of what my father said, I think I need to go to Paris, too. I can help you find whatever information might be in his office. I think he meant for me to try to find the Limping Man, your friend Avon, and since you have the same mission...''

She waited for his refusal, but the blue eyes rested steady for a heartbeat on her face; then he nodded, examining his motives without thinking to question hers, and she began to breathe again.

He had estimated the journey would take three days, but they didn't make the distance he had planned on the first. He called a halt at sundown, finding a location for their camp near another stream, enough like the first to cause a slight shiver when she saw it.

She dismounted quickly, fighting memories of the previous twilight. Her skirt caught on the saddlebow, and she struggled to release it, not thinking about the length of slender leg the mishap had revealed. When she had freed the material, she glanced at her companion and realized he was still in the saddle, watching her.

He lowered his eyes, ashamed of that natural reaction. He knew he was losing control where she was concerned, and he wondered how he was going to manage this journey he had foolishly agreed to. He hadn't realized what a test of his restraint living beside her for days was going to be. But he hadn't been reluctant to agree to her suggestion.

Unconsciously, he shook his head at the confusion of emotions she evoked. Protection, he reminded himself grimly as he dismounted. She's under my protection.

"If I ever get back to England," he said, stretching rather obviously the long muscles in his back, "I'll never sit on a horse as long as I live. Have I told you that? As long as I live. And I used to think of riding as a pleasure."

He rolled his shoulders, the material of his shirt smoothing tight against the flexing muscles of his upper arms. He began to strip the equipment from the two horses, accomplishing the task with an economy of motion that argued long practice. She watched his efficiency, the easy movement of his strong body, but she saw again in her mind's eye the scars. It was hard to imagine him wounded, incapacitated. He was too vital, too strong. Even in the Gypsy's camp, even after he'd been shot, there had been no doubting his strength. Or last night when he'd rescued her again.

She realized that he'd finished staking the horses and was studying her face. She'd been staring at him. Not seeing him today, but remembering scenes from the few days he'd been a part of her life. Daydreaming about him, she mocked herself. He'd think... She could imagine what he'd think, so she forced her eyes away from his face and made them focus on the stream that reminded her of last night's camp. She shivered suddenly.

"What is it?" he asked. There was something haunted about her face.

"I was just wondering," she answered, trying to think of any topic of conversation she could introduce to cover the awkwardness. Her fascination with him seemed to be robbing her of her ability to think.

"Do you think there might be fish in that stream?" she tried to ask matter-of-factly. "I have to admit the prospect of dining again off the provisions in that pack is not thrilling. Are you a fisherman? Or shall I try my hand?"

The blue eyes continued to examine her face a moment and then moved to the stream as if considering her suggestion. They came back to smile into hers, giving in to this deception. Fishing had been the last thing on her mind a moment ago. That much he was sure of.

"I am probably," he said lightly, "the best fisherman of your acquaintance. I've caught fish when everyone else had despaired. All we need," he said, looking around the clearing for a slender branch that would be supple enough to use, "is a suitable pole."

"If you're any fisherman at all, you're the best of my acquaintance. I doubt any one of them has ever even attempted to catch a fish, and certainly not one to eat. While you're providing our supper, I think I'll find a spot downstream and clean up."

She forced herself to move away from him. She knew she had to stop thinking about him, stop dreaming about what could never be.

Nothing can come of this, she thought. The distance between our worlds, our experiences, is too great to ever be bridged. It will be better to end it before it becomes something else.

But even as her intellect produced all the logical arguments against what she was feeling, her heart still wanted the something else.

"I can't remember ever before sleeping out under the stars," she said much later. She couldn't remember eating fish cooked over a fire, either, but she had found it delicious. His expertise had not failed him in the catching or the cooking of their dinner.

He sat leaning against a tree while she was cross-legged, poking at the small fire with a stick. She glanced at him as she spoke and saw that his head was back against the trunk, his eyes closed. The firelight gleamed down the exposed column of his throat until its tanned length disappeared into the shadowed neck of the white shirt. He had used her absence this afternoon to clean up also; his sleeves had been turned back to expose strong forearms, and his hair curled damply.

"For a city dweller, you've adapted to camp life very well. Most women..." He stopped, thinking of his sister's elegance now compared to the life she had lived on the Peninsula. Julie would be another woman who would be capable of surviving under those conditions, he realized, admiring her courage and her adaptability. Another woman whose strength would be equal to any challenge.

Most women? Julie was wondering, responding to whatever assessment he intended to make with a reaction she recognized as jealousy. She didn't want to hear about other women he knew. And given his physical attractiveness, his appealing ease of manner, his sense of humor, she was sure there would be many of them. She wondered what the women of his circle in London would have done in her situation. Perhaps he might have preferred that she swoon or have the vapors or throw a tantrum when confronted with everything that had happened.

"Most women?" she asked aloud, deciding perversely that she wanted very much to hear the completion of that thought.

"Sorry," he said, "I was thinking of something else. I don't remember what I intended to say."

"Something about most of the women you know. Or are there too many to make a general statement about their possible reactions?" she asked with a touch of tartness.

"Too many?" he repeated, laughing. "If you're imagining that I know a number of women… I'm not a rake, if that's what you're implying. As a matter of fact, there was always only one—"

The amused voice stopped suddenly. The silence beat painfully against her heart. *Always only one.*

"I think if we're to make an early start tomorrow," he said, his tone emotionless now, "then we better get some sleep. You have the other blanket, don't you?"

"Yes," she said, ignoring, as he had done, the chasm that had opened between them. "I have it."

She wrapped her body in the rough blanket and lay down beside the fire. She knew that no matter what nightmares or remembered images disturbed her rest tonight, she would not seek the comfort of his arms. He had put the barrier there, not deliberately, she thought, but with his unthinking response to the ridiculous notion that he might be attracted to anyone other than the woman whom, it had been obvious by his voice, he loved. And Julie was not, of course, that woman.

The only possible relationship she might have with this man was the one the drunk at the fair had surmised. And it was not the one that had evoked the deep tenderness she had just heard.

The next afternoon's rainstorm caught them unprepared. They had been lucky the unpredictable spring weather had been kind until then, but the pelting fury had thoroughly soaked them before Devon spotted the dilapidated barn. He motioned her to follow and then gave the gelding his head. The animal responded with a burst of speed that signaled his annoyance with the sedate pace his master had been carefully maintaining out of concern for the woman who rode beside him.

When Julie breathlessly clattered into the sheltering dimness of the barn, she knew the farm had been deserted a long time. In spite of her city background, she recognized that its smells were all ancient, the air musty from disuse and abandonment.

Like the gelding, she'd enjoyed the hard gallop. Her eyes were full of laughter as she allowed them time to adjust to the interior gloom. When her vision cleared, she saw that Devon had already dismounted and was standing at her stirrup, ready to help her down.

"Why did you do that?" she asked, still smiling. "We were already soaked. We couldn't have gotten any wetter."

"I don't know," he admitted. One of the filtered shafts of murky light that intruded like fingers through the missing boards of the roof caught in her hair, glittering in the damp jet of her curls. Her eyes were rich with humor, inviting him to confess to the little-boy exuberance for speed that had made him release his horse's head.

"I just thought of shelter and wanted…" He paused, finishing mentally, *To get you inside, safe and protected.*

"Come on," he ordered softly instead of telling her what he had been thinking. After all, she'd made it clear that she didn't want the protection his friendship for Avon obligated him to provide.

She considered that invitation and wondered if he were thinking about the privacy the shadowed building offered them.

He lifted her from the saddle, his lean hands almost spanning her slender waist. She rested her palms on his shoulders, and for one long moment as he supported her, their eyes locked. Finally he allowed her feet to touch the floor and released her. And instead of looking down into the fathomless depths of his blue eyes, she was looking up into a face that was again guarded and closed. But for an instant, she thought, for a moment, he had been unable to hide what was there. And then the control was back, and with it the distance.

"I don't think this will last long," she said. "They seldom do. Afternoon storms, intense but quickly over. One moment it's black and terrifying, and then the next, the sun's out, and it's hard to remember what went before."

She was talking too much, but she was too aware of his carefully imposed restraint. His self-discipline. Suddenly, dangerously, she didn't want him to be disciplined. She wanted whatever he would give her. Whatever of himself he would share with the Gypsy girl who, for the first time in her life, desired something she couldn't have.

Except, of course, she could. She had known that from the beginning. She knew from his physical responses that she could seduce him, could grasp with both hands the opportunity this journey had offered, and then… But that, of course, was what he had known from the beginning, Julie thought, and, in his inherent nobility, had resisted. There would be, for them, no "then." Whatever they shared could not be permanent. He was too far removed from what her life had made her.

He had moved away from her to rummage in the pack the Rom had provided. He walked across the hard-packed ground, his steps raising dust motes that danced briefly in the shafts of light he crossed until he was again standing before her.

He held out the peasant blouse, and for a moment she didn't understand what he wanted her to do. She wondered if he intended her to wear the damaged garment.

"Dry your hair," he said. "It's too cold to leave it wet. I'll get you a blanket, and you can at least wrap up."

She took the material, dry and warm, that he handed her and began to blot the water from her face. That accomplished, she raised her arms to rub at the dripping curls. Her nipples, tight from the damp coolness she was just beginning to be aware of, moved upward with the motion, outlined against the shirt.

She glanced up to find his eyes resting on her breasts, which were as clearly revealed under the clinging indigo as if she were standing before him nude. She could see the pulse beating under his jaw and the rigidity of the muscle beside his mobile mouth. Even the breath he eased, unaware that she was watching his every move, trembled slightly. The navy eyes moved upward suddenly, as if becoming conscious of her scrutiny. Then, as he had before, he turned away, retracing his steps to the patiently waiting horses and the promised blanket.

She finished drying her hair and didn't know how lovely the halo of dark curls, clustering loosely around the rain-touched clarity of her skin, was. She only knew that again he had retreated from the tension that was between them, that had flowed between them from the first betraying touch of her fingers over his cheek.

Then he returned with the rough blanket. He stood holding it out to her, and determined to break through the reserve that governed his responses, she dropped her eyes. The practiced sweep of long lashes dipped and then lifted, revealing the coquetry she had used to such effect in Paris.

"I don't think that's going to keep me warm," she began, hesitating as if she were thinking about the best thing to do in the situation, "unless…" She let her voice trail off. Her fingers moved to the open throat of the shirt, and she glanced up again at his face. His eyes were fastened on the hand that was touching the wet material.

She allowed nothing of what she was feeling to show in her face. Instead she pivoted slowly until her back was to him. She removed the shirt and waited.

He had known what she intended. What she was inviting. But something about the delicate curve of her shoulders and the narrow channel of her back, through which the slim, perfect column of vertebrae ran upward to disappear into the dusky curls on the nape of her neck, stopped his breath. She was so exquisite. And in that way lay madness, he thought, fighting for control.

He didn't know why he was resisting. She was obviously attempting to provoke the painfully surging desire that was moving through his body. She seemed to know exactly what she was doing, and that knowledge argued a great deal of experience in the game she was suggesting, so he wondered why he hesitated. He wanted her. God, how he wanted her. But somehow, even in the face of her deliberate provocation, he knew that making love to her here was an action he'd eventually regret, an action that went against everything he believed the mission he'd undertaken required.

She turned, the dark material of the Gypsy's gift held against her breasts, crushed tightly in both small fists, an effective shield. The creamy skin of her shoulders above it contrasted to the wet richness of the shirt's color.

"The blanket," she suggested softly, seeing again the harsh reality of what she was doing to him revealed in the taut mouth and slightly narrowed eyes, in the vein that jumped in his temple. And she reveled in her ability to affect him this way. She hadn't been mistaken about his feelings.

"Don't," he whispered. "Don't do this unless…"

"Unless?"

"I want you. You seem to be very aware of how much." He stopped because her eyes were suddenly uncertain.

She had never played with this fire, had never flirted in a situation where anything might come of it. She had used her skills only professionally, well-guarded by her father and then by Jean. Her provocations had all been aimed at intriguing the unwary gambler and never the prospective lover. And faced with the tightly leashed passion that was in Devon's face, she realized that she was unprepared for the flame she had ignited.

But seeing her uncertainty, he, at least, was again sure of the path he had chosen.

"I've never taken a woman in a barn before," he said. The pain that flashed through the dark eyes at that brutal choice of words reassured him. He *had* been right. Whatever her actions had indicated, she had not been prepared for that response.

"Don't," she whispered, denying the phrase he'd just used. But she realized that if she had been successful in destroying his control, that's all it would have been. All it could have been to him. He wanted her, but that's all it meant.

Taking a woman. He'd probably had many women through the years, she thought. He'd been a soldier. And she would be only one more. One more in a line of women who had offered him their bodies because that was all they had to give. And he had given only his body in return. Obviously, that was all he intended to give her. *I've never taken a woman…*

"But I suppose that's no reason not to." He lowered his head suddenly, and his lips found the silken skin stretched over the thin bones that spanned her shoulder to the hollow of her throat. His mouth moved, warmly inviting and slightly damp. Her eyes closed in response.

"And we'll probably need the blanket after all," he murmured against her neck, his tongue tracing upward until his breath stirred against the sensitive shell of her ear. His fingers caught the material she still clutched tightly against her body. Feeling the gentle pressure exerted to remove that barrier between her nudity and the hard wall of his chest, she stepped back, away from the very reaction she had set out to provoke.

"No," she whispered. In the blue eyes there was neither surprise or anger. But it was only much later that she would think to try to identify what she *had* seen in their dark depth.

"No?" he repeated.

"I didn't mean…" she said. "I don't…" There were no words to explain. "Please," she begged instead.

"Then you don't want…" He left the question unfinished, apparently as uncertain about what to call what was between them as she.

"No. I'm sorry. I know what I did, but no, I don't want that. I didn't mean…"

"You didn't mean…" he repeated softly, mocking her words. He took the blanket he had brought and draped it loosely over her shoulders. "Then, until you do mean it, I want your word that what's between us won't be allowed to interfere in what we have set out to do. Do you understand?"

"What's between us?" she repeated softly. "And what *is* between us?" She wanted his assessment of what was happening. She knew what she felt for him, but she needed to hear his explanation.

"This," he said instead and lowered his mouth again to hers. His hands locked as they had before over her upper arms, separated this time from the softness of her skin by the rough wool of the blanket. But his kiss was as sensuously moving, plundering her emotions until she again clung, mindless and helpless against the force of what he could make her feel.

And he released her to stand shivering before him.

"When you want to finish that," he said, certain now that she had not really thought about the inevitable results of her actions, "then tell me. But until we reach Paris, our relationship will remain strictly…"

He hesitated, not sure what kind of relationship they might have, now that the barriers had been lowered and a grudging admission of the passion that smoldered too near the surface had been made.

"I understand," she said, humiliated at what he must be thinking. But it really didn't matter what he thought. Because he was right. Until she decided that she could be satisfied with the only thing he could offer her, it was better that she not invite his lovemaking. But she knew she had moved closer to that decision. Until Paris, he'd said. He had left it up to her. The only offer he'd ever make, she thought. The only one he could make, given who she was—and she had until Paris to decide whether or not to accept.

The nearer to the capital they came, the more frequent their contact with people. They chose routes that paralleled the main thoroughfares, but even on those dusty rural byways, they attracted attention. The quality of both the horses they rode and their equipment, along with the combination of garments Julie wore, and perhaps even her exotic beauty, occasioned too many speculative stares.

"I think we'll have to find more appropriate apparel for you before we enter the city," Devon said after the interested eyes of the farm wife they had asked for directions followed their departure.

"I have clothes in Paris. I don't think we need to spend our limited resources on something for me to wear. Besides, what could be more appropriate for our mode of travel than what I have on?" she asked humorously, touching the faintly stained, gaily embroidered collar of the Gypsy's shirt.

"And on the streets of Paris?" he questioned. "I think someone who knows that Fouché is searching France for her would be more concerned not to attract attention."

"Then why not plan to enter the city after dark? We can go to my father's and be inside, safely hidden before day-break."

"Don't you think they'll be watching the casino, hoping you'll return?"

"After all these weeks? I should think they would have given up that idea. Besides, there's an entrance through the cellars. I discovered it by accident when I was a child. I don't know when, or why, or even if my father had it con-structed, but I'm sure he found it invaluable in his endeavors for your friend. We can leave the horses in the shed that conceals the passageway and be inside the house with no one the wiser, not even Fouché's watchers, if they exist. What better place to hide than under his nose? There's something that appeals to me about that."

Devon turned slightly in the saddle to answer her mock-ing challenge to her enemy's omniscience. But, out of the corner of his eye, he caught a glimpse of a detachment of dragoons, their uniforms glittering smartly with gold braid. He grasped the bridle of the mare and, digging his heels into the gelding's side, directed both horses off the road and out of the path of the oncoming troop. They watched from the shadowed verge as the cavalrymen cantered briskly by.

"Devon?" Julie breathed the question as the last of the horsemen disappeared around the bend. She turned to find the blue eyes still on the direction the soldiers had taken, but there was no shock in their calm depths such as she knew was reflected in her own.

"I know," he said softly. "The fleur-de-lis of the Bour-bons has disappeared once more from French arms to be replaced by the imperial eagles. The Emperor has returned."

"You knew," she said, the accusation clear in her voice.

"Before I left England. One of the advantages of working in Whitehall. My position provided me with enough knowledge to be aware of the dangers the Continent holds for the unwary. I wonder how my countrymen who have been enjoying the sights of Paris for the first time since the Peace of Amiens dealt with Napoleon's return."

"And Fouché?" she said, her eyes resting on the calm, sun-browned face of her companion. "I wonder how the Emperor's return will affect the plans of our friend Fouché."

Devon's blue eyes shifted to her face and he smiled grimly.

He thought of what the intelligence reports had suggested about Fouché's plans to stage a coup much like the one that had originally given Napoleon control of France. And in place of the unpopular Bourbon Louis XVIII, Fouché intended to put another royal claimant, the Duc d'Orleans. A puppet ruler, with Fouché pulling the strings. But with the popular Napoleon back in the game... Devon smiled at the thought of Fouché's frustration. He wouldn't be the power behind the throne as he had dreamed. Only Bonaparte's flunky once again.

"I don't think he's going to be at all pleased with the return of his master. Not at all pleased," he finished with satisfaction.

Chapter Six

It was well after midnight of a long third day of travel when they finally reached Paris. Julie led the way to the small lean-to that sheltered the entrance to the secret passage into the darkened casino.

She slipped off the mare and left Devon to handle the task of settling the tired horses for the night. By memory she traversed the dark tunnel, standing a long time in the kitchens when she reached them, breathing in the familiar scents of home. Then, shaking off those ghosts, she pulled the shutters over the windows and left candles lighted that would guide their way back into the house. When she returned to the shed, she found Devon waiting for her, patiently leaning against the rough planks of the wall. The animals were already unsaddled, watered and lipping the grain they'd purchased yesterday.

"What did you find?" he asked, reading in her expression how difficult this homecoming was. She had left this house the night her father died, and she had not been back in all those weeks.

Her exhaustion was also openly revealed in her face, the fine skin stretched tightly over the perfect bone structure. Although she had never complained, he knew how difficult the long hours spent in the saddle and camping in the most primitive of conditions each night must have been. And now she was forced to deal with the memories that the casino represented.

"Everything seems to be the same. It's so strange. It feels as if I've been away a lifetime, but nothing has changed. I almost expect to open the door to the salon and hear the noises." She paused, unsure of how to explain. "I've changed," she whispered, knowing in how many ways that was true, "but everything else seems to have just stood still. As if I could walk into my father's office, just open the door, and he'd still be there. But then I remember..."

Devon waited, watching the memories in her eyes. And then he saw her come back to the present, to realize what he had really asked.

"There's no one there. It's empty. And it should be safe. Even if anyone's watching, they'll never see us enter through the tunnel. And I closed the kitchen shutters."

She looked up to find his eyes on her face, their concern obvious. But he cleared that emotion from them even as she watched, replacing it with the detachment he had used as a shield since they'd made their agreement.

She took one last look around, then motioned him into the tunnel and locked the hidden door behind them.

He was waiting for her in the kitchens. She studied his lowered head as he leaned against the cook's table that dominated the room.

He looked up, the blue eyes gently teasing. "Have I told you that if I ever get home to England..." he began and watched her slow smile.

"That you never intend to climb onto a another horse?" she finished for him.

"No," he said and shook his head, "that I'm going to sleep for a thousand years."

"You can do that upstairs," she suggested, knowing that, although he was probably as tired as she, his intent was only to allow her to rest. And so she picked up one of the branched candlesticks and led the way to the private quarters she and her father had shared above the very public rooms of the casino.

She entered her father's bedroom, and as the candles she held flickered dimly over the shadowed corners, she realized there were no ghosts for her in this room, no painful memories, only a sense of familiarity and peace.

She turned back to find Devon leaning against the frame of the door, taking in the surprisingly luxurious appointments of the dark chamber she had brought him to.

"This was my father's room," she said in explanation. "I think you'll be comfortable. Everything you'll need should—"

"It's fine." He cut off her nervous monologue. He could see the exhaustion reflected in her wan face. "Go to bed, Julie. Things will look better in the morning."

"Is there anything I can—"

"No, Julie," he said softly. "Go to bed. We'll consider what to do in the morning. But tonight we just need to sleep. We both need—"

"To sleep for a thousand years. I know," she said, trying to smile. "You told me. I'll see you, then, in the morning."

She moved across her father's bedroom and through the doorway. He turned slightly to allow her to pass by. The desire to touch him, to feel again the solid warmth of muscle, to allow herself to rest against the comforting, familiar strength of his body was stronger than any emotion she could remember. Instead of permitting herself any of those satisfactions, she brushed quickly by and hurried to her own doorway. She heard behind her in the dark hall the closing of her father's door.

"Sleep well, Dev," she whispered and stood a moment longer, watching the closed door.

After she had dressed the next morning in the carefully selected jonquil muslin, she waited a long time, listening for sounds from her father's chamber that would indicate Devon was awake. Finally, she knocked softly and opened the door.

He was standing by the curtained window that looked down on the street. He turned at her entrance, and she could see that he had used her father's razor to remove the three days' growth of beard. His hair, lightly touched by the sun after several days in the outdoors, was neatly combed, and last night's tiredness had been erased from the tanned face.

His blue eyes studied the slender figure in the doorway. He thought how different she appeared today—no longer the dark Gypsy waif who had ridden uncomplainingly beside him. Her elegant beauty would rival any of the sophisticates who would grace the entertainments tonight in the French capital. She was so lovely in the simple dress, and he felt again the stirring of the emotions he had fought from the beginning, emotions he had thought he would never feel again, hadn't wanted to feel again. So he took a deep breath, forcing himself to look back out the window.

"I think you must be right. There's no sign that anyone has the slightest interest in this building. We should be safe for a while if we're careful to light only the interior rooms at night."

"Why didn't you wake me?" she asked, glancing around the room. There was no evidence of his night's occupation in the neatly made bed or in the items arranged in order on the dressing table.

"I thought you needed the sleep. You looked as exhausted as I felt last night."

"Thank you," she said with a laugh. "You are definitely not a rake, not with that unflattering turn of speech. And I thought that wasn't allowed."

"Not allowed?" he questioned, smiling.

"Anything personal."

He studied her face and knew that in spite of the amusement in her voice, there was also a message in her words.

"Forgive me. I know that you don't need or want a knight-errant. I'll try not to forget in the future."

His tone had been as light as hers, but she knew she had widened the gulf that lay between them. She asked, dangerously revealing that she cared, "And do you prefer your women helpless and clinging?"

"I told you. There are no women," he said, his voice closing the door to whatever lay in his past. "If you would, I'd like to look in your father's study. It's possible he may have left something I might use to help me locate the duke."

"Of course," she said in the face of his coldness, and she led the way down the stairs to the room behind the casino where she had last seen her father. She opened the door for him, but at the sight of the familiar chair and the desk covered with the dust of the last weeks, she turned away, leaving him to search alone.

After four fruitless hours, Devon admitted defeat. The papers that remained all concerned expenses and profits, debits and credits recorded precisely in the hand of a meticulous scribe. If there were any records of the less innocuous dealings Julie's father had directed for Avon from this small room, he had been unable to find them. Either these rows of figures represented a code he couldn't break, not even with the intelligence the duke had prized so highly in his espionage work in London, or anything that might have proved the old man had indeed been the Spider had been destroyed. There were no papers in the safe and no hidden drawers or doors that he could discover.

He found Julie seated at one of the gaming tables in the enormous, shadowed salon of the casino. She had dealt endless hands of patience through the long hours. Devon stood silently and watched as she was defeated again by the cards.

"Patience," she explained, smiling at him. "It's a virtue I've tried to cultivate. But I do so hate to lose."

"I would think someone with your skills could manage to win every time," he said, returning her smile.

"But to do that, I would have to cheat. And to cheat at patience would be gulling only myself."

"I didn't mean to imply—" he began, remembering her reaction to his accusation at the Gypsy's camp.

"It doesn't matter," she interrupted, her fingers laying out the next game. "Everyone assumes, I suppose, that those who make their livelihood at the tables have no inner strictures against taking whatever advantages their hard-earned skills might provide. My father's house—" Her voice broke suddenly at the memories, and she looked up. "My father didn't cheat. Nor do I. In spite of what I was forced to do for the Gypsy."

"Julie," Devon said, seeing the pain revealed in the dark eyes, "I didn't think—"

"What did you find in my father's office?" she asked, her eyes on the cards she manipulated quickly across the broad surface of the table.

"Nothing," he answered, giving in to her change of topic because, under the conditions of the agreement he'd proposed, he had no choice. He couldn't take her in his arms and kiss away the painful memories. "At least nothing that seemed to have any bearing on his work for Dominic. He seems to have destroyed all evidence of those activities before Fouché's men came. Or Fouché now has whatever papers might have provided that connection. I found indications that I wasn't the first person to evince an interest in whatever the office might have held."

"Someone else searched my father's papers?" she asked, the movement of her hands over the cards arrested. "Of course," she whispered, "I should have known that was inevitable. It seems such an invasion of who he was."

"He would have expected it. He knew the game he played was dangerous. And that those he opposed were ruthless."

"He was very ill," she said softly. "I think that at the last he held on only for whatever service he could provide for his country. A last act of expiation, perhaps. But I don't think he had any regrets when he pulled that trigger, Dev. That's the only thing that's made me able to accept his death. That and the fact that his life meant something, had been valuable to your friend's efforts."

"Expiation?" Devon questioned. "Expiation for what?"

"Someday," she said, her eyes again on the cards that rested, waiting under her fingers. "Someday I'll tell you my father's story. But not today. I think I've dealt with enough ghosts today. Would you like to play a hand against the house?" she offered. "You may choose. Whatever you like—ecarte, baccarat, basset, faro, piquet."

As she talked, the small, graceful hands picked up the lines of patience and then shuffled the cards in long, ruffling falls, almost faster than his eyes could follow. She dealt the four aces in a row across the table, and he wondered how she had arranged the deck so those cards fell at the top. Her voice broke into his fascination with her skills.

"Hearts, truly loved; diamonds, ever courted; clubs, blissfully married; and spades, forever single. Would you like for me to tell your fortune, Devon? There are so many ways for the cards to talk, to reveal the secrets they hold," she said.

"These are the ancient kings," she continued, glancing up under her lashes at him. She then began to place the next four of her fixed deck in a row below the aces of the suits she had just named. "Charlemagne," she pronounced, laying the king of hearts under its ace. "Caesar." She placed the king of diamonds. "Alexander and David," she finished and began to shuffle the remaining cards.

"And the knights," she said, leaving a space between the kings and the cards that she began to place below them. "La Hire? Hector? Lancelot?" she asked, her voice teasing as she smiled up into his eyes again.

He shook his head as he recognized her association of him with the heroes the French face cards had traditionally represented.

"Or are you Hogier?" she suggested, placing at last the jack of spades.

"Distinguished company," he said, smiling, "but too courtly for a simple soldier."

"But most of these were soldiers, too—simple or otherwise,'' she argued, gesturing to the kings and their matching knaves. Her hands began again to ruffle the cards in colorful streams between her fingers.

"And having seen your back,'' she began, and then stopped, remembering his reluctance to discuss what had happened to him on some distant battlefield.

"It's all right,'' he said at her pause, wondering why she would refer to something his reticence had clearly placed off-limits. But then Julie's matter-of-fact acceptance of his scars had also been surprising. "Having seen the damage to my back, you think…?''

"That you belong in this distinguished company.''

His laughter at the compliment he thought ridiculous was genuine. "And your fortune, my lady of the cards? Where is your portrait?'' he asked, because he knew the assembly of heroines the French queens encompassed.

"I'm not here,'' she said, still smiling, placing the queens in the space she had left under their corresponding kings. "Perhaps the women you know in London are here, but for my representation we'd need another game. The As-Nas deck has the dancing girl,'' she said easily.

"*And* the soldier,'' he answered. Her eyes lifted to lock suddenly on his face. And he added softly, "Perhaps we both fit better there.''

The silence that followed his suggestion was finally broken by her low laugh. "You know the cards,'' she said, gathering up the display she had made with the face cards.

"I told you. I was a soldier. I've played cards all over the world. With a hundred different decks in a hundred encampments. And I understand a little of their mystique.''

"Then you're an unusual Englishman. I thought silver loo and whist were your limits. And faro considered very daring.''

"What a poor opinion of my countrymen you have.'' He laughed. "Surely we're more sophisticated than that.''

"My father was English. And, I suppose, so am I. I've never thought about my nationality beyond the circumference of these rooms. What I do with the cards opens many doors. Even those curtained doorways of the Gypsy's camp."

"For someone with your talents," he agreed.

"And what would those talents be worth in a London drawing room? I neither paint nor sew nor play the pianoforte. I have none of the skills of your world."

"My world?" he questioned, laughing. "Do you honestly believe..." he began and shook his head again. "Julie, I don't belong to that world any longer. Mud and heat. Tents and campfires and half-cooked game. Dysentery and fevers. My God, surely you're not picturing me at an afternoon's musicale listening to some simpering debutante's efforts? What we did on our journey to Paris was far nearer what my life has been than that."

"And to the life of the woman you love?" she asked.

At her question his teasing smile faded.

"The woman I *loved* married someone else," he said, emphasizing the past tense of that verb, but she misinterpreted what was in the shadowed eyes, mistaking his bitterness over that betrayal for pain occasioned by loss.

"Why?" she asked, unable to conceive that any woman would be so foolish as to refuse his love, if it were offered.

"And on the day you tell me about your father, I'll tell you that story," he said, closing the door to her questions.

"Play cards with me?" she said suddenly, accepting his refusal. "Piquet," she suggested, her favorite. "You're safe there, I promise, from any tricks I know. Only mind to mind with piquet. The cards—"

"The cards don't lie. And they don't cheat those who respect them," his quiet voice interrupted. "I'll play with you, Lady Luck, but you may find my skills paltry compared to yours."

"Did you win their money, Dev, when you played before battles? Were you lucky?" she asked idly.

"'Lucky at cards, unlucky at love,'" he quoted lightly

and pulled out one of the elegant chairs at the table and sat across from her.

"My unlucky knight of the spades," she suggested, laughing, and dealt by twos the twelve-card hands.

"And what do you suppose those would reveal about our respective fortunes?" he asked as she quickly placed the remaining cards facedown between them to form the stock.

She met his eyes and said, "Look and see. It's your play, Dev."

She watched as he examined his hand and discarded. He quickly took the allowed cards in the stock, studied the others, then smiled to signal his consent to her play.

"Carte blanche," she said, announcing that her hand contained no face cards. She glanced at him to smile with the question. "I think that term has another meaning in London?"

"Yes," he admitted, "but it's not a term I've ever had occasion to use, except in cards."

"No London mistress, either," she correctly interpreted his comment. "Unlucky in love, indeed," she said, making her own exchange from the stock. "And I think I'll leave you in the dark as to what remains here. One should never reveal something an opponent can later use for his triumph."

As the game continued, she found him to be a worthy opponent. He was coldly logical, his play was faultless, and he seldom took chances that went against the odds, which, she realized, he was able to calculate as quickly as she.

At the end she was the winner, but only due to a lucky *carte rouge* on the last deal.

"And today," Devon said, acknowledging his defeat, "not even lucky in cards."

Their conversation through the hands had been limited to scoring, both too intent on the play to continue the double entendres that had begun the game.

"But you're very good," she said. "I had the better

cards, not the superior skill. Will you play me again some
time?''

''Any time you wish, Lady Luck. I think we'll have som
hours to while away as I try to decide where we go from
here. I'm no closer to finding Dominic than I was when
entered France.''

''If Fouché is responsible for my father's death, and if h
was working for your friend...''

''Then Avon's disappearance can certainly be laid at Fou
ché's door,'' he agreed, having already come to that fright
ening conclusion when she had first shared the story of he
father's death. Neither Fouché nor Napoleon could allov
Avon's intelligence network to reveal their very separat
plans. One of them, probably the minister of the secret po
lice, had begun to unravel the network. He had lured Avor
to France where he had disappeared, unable to warn th
allies about what was about to happen to a Europe tha
thought they'd seen the last of French upheaval.

''Fouché's a very evil man, Dev, if one believes half th
stories that circulate about his actions. One who will sto
at nothing to advance his plans. If he captured the duke—'

''I know,'' Devon said, ''but I have to believe that Avor
is still alive. And I have to find him, Julie. I owe him mor
than I can ever repay. And I can only pray that it's not to
late.''

''How long has he been missing?'' she asked, but his eye
didn't lift from the long fingers that were gripped togethe
on the surface of the gaming table.

''More than three months,'' he answered, and his lip
tightened with that admission.

''Three months in Fouché's hands? My God, Dev.''

''No,'' he said sharply. ''Whatever you're about to tel
me about Fouché's methods, I don't want to hear. I'v
wasted enough time. What I would like to hear are som
suggestions as to where he might hold a prisoner of Avon'
value. Do you know?''

''Almost anywhere in Paris. He has that kind of power

But I would imagine that it would be somewhere other than the official prisons. Especially—"

"Especially with Bonaparte's return. Fouché's power is certainly curtailed by the Emperor's," he said, thinking out loud.

"But Napoleon has a history of forgiving him. He's done so time and again. But it's said that Bonaparte has his own spies within Fouché's network, so that he always knows what's being plotted. They're all intriguers. It's their life's blood."

"So Napoleon would be aware of everything his ex-minister of police is doing? Is that what you're suggesting?"

"That's what the gossip suggests," she corrected.

"And is the source of that gossip reliable?" he asked.

"You'd be surprised at the powerful men who have visited these tables. And at the things they discuss quite openly before a woman who deals cards. I suspect that my father's value to the duke was originally founded on the tidbits of information he picked up in these very rooms when he ran the casino. But I don't see how knowing that Bonaparte will almost certainly be aware of your friend's whereabouts can be helpful."

"No," he admitted finally, "nor do I. But I learned from Dominic that all information is valuable. And we have little enough. I wish," he began bitterly and then stopped, trying to think of any other avenue he might explore.

"That you'd never become involved with a boy stealing apples," she suggested, imagining how frustrating the lost days he had spent on her rescues must be to him now.

But his answer surprised her.

"No," he said, smiling. "I think becoming involved with your plight was the most incredible piece of luck I've ever had. The few names I'd been given when I left England couldn't be traced. Those agents had disappeared long before I tried to contact them. You led me to the Rom, whom I would never have found on my own, and who will always be available now to help. And you know far more about

Paris than I. I can only hope that you'll be willing to hel[
me continue the search here.''

She smiled at his doubts about her cooperation. ''I wis[
I felt that I've been as valuable as you suggest. I have a
much reason to want to do Fouché a disservice as you dc
I'll help find your friend, if only as revenge for my father'
death.''

''To our continuing partnership, then,'' he said and hel[
his hand across the table. She hesitated, wondering if h[
remembered that their agreement was only until they ha[
reached Paris. Perhaps that's what he was implying.

When she failed to answer, caught in the confusion o
emotions, he said, laughter coloring his voice, ''Or like m
friend the Gypsy, do you think we should seal our bond i[
blood?''

Her eyes lifted to his face, and she shook her hea[
slightly. ''No, Dev. Remember? I'm the dancing girl. W[
seal our oaths with a kiss.'' And saw the laughter die in hi[
eyes.

''I don't think that's very wise,'' he said softly.

She smiled at his refusal. ''Only a kiss, Dev,'' sh[
mocked. ''Nothing else. No other commitment. Just a kis[
for the dancing girl. I assure you, I know my place,'' sh[
said with a carefully controlled bitterness.

''For days that place has been at my side,'' he said qui
etly, acknowledging her courage and endurance. But tha[
was not, of course, what she wanted.

''Are you afraid?'' she asked, goading him. She was tire[
of his nobility. She wanted the touch of his mouth. *Hi[
whore.* The drunk's words at the fair suddenly leapt into he
mind. She could never be anything else to him, so why
shouldn't she have the crumbs from this table.

''One kiss,'' she offered again, and her eyes were sof[
and dark with the dangerous invitation.

Although he understood that danger very well, he, too[
wanted what she'd suggested. He had thought about touch
ing her, making love to her, too many long hours afte[

hey'd stretched out, carefully separated by the fires he'd
built each night. One kiss. What could it hurt? He couldn't
want her any more than he already did. His control had
proved strong enough in the long nights to fight that temp-
ation. Surely it would be strong enough to cope with one
kiss.

And so, against all his self-imposed limits to their rela-
ionship, he stood to again offer her his hand.

"Lady Luck," he invited softly.

She put her fingers into that strong grip, and he helped
her rise. She hesitated a moment, wondering if he really
meant to give her what she had asked for. And then the long
fingers that held hers tightened and, using their strength, he
pulled her around the table to stand before him.

He raised her hand to his lips and kissed the fingertips.
She was watching his face and saw the question appear in
the slanted brow, offering her one more chance to change
her mind.

"Perhaps you should…"

"No," she said softly, denying his suggestion.

"Then so be it," he agreed finally, giving in to his own
desires as much as hers. He placed her fingers against his
chest. She allowed her palm to flatten, and her hand moved
upward to lie warmly touching his neck. Her thumb brushed
along his jawline, delighting in the slightly rough, masculine
texture of his chin.

He could see the pulse in her throat increase as she looked
up, and at what was revealed in her eyes, his heart lurched
against the wall he had tried to build around it.

His head lowered to her mouth, which moved, sweetly
caressing, over his own. He could feel her soft breasts press
into his chest. Her hands found his shoulders as she stood
on tiptoe, and then his arms, unbidden, circled her body
protectively. So small, he thought, and so alone.

His tongue moved against her lips, pushing to get inside,
and they opened, inviting his invasion. Her tongue began to

answer the movement of his, tenderly matching his sure
mastery. And finally, fighting the tide of passion that had
too quickly flooded his body, he raised his head to look into
her face.

Her eyes were closed, and the tip of her tongue appeared
from between her lips to touch the moisture the kiss had
left on the soft, full underlip. Her eyes opened to reflect
unmistakably the same emotions that had shaken his resolution.

One small hand found the back of his head to pull his
mouth down again to her body, to invite its brush over the
pulse whose fluttering movement he had watched earlier.
Suddenly he was lifting her to bring the smooth ivory of
her skin in contact with his hungry lips. They traced over
the hollow of her throat, and then his tongue trailed lower,
burning against the tops of her breasts and finally into the
dark cleavage between them.

She was lost in the sensations. How she had wanted this.

She turned her cheek against the silk of his hair and whispered his name, but it was not in denial. And he carefully
lowered her body to see what was in her face. He touched
her with his thumb, moving it caressingly from the still-
throbbing hollow of her throat into the valley between her
breasts, which his lips had just deserted. He saw the quick
inhalation of reaction.

Again a shuddering breath shook her slender frame, and
she stepped back, away from his thumb's touch. He allowed
his hand to drop, and then he waited.

"Julie?" he whispered, questioning, and finally she met
his eyes.

"Yes, Dev," she said, agreeing to what she had denied
in the barn that day, knowing that what she felt was beyond
her control. And that she could destroy his.

Lost in the feelings that had been created in the shadowed
room, neither heard the entrance of the man who listened to
the whispered exchange. And who had watched what had
gone before.

Devon's only warning was the widening of her dark eyes, and then he was pulled around by a strong hand on his shoulder and the first blow struck his unprotected chin. The second was a right that landed solidly in his stomach and sent his body crashing into the gaming table, its edge striking against the back of his head.

Julie, he thought, as he went down, and the last thing he heard before he lost consciousness was her scream.

Chapter Seven

When Devon came to, Julie was pressing a handkerchief against his bleeding mouth. For a second he couldn't remember why he was down, but then the image of a dark, scarred countenance and of a fist driving into his chin created a surge of adrenaline. He tried to rise, and with that movement was forcibly made aware of the results of the second impact.

"Julie?" he whispered, his eyes closed briefly against the pounding darkness in his skull.

"Shh," she said, "it's all right. There's nothing you need to worry about. Just lie still. I promise you everything's all right."

"Who?" he finally managed, relieved that, although her eyes held concern for him, there was no fear.

Her hesitation was a little too long, and then she said simply, "A friend. An old friend of my father's. He thought…"

And watching the rush of color stain the translucent skin, Devon said, acknowledging his guilt in the situation, "I know what he thought."

"I explained," she began, and then her voice faltered. "I told him that I had asked you to…"

He took the cloth from her hand and pressed it tightly to his lip. The sting was a welcome distraction from the cres-

cendo of pain in his head. Despite that, Devon put his other
hand against the floor and pushed himself up, leaning back
gratefully against the table that had inflicted the damage.

And he saw again the sardonic smile of the man who had
hit him. He was standing near enough to have heard their
conversation, and his opinion of Devon's actions was clearly
revealed in the glittering eye.

"We still thrash cads in France," he said softly in English. "Or horsewhip them."

"Stop it," Julie commanded angrily, turning from her
attention to Devon's injuries to face him. "Haven't you
done enough?"

"Apparently not," he answered mockingly. "He still appears to be alive."

"I told you—" she began furiously.

"I know what you told me. And I know what I saw. And
you, *monsieur,* I wonder if you would treat a woman of
your circle as you just treated Julie."

There was no easy answer for that soft accusation. Devon
had acted in a way that certainly broke his personal code,
if not the mores of his society. Because of Julie's occupation
and her past, because she was a woman who was surely not
innocent of sexual pleasures, most men of his class would
view her as fair game. But he had agreed to bring her to
Paris, under his protection, to help him find Dominic and to
avenge her father's death. Under his protection, his con-
science reminded him, and he had violated his own definition of what that implied.

"No," Devon said softly. The honesty of his regret was
revealed in his blue eyes, which did not drop before the
indictment in the hazel intensity of Jean's. "No," he repeated, and turned to look into Julie's white face.

"I hope you'll accept my apologies," he said to her.
"Please believe that what happened between us in no way
reflects a lack of respect for you or for the invaluable help
you've been."

"Don't," she said bitterly. "Nothing happened between

us. Do they write that speech out for you to learn? What to say on being caught kissing the upstairs maid? I don't even know what you're apologizing for. I asked for a kiss, and you gave it. You don't owe anyone an explanation of your actions. I enjoyed your kiss, my soldier knight. The dancing girl thanks you."

And she turned defiant eyes to the man leaning gracefully against the wall.

"Very pretty," he said mockingly. "I'm sure your father would have been enchanted to hear you characterize yourself as a 'dancing girl.' Or have you changed so much since his death?"

"You're right," she said, her tone as cutting as his. "Not a dancing girl. A faro dealer. My father made me that. Whatever dishonor lies in who I am, you're creating, Jean. Not Dev. In the days I've spent with him, he has treated me with—"

"In the days?" Jean interrupted, repeating her words in disbelief, and his posture was no longer relaxed. He looked again like the avenging angel he had perhaps pictured himself when he had knocked the Englishman to the floor. Very definitely a fallen angel, but a man who still had enough integrity not to make love to an innocent girl. As this man, apparently, did not.

"Are you telling me that you've spent these weeks I've scoured France for you in his company? And during those days I was... *Mon Dieu*, Juliette. *Mon Dieu*," he repeated incredulously.

At the look on her face and at the pause that stretched as he waited for her denial, he finally turned to the man he had hit and sketched him a mocking bow.

"I owe you an apology. This is an *affaire* of long standing, I take it. Forgive my untimely interruption. I had thought that I was protecting Julie from your unwanted advances. Apparently I was only witnessing—"

"Don't say anything I'll have to force you to be sorry for," Devon warned quietly.

The low laugh from the man he had just cautioned was caustic. "Pardon me if I doubt your ability to carry out that threat. You hardly appear to be in any position to do so."

"But looks are deceiving, as I'm sure you know. There has been nothing in the nature of an affair in my relationship with Julie. We..." Devon's voice ground to a halt, because he had realized that, without the intervention of this arrogant Frenchman, that accusation would almost certainly have become a reality. The silence in the shadowed room lengthened uncomfortably.

"Yes? I assure you I'm awaiting the revelation of your amatory adventures with ill-concealed impatience." The eyebrow on the unscarred side of the Frenchman's face slanted upward with his sarcastic prompting.

"I should hate to have to kill you," Devon said softly, the tone of quiet regret devoid of any other emotion. But there was no doubt in the minds of either of his listeners that he was deadly serious.

"And I think that perhaps that threat might better come from my mouth than yours. You have spent some time with him, unchaperoned, I assume?" Jean paused to ask the girl, who was still kneeling beside the man he had knocked down.

"You may *assume* whatever you wish," she answered, emphasizing his choice of verbs. "You're going to, no matter what I say."

"Several days, unchaperoned, in the company of a young woman for whom I am responsible," the Frenchman finished, ignoring her taunt.

"For whom you're responsible?" Disbelief colored Julie's question. "By virtue of what, may I ask, do you feel yourself responsible for me? Not only do you *assume*," she repeated more sarcastically than before, "you also apparently presume, Jean. You were my father's employee. And that's all you ever were, to me or to him."

The impact of her words was clear, briefly, in the dark face. And then he controlled his pained response. The unscarred corner of his mouth moved into a bitter smile. "I think that is not the entire truth, *petite,* and you know it. I'm sorry what I've said today has hurt you enough that you would deny what your family meant to me."

He waited a moment, but she was silent, a silence prompted by her knowledge that she had given a less-than-honest evaluation of their relationship. But she didn't acknowledge his right to judge her. Or to condemn Devon.

"Your father told me to take care of you, whether you want to believe that or not. They were the last words he said to me before he asked me to send you to his office, before Fouché's agents broke in. But when I looked for you, after your father's death, you were gone. And I searched for you—believe me, I searched."

"I'm sorry," she said softly. "He told me to disappear, to hide myself as far from Paris as possible—and to trust no one."

She waited and saw the negative movement of his head. The low light cast blue-black glints into his hair as he denied the implication.

"But you must have known that he didn't mean me, Julie. Surely you knew that I would do anything to protect you."

"I didn't know what to believe. I never thought that you might be looking for me. And then I met Dev."

Her eyes returned to rest on the face of the man who had become an interested, if silent, spectator to their exchange. Her lips moved into a slight smile, unconsciously revealing what the memory of that meeting meant to her.

"Or rather he found me," she amended softly. "In the grasp of one of the agents Fouché sent to find me. And he rescued me. We decided to travel together. That's all there was."

But the Frenchman had watched her eyes as she talked. Because he had known her so long and, although she had never been allowed to suspect, because he had loved her, he had recognized what was revealed there.

His gaze searched, too, the handsome, unmarked face of

the Englishman, and then he hid the bitterness of his discovery in his sardonic questions.

"And if you had spent some days in the company of a woman of your acquaintance, a woman of your class? Some days in the company of young woman of your circle in England? What would be your response to the concerns of her family, I wonder? As a result of her father's last words to me, I still consider myself responsible for the Viscount Ashford's daughter."

The blue eyes had turned to ice at the beginning of that speech, but the Frenchman had not misjudged his target. And Devon's smile became as dangerous as Jean's as he considered the challenge in the revelation of who Julie was.

"The Viscount Ashford," he repeated finally, and at the recognition of all that name stood for, a recognition clearly revealed in his tone, Julie heard again what her father had faced before he had been driven from his country. "I think I'm beginning to understand," Devon finished, the pieces to the puzzle Julie represented falling finally into place. She was, as the Frenchman had pointed out, a woman of his own class. And she was certainly not responsible for the actions of her father. Or for whatever direction her life had taken as a result of those actions.

There was no response except a mocking half bow and the slight movement of the undamaged side of the mouth that had asked those unanswerable questions.

Devon took a deep breath and turned to the woman who was still watching the Frenchman. He couldn't tell what she was thinking from the still, alabaster paleness of her profile.

He took her hand and saw her come back from whatever memories of her father's bitterness had made her, momentarily, unaware of him. Unaware of what he must now be thinking. She had never intended that he should know who she was. There was no need for what Jean had done. For that betrayal. Devon would have gone as soon as he found Avon, and he would never have had to know that her father was the center of a scandal that had rocked London.

"Julie," Devon said softly, aware suddenly of the tears tangled in the dark sweep of her lashes. His heart beat once, hard, and then he caught the breath her pain had robbed and raised the hand he held to his lips.

She watched his movements, and he saw her throat move as she swallowed, trying for control.

"Julie," he said again in concern, and he smiled into the eyes that finally met his and waited like an animal at bay for whatever he intended to say.

"Would you do me the great honor of trusting yourself to me in marriage? I promise that I will, from this moment on, do everything in my power to make you happy. Will you marry me, my beautiful Lady Luck?"

She had never dreamed that he would offer her marriage. But, she realized suddenly, she should have known. Everything he had done since she'd met him had indicated that this proposal would be demanded by his concept of honor. Not because he wanted to marry her, of course, but because it was somehow, to him, the right thing to do. There was probably no other gentleman in London, she thought, who would have offered marriage to a woman of her background, despite the nobility of her birth. Her father's dishonor and her own past would have made that idea an anathema to anyone else.

Only you, she thought, tracing again his features. And I will never allow you to make that sacrifice.

Her eyes swam with unaccustomed tears, and he watched one escape its shimmering pool to trace downward over her paper-white cheek.

I never cry, she had told him, and thinking that he knew what those tears signified, Devon smiled at her again and raised her fingers to the gentle touch of his lips.

The small hand was ripped from his hold, and she was on her feet before he realized her intent. She walked to stand trembling before the Frenchman. His face was free of the mockery he had so effectively employed against the Englishman. And then she slapped him as hard as she could, the blow resounding in the echoing emptiness of the casino's vast salon like a pistol shot.

The imprint of her palm showed white against his dark skin.

"You bastard," she whispered. "You bastard," she said again more strongly, and then she ran from the room, leaving the two men, enemies from the inception of their acquaintance, alone.

Jean had not reacted in any way to her assault other than the involuntary recoil of his head in response to the force of her hand.

Devon watched as the Frenchman put his hand up to the mark she had made, and he was pleased to note the slight tremor in those long fingers. They finally touched the blood that had begun to well from the corner of his lip.

"Yours, I believe," Devon said, holding out the stained handkerchief he had used on his damaged mouth. "At the moment, you seem to have more need of it than I."

He was satisfied to see the mockery had also disappeared from the hazel eye. The Frenchman took a deep breath, and his fingers moved to touch the black patch above the scars.

He waited a long moment and finally moved to stand over the fallen man. Jean took the handkerchief, but instead of using it to blot the blood from his lips, he returned it to his pocket.

And then he put out his hand and allowed the tanned fingers of the Englishman to lock into his.

When Devon was standing, the blue eyes rested again on the brutally scarred face.

"I haven't made love to Julie. What you saw..." Devon paused, wondering why he felt compelled to explain his actions to this man when Julie had denied his claim to speak on her behalf.

The Frenchman found himself believing that quiet assurance. He recognized that he had, in his impetuous defense of Julie's honor, probably marked paid to his own hopes.

"Then why did you offer? There's no one but we three who know."

"Maybe," Devon said, "but I can't be sure of that. We traveled together. We shared our meals, our resources and—" He remembered the times he had kissed her, the night he had held her trembling body against the warmth of his.

He acknowledged to himself, at least, the real reason he'd made that offer. He loved her. He'd fallen in love with the woman who had ridden by his side these last days, in a situation, like battle, in which one's true character could not be disguised or hidden. And he knew that she was not indifferent to him. She had revealed that in her response to his every touch. But discussing his feelings was not something he intended to do with this arrogant Frenchman.

"And Arthur Ashford was a friend of my father's," he substituted instead of confessing what he'd been thinking. "She didn't use that name when she told me her story. Believe me, I had no idea who she was."

"Very revealing. Thankfully we've abandoned those class distinctions in France. Had you known she was one of your own, you would never have—"

The words were cut off at the sudden blaze of Devon's blue eyes that warned him against a further defamation of character.

"She's always used her mother's name," Jean said, realizing he'd overstepped the boundaries he had tacitly agreed to. "Her mother was French, one of the old families. Despite the name's aristocratic associations, Julie found it better for her work here."

"Perhaps because it wasn't familiar to the Englishmen who frequented these rooms."

"The event that drove her father from London is a very old scandal," the Frenchman suggested. "I'm surprised that anyone remembers. Or cares."

"A peer caught cheating the members of his own club?

I should think that would be remembered even in Paris.'' Devon said and saw the quick amusement.

"Certainly a brief notoriety, *even* in Paris,'' Jean admitted. ''But a twenty-five-year-old story about a minor aristocrat would hardly be *au courant* in France. You were only a child when it happened, and yet you recognized the name immediately.''

"I told you. Ashford was a friend of my father's. I heard the stories about my father's friend as I grew up. But my father never discussed the incident at all.''

Realizing fully, perhaps, what, in his anger, he had forced the Englishman to do, Jean spoke aloud the question Devon had already begun considering.

"And what will your father say about your marriage to the Viscount Ashford's daughter?''

The blue eyes glanced up, and Devon smiled at the Frenchman for the first time since their encounter had begun.

"I think I'll worry about that after I've secured the lady's acceptance. Do you know where I can find Julie?''

"If I did, I wouldn't tell you. But I'm beginning to believe you were telling the truth. And if so, then there's really no need for that very gallant sacrifice,'' Jean mocked. ''I think for Julie's sake it would be better if you left her in my protection. In view of the scene I interrupted, yours seems to be suspect.''

"And I really don't think that your opinion of what lies between Julie and me is going to affect what I think is necessary.''

"Necessary?'' Jean broke in, his tone biting. ''But that, my English nobleman, is exactly what I object to. You'd marry Julie because you consider it necessary to satisfy your ideas of honor and the image you have of your own nobility. And I think that she deserves more than a husband who will wallow in his self-sacrifice and never let her forget what he gave up for her sake.''

"A husband—such as you?'' Devon questioned, smiling.

"I think I'm beginning to understand your objections here. You want her for yourself."

"I want what's best for Julie," Jean argued. "I know Julie. I understand what her life has been, and I value her for who and what she is. I want her, but not because of some twisted idea of honor. I think Julie deserves more than that."

"In other words, you think what I'm offering isn't good enough," Devon said quietly. "That your motives are somehow more..." He paused, searching for a word that wouldn't denigrate what the scarred gambler wanted to give her, because he had recognized the sincerity of Jean's concern.

"More honest," the Frenchman finished for him.

"You'd be surprised at the honesty of my motives," Devon said. "But whatever they are, I think I have the prior claim. Until Julie refuses my offer."

"And you expect me to wait patiently in the shadows while you convince her that, in taking her to London as your wife, you'll be doing something fine and noble. I'm sorry, but I think you should understand that I intend to do everything in my power to show Julie the worst possible thing she could do is to allow you to marry her out of your noble sense of guilt."

"Then," Devon said finally, "I suppose I should begin my convincing. Are you sure you don't know where I might find her?"

"Go to hell," the Frenchman said softly. "You'll bring her nothing but the bitterness her father lived with. Leave her alone. Go back to London and a world you understand. You know nothing about hers. You'll only hurt her if you stay."

The Englishman didn't answer that accusation because he was afraid there was some logic there. But he had seen the hunger that had briefly flared in Julie's eyes when he'd asked her to marry him. And in spite of what the Frenchman thought, there had been no self-sacrifice in his proposal. On the contrary, for once in his life, Devon had done exactly what he had wanted to do, with no considerations for his family, his honor or his country.

Devon nodded slowly, not in agreement with what Jean had said, but in acknowledgment of the conditions. And then he turned and left the room.

Behind him the shadowed salon was silent. Finally the man standing there alone flicked one of the cards Julie had left on the table, and under his expert fingers it turned to lie mockingly, face up, revealing the king of hearts. And the laughter that echoed under the high ceiling and bounced back from the empty spaces was bitter.

Jean found Julie a short time later where he had known she would take refuge, in the small room she had long ago claimed as her domain in the vast maze of salons and private parlors that occupied the lower floor of the casino. She was sitting at the elegant secretary where she had once placed the orders for the choice delicacies and the fine wax candles and the expensive sea coal used to fill the huge fireplaces— all the details that were necessary to run the successful business she'd directed for the last three years.

He entered quietly and stood a moment watching her. Although she was certainly aware he was there, she made no acknowledgment of his presence. The anger she had expressed over his interference was no longer apparent in the small body. She sat, lowered head resting in both palms.

"Surely you're not grieving over rejecting that sanctimonious *aristo's* proposal. Did you really want to trail him to London, kissing his hands in gratitude every day, properly humble because he was honorable enough to marry you despite your father's fatal mistake?" His voice was as mockingly sardonic as it had been downstairs.

"He's not an aristocrat," she answered. But she had known, despite his denial of a title, that Devon was.

"Oh, God, Julie, of course, he is. You've dealt with

enough London fops to recognize one by scent alone. He fairly reeks of wealth and position.''

''He's a soldier.''

Jean's laugh was short and pointed. ''And so is Wellington, who is also an English nobleman, as are most of his officers. Do you imagine your nobleman as a recruit? That arrogance brooks no impudence from the rank and file. He's accustomed to command, all right. Probably staff. Christened with enough names to choke his own charger and related to half the peerage. No matter what he told you, that noble air is too inbred to hide.''

''It doesn't matter. Whatever he is, he's beyond my reach, and I know it.''

''But what matters is that, clearly, you want him,'' Jean said, his amusement evident. ''Buy a hair shirt. It's cheaper. And when you've had enough pain, at least you'll be able to take it off. Unlike matrimony with your nobleman who'll require a permanent penance for who you are.''

''You *are* a bastard,'' she accused bitterly, still without raising her head.

''Of course,'' he agreed, laughing. ''I thought I'd told you. My mother professed to have had no idea—''

''Why must you mock every human emotion, everything that's fine and decent and noble?'' she asked, her eyes raised in fury to meet his, her voice echoing the contempt he had earlier instilled in the word ''noble.''

''Perhaps because I am none of those things,'' he said, relieved to see that flash of fire back in her dark eyes. He moved to prop himself gracefully against the edge of the desk at which she was sitting, looking down on her. ''Or because I've come to believe that most of the people who profess to possess those qualities are hypocrites. As he is. Surely, Julie, you don't think there are still knights on white chargers waiting to ride to your rescue. As you told me, you're a little old for fairy tales.''

''I'm a little old for everything. But that doesn't mean

that I can't believe there are still good and honorable people in the world.''

"And the man I just found putting his lascivious mouth on your body? Do you classify him as good? Somehow that wasn't my impression. But then I have been, perhaps, more disillusioned by my past than you. I had always thought you understood the ways of the world. That you and I were alike in that,'' he finished gently, inviting her to remember the rapport they had once shared.

Her eyes searched his face, and he allowed their scrutiny, although she knew his inclination would be to turn away, to hide, as always, the damaged profile from the interested or horrified stares it evoked. But Julie had seen his scars, at least the external version, for years, and so he endured her gaze.

"I know,'' she whispered finally and touched the small smudge of dried blood in the corner of his mouth, the only physical evidence remaining of her anger. "I know that we are. That you and I are alike. But he's not what you believe. He's like my father. Surely, Jean, you can't deny my father's standards were unusual in our world. He—''

"He cheated his London friends at cards and then spent the rest of his life trying to make up for it. He raised his only daughter in an environment most men of his class would never have permitted their women to know about, much less participate in. And he did that because he was selfish enough to want the support of your love, your daily presence. He apparently also worked to defeat his adopted country, spied on the nation that had taken him in when his own had kicked him out, had exiled him because of that very nobility you're now so enamored of. Do you want to know why your father became the bitter old man he was? Look at your hero if you want to see the cause of your father's heartbreak.''

"Then if you believe Devon is the villain you've just painted him, why would you make the ridiculous suggestion that he marry me?'' she asked, and again he could hear the bitterness that underlay her question.

"Because... God, Julie, I don't even know any more what I felt when I walked in and found him making love to you," he said harshly.

"Jean," she protested, and he interrupted, knowing what she was about to say.

"All right," he acknowledged. "You tell me that nothing has happened between you, and I believe you. But I was so—I don't know. Furious. Jealous," he suggested finally, and her brown eyes widened at the word.

"Jealous?" she echoed, unbelieving.

The unscarred side of his mouth moved suddenly, the ability to mock himself undiminished by the real feelings he had for her.

"Ironic, isn't it? Especially after the lecture I just read you. But I had always believed, had at least hoped, if anyone could succeed in melting the cynicism that has encased your heart in ice, that I would be that someone. I waited so long. And then I walked in here today, after weeks of searching for you, and find you in the arms of another man, apparently enjoying his lovemaking."

Her face, when he glanced down to read her reaction, was very still, but her eyes held no trace of amusement or disbelief.

"Then why..." she whispered.

"Why would I demand that he marry you? Because I thought he'd refuse, and you'd see him for what he was."

"And if he had?" she questioned, and he smiled at her before he answered.

"Then I thought you'd realize there is someone else who loves you. I know the idea of taking your place in London society at the side of a man who has a right to be there is far more romantic than the thought of living with a scarred bastard who was raised in the stews of Paris and has known nothing of that nobility you seem to admire. I know that

I'm no woman's image of a white knight, especially someone as idealistic as you.''

"Idealistic," she repeated, laughing. "Of all the terms anyone has ever applied to me, that—''

"—is the one the person who knows you best in all the world would choose," he said softly. "I just hope, Julie, that when you eventually decide you're going to survive this infatuation with that very noble Englishman, you'll think differently about someone who has loved you for a long time. Someone who will accept you with no caveats or restrictions on who you are or on the woman you will eventually become.''

Finally she smiled at him. "And when I decide I'm over that infatuation," she invited softly, "what do you suggest?''

"I had thought," he said speculatively, a slight smile hovering over his lips, "a small and very select card room...''

"Perhaps somewhere near the Palais Royale," she pretended to muse, "very exclusive, only the most *noble* clientele. Is that what you had in mind?" she asked, smiling at him.

"Exactly. When you're ready, I'll order the wine, my darling," Jean promised softly, the only endearment he had ever used to her, "and deal the first hand.''

Chapter Eight

When Jean had willingly allowed himself to be dispatched to care for the horses and to buy in the nearby Les Halles market the provisions they would need to remain safe in the midst of their enemies, Julie decided she'd hidden long enough. Devon would eventually have to be faced, and the proposal Jean had forced him to make would have to be answered.

Remembering the gambler's carefully worded avowal of his feelings, she knew that she was better prepared for that ordeal than before Jean had sought her out. Again he had provided support. Not the protective cotton wool Devon seemed to feel her situation called for, but a reassurance of his willingness to stand behind whatever decisions she made. And so, taking a deep breath, she left the sanctuary of her private office and returned to the main salon where she knew Devon would eventually find her.

She automatically began to gather the cards she'd left scattered on the surface of the table, scarcely noticing the upturned king of hearts. When she realized what she was doing, she stacked the deck and left it. She walked across the salon and into the dimness of her father's office where Devon had looked for some trace of information that would help him find his friend. The afternoon sun was filtered by the heavy draperies, and the resulting gloom softened somewhat the impact of entering the room where she had spent so many happy hours.

She thought again about the judgments Jean had made of her father's actions, ideas she had never even considered. She knew she had blindly accepted that what her father had done was right, accepted those decisions because he was her father and because she loved him. But she wondered what her life would have been had he left her with the nuns. Would it then have been possible, as clearly it now would never be, to have what she wanted? As if conjured by her thoughts of him, she heard Devon's voice from the doorway.

"I think we need to talk," he said simply, walking across the small room to stand before her. He was somehow relieved to find no trace of tears, despite the emotional scene in the salon. He thought he understood something of what, between them, he and Jean had done to her.

"I know," she said softly.

"Somehow, when I finally asked a woman to marry me, I didn't expect it would occasion flight. Is the thought of marrying me that terrifying?" he asked, smiling slightly.

She allowed her eyes to rest on his face a moment before she replied.

"I should think it would be the other way around," she said softly.

"And I had thought you'd decided that I'm really not a rake. I don't offer for women I'd be terrified to marry. You're beautiful and brave, intelligent—"

"And I deal faro and vingt-et-un in the most notorious gaming house in Paris. I wonder how your family would respond to your bringing home a wife with those credentials."

"I think I'm old enough that I don't need my family's approval of the woman I choose to marry. I asked you to marry me, Julie, and I'm still waiting for an answer," he said.

When he had met her tear-glazed eyes, he had known that his proposal had been a matter of his emotions and not his honor—emotions he had fought throughout their journey to Paris. And he was tired of denying what he wanted. During the last two years, he had certainly been shown that life was too precious to allow conventions to stand in the way of living.

Caring for Julie was, he had realized sometime in the difficulties of the last week, exactly what he wanted to spend the remainder of his life doing. Something in the French-man's calm assertion that he would be better able to make her happy had made Devon grimly determined to prove that allegation wrong. Given the chance, he had no doubt he could ensure her happiness. Her responsiveness to his touch had shown him that she was as emotionally involved as he

Her hand lifted involuntarily, wondering what he was thinking, and the slender fingers touched the bruise that was already beginning to darken the side of his mouth. When she felt his smile move against her sensitive fingertips, she forced her hand to drop.

"And old enough, I think, to know what would happen if I said yes." She added reality to his list. "I've known no other life than the one I've led in these rooms, but I saw what exile from his world did to my father. I couldn't do that to you, Dev. Even if I thought this sudden desire for my hand was prompted by anything other than your mis-guided nobility."

"My nobility," he said mockingly and shook his head. "That wasn't nobility between us in the salon today. You know better than that, Lady Luck. And I'm not really con-cerned about my family's approval of whomever I marry. They would be the first to support my right to make that decision."

"Because?" she asked, trying to read what was hidden in his tone.

He shook his head again. "Marry me," he said, smiling invitingly, "and I'll reveal all my family secrets."

"And all your own?" she asked, cherishing his slow smile.

He was a man who didn't undertake promises easily or make oaths without considering the costs.

But he pledged finally, "And all my own."

It was a vow whose implications she recognized and valued.

She wanted what he offered, all that it represented, and most of all, of course, she wanted him. She fought to keep her fingers locked around the fold of yellow muslin they had found, fought to keep them from touching again the bruised mouth or the faint lines that fanned from the corners of the dark blue eyes.

"And would your sister, who calls you Dev, welcome me into your family?"

"Of course," he said easily, but somewhere in the back of his mind a faint whisper of doubt about Emily's reaction stirred.

"And your brother-in-law, the Duke of Avon? Will he take me to court on his arm?" she questioned.

"He'll adore you," he assured softly, knowing Dominic's abilities too well to doubt his recognition of her quality.

"And perhaps I can open a small card room, something very private and exclusive. For your friends and his?" she suggested, thinking of Jean's response to that same proposal. But instead of the support the Frenchman had offered, she saw the faint crease grow between his brows.

"Julie," he began doubtfully and realized from her eyes that he had walked into the trap she'd deliberately set. He cleared the question from his voice and said, laughing, "Won't that take a lot of money? Remember you're marrying a simple half-pay soldier. Not even a minor title."

"I can imagine the titles your friends would bestow on you if you were foolish enough to marry me, Dev. I wonder how many faces I'd meet across the dinner tables of London that I've faced across the gaming tables of Paris. And I wonder how many of them you'd be forced to meet on some deserted field at dawn to protect my honor," she said, and saw a pained reaction to her words move across his carefully controlled features.

"Think," she demanded forcefully, knowing her arguments were having some effect. "Think what you're suggesting and what it will mean to your life. I can't live with you in London, and with Bonaparte's return, I don't think you want to live here in Paris. Venice, perhaps, or Florence?" she suggested, imagining how he would hate the separation from his country and his family. "Think, Dev, if you want that exile. That loss of who and what you are. The loss, perhaps, of everyone and everything you love."

She waited. His lips tightened, and she saw him swallow, the movement too strong and sudden. And then the blue eyes were smiling again, their serenity unbroken.

"You haven't answered my question, Julie. Will you marry me?" he asked calmly, as if she had never spoken. She could see none of the images she had sought to create in the lucid blue.

"No, Dev," she whispered, and finally she allowed her hand to touch his cheek. "I won't marry you, but I will never forget that you asked me. I'll never, ever, my beautiful soldier knight, forget that you asked."

She watched his lips tighten and the blue eyes drop before hers. But she had always known that he wanted her. She had had no doubt from the first about the sexual attraction that had flowed between them. But he'd said nothing about love. *"The woman I loved…"* Perhaps he was still in love with that woman. She'd never know. She only knew that she couldn't marry him. Marriage to him would be exactly what Jean had said. A hair shirt of punishment. His in answering the slights made because of what she had been, and hers because of what that would eventually do to him. It would be better, then, that nothing come of what they both felt, rather than that pain.

"And I think that perhaps your gambler friend found you first," he said, and she looked up from her regret to find his eyes calmly searching her face.

"Jean?" she questioned softly, lost with the sudden shift of subject. She couldn't know of the antagonistic understanding the two men had reached regarding their very different plans for her future.

"We talked. He knew where I'd be," she explained. "Where I always go to hide, to think."

Her words revealed something of their shared history, an affirmation of their closeness that Devon would rather not have heard. He found himself wondering suddenly about their relationship. He blocked the thought of whatever might have happened between them in the past. In that way, too, lay madness. A particularly dangerous insanity for their situation.

If he accepted his love for Julie, it would have to be with a blindness for whatever romantic liaisons her past contained. Or the Frenchman would be right. If he couldn't control the images of someone else's possession of her before he had entered her life, then he had no right to seek to make her his. He would only end up punishing them both. But because his inner strength was very great, having been tempered in fires of self-examination that few men are ever forced to confront, he buried that question and smiled at her.

"Then apparently he's had an opportunity to produce some compelling arguments against your acceptance of my proposal," he said. His comment invited her confidence or her assurance that nothing important had been said between them. He could tell by the slight flush that spread upward from her throat that she wouldn't be able to offer that comfort.

"I see," he said finally as she allowed the silence to grow. "Somehow I think I prefer his assessments of my character be made in my presence. And I don't like the idea of your discussing my suit with someone who's made it clear he considers me obligated to marry you, but at the same time unworthy to touch the tips of your fingers."

"We weren't discussing *your* suit," Julie answered softly, her emphasis clear.

"And was he more successful in pleading his cause than I've been?"

"No, but Dev, you don't understand—"

Her voice cut off in unconscious appeal, and he waited a long time for her to go on. Finally his grim expression softened.

"Do you realize how much you've been asked to deal with in the last few weeks? Your father's death, your flight and its dangers, my rather clumsy attempt to offer you both the protection of my name and my physical protection from Fouché. And now, apparently a counterproposal from someone who has known you far longer than I," he said, trying for a lighter tone than the deep disappointment he felt. "But I want you to remember you don't have to make any decisions you're not prepared to make. I'm not going to push you into anything, Julie. I hope you won't allow your friend to, either."

Listening to that quiet commitment, she knew, despite the proposal she had just received from someone far more knowledgeable about who and what she was, that she had not mistaken her feelings for this man.

"Dev," she said softly, "could we go back to the way things were before, to whatever there was between us before Jean came? I want what we felt then. Not what he's blackmailed you into offering out of your sense of honor."

"You'd be surprised at my motives in offering for you, Lady Luck. I was rather caught off guard by them myself," he admitted softly. "But I think you're right. Perhaps what you need now is the assurance that you can count again on my self-control. And as soon as I've told you that exercising that control is going to be the most difficult task I've undertaken in some time, I'll begin. And I think this time..." he said, holding out his hand.

She looked down at the outstretched palm, the red line of

the Gypsy's knife still clear, and laid her fingers against the scar.

He turned her hand in his and raised it to his lips for a brief kiss.

"Until I find Dominic, my Lady Luck, you're safe from *my* proposals," he promised, stressing the pronoun.

"And do you have a plan for achieving that, now?" She removed her hand to gesture at her father's office.

She was sorry she had asked when he shook his head, his lips tight with frustration.

"I didn't believe I'd simply come into France and find Avon's agents ready to help me locate him. Nor did I think I could just walk out of a hostile country with Dominic in tow, but I did hope there would be something or someone remaining that might offer a clue. It's as if the duke and his network have simply disappeared."

This time they both heard the footsteps crossing the salon. Devon turned so that his body was between Julie and whoever was approaching through the vast room beyond the office.

"It's Jean," she said, brushing by him to prevent any more of the hostility that had been so evident between them when she had fled upstairs.

Devon watched her walk quickly to meet her friend and felt a sudden jolt of anger at the thought of her rushing to greet the Frenchman. Jealousy, he admitted, mocking himself, but he didn't bother to deny the validity of his identification of the emotion that was tightening his stomach muscles.

"Dev, come and eat," she called, her voice coming from the shadowed passage that led to the kitchen.

He took a deep breath to banish the possessiveness, which he acknowledged could destroy any chance of happiness between himself and Julie. He realized he had been gripping the frame of the door so hard that its ridges were still clear on his fingers when he removed them. He looked at those marks a long time, and then, obeying Julie's suggestion, he forced himself to walk across the wide salon to join them in the shuttered kitchens.

He found Julie unpacking supplies on the huge cook's table. He didn't even glance at the man who stood leaning against the wall, also watching her.

"Jean's brought enough so we won't have to venture out again for a few days. We may not enjoy a wide variety, but at least we won't go hungry. You know I can't cook," she said, looking up at him from under those impossibly long lashes.

"I can," he said, smiling at her confession, and he knew she was remembering, as he was, the simple meals they had shared on their journey. "I don't think, however, that building a fire would be a very wise move on our part."

"I agree," said Jean. "That's why there's nothing there that requires cooking. I suggest that we eat the meat pies first and save the less perishable items for later."

"Of course," she said and held one of the still-warm pastries out to him.

When he had accepted it, she unthinkingly licked the gravy off her fingers and lifted another pie from its wrappings to hand to Devon. When she realized that she was holding this pie in the same fingers she had just delicately cleaned with her tongue, she pulled back the offering just as his hand reached for it.

"I'm sorry," she said, embarrassed by her lapse of manners in front of him, conscious that she had forgotten to maintain the social niceties with this man with whom she had lived so intimately.

The corners of his mouth moved in quick amusement, and his brow quirked in question.

"I don't think you need be so concerned about your fingers. After all…" he suggested, daring her to remember that her tongue itself had only recently caressed his mouth.

But she, at least, was very conscious of the man who had stood watching throughout the exchange.

Devon took the pastry she held out to him, and then with

his other hand he quickly captured her fingers, licking the pie's juices from them, all the while holding her eyes with his.

She was fascinated by the texture of his tongue against her skin for a heartbeat, and then her fingers struggled, demanding freedom, and he released her. Her knees were weak, and there was a peculiar sensation in the pit of her stomach, but she turned and found the third of the pastries in the grease-stained paper.

She didn't look at Devon again, and finally she heard him move to prop one hip casually on the top of the table while he ate.

"Devon," she said finally to break the oppressive silence, "Jean thinks that you were right. There seems to be no one watching the casino. Apparently Fouché—"

"Devon?" Jean's voice questioned harshly, shockingly forceful in contrast to her casual comment.

Two sets of eyes, velvet brown and hard blue, locked on his face.

"Devon?" he asked again, more softly but with more meaning than the first startled response to the use of the Englishman's full name. "Is that a common name in England?"

Julie's eyes flew to the narrowed blue gaze that seemed to be searching the question for any hidden aspects.

"No," Devon admitted at last. "I was named for my mother's family estate. It's not really a proper Christian name at all, not one that I've ever—"

"Devon," the Frenchman said again, smiling. "And did you really come from the pits of hell?" he asked, the mockery full and derisive in the soft question.

"Jean," Julie whispered, shocked by what he had asked. She hadn't understood the comment she took to be an insult, but she saw Devon's face drain suddenly of color and the pupils widen, a contrast to the diminishing ring of cobalt surrounding them.

He never stopped to consider what he might be revealing.

He was too relieved to consider the consequences of letting this man, whose convenient appearance had already made him suspicious, know more than he apparently already did.

"Where is he?" Devon asked dangerously, and watched the smile that lifted only the undamaged side of the Frenchman's lips. "Where the hell is the man who told you that?"

"But he didn't tell me, *mon ami*. I was simply in a position to overhear his delirious ravings. Your name and that phrase repeated over and over."

Julie wondered how someone could move as quickly as Devon did then. He was across the space that had separated him from the Frenchman and was holding Jean's wrist almost before her eyes had registered the motion.

She watched Jean's eye move from an unintimidated confrontation with the furious blue ones to rest pointedly on the fingers that held him captive. Eventually Devon released his grip, and she saw his struggle to regain the control that had, at the Frenchman's words, deserted him. He stepped back, allowing a less threatening space to open between them, and waited until the flush had died from the high cheekbones of his adversary before he spoke again.

"The man you just spoke of," he said quietly, exercising an enormous force of will to modulate his tone, "is my friend. And I owe him more than my life. I'm sorry for what I just did, but I have to know what you can tell me about him. You said he was delirious?" he asked, feigning a calmness he didn't possess and waited again.

"And what would you give for the information you seek?" the equally restrained voice asked.

"Anything," Devon answered without hesitation. "I told you. I owe him more than my life. I'll give you anything you want—anything I have."

The scarred lips lifted in the bitter, one-sided smile, and the tone of the answer made the girl listening shiver suddenly.

"Julie," he said simply, and at first she thought he was speaking to her. But then he finished with even darker malice coloring his words. "Will you give me Julie in exchange for your friend?"

"No," she whispered and was forced to clear her throat against the sudden constriction. She didn't want to hear whatever answer Devon might have made. "No," she repeated, louder than before, and they both turned to her. "He doesn't have me to give, Jean. I control my own fate. I'm not a stake to be fought over. You tell him or not, but don't bring me into whatever you're doing here. I won't be a party to this."

Jean looked at the pale face a moment. Some of the tension seemed to leave his body and he, too, stepped back, widening the distance between them.

"Your friend was Fouché's prisoner. He was being held in the Luxembourg Palace. After the raid on the casino, I was briefly incarcerated in the same cell, held for questioning because I worked for Julie's father and was therefore suspect. That's all I can tell you. Except that, if you're planning to try to liberate that man, I will warn you you'll never succeed. You'll never get him out of France, or even out of that building, alive. And I'm urging you not to try. You can't beat Fouché, not alone and not with the odds all in his favor. And not given the condition of your friend. Go home and forget him. Your friend is beyond your help. Beyond anyone's help. And you might as well accept that."

The blue eyes considered the sincerity that rang in the quiet voice. Julie was holding her breath and didn't realize it until she watched the slow smile break the rigid control Devon had forced over his features.

"In the pits of hell?" he asked quietly. "Is that where you're suggesting Dominic is? But, my friend, I've already been there," Devon said truthfully. "And returned. Thanks to Dominic. And nothing you can say will make me leave him in Fouché's hands. And whatever I choose to do with the information you provided is surely, after all, my choice." He waited for his opponent to absorb that idea, and then he finished softly, "Will you tell me about my friend?"

The Frenchman stood still, held by the surety of that calm voice, which Julie had seen affect all those with whom they had yet come in contact. And then, almost imperceptibly, he nodded.

Jean's story was told without embellishment, and most of it could have been predicted by the other two based on their experiences in avoiding Fouché's reach. He had left the casino the night Julie's father had died, his sense of danger too well-honed to think he would get away unscathed by whatever was happening. He had disappeared during the aftermath that followed the agents' break-in and the patrons' shocked response to gunfire in the middle of a peaceful night in this well-run establishment.

"My first thoughts were of getting you out, Julie, before you could be taken for questioning, but you weren't here. You'd disappeared. I watched the casino for several days, and there was still no sign of you."

"My father told me to leave Paris, but we hadn't had time to discuss where or how. He only had time to issue the warning and then to give me money. Enough for several weeks, but it eventually began to run out."

"And then you met Devon?" he probed.

"No," she answered, laughing. "Then I became a boy."

"A boy?" he questioned, considering the vision of femininity she presented in her fashionable gown.

"A very believable boy," she said lightly. "I have it on the best authority."

Her eyes rested teasingly on Devon's face, and it was obvious that she was reminding him of some shared memory. That thought was enough to cause a strong surge of jealousy in the Frenchman.

"But why?" he asked.

"It seemed safest. And I thought no one would expect it of me," she explained.

"No wonder I had no luck in finding you," he said. "I'm looking for the most beautiful woman in Paris, and she's pretending to be a boy. Pardon me, *petite,* but in spite of your friend's assessment, I personally can't imagine you in that guise."

"If you had seen the dirt under her nails and had smelled…" Devon began. It was the first time he had spoken since he had demanded the Frenchman's story, and Julie was glad the darkness of his vow was gone from his voice.

"I beg your pardon," she interrupted in response to his description. "I assure you I did not smell. I was a very clean urchin, at least below the surface dirt I carefully applied."

"Your hair smelled of flowers," he said softly, remembering. "That was the first indication I had that the child I had just stolen from his enemies was something other than he appeared."

"And the second indication?" Laughing, she invited him to confess.

"The second was perhaps a certain *je ne sais quoi*—a certain echo of womanliness," he finished, smiling.

"That's not—" she began, still smiling at his reluctance to admit what he really meant.

"We seemed to have strayed from the point," the Frenchman interrupted bitingly, aware again of the teasing intimacy of the verbal exchanges between his companions. "Or are you no longer interested in the whereabouts of your friend?"

"Did it appear to you that my interest had waned? If so, I assure you, you're mistaken," Devon said quietly, his eyes no longer on the girl's face. Instead they rested with somewhat bitter inquiry on the scarred countenance of the man who had just spoken. "I await the point in your narrative at which you arrived in Fouché's prison with much anticipation, I promise you."

Jean's mouth tightened slightly in anger, and then his control was reimposed. However, that icy discipline didn't prevent his longing to see the Englishman stretched out at his feet, the victim once more of a fist that was itching to wipe out the polite boredom, which was the only emotion the handsome features now displayed.

"I came back to the casino finally because I had nowhere else to look. I had exhausted every acquaintance of yours I knew and had asked as many questions as I dared. I was afraid that my search might direct theirs to wherever you were so successfully hiding. But then I made the mistake of entering this building, and of course they were watching. They took me to Fouché, but since I was not who they'd been waiting for, they seemed unsure what to do with me. They knew I'd worked for your father, which naturally made them suspicious of my activities. But their questioning was cursory, if rather painful. And then they threw me into a cell, a cell occupied by what appeared to be a still-breathing corpse."

He stopped at the strength of that memory. As cynical as he imagined himself to be, he had been affected by his encounter with the man in that cell. But it would be impossible for him to admit that.

"And?" Devon prompted, wondering at the look in the hazel eye, a look he had not seen before in his rather hostile dealings with this man. But with his question, the emotion, whatever it had been, cleared, and Jean went on with his story.

"He was in high fever, suffering from what appeared to be an inflammation of the lungs. And he was delirious. I honestly doubted that he would live out the night. I found out later that Fouché, only a few hours before, had him brought from the dungeon. Apparently he'd changed his mind about letting him die. But he cut it close." His voice fell almost to a whisper as he repeated, "Damn close."

There was a long silence at the unexpectedness of the feelings revealed in that whisper, and then the Frenchman seemed to shake off the memories of that experience.

"What had they done to him?" Devon asked, knowing that if he were to be successful in freeing Avon, he had to understand what he would be dealing with. And in light of Jean's earlier warning, he had to know Avon's physical condition.

"They'd inflicted some damage, apparently, in the capture. They'd taken him in the street outside the casino. Obviously, they'd been waiting for him to contact your father. He fought them. He recalled a blow to the head and something—" he stopped and looked at Devon's carefully controlled face "—some injury to his leg. I don't know what kind of damage because I have no idea what it was like before, but…" Again he paused, and the slight shudder was involuntary.

"Go on," Devon said, his voice rigidly emotionless.

"Fouché used cold water to bring him around during the interrogation, and his clothing was soaked. Then they threw him into that hole," he said, looking up suddenly.

"And?" Devon prompted softly.

"They fed him. At least they put food in the cell and he crawled to it. As long as he was able to crawl. I don't know how he'd stayed alive as long as he had. Sheer force of will, perhaps."

"Yes," Devon said again, his voice even softer than before.

"And the thought of someone named Devon who had promised to come from the pits of hell," Jean finished his story, watching the face of the man who knew better than he the meaning of that determination. "And you are that man?"

"Yes," Devon admitted, "and knowing what you've just told me, you still think I should leave. You believe I should let him remain in the hands of the man who arranged that imprisonment. Do you know who Fouché's prisoner is?" he asked suddenly, hoping to catch the Frenchman off guard, to surprise information from him in the midst of what appeared to be honest emotion.

"No," he said simply, and a remembered amusement lightened his voice. "He told me it was dangerous to know him. I assumed, because they had questioned me about espionage for the English, he was involved in that. Especially when I learned Fouché had stationed a guard outside the cell we occupied in hopes he might overhear something that would link me to his prisoner. They knew we were both connected to the casino, and they hoped I'd reveal something that would allow them to hold me. Luckily for me, Fouché's listener was disappointed. And to give him credit, your friend warned me, as soon as he was able, about what Fouché was doing. I'm afraid it had never crossed my mind he might have had ulterior motives in placing me in that particular cell.''

"And then they let you go? Are you trying to tell me they released you with no more assurance that you were not involved in the passing on of information to the English, than a lack of conversation? Frankly, I find that very hard to believe.''

"And I really don't care whether you believe it or not. By that time, I think Fouché had other things besides external enemies to consider. The Emperor had returned, and Fouché might have simply lost interest in your friend. But since you are far more knowledgeable about my cellmate's importance to your government than I am, you're the better judge of that. He certainly lost interest in me. I was released after little more than two weeks' internment. I didn't question my good luck. And I don't care if you do. I was happy enough to leave his hospitality. But I don't think your friend will be as lucky.''

"No,'' Devon said, shaking his head. "Fouché knows very well—''

The words were cut off when Devon realized he'd been thinking out loud. He didn't trust this Frenchman. He wasn't sure how much Jean knew and how much he had surmised from Avon's delirium. Either way, Devon didn't intend to add to his knowledge.

So he asked instead, "Who had access to his cell? Who entered it each day? Who has freedom of movement within the prison? Guards, officials, anyone else?'' He halted the running questions as the other man simply shook his head and continued to shake it in response.

"No one. The guards slid the food each day through a slot in the door. No one entered. Not in the entire time I was there, except—''

Devon smiled in satisfaction as the significance of Jean's sudden pause was clear to all of them.

"Who?'' he asked softly. And at the continued hesitation, he said again, "Who? You obviously thought of someone who was allowed to enter.''

"A doctor,'' Jean answered, his disdain clear. "Some pompous, arrogant poltroon who tried to bleed him.''

"To bleed him,'' Julie repeated in disbelief. "I should have thought that would be the last thing a man in his condition would need.''

"Yes.'' Jean smiled at her. "So did I. I'm afraid I rejected his professional services,'' Jean admitted grimly.

"Then you probably saved Dominic's life,'' Devon said quietly. "And for that alone, I'm in your debt.''

"What I did for your friend I would have done for anyone. I don't want your gratitude or your friendship. Save it for your hopeless mission.''

"Why hopeless?'' Devon answered easily, ignoring the hostility. "Now that you've just given me a way to get in. Another doctor, a repeat visit.''

"And if Fouché has already sent another physician? Or if your friend has staged a remarkable recovery, although I can't tell you, given his condition when I left two days ago, how remarkable that recovery would be. Or perhaps, by now, he has instead—''

"No,'' the Englishman interrupted, "and you don't believe that, either. He's waiting. Just as he survived in that hell Fouché put him through, Dominic will be gathering his reserves of strength and waiting for me because he knows that I'm coming. There is not now, nor has there ever been, the least doubt in his mind as to that fact.''

"You're a fool," the Frenchman said softly. "You'll never get him out. For one thing, he's in no condition to walk out, and they certainly aren't going to stand by and watch you carry someone out, no matter what role you're playing. Even the guards aren't that stupid."

"I won't have to carry Dominic out. He'll do it. Don't doubt what he's capable of. I should think that even a brief meeting with him would have convinced you of that."

"You haven't seen him. You can't imagine—"

"But I know him. He'll walk out. All we have to do is come up with the plan that will give him that opportunity."

"All right," Jean said abruptly. "Even if I grant you his physical ability to leave his cell, what makes you think you can get him past the guards? Don't you believe someone will recognize that the man who's walking past them is the prisoner they've guarded so long?"

"But you just said that no one ever entered the cell. The guards carried an unconscious, delirious body upstairs. Not a man. It's a chance we have to take. And the guards aren't hired for their intellect."

"If he's important to Fouché, and only you know how important he might be," the Frenchman argued, "then our friend won't be careless enough to allow you to walk out with him. No matter how distracted he is with Napoleon's return."

"Jean, I want your help in getting Devon's friend out of prison," Julie said, and they both turned to her in surprise. She had been so quiet throughout the last part of the discussion that they had almost forgotten her presence. "You have more information than we about the conditions under which he's being held. Your assistance can be invaluable."

One corner of the scarred mouth lifted in the familiar mocking smile as he asked, "And why should I do that, *petite?* Because you wish it? Do you think that's enough reason to convince me to help a man I don't like?"

"No," she answered softly, rejecting his cynicism. "I expect you to help a man whom you clearly admire. A man who is still suffering in Fouché's hands. I'm going to help because Fouché was responsible for my father's death, and you're going to help because that man's life came to mean something to you. That was evident in your voice when you told that gruesome story. You left him in better condition than you found him in because you took care of him. And I know you well enough to fill in the parts of the narrative you deliberately left untold. You stopped the doctor, and then you accepted the responsibility for the life you'd saved. You're going to help Devon rescue him because you couldn't prevent yourself if you tried. We are too much alike to hide our feelings from one another.''

"You think you know me so well," Jean said, his voice caressing. "I wonder what it would take to surprise you."

"Only the thought that you could let someone die out of jealousy or anger. That would truly surprise me," she said.

"I hope you're not endowing me with the noble sentiments you believe you see in your own rescuer. I'm not your knight, *petite*. And I never will be.''

She studied the saturnine features, familiar and well-loved, before she answered. "But I never wanted a knight. However, I do want your help. And I think you have all the attributes necessary to play this role. It doesn't call for nobility at all. Only a certain single-minded determination and a great deal of shrewdness. Those qualities you have in abundance. And unlike us, Devon lacks certain skills. Skills like thimblerig, which make people think they see one thing when in reality…'' She stopped, knowing that he understood what she was suggesting. "He needs our help. And I need yours. It really is a very simple choice."

"Then if this is what you desire, my love, I shall be delighted to help your white knight. How could you ever doubt it?"

"I never did," she said and smiled at him.

The Frenchman's voice had been light, but something had underlain the amusement, something dark and haunted. Again Devon felt the apprehension he had had from the first moment he had learned about Avon's mission. However, he was too relieved by Jean's agreement to endanger that co-operation by any questions. He'd let Julie deal with her admirer. And he would stand by, for Avon's sake, and grit his teeth while she did.

Chapter Nine

The plan they finally devised was simple. Devon would enter the prison posing as a doctor and, using Jean's directions, go to the cell where Dominic had been held. They hoped that his assurance in finding the place would, in itself, be convincing as to his right to be there.

"The passage from this entrance leads straight to the few remaining cells. It's a busy corridor, used by people in the building who have no connection to the prison. You'll probably be challenged somewhere between your entry into the building and the cell. The more unconcerned you are about answering those questions in any detail, the better. Your attitude should be, how dare these peasants ask a man of my learning and position his business. Use Fouché's name. You have nothing to lose by showing them contempt. If they doubt you enough to check, it's already too late."

"I can't believe you think you can just walk in," Julie argued as she had for the last twenty minutes. They planned no diversion, no attempt to occupy the guards' attention. A straight bluff that, gambler though she was, she couldn't believe would succeed.

"This isn't the Conciergerie. There," Jean said, shaking his head, "there is a real prison. With a lot of experience at keeping its prisoners and foiling escapes. This would never work in that atmosphere. Luxembourg, however, was designed as a royal residence. With the requisite dungeons, to be sure, but the main building itself hasn't been used as a prison in nearly ten years. You're lucky that Fouché wants to keep his affairs secret. We may have a chance at the Luxembourg."

If Jean had been reluctant before, it seemed that once the decision to lend his aid was made, he entered into the planning with every appearance of enthusiasm.

"The key is your ability to overpower the guard who is stationed outside that cell. The door is solid, except for the high grill. If you can get him inside, where you'll be hidden from sight. And if you can manage—" Jean began, and then halted. Having made his evaluation of the Englishman's fighting skills, based on the success of his own surprise assault, he seemed doubtful that Devon would be able to carry off this vital aspect of the scheme.

He looked up from the rough plan of the prison rooms in the Palais du Luxembourg to find a pair of amused blue eyes. A quick drop of lashes hid the expression, but Devon's voice when he answered the implied doubt was calm and absolutely sure.

"He'll come into the cell, and he'll remain there when we leave. Avon dresses in the doctor's clothes and exits, following the route by which I entered. You'll be waiting outside in the hired carriage to drive him to the Gypsy's encampment. In the meantime I change into the clothing concealed in the false bottom of the satchel I'll carry, and leaving the guard unconscious in the cell, make my way out some other entrance as unobtrusively as possible. And I'll ride to meet you at the Romany camp."

"The key..." Jean began again.

"The key is my performance at the prison. But I'm the only one who can do this. And I will do it, despite your doubts. Your face might be recognized, and Julie, while having managed to become a believable boy, is going to fool no one masquerading as a doctor. I understand. And I'll get him out."

"Or become Fouché's prisoner yourself," Julie said softly.

"No," Devon promised, but she wasn't comforted by the smile that accompanied that quiet denial.

"This is your one chance. And his. If you fail…" Jean said.

The Englishman's smile widened slightly, and his eyes rested on the dark, marred face.

"If I fail, then you get what you want, don't you? Or is that what you're hoping for?" he asked quietly.

The eyes of the two men held for a long time, and it was Jean who broke the silence.

"Not that way," he said, and finally the Englishman nodded.

"Then tomorrow," he agreed quietly.

"I'll have to go out again to get the props you'll need and to arrange for the carriage," Jean said.

"And to find a suitable stick," Devon commanded.

"A stick?"

"For Avon. A walking stick. Make sure it's sturdy," Devon instructed. "And Jean," he added as an afterthought, and again the Frenchman waited. "See if you can find one with a silver head." He didn't bother to answer the quizzical look that met his, but he smiled, and the Frenchman shook his head over whatever had prompted that ridiculous request.

Julie followed Jean into the tunneled passage to secure it from the inside and to make the necessary arrangements as to when she should again open the secret entrance for the gambler's return.

It seemed to the man who waited in the kitchen that she took a long time over that task. Devon forced himself to bury the anxiety caused by the minutes she was spending alone with a man who had also offered for her hand. The sooner he removed Julie from the influence of that dark gambler, the better he'd like it. But until they had rescued

Avon, he knew he'd have to be patient and trust her not to be swayed by the Frenchman's arguments. But that didn't mean he had to enjoy exercising that patience.

He glanced up to find Julie standing in the kitchen doorway watching him.

"I still think—" she began.

"No," he said too sharply, "for the thousandth time, no. You'll meet the carriage at the Observatory. If, for any reason, we aren't there at the agreed upon time, you go to the Gypsy. I don't want you anywhere near that prison tomorrow. I mean it, Julie. And I want your promise that you'll do exactly as you've been told."

"Exactly as I've been told?" she repeated incredulously. Had he known her longer, he would have recognized the dangerous undertone. His response to her suggestions for how she might help tomorrow had been so different from Jean's. And she felt a surge of anger at Devon's refusal to consider what she'd been urging since they'd begun planning.

"And have I given you the right to dictate my actions? Even had I agreed to your ridiculous offer, would that have given you the right to tell me where I'm allowed to go or what I'm allowed to do?"

"My ridiculous offer?" he asked, his voice as revealing of his dark mood, provoked by her prolonged absence, as hers had been. "And why do you find my proposal so ridiculous?" he asked, wondering how seriously she was considering the other that had been made.

"I suppose it was occasioned by your desire to take as your wife a woman of my background. You know why that proposal was ridiculous."

"Your father is dead because of his efforts on behalf of my country, and you've been left with no one to protect you. You traveled in my company for several days without proper—"

"And so you feel compelled to offer for my hand? Because my father is dead? Because we traveled together?"

he laughed a little bitterly before she continued. She had nown there were no other reasons for his offer, but to hear im acknowledge that so openly hurt unbearably. "Or is it ecause your lover married someone else? And I'm even eginning to suspect why she did that. She probably discovered how pigheaded you can be," she mocked.

"Pigheaded?" he repeated furiously. "Because I don't vant to take a chance that you'll be taken by Fouché? Do ou know what would happen to you in a prison? Do you ave any idea of the treatment the guards submit female risoners to?"

"Of course, I know what would happen to me. Believe ne, I know." She stopped. Why reiterate that she knew far nore about the underside of Paris than he did? And arguing vith him, now that they had so little time, was not what she ad intended. She had only wanted to help tomorrow, and he knew she could, but for his stubborn, idiotic English ride.

"Do you know that they would take turns," Devon began, remembering the atrocities on the Peninsula and with he image, sudden and sharp, of that happening to Julie, his oice lost the anger that had colored it. The diversion she ad offered might make it easier to get Dominic out. But ot at the expense of Julie's life, he thought. Not at the cost f even one hour in a French prison.

"I can't stand that thought, Julie," he whispered and ulled her tightly against the solid warmth of his body.

Just as I can't stand the thought of losing you tomorrow, he thought, but you don't want to allow me to help. And can. Tomorrow she would watch him walk into Fouché's rivate hell, and she didn't know if he would ever walk out gain, but she knew that she intended to do everything in er power to make sure he and Avon would escape. Escape o return to their London world of safety and nobility. Away rom the lies and deceptions of her world that he found so epugnant.

She allowed herself to rest against the hard strength of

his chest a moment, listening to the heartbeat that was dearer than her own.

She stepped back and found his eyes, still clouded with his vision of what could happen to her if he allowed her any role in tomorrow's rescue. But she had no doubts about her ability to survive, to carry out the plan she'd devised. Because she had been surviving without his protection for a long time now. She wished suddenly that she was the sheltered, protected lady he deserved. But she wasn't. And never could be.

"Please let me help," she whispered and watched the slow, negative movement of his head. And when his mouth lowered to find hers, as she had known it would, she turned her face away, avoiding his touch. She pulled her hand free and walked across the kitchen without another word.

I don't need or want a knight-errant, she thought again. And I make my own decisions. The Gypsy girl will be at the Palais du Luxembourg long before you arrive, Devon. Bluff and counterbluff, my darling. Never wager against the professionals.

They had all been subdued at supper, each lost in private thoughts about the endeavor they would undertake in a few short hours. Julie was conscious that Devon's eyes rested frequently on her face, and she knew that he regretted as much as she did the bitterness of their last exchange.

She didn't want to let him walk out of her life with that memory between them. But she had responsibilities to carry out in the morning, and if she allowed herself any intimate moment with him, she feared the loss of the control that must be used to keep her intentions secret.

He had been forced to offer her his name, a marriage that could only take place at a cost to him that, based on her father's life, she was certainly in a position to weigh. But she wondered how she had found the resolve to refuse what she wanted more than breath or food or life. And tomorrow

e would be gone—by her choice and because she loved
im.

Jean watched her as, head lowered, she picked at her
ood. When she looked up, she smiled questioningly at him,
ut he simply allowed his considering gaze to rest on her
nhappy face. There was nothing he could do to alter what
vas happening here. She was in love with the Englishman,
s incredible to them both as that might seem. And the only
ope for the fulfillment of what Jean wanted was if Devon
nd his friend were successful in leaving France tomorrow.

"I think I'll make it an early night," Devon said finally,
iding his frustration over Julie's refusal to meet his eyes.
Ie pushed up from a gaming table in the salon where they
ad spread the remaining selection of foods Jean had
rought from the market. "Unless, Julie, you want to try to
mprove my accent over the next several hours?" he asked,
slight smile on his lips as his eyes rested on her averted
rofile.

"No," she said simply. "Jean can try, but I'm going up,
oo. It's been a long day." She didn't turn to face him, but
ontinued to play with the edge of her wineglass as if it
vere the most fascinating object she'd ever encountered.

"No," Jean said, his eyes still on her face. "Parisians
on't think anyone else speaks French anyway. Your ac-
ent's good enough that the guards will assume you're sim-
ly another provincial. And it's too late for any last-minute
nkering. It either works, or we end up as fellow guests of
'ouché."

"Then good night," Devon said, and he stood a moment
vatching her, waiting for some indication that she felt as
egretful about their estrangement as he. He didn't want to
valk out that door tomorrow with her anger as the only
egacy of the time they had spent together. Despite his as-
umed air of confidence, he was well aware of the odds of
is leaving the Luxembourg Palace tomorrow.

Give me something, Julie, he thought, some sign that all
hat remains between us isn't this brittle politeness. He

waited a long time, and then became aware the Frenchman was watching him with that mocking half smile. His eye fixed for a moment on that arrogant face, and then he nodded his good-night and left the room.

It seemed she had made her choice, he thought as h walked away, and maybe that was for the best. At least ther would be someone who would look after her when he wa gone. Someone who cared perhaps as much as he did.

Devon was used to imposing his will by the sheer forc of his personality on those around him. Early in his caree his superiors had recognized that he was a born commande his troops ready, if he led them, to attack hell itself. Fo him, leadership had always been easy. But with Julie, h acknowledged, he might as well be trying to force his wil on Dominic.

With a reluctant grin, he contemplated what an interestin combination of personalities that would be. If only, h thought grimly, I can bring that meeting off. And then h began the climb to her father's bedroom to face a long nigh spent trying to forget what would occur in the morning— and the very real possibility that after tomorrow he migh never see her again.

"Dev." The voice floated to him in the middle of th horror that held him, its concern pulling him away from th chains that confined him. He couldn't move, couldn't resis their weight, which was crushing the life out of him. H couldn't breathe. The darkness sat on his chest, hot an fetid, but he was helpless to fight its hold. Helpless.

"Devon," she said, and he struggled to find her voice, t use it to fight his way out of the mists of the nightmare. H hadn't dreamed about the paralysis that had been the im mediate result of his injury in so long. He had pushed i deep into his mind, had buried it, denying its power to mak him again its prisoner. And now once more it was here, it horror undiminished by the months that had passed.

"Devon, please. Wake up, darling. Whatever it is," sh

whispered, frightened by the shivering convulsions that still shook his entire frame.

He was drenched with sweat, the sheet clinging like cold hands to his nude body. It was always that way. God, he hated it. Hated the helplessness of that endless battle.

He was aware enough to know that her warm hands were touching him. He could feel them caressing his cheek, and he needed to know if he could also...

He took the slender fingers in his own and forced them over the muscles of his bare chest. He pushed hard against their softness, grinding his hand down over the light bones of hers, forcing it lower, over the ribs and then to the flat, ridged plane of his stomach. He had to know that he could really feel her touch against his skin.

And he could—not paralyzed, not helpless. With that realization, he suddenly relaxed his hold. He released her hand and allowed his own to fall to his side. He tried to breathe naturally, to control the harsh gasps he could feel. He knew he was frightening her.

"What is it, Dev?" she said, her hand moving of its own volition against the smooth skin that covered the strength of his body, her intent not to arouse but to comfort, to soothe away whatever terror had gripped a man she knew to be absolutely fearless.

She shook her head at the frightening remembrances of his reckless courage. Whatever had caused this man to react in the way she had just witnessed was beyond her imagination.

She eased down on the bed to sit beside him. He was still breathing as if he had run a race. Long, hard breaths that shook his body. She could feel the clamminess of the sweat-drenched sheet against the warmth of her hip. She leaned over his chest and took his right hand in her left and felt the long fingers close tightly over hers. Her right hand continued to stroke the damp satin of his skin. And finally she watched the rigid muscles begin to relax under her touch.

Unconsciously, her thumb found the small peak of his

nipple. She brushed over and around it, her eyes following
the circling movements of her fingertips against the darke
brown that surrounded it and then over the nipple itself
which suddenly pearled hard under her touch. She looke
up to find the blue intensity of his gaze, aware now, on he
face. This, at least, she would have to remember. She ha
touched him, had felt the strong, masculine length of hir
under her hands.

"It's all right," he said softly. "I'm sorry I woke you. I
was just a nightmare."

"I thought I had seen nightmares," she teased gently
smiling at him, "but that—"

"I'm sorry. Did I—" He stopped the question, but sh
knew what he wanted to know and how much he woul
hate to ask.

"I heard you. I thought at first you were talking to Jean
and then there was something strange about what I heard
Your voice wasn't loud, but different. I didn't know wha
was happening, but I knew something was wrong. Do yo
want to tell me about it?" she invited. Her hand move
lower, fingertips following of their own accord down th
ribs that were clearly marked under the overlaying muscle
Her thumb traced along the center channel of his chest t
pause when it encountered the rough hair that began abov
his navel and disappeared under the twisted sheet tha
wrapped his hips.

Her touch was soothing to him, reassuring with each incl
her fingers caressed that it was over, that he could feel
could move his legs, his arms, his hands. He raised his lef
hand and watched as the fingers flexed easily under hi
brain's command. God, he thought. I wonder if anyone eve
appreciates what that means unless…

"Dev?" she said again, arrested by the wonder in th
blue eyes. At her question, his gaze left the contemplatio
of the movement of his own fingers closing into a fist. H
touched her chin with his knuckle and then used his thumb
to trace over the softness of her bottom lip.

"Do you know..." he began, and his fingers spread to pan the side of her face, to feel the fragile cheekbone, the ɪne brow, the small, delicate curl of her ear, the soft black ſtrands of her hair. She allowed her head to lean into his touch, and turned her cheek to rub slightly against the palm.

"Do you have any idea how much it means to be able to touch you, to feel your smile start under my fingertips?" he asked softly, the motion of her lips against his thumb preceding his words by only a fraction of a second.

"No," she said, loving the tenderness in his voice, "but ɪ'm willing to have you explain."

"It's like being dead and then coming to life again. Can you imagine what you would feel?" he asked.

She shook her head, and his palm cupped her face, savoring that movement.

"Did you dream you were dead?" she asked softly, thinking that would be horror enough, perhaps, to cause what she had seen.

"No," he whispered, "but I wanted to be. And I couldn't even manage that." The grim smile that lifted his lips was not directed at her, but she shivered at whatever emotion had caused it.

"Dev," she said again, to bring him back to her, and finally his eyes focused on her face.

"You must think—" he began, and then his eyes closed tight. "God, I can't imagine what you're thinking."

She looked down at the man she loved, and finally she whispered, uncaring of the consequences, "I think I'm about to show you what I think, my heart."

His eyes opened then at what was revealed in the husky whisper. She leaned down, giving him the opportunity to avoid her kiss, as she had moved to deny his today. Instead, his mouth opened, welcoming the hesitant invasion that remembered all they had shared before. His tongue slid smoothly, hot and demanding, against the brush of hers. She was so warm, so alive. And he had been so cold.

Her hands found his, locking tightly together with them

to rest against the pillow on either side of his head, small fingers intertwined with strong brown ones. He used those locked hands to pull her down to lie against him, never stopping the cherishing movements deep within her mouth.

Her breasts, covered only by the thin silk of her night gown, pressed into the steel of his chest. And at their contact she could feel the searing breath he took and heard the low groan from somewhere deep in his throat.

Life and death. The agony of the past and the uncertainty of the future. They were all mixed up in his mind. He hadn't had time to escape the throes of the nightmare, to find the control he needed to resist what she was offering, the temptation of feelings that were so much a part of what it meant to be alive.

And so he buried his tongue in the softness of her mouth as he wanted to bury his body, hard and tight, into the dark honeyed warmth of hers. It had been so long. Such a long aching, lonely time, and he knew that this woman had been made to ease that loneliness, had been created for him to love and to protect. He had never been as convinced of the rightness of anything in his life as of the rightness of Julie in his arms. No matter what the past, no matter even the future.

She raised her head and smiled into the smoky, sensual midnight of his eyes. He lay still as she touched her tongue to the corner of his mouth where his slow smile always began. She had wanted to do that for so long. She couldn't remember when she had first known that she wanted to touch him there. She dropped small kisses, relishing the salt sweet taste of his skin. Her tongue smoothed across the skin of his eyelid and then down his nose to meet his mouth which lifted, open to welcome her.

"Julie," he breathed as his lips moved, turning slightly to fit, as if they had always known their place under her mouth. His hands freed themselves to find her body. One slid possessively into the short, dark curls that touched her neck. His fingers opened until they cupped her head, holding

er against the sweetly ravaging kiss. The other spread wide
gainst the small of her back, hard fingers pressing insis-
ntly into the depression at the base of her spine. She
rched into their touch like a cat.

He tightened his hold around her body and rolled, pulling
er completely onto the bed with him, so that she lay on
er back, the strength of his broad chest and wide shoulders
eaning over her. His eyes watched her face and then, smil-
g, he lowered to find her lips.

Her hands moved to fit along his shoulders and then to
teal around his neck, feeling the long line of the muscle
hat led from under the thick hair curling over his nape. Her
ngers found, and had forgotten, the ridges of the scars she
ad seen that morning beside the stream. And they paused,
fraid to hold, to smooth, to touch there, as she had been
llowed to caress the rest of his body.

She became aware that his mouth had deserted hers, and
hat the blue eyes were shadowed with some question, but
e waited. Finally with one finger she gently followed the
ongest of the weals she had felt.

"I'm afraid I'll hurt you, Dev," she whispered.

"They don't hurt," he said and then hesitated. "They're
ot sensitive, but if you'd rather not touch me there—"

She lifted her mouth to cover his, to stop whatever he
ad been about to suggest, and her hands moved across his
ack, unhindered by fear. She felt his muscles clench be-
eath her fingers as she deliberately deepened the kiss,
rawing from his lips the reassurance that he wanted her.
n spite of whatever motives had prompted his offer, in spite
f the woman in London, here and now, at least, it was she
e wanted.

"I want to touch you. I want to feel my lips on your
ody," he said softly. "I want to see you. Julie, just let me
ouch you. I just…"

As he whispered, his fingers found the narrow ribbons
hat held the tube of silk. They grazed against her skin as
e used his thumbs to slide them over her shoulders and off

her arms. And then his hand lifted to smooth the cool touch of the material away from her body.

Her breasts were small and perfect ivory globes, the tips touched with rose. As he watched, the nipples lifted as if straining toward his lips. She saw the smile catch the corner of his mouth, and felt the breath he gathered and held.

"I knew," he said softly, awe filling the deep voice, "I knew you would be this beautiful."

Her throat closed tight and hard. Touch me, her mind begged, but she couldn't speak, lost in the wonder she saw in the hard contours of his face.

And finally his thumb moved, as light as the breath of summer breeze, against the tip of one waiting breast. It rested there a moment, caught in the spell of her.

His fingers caressed under the milk white globe, lifting slightly, while his thumb moved, teasing, over the growing hardness of the rose nipple, exactly as hers had moved before against his body. Sensations, gliding like silk pulled through a ring, rippled deep, low inside her body. Her breath was thready, and she was mesmerized by what his eyes said and by what the hard fingers were doing. The smile she loved tilted the corners of his mouth at the pleasure that began to glow in her dark eyes.

And then slowly, her anticipation so great that his slowness was almost cruel, his head lowered. His tongue, warm and wet, circled where his thumb had been and then flickered with deliberate strength over the hardened bud. Some sound like the caught breath of a child before the first tears, moved through her throat, and in response to that appeal, his tongue laved again, rough against the smoothness, soft against the hardness.

She watched the intimate movement of his mouth against her breast without any sense of reservation or of shame. This was Dev, and it was right.

With my body, I thee worship. The words came to her from some shred of memory, unfurling like ribbon in a brain that had almost ceased to think, lost in a body that craved nly feel, touch, caress—but she knew with unshakable certainty that worshiping was what he was doing. With my body...

The waves of sensation that had begun to curl somewhere deep inside moved, arching upward to flicker like summer lightning into her stomach and downward through her thighs. Her knees were boneless, floating, and only he was aware that they had opened, already welcoming what he knew she wasn't ready for.

Not yet, my sweet, not now. But no one else will ever again touch you like this, he vowed silently. No one else. You are forever mine.

And thinking that, he allowed his mouth to finally possess her, to close over the reaching peak he had created. He suckled and heard again the softly gasping wonder of her response. His teeth found and captured, gently teasing as her body arched beneath his touch. He could feel his control slipping, draining from his mind as his body filled with desire, taut and demanding. If he didn't stop now...

And so the movement of his hard lips stopped; his tongue caressed once, twice, and then lifted away. He took a shuddering breath, its strength vibrating through the entire length of his body. Finally the blue eyes, starred as the night sky, raised to find hers, whose black lashes sparkled again with the diamonds of her tears.

"Julie," he said, leaning to kiss the moisture away, first one eye and then the other, tenderly caressing against the movement of closing lids. He moved back, and when she opened her eyes, he was smiling at her.

"Why are you crying, my beautiful Lady Luck? I'm the one who should cry. I have never seen anything as lovely as you are. Do you have any idea what you're doing to me?" he asked softly, trying to restore the discipline her shivering reaction to his mouth had destroyed.

Slowly she shook her head. His smile widened lovingly at what was reflected in her face as he took her hand and guided her fingers to brush lightly along the hard evidence of how much he wanted her. She pulled away from his hold as if she had been burned, and then she knew that she had. Branded by the knowledge that she could do that to him. He had made no effort to keep her fingers. She was so trusting in his arms, allowing him to do anything.

And with that thought, he realized he had been doing exactly what that bastard had accused him of. She wasn' his. At least not in the eyes of the church and the state. No yet. But under heaven, he vowed, she will be. Because she is mine. We just proved that beyond any doubt. Regretfully he lifted the slender straps over her shoulders, the tempting beauty of her body at least covered by the sheer gown.

"I thought..."

"Don't," he whispered. "Don't say it. There are limit to whatever fragments of control I'm piecing together here And the imposition of that control is a second-by-second operation. And you, my delight, are trying to shatter what ever I have left."

"I don't want you to have any control. I want to feel your mouth against me, Dev. I've thought about having you touch me there, wanted you to, since you kissed me in the salon. Oh, God, Dev, I'm so afraid that this will be all we'l have," she said. Tomorrow had intruded, had broken against the constraints they had placed on the world that had, until now, encompassed only this room, this bed.

"If—" he began.

"No. No if's. I don't want to hear them. We have tonight You know this may be all we ever have. Please, Dev. No if's." And she watched his eyes, and hoped.

His face was relaxed, the harsh emotion of the nightmare defeated by the effects of what they had just shared. She knew he had forgotten whatever horrors had driven him into her arms. Whatever had stolen the self-control he had prom ised. He lay on his side beside her, the long length of his body touching hers. She could still feel the heaviness of his erection against her thigh.

He was silent a long time, and she wondered what he was

thinking. And then his hand lifted to find her trembling lips, already anticipating its movement against her body. He let his fingers follow the line of her throat, the silk of her skin contrasting to the rough, callused palm that paused briefly to hold the slim column of her neck, savoring the movement of the pulse at its base. He allowed his hand to brush down her body, and it was large enough to span the peaks of both breasts. He felt their response and saw her eyes close, the lids dropping suddenly at the flood of warmth, stealing again, coiling hungrily in her body.

Down to touch the depression of her navel, outlined against the fine material of her gown. His hand turned, the fingertips moving lower to rest at the beginning of the V made by the joining of her slender legs that were still relaxed, waiting for his body to move between them. Empty and waiting for him. And then he stopped, his palm holding the slight convexity of her belly. She opened her eyes finally, wondering why the seductive movement of hard flesh against the smooth glide of the silk had ceased.

"And what if..." he began, and the picture that had stopped his hand, the image of her slender, perfect body filled, tight and hard, with his child, caught at his throat. He wanted to make love to her more than he had ever wanted any other woman. But she was, he discovered, capable of arousing emotions he had never felt before. He had never even dreamed of creating a child, never even thought of how he would feel to hold the turning movement of his son under his palm, inside the body of the woman he loved, separated from his hand only by the warm velvet of her skin. And now the vision was so strong he could almost sense the stretching movement of tiny limbs.

"I'm not walking into Fouché's hands tomorrow with the possibility that you're carrying my son, a son I might never see."

She hadn't realized what he had been thinking. His touch had been so gentle that she had simply been lost in the caressing tenderness of whatever he was feeling, but this...

Only after he spoke did she know how much she wanted the reality of the image he had just created.

"Dev," she whispered and lifted to kiss the lips that had just given birth to a dream.

He met her mouth, allowed a brief and insubstantial touch against all she had hoped for. And then he moved away from the reach of her lips and removed his hand from her body.

"After tomorrow. After I find Dominic. Then, Lady Luck, you and I have an appointment," he promised softly.

"But—"

"You're my luck. After tomorrow," he said and touched a finger against her mouth to stop the questions he could see in her eyes. "Go back to bed before I forget all my good intentions. And Julie, I don't want to see you in the morning. If—" he began, and remembered that she had rejected those possibilities. And said instead, "I want to remember only this. Here and now."

And because he had given her no choice, she nodded.

He lowered his head suddenly, and his lips closed around one small, rounded breast. His mouth pulled strongly, the silk no barrier to the movement of his tongue against her skin. She cried out softly against the sudden heat that jarred deep within her body, roiling and arching, so intense it was almost on the edge of pain. She hadn't known anything could feel like his mouth, moving warm and darkly demanding against her softness.

She wasn't aware that her fingers had found his shoulders, nails biting deeply into the scars she had touched so tentatively before. Unaware and uncaring now that she was hurting him. She wanted into his skin, to become a part of him, and she would not even have known how to find release for those feelings. She only knew she wanted, and he was leaving her unsatisfied. Unsatisfied as he was.

She heard his quiet, delighted laughter at her response, and then he had encircled her body in hard arms that held her crushed tightly enough against him to deny the possibility of any separation, protected as only Devon could.

"After tomorrow," his lips promised against the smoothness of her skin. She could feel his warm breath on her temple, and then his mouth rested over her own to whisper, "After tomorrow, I promise, my Lady Luck."

He leaned back and lifted her hand like a courtier. She stepped down from the high bed, one bare foot finding the floor, hoping her trembling knees would be strong enough to support her.

She thought nothing in her life had been harder to do than to leave the shadowed safety of this room, but because she loved him, she trusted him and, for once, obeyed. But she touched him again, slender fingers tracing lightly across the shivering skin of his chest, and then she moved away, beyond arm's length, removing herself from the temptation that was his body. She turned finally and slipped across the room, her bare feet making no sound on the thick carpets.

He lay awake a long time after she had left, her body's perfume tangled in the sheet he pulled up over the stinging marks she had made on his shoulders. The image of Julie cradling a child they had created moved into all the dark corners that his nightmare had occupied and erased the premonitions about tomorrow. He fought the force of his blackest memories with the promise of ones yet to be made, and finally, when he closed his eyes, there was nothing of that darkness that remained.

Chapter Ten

The doctor's elegant carriage stopped close to the service entrance of the palace. The morning's cold had already given way to a springlike sunshine that made the guards on duty relaxed and desirous of escape from their posts along the gray portico at the rear of the building. The entertainment that had begun in the courtyard almost a half hour earlier had pulled everyone who wasn't as confined as they to watch the Gypsy girl's hands tantalize even the wise eyes of this urban audience. From the kitchens and offices of the gracious stone edifice the watchers had wandered, drawn by the sense of excitement that had floated like a pleasant aroma through these businesslike halls.

And now, almost the only workers who were not being entertained by the laughing eyes of the magician who moved the shells over the elusive ball were those standing disconsolately isolated from the amusement, still tied to the duty of guarding the entrance to the corridor leading to the prison area.

The figure that stepped down from the coach was tall and stooped, bent perhaps with age. And then the guards noticed the heavy cane and the way the lean body rested painfully against its support a moment, gathering strength before he would be forced to begin the halting journey to their door. The black satchel marked his profession for them, confirmed by the severity of the finely cut frock coat and the elegant hat he wore.

The doctor allowed his eyes to glance toward the crowd at the far end of the square, which was formed by the shape of the building's wings. The Gypsy girl's dark curls were occasionally visible through the heads of the taller watchers who surrounded the portable table. He could hear her laughter clearly, along with the morning noises of bird song and the traffic along the street. And then, as if pulling himself back to the unpleasant demands of his duty, he limped heavily to the guards' station.

He waved a dismissing hand at their challenge, and at the assured gesture, the barrels of the rifles they held lifted away from the doorway across which they had perfunctorily dropped. The soft, muttering explanation he had begun was halted as he thrust the bag he carried in his left hand at one of the guards. He never looked at the man whose fingers closed over the handle in automatic response. Instead, with an eloquent groan the doctor used his left hand to lift the crippled right leg up over the threshold of the entry. Then gripping the stone facing with that same hand, he used that and the cane to support the leg as he pulled the left one up alongside it. That painful maneuver accomplished, his fingers fumbled in his waistcoat pocket for a large white handkerchief with which he wiped his forehead, careful not to dislodge the gray wig he wore.

"Gout," he grunted finally in explanation, calling forth a smiling condolence from the younger and a head-shaking tsk from the other. "The disease of kings," he offered, stuffing the handkerchief untidily back into his vest pocket. He reached for the satchel, which was politely replaced in his outstretched fingers.

"But not of emperors." The guard laughed as he released the bag. Louis XVIII's suffering from that infirmity was widely known, but as the soldier reminded them all, no longer of concern to any loyal Frenchman. Bonaparte was not a victim.

"Thank God," the doctor said softly and, leaning on his stick, took two steps into the shadowed hall. He paused as if confused and asked over his shoulder. "Fouché's pet?" he questioned and hoped.

"To the left along the corridor and then the first right. The third cell. It's rather a distance." The young guard's apologetic voice hesitated.

"No matter. When Fouché commands..." the doctor said and began his limping journey.

As the visitor disappeared into the gloom of the interior corridor, the guards turned back, their attention once more directed toward the laughter of the crowd in the courtyard.

Devon paused briefly at the turning, as if resting. His performance down the secondary hallway was as convincing as his earlier one. There was a quick flare of interest in the eyes of the huge guard who stood duty before the door of the cell he sought, but he could almost see the mental relaxation as the mud-colored eyes appraised the limping figure. He wondered briefly if Jean's doubts about his ability to handle this giant might have been justified, and then he no longer allowed himself to even consider the possibility that he could fail. Not now, he thought. Not this close to success.

He gestured imperiously at the door when he reached it and again made a show of mopping his forehead, a show that had effectively hidden his features, as he waited while the thick fingers fumbled for the key.

When the metal latch released with a discernible clang, he waved vaguely back along the passage he had so painfully traversed.

"I'll need water, hot water from the kitchens," he ordered, and then entered the cell without waiting to see if his command had been obeyed. He was not surprised, however, to hear the retreating footsteps fade into the distance over the stones behind him. A few minutes alone with Dominic, to assess his strength and tinker with the plan according to what he judged the duke would be capable of.

His eyes gradually adjusted to the dimness to find the figure of his brother-in-law. The Duke of Avon was sitting on the low bed that appeared to be the only furnishings of the room. His shoulders, covered by a coarse cotton shirt, were propped with his usual elegant grace against the wall behind the bed. His right leg was stretched out along the mattress, but the left had swung off the bed to touch the floor. Devon was relieved to see that he was dressed, dark trousers covering the long length of leg and his feet in low boots. Except for the terrible thinness and the increased spread of silver that fanned back from his temples into the coal-blackness of his uncut hair, he appeared, reassuringly, the same.

The silver eyes rested without surprise on his face, but the firm lips were touched lightly with his smile.

"You have every right to ask," Devon said softly, and watched the familiar lift of one dark brow in questioning response.

"To ask what took me so long." He explained his attempt at humor. Almost before the words had left his mouth, the eyes of the man on the bed shifted to the right, and the cold muzzle of a rifle was thrust against the artery that pulsed under Devon's jaw. In the sudden stillness he could feel the increased tempo of his heartbeat thud against that rigid tip.

Avon's silver eyes were again on his face, and Devon managed to whisper past the sick disappointment of his failure, "How long?"

"They've been here over an hour," the duke answered softly. "Waiting."

Betrayed, Devon thought bitterly, and his hot rage made him wonder fleetingly if he could move quickly enough to wrest away the muzzle. But his hands were still encumbered by the props he carried, and the rifle of the other soldier rested with unwavering certainty on Avon, who might be unable to move quickly enough to escape a ball if he started anything. And with the report of the gun, the other guards would come. Betrayed, he thought again with hatred, as the options presented themselves in a series of lightning images, each of which was rejected by the quick fighter's brain. No chance. Not now. Not and get Dominic out, too. And so he waited, praying that there would be another opportunity.

The door opened behind him, and the guard reappeared, without, of course, the requested hot water. At a gesture from one of the soldiers standing in tableau to Devon's left, his massive figure lumbered across the cell and lifted Avon in his muscular arms. The duke quickly hid whatever emotion had stirred momentarily in the too-thin, harshly controlled face. Pain or humiliation or both, Devon wondered briefly, as Dominic was carried, as easily as if he had been a child, across the stone floor. The increased pressure of the muzzle was used to guide Devon out of the way, but the soldier's eyes never left his face, anticipating any sudden action.

The giant skillfully turned the long body in his arms to facilitate their movement through the doorway, and then he and his burden disappeared into the shadows.

The soldier's eyes directed his prisoner to follow. Devon moved also through the cell door, the satchel and stick still held loosely in either hand. His long stride, however, in no way resembled that which he had adopted in his passage down the corridor.

"Fouché's orders." The familiar mocking voice was audible now. The sunlight ahead of them filtered from the open courtyard into the gray recesses of the prison. The speaker was silhouetted against the entrance, explaining something to the guards who had been so sympathetic to the physician's disability. Devon's mind identified and accepted the reality of the voice, and with an unspeakably painful effort he fought to restrain his rage.

"And I'll sign for the release of your prisoner," the speaker continued, folding and returning to his breast pocket whatever document he had been showing. "We intend to interrogate all of them at the ministry. Your cooperation in the capture of these additional conspirators will be noted on your record of service. My congratulations on a job well done.''

The trace of officious condescension in Jean's voice had been obvious to both Englishmen, but the soldiers appeared to preen under his commendation, accepting his praise as sincere and as their due.

The Frenchman moved away from the door to allow the enormous figure room to maneuver the prisoner he carried through the entryway. The duke's silver eyes rested briefly on the scarred face that quickly disappeared from their gaze as Avon was carried into the sunlight and toward the waiting carriage.

Devon, however, had the opportunity to convey all the contempt he felt for the man who had betrayed them. His cold blue eyes locked on that marred face. The hazel eye allowed the meeting, lazily and sardonically accepting his hatred. He bowed with courtly elegance to the Englishman who walked under the watching bores of the two rifles trained on his spine.

''And I think you may safely relieve our friend of his theatrical trappings,'' Jean instructed. Devon allowed the props to be taken from his fingers, and removing the wig, handed them that also. His hands, now, at least were free. As he moved toward the waiting carriage, Devon's mind began to hope. The Gargantua was carefully arranging Avon into the seat, and Devon could see the cost of that procedure in the perspiring features of his friend. But he knew that if they allowed him to also enter those confines, he could count on Dominic's support of whatever he could devise that might give them a chance. Their opportunities were surely better in the carriage, a conveyance that offered a means of transportation for the duke, in spite of his condition, the seriousness of which was becoming more obvious with each passing minute.

Wait, Devon urged against his anger. Wait and think. You'll only have one chance, and it must be the right one.

"Get the Gypsy." The traitorous voice spoke from somewhere behind him. "She's one of them, too. A diversion."

A soldier who had been standing by the carriage when they emerged from the building started toward the crowd, still focused on the flashing promise of the shells.

They all watched as the trooper efficiently scattered the spectators to their forgotten obligations and pulled the slim, writhing figure across the cobblestones that separated them. As she had in the village, she fought every foot of the way, but she was too small to do any real damage.

Devon flinched against the casual backhanded blow the guardsman gave her when she managed to bite fingers that had foolishly moved within reach of her teeth. The rifle's muzzle, which Devon had felt sliding down his shoulder, and by which he had been judging the distraction of the two soldiers behind him, shifted again into vigilance at his reflexive response to that slap. Not wise, he reminded himself and fought to relax the tension that corded the muscles of his shoulders.

The soldier laughingly controlled her, and the struggling duo moved closer, ever closer to where he stood waiting. And it seemed that his prayers were about to be answered as she was being dragged to become a passenger in the coach on which now rested the frail hope of escape. And then the dark voice spoke again behind him.

"No," the Frenchman ordered authoritatively. "Not in the carriage. She'll go with me. Put her on one of the horses. I have some special entertainment planned for the girl."

All he had to do, Devon thought, the plan instantly leaping into his mind at the implication of those words, was to inflict enough damage on the three people surrounding him to allow Julie to reach the driver's seat. Or if Dominic must be sacrificed, to reach one of the waiting horses and to make a bolt for freedom. The huge guard who had carried Dominic had disappeared somewhere behind his line of vision, but he couldn't be sure he had reentered the building. However, it was a chance he had to take. In the distraction he planned to cause, Julie should be able to break away from the one soldier holding her.

Think, my darling, he prayed, the muscles in his legs gathering for the movement that would provide the distraction that might allow her to take the opportunity to flee.

The odds seemed fair, as long as Julie would be safe. And if this failed, they would be, perhaps, no worse than they were now. At least he would have the opportunity to get in a blow or two on that scarred bastard.

"Too bad all these elaborate plans were destined to fail, my friend," Jean's voice taunted, closer to him than he had dared hope.

Devon knew where the enemy was, and he could still feel the tip of one of the rifles resting lightly against his shoulder. He dropped suddenly, his body turning and his quick hands reaching to grasp the muzzle. He used it like a scythe, swinging in a hard arc against the temple of the man from whose surprised hands he had wrenched it. And then back, to strike with a thud against the skull of the other soldier who had stood dumbfounded by the speed of the attack.

He turned then to the Frenchman, and allowed himself a brief moment of satisfaction at the shock that had, as yet, arrested any reaction. Two down, he thought grimly and swung the improvised club again. Jean lifted his arm to ward off the blow that struck painfully against his raised forearm instead of the side of his head.

Before Devon could recover from the momentum of that swing, the Frenchman dropped street-fighter quick and barreled his shoulder into the Englishman's stomach. The movement threw Devon back to crash heavily against the side of the coach. As always in battle, the adrenaline was pouring into his system so that he was barely aware of the pain. He managed a hard right into Jean's gut and heard the grunting response. Due to the closeness of the carriage door behind his elbow, he had not been able to get enough force into the blow to do a great deal of damage. He worried briefly that the remaining soldier hadn't joined the fight. Surely, with this going on, he wasn't still holding Julie.

"You stupid, arrogant son of a bitch," Jean said under his breath. He then began to curse softly and very fluently while he struggled to control the muscled arms that fought to free themselves enough to strike another, more successful, blow. Neither was aware that the carriage door on the far side had opened to welcome the scrambling figure of the girl, who was helped into the safety of its enclosure by the man inside.

"Get into the carriage, you idiotic bastard," Jean ordered desperately and was relieved to see, finally, the third soldier appear peripherally in his line of sight.

"Help me get him into the carriage," he grated in relief, just before Devon's knee slammed up hard into the vulnerable area between his legs. The Frenchman's body went limp with the agony of the blow, and he fell to his knees, retching, against the cobblestones. Devon turned to meet the advance of the remaining member of the opposition, who appeared to be approaching with reluctance.

The Englishman backed against the coach, waiting in the loose, relaxed crouch of a born fighter. He was surrounded by the groaning bodies of three of the soldier's comrades. The remaining man looked as if he might be considering whether he was getting paid enough to get killed.

Strong fingers reaching from the window of the coach at his back found the vital arteries on either side of Devon's neck and pressed hard, skillfully blocking the passage of blood to the brain. Devon's hands lifted to pull against their constriction, but already the air was beginning to shroud with mist and the scene before him to darken. The soldier, suddenly realizing his opportunity, darted daringly to direct a fist against the unprotected chin. Devon's head rocked back with smashing force against the frame of the carriage door, and he dropped like a stone, a victim of the combined assault.

''Dev. My God,'' Julie cried from inside the carriage as he fell, ''you're going to kill him.''

Through the efforts of the soldier and of the huge guard, who had finally responded to the commotion, his limp body was lifted easily, if not gently, into the coach. She could see the giant toss a comment over his shoulder to the guards at the door, who had started to come out into the square. At whatever he said, the two returned to their positions. It did, indeed, appear that the fight was over.

As Julie cradled Devon's head in her lap, wondering what damage had been done in the struggle, the men who had just loaded him into the coach turned to help Jean. In response to his angry rejection of their attentions and his agonized whisper, the soldier mounted the driver's box while the guard helped the two who had been injured by Devon's improvised club. But it only took a few minutes to gather their weapons and mount the waiting horses, the proceedings watched by the prison guards, except for the giant, who had disappeared into the palace.

In short order the small procession, led by Jean, whose fury was clear both from the set of his shoulders and from the livid features, was riding out of the sunlit courtyard and into the main thoroughfare that would lead to their destination.

The man seated opposite Julie in the carriage watched her slim fingers smooth Devon's disordered hair as she bent to kiss his lips, slightly parted in unconsciousness. When she raised her head, she met for the first time the impact of the Duke of Avon's silver gaze. One dark brow rose in response to what was in her face.

''Why did you do that?'' she said, disbelief coloring her voice. She had just watched the Avon's sure fingers render his friend, his rescuer, his brother-in-law, unconscious. ''How could you possibly...'' She stopped as the amusement he had been feeling at her genuine puzzlement was allowed to move finally into the dark, classically perfect features of the man who watched her from across Devon's body.

"Because someone had obviously made a serious error in judgment. And if I didn't do something rather quickly, I was afraid our friend here was going to spoil it all. And it was such an entertaining farce, my dear. Your idea?" he suggested softly, smiling at her.

Her mouth was suddenly dry at the force of that smile and at the intelligence in the unusual gray eyes that rested on her face in absolute enjoyment and with sincere compliment.

She nodded slowly, arrested by his reaction, but compelled to answer by some force in the gentle question.

"But Devon wasn't allowed to know all the details?" the low voice continued softly. "And no one, of course, thought that he would be foolish enough to take on a garrison?"

She shook her head, ashamed now that she had agreed with Jean's assessment of the Englishman. She, who had seen, who had known what he was capable of, had allowed Jean to make her doubt him.

"We never dreamed..." she began, then faltered as the duke's beautiful mouth slanted quickly into a smile.

"Then I assume your acquaintance with my brother-in-law has been brief," Avon said, amusement in the rich voice. "And he nearly carried it off. I wonder what you would have done had he left the members of our escort too seriously injured to carry out their pretended duties. If they had been replaced by real soldiers from the detail assigned to the palace—"

"Don't," she begged softly, shivering. "I didn't think— No one would have believed he could—"

"I would have," the duke said with conviction, "but then obviously I know him far better than you. I would have known exactly what action Colonel Burke would have taken under those circumstances. You should have told him, Mademoiselle de Valmé. It would have been far easier on him." His eyes dropped deliberately to watch the slim fingers, which had been unconsciously caressing Devon's face. "And, I think, on you."

"How do you know who I am?" she breathed, but it took him a moment to answer.

Color stole suddenly into her throat and cheeks when she noticed, as he had, of course, intended, that he was watching her touch his brother-in-law with the familiar, rather possessive fingers of a lover. At that unexpected blush, Avon, who was very wise in the ways of women, revised his opinion of the one seated opposite him, an opinion that had been based on her profession and on her reputation.

Whatever his sources had led him to believe about Ashford's daughter was obviously not the entire story. Not considering that revealing blush, and certainly not if Devon were involved with her. The duke pulled his thoughts away from that interesting possibility to answer her question.

"Who else could you be?" he suggested softly. "Besides, I was in Paris watching your father's establishment for several days before Fouché—" He stopped suddenly, the remembrance of all that had been done to him blocking his explanation with a flood of emotions so strong he was powerless against its force. He closed his eyes, fighting the weakness that had stolen his usual iron discipline, and then locked the dark door of those memories.

Julie watched him struggle to regain control. He made himself open his eyes and continue the answer he had begun. "And I had heard a variety of descriptions of the Divine Juliette."

He had meant nothing disparaging by his use of the nickname all of Paris called her. But had he not been lost in a battle with his own demons, Avon would never have unthinkingly inflicted the pain that was reflected in the white face raised to his.

She blocked that reaction to his knowledge of her reputation to ask the obvious question.

"But even so, how could you possibly have known that

they weren't Fouché's soldiers? That it was all..." She stopped and shook her head.

"Some slight difficulties with their uniforms. A grenadier's belt on an infantryman's uniform. A minor problem with regimental insignia on another. Who are they?" Avon finished his critique to ask.

"An out-of-work actor, a mountebank, gamblers Jean knew. I don't really know. They all owed Jean money. I suppose it must have been a lot of money to make them willing to take the chances they did. The uniforms came from a rag shop. We thought they would..." She paused, embarrassed by their obvious errors.

"I had a great deal of time to study them," the duke said forgivingly. "But Dev... It would have taken Devon only one glance to sum up their deception. I'm sorry that he didn't have that opportunity." His eyes moved consideringly to his brother-in-law, whose head still rested in the girl's lap.

Her eyes followed his, and their drop allowed the duke the opportunity to study her. He saw the small thumb brush over the abrasion on the chin of the man she held.

Dev looked so helpless, she thought, so defenseless. And then she smiled slightly, thinking that he had been anything but defenseless. He had almost foiled it, had almost defeated them all. He had only been stopped by the collusion of someone who knew him so well and who, for his sake, had mounted a rear assault.

"God, I hope..." she said softly, thinking out loud, and then she paused, knowing how Devon would hate any expression of concern about him.

"He'll be all right," Avon reassured, wishing he were as certain as he sounded. "He's survived far more serious injuries than that."

"I know. I've seen—" she began softly and then stopped in embarrassment. The duke's eyes lifted suddenly to her face at that unconscious disclosure of the intimacy of her relationship with Devon.

"But don't tell him I told you that," she finished, knowing it was too late to deny what she had just revealed. And then for the first time Avon was exposed to the teasing sparkle in the smiling eyes that had enslaved half the men in the French capital.

The duke glanced again at his brother-in-law, lying in the arms of a woman who clearly loved him very much. His eyes closed tightly as the memory of Emily in his arms flooded his body, hot and demanding, moving with all its remembered heat into his groin. He took a deep breath and looked up to find the girl watching him anxiously.

"Are you all right?" she asked softly, concern for him written in her features. This was Devon's friend.

"No," he whispered finally, "but I will be. If I can just get home, I will be." He leaned his head against the side of the coach, suddenly exhausted, the limits of his uncertain strength reached, as they often were now, without warning. "If…" he breathed.

"No *if's*," she said softly, seeing the beautiful profile revealed in sharpened purity by his ordeal. Although he didn't answer or lift the fall of thick black lashes that hid the charcoal-rimmed silver irises, she knew he had heard her. The corners of his mouth stole upward in response, and watching, she thought irrelevantly that she liked his smile also. She wondered if she might watch for it with the same anticipating pleasure with which she had always waited for Dev's.

With that thought her eyes fell again to Devon's face. No, she revised, there will never be anyone whose smile I'll long to see as I do yours. She remembered the gentle weight of his hand resting against her stomach and thought about a child of his growing there. She tried to banish that image, and then suddenly wondered why she shouldn't be allowed to think about what he had suggested.

Everyone is entitled to dreams, she told herself. Even if they are aware that they'll never come true, everyone is allowed to have them. She brushed the tips of her fingers

against his forehead, the sunlight from the carriage window
alternating there with the shadows cast by the tall trees that
lined the road they took. And at the end of that road, she
knew what she had to do. But until that time...

Until that time, my darling, at least I, too, am allowed to
dream.

Chapter Eleven

Julie didn't open her eyes again until the motion of the coach began to slow. She didn't think she had slept, as her companions still did. Surely Jean wouldn't have called a rest this close to the city.

When the carriage had come to a full stop and was standing under the shadows of the trees, the voices that floated back to her weren't loud, nor should their indistinct cadences have been enough to cause the frisson of fear that was her immediate reaction. That was caused because she knew that whatever was happening now was not part of the carefully devised scheme she had outlined in detail to Jean.

She glanced down at Devon and was surprised to find that his eyes were open, watching her face. And he was obviously listening with the same breathless concentration that held her motionless to whatever was now happening in the road before them. They heard the clattering movement of several horses, the unmistakable jingling noises of armed men riding. Then through the windows they watched as their disreputable crew of mock soldiers was replaced by a group whose extreme efficiency of maneuvering left no doubt that here, at last, was the real thing.

The coach began to move again, and the pace was far sharper than that at which they had been traveling. It no longer mattered, it seemed, if they attracted attention. In-

deed, it would be impossible not to, surrounded as they were
by a detachment of hussars.

She was unprepared for the upward movement of the
body that had rested so quietly in her lap. Devon had noticed
Avon half-sitting, half-lying on the facing seat. The duke's
eyes were closed, and he rested against the wall of the
coach. It was apparent by the unchecked motion of his head
in response to the pitch of the rapidly moving vehicle that
he was unconscious.

Devon grasped Dominic's thin, white wrist, which lay
limply in his strong fingers. She could read the worry in his
face as he felt the faintness of the pulse. His eyes, filled
with concern, lifted to meet hers. "Julie?" he asked, but
she shook her head.

"He talked to me," she said, watching the man she loved
care for his friend. She smiled in remembrance of the duke's
gentle teasing. "And then he just went to sleep. At least, I
thought he was asleep. What's wrong with him, Dev?"

"I don't know. Maltreatment. Starvation. The results of
the fever Jean described. But surely by now…" he began
and then discarded the possibility that Avon might be more
ill than he had thought.

"Maybe it's just exhaustion. He was strong enough to—"
she stopped suddenly, and the blue eyes swung to her face
at the hesitation.

"Strong enough to what?" he questioned.

"He's the one who stopped you. He did something to
your neck, and then the soldier hit you. I think the coach
really did most of the damage."

She stopped, his face clearly indicating that what she was
explaining made no sense.

"Avon stopped me? Is that what you're suggesting? That
Dominic would try to keep me from getting us out of
there?"

"No," she said, smiling, "but he would try to stop you
from ruining everything. And you almost did. It was a trick,
Dev. Deception. The prison officials thought they were help-

ing foil an attempted escape. Jean had forged papers ordering them to cooperate with him, to catch you trying to free
the English spy. He hired the fake soldiers, bought the
forged documents, everything.

"But we thought that it would be more believable if you
reacted naturally. If you thought you really had been betrayed. We couldn't be sure, of course, of your acting ability. I'm sorry, Dev, but we never dreamed that you'd react
like you did. And then no one could stop you. So the duke
did," she finished her explanation.

"Then if what happened at the palace was a deception,
what's taking place now?" He halted, waiting for her explanation.

"I don't know," she admitted. "It's not part of anything
I planned," she continued. "I don't—"

"You planned?" The disbelief was dangerously evident.

"It was my plan we used for the escape. Jean had to carry
out the details. He was the only one who could go into the
city to make the arrangements. But the plan was mine. I
thought your scheme needed a few diversions, a little deception," she mocked, suddenly tired of his continued denial of her values, of the methods used in her world. "What
we did worked. At least until you decided to slay dragons
instead of giving in to overwhelming odds, as we'd anticipated any sensible person would. Jean said if you'd been a
soldier, it would be obvious to you that there was no
way…"

Her voice faded. Overwhelming odds or not, he had defeated them. Had it not been for Avon's intervention, Devon
would have accomplished what they had never even
dreamed he might attempt.

"Then you have no idea who these soldiers are or where
they're taking us?" he asked.

"No," she whispered. "But I'm afraid that, in spite of it
all, we haven't succeeded."

"Fouché," he said softly. "Damn him. He has probably
expected an attempt to rescue Avon since he was captured.

He's probably just been lying in wait for whoever was foolish enough to try it.''

''We knew the odds were very long.''

''Which is why I never wanted you involved,'' he said softly. ''Why didn't you listen to me, Julie? By now, you'd be safely away in the care of the Gypsy.''

''Because,'' she told him truthfully, ''no matter what happens, I'd rather be here with you. No matter what, Dev.''

Devon recognized where they had been brought as soon as the carriage and its escort wheeled into the entrance. The Emperor had made the Tuileries Palace his headquarters when he'd entered Paris. Fouché would almost certainly have rushed here to reestablish the old comradeship with Napoleon.

Soon, he supposed, they would be forced to face the man who had led them all to this moment by plotting his own climb to power months ago. A climb that had been threatened only by the existence of Avon's network. Devon suspected Fouché feared his proposed coup, which would replace the Bourbon king with a claimant controlled by Fouché himself, would be exposed to the outside world before it could be carried out. So he had set out to destroy the network, and then, having lured the duke to Paris, to destroy Avon himself.

But with the arrival of Napoleon in France, Fouché had obviously decided that Avon might be more valuable alive than dead—hostage, pawn. No one would ever know why that twisted mind had made the decision to move Avon from the dungeon. Perhaps, as Jean had suggested, the duke had been carried up to share his cell simply as a test of the gambler's involvement. But whatever its original purpose, that move had brought the duke within reach of rescue. A rescue that had now, apparently, failed.

Devon's speculation about Fouché's motives was interrupted by the halting of the carriage. He glanced again at

Avon's pale face, and his lips tightened in frustration. Dominic had already suffered so much at the hands of the French.

They were very professionally guarded as they unloaded the coach, and the litter on which the soldiers carried the duke inside had disappeared before the others were herded into the courtyard.

The room to which they were finally brought was a simple office. Maps and charts and dispatches were spread in a seemingly careless array over the surface of the huge table that dominated. The rest of the furnishings were plain, almost Spartan, in comparison to those of the rooms they had passed through on their way here.

The small, dark man standing behind the table looked up briefly at their entrance. He took the time to make a carefully considered mark on the map he was studying. Then he gestured dismissal, and the young officer who had escorted them here saluted, turned on his heel and, closing the door behind him, left them alone with the Emperor of France.

Napoleon's black eyes had dropped to his map again even before the young lieutenant shut the door. He rubbed his chin a moment and moved to another position to study from a different angle the terrain and then the notations he had made. And finally he seemed to become aware of the presence of the three who waited before him.

"I am led to understand that you carried out quite an entertaining diversion at the Luxembourg Palace this morning. Let me congratulate you on the daring of your attempt. However, I'm sure you must realize that I could not allow you to spirit such a valuable political prisoner out of France."

"Then they weren't Fouché's soldiers," Devon said softly, trying to think what the Emperor's hand in the game might mean.

"The Duc d'Otrante," the Emperor corrected carefully, using Fouché's proper title, which he himself had bestowed, "*has* no soldiers. Only Bonaparte commands the soldiers of France," he said. "My minister of police seems to have forgotten that. He arranged for your capture and conveyance here. He had also hoped to meet with you personally, but I'm afraid he has been...detained.'' His slight smile suggested his amusement at the thought of Fouché's frustration over his interference. Devon remembered what Julie had told him about the relationship between the two. Napoleon used Fouché, but he didn't trust him. He even spied on his own minister of police. Apparently that was how he had known of their capture. But he couldn't imagine why Bonaparte had chosen to interfere.

"I've sent a physician to see to your friend,'' Napoleon said to Devon, the accent of Corsica still coloring his French. "Not my personal physician, who unfortunately is not in attendance at the present. But an army surgeon, a very good one. I understand that the duke's treatment since his capture by the minister of police has not been particularly gentle."

"Fouché wasn't your minister of police when he imprisoned the Duke of Avon,'' Devon commented carefully. By the slight tightening of the Emperor's lips he knew that both the points he had just made had been acknowledged.

"The Duc d'Otrante has occasionally been known to assume powers that do not rest within his domain. I am aware he was not acting in an official capacity when he imprisoned the duke. However—''

"The Duke of Avon is a fully accredited representative of the Court of St. James's. I am sure that, as such, he falls under the protection of the sovereign of France. Although, of course, it was not to this government that his diplomatic mission was undertaken. Even so, an ambassador of His Royal Highness, the Prince Regent, would certainly not be subjected to any further disrespect by the French Crown.'' Devon's face was perfectly calm. It was the highest level of bluff. A game of diplomacy played against a master.

"An ambassador from the Court of St. James's?'' the Emperor questioned softly, his amusement deliberately revealed at this reckless maneuver.

"Indeed, Your Majesty. If, however, you would care to
assure yourself of the Duke of Avon's credentials, I'm certain—"

"Of course. We are all certain." Bonaparte gestured
impatiently at the formal language of the protest. "But
whatever the English Crown would now claim, you and I
both know why Avon came to France."

"I know if an accredited diplomat who holds one of the
oldest titles in England suffers any harm while in your court
what the nations assembled at Vienna will do."

Devon was aware that he was threatening the man who
had controlled almost all of Europe. A man whose power
over their lives was still undisputed. He could do what he
liked here and worry about diplomatic repercussions later.

"Do you think they could hate or fear me any more than
they already do?" the Emperor questioned softly.

For the first time Devon was allowed to feel the power
that emanated from this potbellied, insignificant-looking
man, dressed in the simple green uniform of his own Chas-
seurs of the Guard, who was leaning, both hands resting on
the annotated map before him. And Devon knew that he
was deliberately being made aware of the Emperor's displeasure.

"And you?" The Emperor's soft voice was not in any
way threatening, but Julie shivered suddenly. "And are you,
too, an accredited representative of the English Crown?"

Both Devon and the Emperor were aware that whatever
protection the Court of St. James's chose to exert on behalf
of the Duke of Avon, it would not extend to his brother-in-
law. And so Devon told the truth, a truth that he hoped
would still mean something to Bonaparte.

"No," he said, and there was a quiet arrogance in the
claim with which he answered Napoleon's question. "I'm
not a diplomat. I'm only a soldier."

There was a pause while that information was evaluated.
Devon's carriage and something indefinable about the pride

with which he had brazenly spoken appealed to the general's mind which still dominated Bonaparte's thinking.

"But my soldiers wear uniforms. And you don't appear to be wearing one. Perhaps you have fought for your country in a different way. Perhaps you, like your friend, have chosen espionage as your method of service to the English Crown," Bonaparte said gently.

"I am not, nor have I ever been, a spy. I told you. I'm a soldier. Nothing more."

Everyone was aware that one of the Emperor's favorite conceits was the idea of himself as, still, only a soldier. It was Bonaparte's often-noted affinity for his fellow soldiers of any nationality, that Devon had been gambling on.

"You enter my empire under false pretenses, attempt to rescue the man credited with directing England's intelligence activities and then tell me that you are 'only a soldier.' And I wonder, my English friend, why you think I would accept that claim, in the middle of this entire web of deception, as true?"

The silence, disturbed only by the ticking of the gilt and marble clock on the mantel, was complete as they waited for Devon to answer the Emperor's question.

Pride, Julie thought, suddenly afraid. Your stubborn English pride is about to cost you your life. Show him, she urged mentally, *prove* to him that you are exactly what you've said. But the silence stretched dangerously.

And when he didn't speak, the quiet waiting was shattered by her voice, which rang clear and calm.

"Make him show you his back," she said to Napoleon, knowing that was proof beyond dispute of Devon's assertion, and that the Emperor would certainly be able to identify the cause of those scars.

Bonaparte's gaze had moved to the girl's face and softened unexpectedly. He had a notorious weakness for beautiful women. And in spite of the nature of her rather bizarre costume, this one was very beautiful. Judging by her speech and manner, she was not what she appeared to be, either

This was turning out to be far more entertaining than he had anticipated. He smiled at her and was treated to a practiced and very provocative dip of dark lashes and then an up-sweep, which revealed smiling eyes.

"Take off your coat," he said to the tall Englishman, his eyes still resting on the girl's heart-shaped face. Far paler than he would have thought with that black hair, but re-markably beautiful.

"No," Devon's soft voice answered, and the Emperor's surprise pulled his attention from the eyes of the girl, which had suddenly widened.

"Don't be a fool." Devon heard Jean's whisper from behind him, but he was so furious he was almost trembling.

"I can always have someone remove it," Bonaparte said simply. He didn't seem to be particularly angered by the refusal. "But I don't think you would enjoy that. And to preserve your own dignity..." he suggested.

Julie held her breath until the long fingers began to re-move the dark coat he had donned this morning for his role as doctor. Devon dropped the coat and reached behind with one hand and, locking his fingers into the material of the shirt, pulled it over his head in a single, furious jerk.

He heard Jean's quickly suppressed gasp behind him, and then he turned slowly, so that his back, held as straight as if he were on parade, was to the Emperor. His ice-cold blue eyes locked on Julie's, and by the bitterness that was re-vealed in his she knew how much he hated what she had just forced him to do.

But in watching her reaction, Devon missed the soft foot-steps that crossed the carpet behind him. The gentle touch of fingers tracing the ridges of scar tissue sent a shiver across his marred back, like the flickering skin of a horse that has felt the touch of the spur.

"I think sometimes it's a very hard thing to be a soldier," one old veteran said finally to the other and, bending, the Emperor of France lifted the discarded shirt and draped it gently over the English colonel's shoulders.

He walked by Devon, who was still trembling slightly with reaction. Bonaparte's eyes deliberately did not look at the face of the Englishman, but he allowed his gaze to openly study the scarred countenance of the Frenchman.

"And I think that's something you, too, understand," he said to Jean. "I remember your face. Before those scars." He paused and met the unwavering intensity of that hazel eye. "It was in connection to a certain position at Wagram, a position that had to be held at all costs, and a young captain who promised that it would be."

There was no answer for a long time, and then Jean said softly in response to that memory, "And it was."

"Yes," the Emperor acknowledged the quiet pride of that claim. "It was. I understood that you had been wounded. I looked for you, but the surgeons hadn't expected you to live. You'd been sent from the front, and I'm afraid I assumed…" he paused in the midst of that remembrance. "But I must confess, I'm surprised to see you in this company, or have your loyalties changed so much since then?" And he lifted one hand in a brief gesture at the burns that marked Jean's face.

"I hope you know that they haven't, sire. But there are extenuating circumstances," the gambler said, smiling slightly in return.

The Emperor's dark eyes watched the twisted movement of that damaged mouth, and then he nodded. "There always are. We are seldom allowed to do the things we believe are right without extenuating circumstances. I assume you also would like for me to intervene with the minister of police on behalf of you and your companions."

"If…" Jean paused, unwilling to ask.

"If I remember what I owe you?" the Emperor finished for him.

Jean's gaze fell before that ready acknowledgment of that debt, and then he glanced up to say, "I would never ask, but…"

"Extenuating circumstances?" Napoleon suggested softly.

Jean hesitated.

"It doesn't matter," the Emperor said, watching the conflict in that dark face. His eyes traced the seared flesh and the black patch. "I don't forget deeds of valor. And whatever business Fouché has with you, I think he can be compelled to forgo its completion."

"And the woman?" Jean asked into the silence that followed the Emperor's promise of his freedom.

"And is she the circumstances that drew a loyal Frenchman into this nest of spies? Perhaps, if love is involved, your lack of judgment is explained," the Emperor suggested, smiling.

Jean allowed his eyes to turn to Julie's for the first time since he had seen, overlying the brutal damage the shrapnel had inflicted, the fresh marks of her nails on Devon's back and shoulders. He knew she had not been aware of them, or of what they had revealed to him. Her concern had been for Devon, and not for him.

But Jean had loved her for a long time, and he wouldn't abandon her now. The Emperor would let her go if he claimed her. No matter what he decided about the two Englishmen, Napoleon would give him the girl.

"Yes," he said softly. Her eyes met his, but nothing was the same.

He held out his hand, and her small fingers locked into it.

Seeing her response to the Frenchman's invitation, Devon looked away, his mouth as rigidly controlled as that straight, scarred back.

And Napoleon again considered the Frenchman before he smiled at the girl.

"Make him tell you some day how he got those scars. It's an interesting story."

"I will," she promised softly.

Suddenly the door that led to the Emperor's private quarters behind this office opened. It was the military doctor Bonaparte had sent to examine the duke, and they all turned at his entrance. Even Devon, who had not touched the shirt that had been thoughtfully placed over his shoulders.

The surgeon's eyes seemed to rest on Devon's figure a moment too long, but after all, it was certainly unusual to find a half-dressed man in the presence of the Emperor, and his gaze eventually shifted to his commander's face. Bonaparte's black brows lifted in question. Again the physician's hesitation was almost noticeable.

"Let him go," he said softly.

"I've told you who he is," Bonaparte began, and the surgeon interrupted, an obvious sign of the respect in which his opinion was held.

"He's not a threat to you. Not any longer. Let him go," he said again.

The Emperor waited, considering the options available to him and the English soldier's warning about the possibility of international repercussions. Perhaps it was the simplest way, after all.

"He's dying. I don't know that he'll survive the crossing." At the involuntary reaction of the man standing nearest him, the man whose bare chest heaved hard once, reacting as he had seen men react to a saber thrust, the surgeon paused, and his next words were clearly addressed to Devon.

"There's an abscess of the bone. It's too deep for surgery. And for the hip, of course, amputation, which is the only treatment, isn't possible. Take him home. I'll give him something so he can stand the Channel."

Devon nodded once.

Having made his decision, the Emperor walked back to the table and, finding materials, wrote a scrawling message that represented freedom for them all. He turned and gestured to Jean, who released Julie's hand and moved to accept the document.

The Emperor's lips lifted slightly, and he rested his hand

a moment on the shoulder of the man whose scars would make an interesting story. One he had no doubt the girl would never be told. And smiling, he patted the hard arm and turned back to his table and the endless maps and charts. They had been dismissed, and the surgeon and Jean were certainly aware of it.

The doctor moved his head in a slight gesture toward the front entrance, and Jean knew that he would arrange for Avon to be carried there to meet them. He walked across the room and touched the English soldier's arm. Devon started slightly and, still in shock, followed him.

Julie waited until the two men had passed, and then she turned to the man who stood looking down on the Empire he must try to re-create. Re-create without his *Grande Armée*. Without many of his most experienced marshals, who had refused to break their oaths of loyalty to the Bourbon king. Without his wife and son, who would not, of course, be allowed by his Austrian father-in-law to rejoin him.

Julie knew that the people who had been judged here this afternoon had already been forgotten, but she said it anyway, whispered the words that no one else had thought to say.

"Thank you, sire," she said softly, and in the Gypsy skirt that was so short it touched well above slender ankles, she gracefully performed a deep and formal court curtsy. And held her position until the dark eyes, enjoying the picture she made, smiled their reply.

It had begun to drizzle rain, and the courtyard was dark with the heavy clouds that overhung the city. Under the direction of the military surgeon, the soldiers were carefully transferring the English duke into the waiting carriage, one clearly marked with the imperial crest, larger and more accommodating transportation for the sick man.

When the three of them reached the coach, Jean put out his hand to help Julie inside. She hesitated, looking at Devon's set face.

"No," she said softly. "I'll ride. The air will do me good. I need…" She couldn't think of an excuse for her sudden desire for hours spent sloughing through the muddy roads. But it really didn't matter.

"You ride inside with the duke," she said to Devon and walked toward the waiting horses, who, sensing the coming storm, milled against the experienced hold of the soldiers. One of the imperial guard eagerly helped her mount the gelding, which she had instinctively chosen, and the young guardsman blushed in response to her smiling thanks. She forced her eyes not to return to the man standing beside the Emperor's carriage.

Jean's hand grasped her bridle suddenly, and she watched the raindrops pattern against his dark skin. She couldn't meet his eyes.

"Why?" he said. "Why in God's name did you do that?"

"To save him from a firing squad," she answered. "I thought it was the only way."

"You must have known how much he'd hate being forced to show those scars," Jean said, thinking that if anyone understood what Julie's suggestion to the Emperor had cost the Englishman, it was he. "He'll never forgive you," he warned.

Her eyes rose to meet his, and she pushed at his hand, demanding her release.

"It doesn't matter. It was just a dream. You've told me from the first how impossible…" she began and then shook her head.

He held the bridle until the restive protests of her mount finally broke through the confusion of his thoughts. He released his hold and watched her calmly soothe the gelding's display of temperament.

"It doesn't matter," she whispered again, the rain beading in the dark curls, and he couldn't tell whether those drops caught in her lashes were rain or tears. But her eyes were clear and wide on his face. He stepped back and mounted the horse the watching soldier held and waited for the signal that would allow them to leave Paris behind.

Devon climbed into the carriage, and hidden finally from those who had surrounded him since the surgeon's diagnosis, allowed his eyes to close against the sting of unshed tears. Only for a moment, here alone, would he allow himself to remember Avon's hand holding his through the long horror of surgery. To remember the hours he and Dominic had spent that fall and winter in London as they had sought the traitor who threatened the lives of British soldiers fighting to defeat the monster whose presence they had just left. Who was not, of course, a monster at all.

"Put your shirt on," the French surgeon commanded softly. He was leaning in to make a final check of the placement of the pillows the soldiers had piled on the seat to cushion the duke from the jolting of the carriage over the rough roads. His dark eyes moved from Avon's limp form to Devon's.

"I should hate for my best work to have been in vain," Larrey, Bonaparte's chief military surgeon, said softly. "In spite of the confidence I expressed when the Duke of Avon asked me to go to London to operate on his brother-in-law, I didn't believe the results would be this good. You owe him a great debt."

"And you and your skills. I am grateful. I would be more grateful if there were anything you could do—"

Devon stopped because he saw and didn't understand the twinkle that began to grow in the physician's eyes. And then his smile.

"I'm a hell of a surgeon, Colonel Burke, but diagnostics is not my forte. Get another opinion when you get to London. It's highly possible that I may have made a mistake. But I shall leave it to you to protect my reputation," he said softly. He withdrew his upper body from the coach and closed the door. He signaled the driver, and the carriage and its outriders clattered out of the courtyard.

"He told me what he was going to do," Avon's voice

spoke from the shadows of the opposite seat. "I was afraid you'd try to kill Bonaparte and then fight your way out of the palace. Those were the longest minutes of my life." The familiar amusement colored the confession.

There was no response from the man who sat, elbows on his knees and his head bowed in his hands. No sound at all except the rain against the roof and the horses' hooves ringing on the stones outside.

The duke reached carefully and touched his knuckles lightly against one of the hands that held the lowered head of his friend.

"Dev?" he questioned softly.

And finally, after a great while, the voice of his brother-in-law, who sat shivering, still bare to the waist, spoke into the silence.

"Just give me a minute, Dominic. I'm having a little trouble adjusting to the idea that I'm not going to lose you, too," he said softly, remembering Julie's small hand, which had been placed so trustingly in the gambler's.

The silver eyes watched that bowed head a long time in the dim interior of the coach. And then they closed, content because Avon understood Devon's strength and knew that he would somehow manage to deal with whatever had happened in the Emperor's office.

Chapter Twelve

The weather called a halt to their progress long before the lieutenant, ordered to see the party safely to the coast, made the distance he had hoped to cover. But he had received explicit instructions from the surgeon as to the care he should take of the sick man inside the carriage, and the condition of the roads had certainly gone beyond those proscribed limits. The small inn had appeared almost miraculously, but the weather had also guaranteed its crowded conditions.

The soldiers were perfectly willing to bivouac in the attached stables, but a private parlor was all that the officer could convince the host to make available to the travelers in his charge. Under his direction, his men made up a pallet not too far from the parlor's welcoming hearth with sheets and blankets provided by the innkeeper. Those and the pillows from the coach ensured a suitable bed for the duke.

When the four travelers were finally alone, there was a decided lack of conversation. Julie stood with her hands outstretched before the blazing logs in the fireplace.

"Do you know where we are?" she said as her fingers began to thaw.

"Somewhere near Argenteuil, I think," Jean answered, watching the slim, straight back. She had thrown off the heavy military cloak one of the troopers had finally persuaded her to take against the cold rain, but the thin peasant blouse was slightly damp, the vertebrae of her spine outlined by the clinging material. And the vision of another back, broad and scarred and scored by the marks of her nails, intruded into the room.

"I think we need to discuss what happens when we reach the coast," Jean continued, and she turned from her contemplation of the fire.

"I don't believe that's anything we need to decide tonight," she began.

"But I do," he said, challenging, and watched the sweep of color in her cheeks.

"No, Jean," she begged softly. "Let it go. At least for tonight. Everyone's exhausted, and—"

"I don't understand the problem," Devon broke in. His voice was calm and reasonable in contrast to the Frenchman's obvious anger. "Dominic and I cross the Channel. After that, you're free to follow whatever agenda you were pursuing before. Unless you want asylum. If you think Fouché will try to take some sort of revenge, in spite of the Emperor's intervention."

"I'd be delighted to arrange protection in England," the duke offered. "Considering all that I owe you, it seems the least I can do."

"You owe me nothing, and I'm not interested in asylum," Jean denied, "but you haven't mentioned what Julie should do."

"I thought Mademoiselle de Valmé had arranged her own future," said Devon.

"And your offer?" the Frenchman asked, the mocking sarcasm back in force.

"I think any offer you coerced from Colonel Burke in Paris has certainly been negated by the events that have intervened," Julie said calmly.

Don't do this to me again, she begged silently, her eyes

eld on his scarred countenance by sheer force of will.
Don't make him ask again what he certainly doesn't want
o ask. Don't, Jean. Not if you care about me.

"On the contrary, my dear. Whatever event left the marks
of your nails clearly visible on his naked back seems to me
o demand some response. Unless, *monsieur,* you managed
o introduce into the casino last night some other female
whose lust for your body left it further scarred with that
distinctive signature of shared passion."

Julie realized then that in forcing Devon to reveal to the
Emperor proof of his military service, she had also led him
o expose what had happened between them. But it had not,
of course, gone as far as Jean was imagining. He would
never believe that now. She didn't remember using her nails
on Dev's back, but considering the emotional state his touch
had reduced her to, she didn't doubt the truth of Jean's
claim.

Unconsciously, in remembering, her eyes had sought
Devon's. And found, instead of the memories of what they
had shared reflected in their blue depths, only a cold formality.

"Of course. Mademoiselle de Valmé is still welcome to
the protection of my name. If she desires it," he said and
bowed slightly, his smile as sardonic as Jean's had ever
been.

"No," she said simply. And the bitter smile widened in
response.

"No," he repeated, "I didn't think so. *Mademoiselle*
made her choice clear in the Emperor's office."

"That's not—"

"There's really no need to defend your decision. And I'm
sure you'll be much happier in your friend's capable hands.
You have so much in common," Devon said, gently mocking.

"But I'm not offering my hand," Jean denied softly. And
only Julie saw and recognized his pain. "I find that I no

longer want her, *monsieur,* now that you've made her you
putain."

At Julie's response, a gasp she couldn't control, Devon'
fists closed, and he made the first step toward the French
man.

Avon's voice interrupted harshly. "Dev," he shouted.

His career had instilled an automatic reaction to that ton
of command, and Devon fought to impose a control he wa
far from feeling, unaware of how revealing of the true stat
of his emotions that unthinking defense had been.

"I would like to offer Mademoiselle de Valmé anothe
option," Dominic said softly.

Devon's gaze swung to Avon's calm face and rested ther
unbelievingly.

"*Mademoiselle,* your father worked for me for years.
would like to offer you a home, a refuge from the danger
you've recently faced because of his employment in m
service and for his country. I hope you'll come to Englan
as my ward. I promise you that my protection is given will
ingly and with no conditions attached. You will be free t
come and go as you wish, and you will be welcome to m
hospitality and my support as long as you like."

"As your ward?" Devon asked explosively, thinkin
only of Avon's reputation before he had married Emily
"You can't be serious," he said.

"Why?" Julie asked quietly, imagining all the wrong rea
sons for the disbelief in that strained voice. "Because eve
the Duke of Avon wouldn't dare take your whore into Lon
don society?"

"God, Julie," Devon said, "you know that you're not—
Don't say that," he commanded softly, his anger dissolvin
suddenly, destroyed by the knowledge of what he had mad
her feel.

"It's what they both believe," she whispered bitterly.

"But it's not true. Why are you saying this?" he asked

"Because it would have been true. Last night. If you adn't…"

And the memory of what he had said, and of the caressing ouch of his hand, destroyed her bitterness, too. She met his yes, and there was none of the coldness that had been there arlier. They were as tender as they had been last night.

Only last night, she thought. So much had happened. She ould no longer depend on Jean's support. And she didn't nderstand why Devon had been so angry. Perhaps, as the renchman had warned her, he would never be able to for-ive her for what she'd forced him to do in the Emperor's ffice.

Only two things were the same. Fouché would still like find her, for revenge if for nothing else, and she could ever become Devon's wife. For it would be a marriage orged out of his sense of noblesse oblige and destined, in ae closed world of London society, to become nothing but cause of bitter regret.

"Marry me, Julie," he said softly, as if in mockery of aat thought. "Let me take care of you." And he waited.

But it was not the reason that might have moved her to hange her mind. She had never wanted his protection. Only is love. And he had never offered her that. She knew he vanted her, wanted to make love to her, but it was not the ame.

When she finally spoke, it was to the man on the pallet, hose silver eyes had watched with concern for them both.

"Yes," she said to Avon. "If you meant it, then, yes, I'll o to London as your ward."

She didn't look at Devon, whose proposal she had re-cted for the second time. And she didn't attempt to explain gain the impossibility of accepting what he had just of-red.

"That's probably a wise decision," she heard Devon say itterly. "As the Duke of Avon's ward your future will cer-inly be assured. My congratulations on the shrewdness of your choice. Ever the opportunist. And who knows, perhap in London an even better offer will come along.''

And because she didn't look at him, she didn't know unt she heard the door of the small, comfortable parlor clos behind him that he had left the room.

She never knew where Devon spent that night. In a care fully maintained silence, she and Jean had occupied th chairs in the inn's front parlor, and Avon's weakness an exhaustion had ensured his night's sleep. But she didn't se Devon again until he met them at the carriage the followin morning. He didn't look as if he had slept at all, the ski surrounding the blue eyes dark and bruised. But he had es tablished a laughing camaraderie with the soldiers who ac companied them, and she supposed he had bedded dow with them when he had left last night.

He walked up to the gelding she had ridden yesterda quickly adjusting the stirrups to their normal position. Th roan reached back to dip his nose gently into the broa shoulder, and Devon whispered into his ear with seriou concentration. He patted the massive neck and then swun smoothly into the saddle. The horse turned, dancing slight in response to the familiar weight of his rider. Devon's blu eyes met Julie's watching brown ones and lingered brief over features that revealed that her night had also bee sleepless. And then he skillfully controlled the gelding's ex citement and edged the horse to a position close to th young lieutenant, who looked up with a smiling welcome

Julie forced her eyes away and found the silver gaze of the duke on her face. He smiled at her as she entered th carriage to take her place across from him.

"I think this will be a good opportunity for us to becom better acquainted, *mademoiselle,*" he suggested softly.

"Of course," she said, closing the door. "But if I'm t be your ward, I think you might begin to call me Julie.

he wondered again why he had made the offer she thought s ridiculous as Devon's.

A twenty-three-year-old woman, especially one who had een as much of the world as she, didn't become anyone's ward. Her acceptance had seemed the only solution to what ad been happening last night, but here in the light of day, he thought he might be as embarrassed by his proposal as he was by her agreement.

Even as ill as he obviously was, it was hard to imagine hat someone whose sheer vitality was so evident in his eyes nd in his intellect had so little time to live. And she would ever allow him to spend one moment of whatever time emained worrying about her future. She was, as Devon had eminded her, perfectly capable of arranging that for herself.

The duke didn't speak again as the carriage began to roll ut of the yard and onto the mire of the road. Their journey vould be as slow today as yesterday, she supposed, staring ut at the rain-washed countryside.

She looked up to find Avon watching her face with some-hing approaching compassion, and so she decided that she night as well put an end to this farce, as well.

"I want to thank you for what you offered last night. I'm orry that what was taking place when you made that offer vas so uncomfortable for everyone. But we both know so-iety will never accept the idea that you've suddenly de-ided to adopt a female faro dealer. And I've no doubt your vife would be less than delighted to welcome me into her ome. I wouldn't blame her."

"I've found that the ton generally accepts anything, no natter how outrageous, as long as it's presented from a po-ition of wealth, birth and power, and with a certain arrogant *ravacherie*. All of which I happen to possess," he said. he could hear the amusement and the gentle invitation to oin him in making fun of his own class.

"I'm sure you could carry even that off, but I don't intend hat you'll have the trouble."

"I assure you, my dear, that I'm quite looking forwar
to presenting you to London society. I think they'll be er
chanted. And as for Emily—"

"No," she interrupted softly, and her eyes were very se
rious. No wonder Devon had been so determined to find thi
friend. He was making plans for her future when his ow
seemed so bleak.

"Am I allowed to know why?" he asked.

"Because you'll have other things you'll want to do. Be
fore…"

There was a delicate pause, and when she looked up fror
her twisting fingers, the gray eyes were alight with laughte

"Forgive me," he said. "You must think I'm remarkabl
slow. But I had forgotten."

"Forgotten?" she whispered.

"My impending fate. My untimely demise. My unfortu
nate—" And at her sudden obvious enlightenment, h
smiled.

"You're not dying," she said frankly.

"I don't think so. And neither did Larrey."

"Then why?" she breathed and knew the only answe
"To save your life. To make the Emperor release you. Bi
why would he do that?"

"I'm not sure my life had a great deal to do with Larrey'
decision. Dr. Larrey was the surgeon who removed the mos
damaging piece of shrapnel from Devon's back. I think, lik
a painter, he couldn't stand to have his greatest masterpiec
destroyed. He'd worked too hard to watch Dev shot dow
by a firing squad. If he could convince Bonaparte that I wa
no longer a threat to him…"

"But Dev had, I think, already convinced the Emperor t
release you. He'd claimed you were an accredited diplo
matic. He seemed very assured that the English Crow
would corroborate that claim. He was extremely convinc
ing."

The duke's slight smile told her, without the arroganc

words would have displayed, that that part of Devon's assertion had almost certainly been true. Avon had been too valuable to the British government for them to deny him any aid.

"So Larrey's deception wasn't necessary," Avon suggested.

"No, I didn't mean that. I think it was the deciding factor." She paused, remembering the scene in Bonaparte's office.

"I *am* interested in what happened. When Larrey told me you were meeting with Napoleon rather than Fouché... I don't even understand how that was accomplished."

"Apparently the Emperor was aware, even before his escape from Elba, that Fouché had been planning a coup. In spying on his minister of police, he discovered our attempt to rescue you."

"I understand the diplomatic repercussions of holding me, but why would Bonaparte decide to release the rest of you?"

"My father and I never knew anything about Jean's background, but it seems that at some time he was a soldier. An officer. Napoleon called him captain. He managed to hold some position in Austria. And in the process... You've seen Jean's scars, which the Emperor indicated were acquired in his service."

"And because of that service Bonaparte was willing to release Jean?"

"And me. He asked if I belonged to Jean. I accepted because I thought if we were free, we had a better chance of arranging for Dev's escape. He'd already ensured your safety. But then Dev said..."

"What?" Avon prodded softly at her pause.

"That he wasn't a spy, but a soldier."

"Which is true," Avon agreed, watching her face, which had drained of all color as she remembered what had happened next.

"But Napoleon wanted proof."

"And?"

"And then I made Dev prove that was true," she whispered, seeing again what had been in his eyes as he had stood, stripped, before the Emperor.

"You made Dev— But how could he prove—" the duke began, and then he knew. "You made him show Bonaparte his back?" The duke's voice clearly expressed his doubts about the possibility of that having occurred. "I would be very interested, my dear, in hearing how you were able to convince Devon to do that."

"The Emperor ordered him to, but only because I suggested it. I thought they were going to execute him if he didn't. But he hated it. Jean said he'd never forgive me."

"I think never is too long a punishment for an action that was undertaken with the best intentions."

"That was when Jean saw... You heard what he saw. But I promise you—"

"You owe me no explanations." Avon interrupted whatever assurance she was about to give. "Indeed, I am the last person to whom you need explain any action you were forced to take after your father's death. I'm only sorry I was unable to offer you my protection then. And I know Devon very well. I know the kind of man he is. There's nothing you need to defend in your relationship to my brother-in-law. I'm well aware of Devon's code of conduct. It certainly extends to his treatment of the woman he loves," the duke said quietly.

"He told me he was in love with someone in London," she said.

"At one time. But she married someone else because of his injuries. If your refusal of Dev's offer was in any way influenced by the thought of that woman in London..."

"No." Smiling, she shook her head. "I knew she existed and I also knew she had married someone else. I refused Devon because I know what marriage to me would mean

You know who my father was. Can you imagine me entering, on Devon's arm, any of the homes of the people who knew my father's story? I wouldn't mind so much for myself, but I would care very much for Dev. And he would hate them for the way they would react to my presence. Hate them enough to kill someone, I think,'' she finished softly.

"And if that barrier were removed?" Avon questioned, watching her face. "Would you accept his offer then?"

"An assumed identity?" She laughed. "Even if no one learned that I'm the Viscount Ashford's daughter, I assure you I couldn't attend a single dinner party in London where some gentleman wouldn't recognize the Divine Juliette." The epithet was lightly spoken, but the duke remembered the pain his use of it had caused. "I don't want him killed in some pointless duel to protect an honor only he believes I have."

"Then you love him?"

"Of course," she said simply, and smiled at him again. 'I thought you knew."

"Forgive me. Sometimes the workings of the female mind defeat me," he said.

"I doubt it," she denied, smiling.

When his soft laughter came, she swept the thick lashes up to show him the hidden sparkle. Somehow she had been instantly at ease with this man. She already considered him a friend. And, she decided, if he were serious, she was going to enjoy being the ward of the Duke of Avon, however ridiculous anyone else thought that might be.

The inn they found that night was almost empty, the sudden clearing of the weather freeing the travelers who had been stranded there by the storm. There were rooms for them all. She knew that Devon had seen to the meal that was carried upstairs to the duke, and he didn't join them in the downstairs parlor. She and Jean ate with the young of-

ficer, grateful for the restraining presence of his company
But eventually he retreated from the warmth and the polit•
conversation to rejoin his men, and she and Jean were lef
alone. She began some excuse that would take her safely t•
her room without having to face what now stood betwee•
them, but he put his hand on her arm, and so she waited.

"I'd like to talk to you," he said. "I wanted to tell yo•
that I'm sorry for what I said."

"I know," she whispered. "But what happened wasn'
what you thought."

"Come with me. When we reach the coast. In spite o
the fool I've made of myself, you know how I feel abou•
you. And if you're really determined not to accept his offer
then let me take care of you. It's what your father wanted.'

Her eyes rested on the face of a man who, knowing ho•
she felt about another, was willing to give her his love. An•
because of what had happened in the emperor's office, sh•
was very conscious again of his brutal scars for the firs
time since she had come to be more aware of the value o
the inner man.

"You were a soldier, weren't you? Like Dev. That'
where you met Bonaparte. You fought for him. And that'
what he meant about the scars. He told you to tell me abou•
this," she whispered, her fingers touching the textured dis
coloration that marred his face. He turned away, move•
slightly so that she couldn't caress his cheek.

She let her hand fall and watched him a long time. An•
then he smiled.

"In the course of the last ten years, almost everyone i•
France has fought for the Emperor. And in spite of what h•
told you, these don't make a very interesting story. But I'•
tell you sometime," he promised, "if you'll come with m•
tomorrow. You know you don't want to go to Londo•
Think, my darling, what your life will be like. You're to•
accustomed to the freedom you've enjoyed so long. You'•
never fit in. And you don't really want to. You can't."

"I'd give my life if I could," she said truthfully, and heard the rasping breath he took when he understood what he had just said. "But I won't marry him. I won't make his life the hell my father's was."

"Then why won't you come with me? What do you hope—"

And suddenly he knew from her eyes what she intended, knew before she confirmed it, her voice stumbling a little over the words. "If I can't become his wife, and you and I both know all the reasons that's impossible, then I'll be his mistress."

"He'll never allow it," Jean whispered.

"I thought you didn't believe he was that noble. And perhaps you're right—maybe he won't want me. But I have to try. It's the only chance I have."

"And if you don't succeed?" Jean asked. He hadn't touched her, but he knew he would. Before he left. Before he let her go to the man she had chosen over him. "What will you do if you don't succeed?"

"I don't know," she said honestly, smiling over the limited choices left to her. "Become a Gypsy fortune-teller," she said, remembering the Romany camp. "Or convince the duke to back a small, very select gaming room in London. I haven't thought that far."

"Julie, my love, if you ever need help with that genteel establishment in London, you have only to send word. You know that, don't you?" Jean asked softly. "Or if you ever decide that you need me for anything else."

"And like Dev, you'll come from the pits of hell for your friend?" she said, reading clearly what was in his face and in the tenderness of his voice.

"Of course," he said, smiling.

She lifted on tiptoe and placed her lips against the cruelly marked corner of his mouth where the damaged nerves created the slanting, one-sided smile.

"I can't feel you there," he said softly, his breath stirring against the gentle touch of her mouth. And very carefully as if she were a fragile piece of porcelain, he enfolded he in his arms. His lips found hers, and his tongue forced an invasion. And a response. For a fleeting moment, she al lowed the comfort of his love to envelop her. But he wasn' Devon, and finally he knew.

He released her and forced himself to smile into her eyes

"I hope he's not a fool," he said. "For your sake, my darling, I hope he has sense enough to know what you are But remember…"

"I know," she said. "And I will, I promise. I'll neve forget."

He was gone the next morning, and although Avon asked she could say quite honestly that she didn't know when he had left or where he was going.

Chapter Thirteen

Despite Larrey's denial of the death sentence he had imposed for Bonaparte's benefit, Devon was still concerned about Avon's health. For more than one reason now, he wanted to get the duke back to London, to put an end to this seemingly endless journey and then attempt to arrange his own future.

He pawned the gold and emerald seal in Le Havre to provide funds for their passage. He arranged for the mare to be sent back to the old man and for the gelding to be loaded on the vessel he had hired for their crossing. Then he returned to the inn where Julie and the duke waited.

"Tell Moss how valuable that seal has been. And I promise to retrieve it for you, Dominic. I'm sure you could simply order our journey on the basis of aristocratic arrogance, but when I showed up on the wharf, they all demanded their money in advance," Devon said, smiling.

"I don't care about the damned seal, and I don't think I could convince anyone to do anything right now, Devon. I can't even seem to command myself most of the time," Avon said bitterly.

Devon recognized the duke's frustration with his continued illness. Avon's inability to make his body recover, to become strong enough to do more than sit up for short spells before he fell asleep like an exhausted child, was, Devon knew, driving him mad.

Dev touched his shoulder in unspoken sympathy, and somehow, at that gesture, they both were back in those small rooms in London where Devon had lived his confined existence before Larrey had freed him.

"Dominic," he advised, knowing very well what the duke was feeling, "give it time. When we get to London—"

"Sandemer," the duke said, and looked up with more of that familiar aura of command than Devon would have believed possible only minutes before. "Not London. I want you to arrange for me to be taken to Sandemer. Send for Moss and for Dr. Pritchett. But I'm not going back to London until I know…"

The blue eyes that met his were carefully controlled. Devon in no way revealed that he was well aware of the fear that had necessitated the decision.

"And Emily?" he asked, watching the duke's face.

"When I've talked to Pritchett," Avon said. "When I know what the hell's wrong with me."

"Dominic," Devon began to argue.

"No, Dev. Whatever you're going to say, whatever argument you intend to make, I've already considered. Believe me. You have no idea how much I want to see Emily, but I want some answers first. Just get me to Sandemer and then get Moss. You've wasted enough time on my affairs."

"I hope you don't mean that," Devon said, anger coloring his voice. "How can you believe that I've begrudged a moment I've spent in this search?"

"You know I didn't mean it. If you want my apology for that idiotic remark, you have it. I just—"

"You don't have to explain. Especially to me. That's a road I've been down, my friend. But if you don't send for Emily, you're going to hurt her more than you ever have before. By now, she's bound to know that something's gone wrong. And if you come back and hide at Sandemer, then she's going to think—God, I don't know what she'll think.

But don't do it, Dominic. You're wrong. Stubborn, arrogant, proud—as always. And wrong.''

Blue eyes locked with gray, and for the first time in their friendship, Avon's fell, hiding what he felt.

"Sandemer, Devon. I know what I'm doing," he said, the blue-blooded aristocrat accustomed to immediate obedience commanding once more.

Devon studied the averted profile a long time, but the duke refused to meet his eyes.

Finally he turned away and found Julie watching the scene. She smiled at him tentatively, but his lips tightened rather grimly. She knew she was just another problem.

Since her refusal of his offer, he had spoken to her only out of necessity, the words polite and formal. As one might treat the friend of a friend, someone whom one was not especially fond of. And she supposed that described their present relationship rather well. Finally she turned away, and she didn't know that his gaze rested on her a long time before he left the room.

When she heard the closing door, she glanced at the duke, but his eyes were closed, the smudged circles of exhaustion dark around their hidden vitality. She wondered about the woman they had been discussing, Avon's wife, who was apparently to be denied the opportunity to care for her husband in his illness. She understood her own guilt, but she wondered what the Duchess of Avon had done to deserve her punishment.

The Channel was rough, the waves chopping whitely against the sides of the small vessel. Devon worried about the wisdom of trying to make the crossing considering Avon's condition, but he knew the duke was a good sailor and more than eager to make the attempt. He couldn't imagine the effects a bout of seasickness would have on Dominic, so he simply closed his mind to that possibility.

But it was not Avon who suffered that indignity. It was the Parisian, the sophisticated cosmopolitan, who had never before been on the sea. Devon had arranged for two cabins, and having helped the willing crewmen install the duke in the narrow bed of one, he had returned to find Julie standing by the rail, fascinated by the activities of the busy docks.

They were barely out of the harbor, the gray-green water churning against the planks of the laboring vessel, when Julie turned suddenly and fled below. Not understanding at first, Devon followed and found her in her small dark cabin where the odor of fish and stale bodies overlay the scent of brine. She was sitting on the bunk, the clammy pillow held crushed against her face. He could see her shoulders beginning to heave as she fought the growing nausea.

He found the bucket, conveniently placed by the door, and knelt before her. He forced her to release the pillow, and at the desperation in her dark eyes, he smiled comfortingly at her. She lowered her head and swallowed hard, fighting her body's betrayal.

Only a few seconds later, her small fingers found the rim of the bucket he held, and then he was holding her, too, as she was thoroughly and violently sick.

When he judged the first paroxysm had eased, he sat beside her, pulling her to rest against his chest, and fumbled in the dimness for the discarded pillow. Its casing, however, proved to be too noisome for his need, and without hesitation he used the sleeve of his shirt to gently wipe her mouth.

She made a token protest with fluttering fingers, and then allowed his strength to overrule her sensibilities. She really didn't care what he did. There could be nothing more humiliating than what she had just been forced to endure.

"Go away," she said hoarsely. Her throat ached with the violence of the attack.

Her hands pushed weakly at his chest, but he didn't loosen his warm embrace. And instead of the smell of fish, which had increased her sickness, the scent of Devon rested under her nose. She breathed in the masculine aromas of his clean body, and wondered vaguely how he managed to smell so good in spite of the conditions of their journey.

She was sure she didn't. And remembering the events of the last few minutes, she was again horrified that he was seeing her like this.

The toast of Paris, she remembered suddenly. What a bitter jest. The one man she had ever cared about impressing, and instead...

"Go away," she said desperately, and managed this time to sit up, to pull her swimming head away from the comfort of his hard chest. He let her up, but she knew he was still there. She could hear his breathing, magnified in the swirling vortex of her nausea. And then the fish. And the rocking motion of the world beneath her.

Her fingers dug suddenly into his arm and she whispered, pleading, "Dev." And miraculously the bucket was there again when the next convulsive retching made her forget everything, her humiliation lost in her gratefulness for his hands, which seemed to know exactly what she needed.

She was sick a long time. A maelstrom of confusion, of being held closely, cherished between the agonizing spasms that robbed her of thought, of dignity, of humanity, it seemed. Until finally, exhausted, she thought it might be over. Her stomach still gave an occasional heaving motion, but there was no longer any need for the bucket. There was literally nothing left.

He laid her at last against the cold sheet. She was aware that she held, with trembling fingers, the warmth of his shirt against her face. At some time during the ordeal, he had removed it to wipe her face, and she had latched onto it as to a lifeline. It was Devon. As were the hands that had held her head, as gentle as a woman's would have been. And his voice, whispering against her icy cheek. She wanted to remember what he said, because she thought it was important, but it had been lost in the devastation.

She was aware that he was kneeling beside the bed. Her eyes closed, so she wouldn't be forced to see whatever was in his face, she said, "Go away. I don't want you. Just leave me..."

"Alone?" he finished softly, and the word echoed somewhere in her consciousness, reminding her of how alone she was now.

"Yes," she said, fighting the urge to just let him take care of her. To just give in and let Dev again protect her. "Go away," she whispered instead.

But he was back almost before she had realized that he really had obeyed her. He lifted her to sit leaning against his chest, as he had cradled her between attacks. He held a brandy flask against her lips and tilted it suddenly so a few drops of the spirits it held entered her mouth. She was afraid she was going to be sick again, but the container was insistently presented.

"Drink it," he commanded softly, and she did, trusting him.

When he judged she'd had enough to relax her, but not enough, considering her empty stomach, to precipitate another bout of nausea, he found the stopper, his arms still holding her against him while his fingers secured the flask and then laid it on the floor beside the bed.

"Sit up," he said in that same soft tone of command. She leaned forward and then he was sitting with his back propped against the wall behind the bed. He pulled her against him, shifting her body so that he could stretch out his long legs beside hers. Her back was against the solid warmth of his bare chest, and his arms encircled her, his hands crossed loosely in her lap.

"Are you going to give me back my shirt?" he asked, his mouth against the top of her head, his breath stirring the fragrant curls.

"No," she said.

"Not ever?" he asked, and she could hear the smile in his voice.

"No," she denied, snuggling closer to the pleasant closeness of his body.

"Why not?"

"Because it's yours. And I like to hold it."

The brandy he had forced her to swallow was making inroads on her ability to think. But it didn't matter. This was Dev. Whatever she said was all right. Was right. Because he was warm. And he was holding her.

"I love you," she said finally.

"I know," he whispered again, and she felt his lips nudge against her temple. She closed her eyes at their touch.

"I'm going to seduce you," she said, and his steady heartbeat against her spine hesitated and then resumed.

"I'm delighted."

"Not now," she explained carefully. "In England. But now... I don't suppose you'll want me now."

"And why would you suppose that?" he questioned, and again she could hear the smile.

"Because how could you?" she said simply. It was so clear. No one could still want someone whom he had... She lost the thought. And it hadn't been very clear anyway. "You know," she said instead.

"No, I don't know. And I don't care. I think I've made you drunk, my darling."

"I like that," she whispered.

"Being drunk?"

"No, the darling part. I wanted to have your babies," she said rather incoherently, and the tears started unbidden, but she blinked them back. There had been that lurching break again in the strong rhythm behind her.

"Little Gypsy girls with dancing eyes," he suggested softly.

"Or soldiers. No, not soldiers. Soldiers get hurt. I don't want our sons—" Her voice broke, and his arms tightened. "But mistresses don't have sons," she finished. "At least in Paris."

"I wasn't planning on having a mistress," he explained.

"But she's married. You can't have a wife who's already married to someone else," she reasoned. "You told me."

"I told you a great deal of nonsense, all of which you

seem to have remembered. And I have my doubts that you'll remember this. But I'm going to try anyway. You're going to marry me. You might as well get used to the idea. You may think that you'll convince me otherwise, but you won't. You won't be my mistress. And you won't fall in love with anyone else. You belong to me, and you know it, and I know it. And you're just going to hurt yourself fighting against that truth. And you're going to have my sons one day. And my daughters,'' he said softly. His palms had found again the curve of her stomach, and he tightened his fingers to let her feel his possession there. "Don't break your heart, my darling, fighting the inevitable. It won't do any good.''

"No,'' she argued softly, and shook her head. She could feel the roughness of his unshaven chin catch a strand of her hair. "You need a shave,'' she said, sounding very much like a wife.

"Yes, dear,'' he whispered, and she wondered vaguely why he laughed. But the feel of that gentle movement against her body was so pleasant that she closed her eyes, and he held her while she slept.

Devon and his shirt were gone when she woke. The motion of the ship had stopped, and she knew they were in England. Her father's home. And now hers. At least for the time being.

She straightened her clothing as well as she could, and wrinkled her nose at the unpleasant odors that surrounded her. She wanted fresh air and the salt breeze against her face. And out of this awful hole. She walked to the door and noticed the bucket he had brought her, washed out with salt water and standing innocently in its usual place. She wished she could remember all he'd said, but she remembered enough, and her eyes were suddenly haunted. She gathered her courage in both hands and climbed the narrow steps to the deck.

She wondered if they had left her. There was nothing and no one in her bustling surroundings that looked familiar.

"My lady," a voice at her elbow said hesitantly, and the sailor had to repeat his assertion before she realized he was talking to her.

"His grace asked if you'll wait on board until the arrangements for transportation have been made. The colonel's already gone ashore."

"Of course," she said softly, wondering how he could possibly call someone as bedraggled as she was "my lady." How ridiculous. And she had long since ceased to think of Avon as "his grace." But, of course, he was.

Once Devon's initial resistance to the duke's plan had been voiced and rejected, he had privately decided that Sandemer's location on the coast might be easier, given the duke's condition. The French captain, however, had adamantly refused to accommodate his unscheduled and unsought passengers by landing them in those unfamiliar waters, so the colonel had been forced to make arrangements for their transportation to Avon's home overland.

When Devon returned, he found Julie sitting on a pile of hempen rope watching the harbor. The look he gave her was slightly challenging, but there was a new element in the blue depths that she hadn't had time to identify before he turned to continue below decks to discuss their imminent departure with Avon.

In the carriage she and the duke slept most of the way, and it was dusk before they turned from the well-maintained road up the winding mile that led to Avon's estate. And she was unprepared for the vast expanse of the structure that suddenly rose before them out of the mists that had begun to gather with the twilight.

Her eyes moved from the imposing sight to find Avon watching her.

"I used to get lost," he said, smiling.

"I can see why," she said, laughing. "You didn't tell me..." She stopped because he hadn't told her anything except that she would have the protection of his name. She couldn't imagine why she hadn't realized his name would entail all the privileges his title automatically carried.

"I know it's an architectural horror," he said. His head was resting back against the corner of the coach, and she knew he couldn't see the castle. Only in his mind's eye. "But it's..."

"Home," she suggested, and he smiled.

"Thank God," he said softly, and the smile faded. "Devon's right, you know."

"Don't you start, too."

"Why not?" she said. "I'm your ward, remember. I'm supposed to be concerned about your welfare. And I'm a woman. I know how your wife will feel."

"I know how she'll feel, too," he said softly. "That's the bloody hell of it."

And wisely she left him alone.

Julie had certainly not grown up in any sort of impoverished situation, but she had not previously encountered anything on the scale of the wealth and the elegance of Avon's estate. Her fingers trailed over the ivory silk hangings of the bed in the enormous chamber she had been carried to. The dignified footman who had escorted her had in no way expressed surprise over the condition of her apparel or her disheveled hair, but she found herself fighting to keep her lips from moving into a smile as she imagined the story he would tell below stairs when she had been safely disposed of.

She noticed her broken nails and decidedly grubby knuckles and quickly removed her fingers from the priceless material before she could damage it. She looked at the inviting tub and the steaming, fragrant water that had appeared, almost like magic, under the direction of Avon's efficient majordomo. She touched the soft lawn of the nightgown that had been laid over the lavender-scented sheets.

Impostor, she thought, but she undressed quickly and lowered her body into the warmth of the water. After she had washed her short curls, she leaned her head against the back of the tub and wondered if Devon were soaking in the soothing warmth of a similar bath. She almost dozed, surrounded by the realization of what it meant to be the ward of His Grace, the Duke of Avon. And then she smiled.

I'm still the dancing girl. No matter what my surroundings, that hasn't changed. And I know it.

She waited until the noises of the house had ceased. And then she forced herself to wait another long hour, carefully measured by the hands of the mantel clock.

The smell of beeswax and lemon oil permeated the upstairs hallway, and her bare feet made no sound on the gleaming oak.

Standing before the heavy door, she wondered briefly if she should knock. But in the silence she decided against that urge, and so she turned the handle and allowed her eyes to adjust to the dimness.

Devon was standing by the window, his body marked by the shadows of the mullions. He didn't turn, and she thought he hadn't heard the opening of the door. The scars on his back were dark fissures against the liquid glow of the moonlight that washed his skin. She stood, drinking in the tall perfection of his body, the broad bare shoulders, the muscled length of thigh under the skintight material of his pantaloons.

"I've been waiting a long time," he said softly. "I was beginning to think you'd changed your mind."

"No," she said, and at the uncertainty of that single syllable, he turned and smiled at her.

"You seem a remarkably reluctant seducer," he said finally into the long silence.

"I had thought you might help," she suggested, smiling.

"No," he denied, and he didn't return her smile. "I want to be courted. I'm tired of being rejected, Julie."

"I've never rejected you," she said.

"Forgive me, but when you accepted Avon's proposal, it felt very much like rejection to me."

"I refused to marry you. That's very different—"

"No, it's not. If you've rejected my name, you've rejected me."

"That's not why. And that's not fair. You know I can't marry you. I've told you what would happen."

"Do you think I care what anyone else thinks? Do you honestly believe that what anyone would say about you would make any difference to the way I feel?"

"Eventually," she said, very sure. Remembering her father's exile.

"God," he said softly. "You have to know—"

"Make love to me," she interrupted. And saw the words stop him.

"Why?" he asked.

"Why?" she repeated, incredulous. "Because I want you to. Because I thought that you— You do still want me, don't you, Devon? What happened on the boat hasn't changed that, has it?"

"Julie," he said, laughing. "Yes, I still want you. Do you remember what I showed you in your father's bedroom?" he asked softly. And saw by her face that she did.

"Would you like me to show you again how much I want you?" he asked, his voice seducing her. This was not what she'd imagined, but it was better. He wasn't resisting as she'd been afraid he might.

She nodded slowly, unable to move. So he walked across the expanse that separated them and closed the door behind her, and then the chamber was lighted only by the moonlight.

His eyes were very dark, and she could barely read his features. He bent to touch his lips gently to her throat, ivory in the silver glow that poured into the room from the tall windows behind him.

Her head fell back, too heavy suddenly for the slender column against which his breath glided, caressing. He hadn't touched her except with his lips. And with the shivering weakness moving into her knees, she put her hands on the strength of his shoulders.

"You should probably pretend to resist. Simply for convention's sake," he said, whispering the words into the soft fragrant skin between her ear and the silk of her curls.

"No," she breathed.

"No," he agreed, his fingers tangling in the ribbon that secured the low neck of the lace bodice.

His thumb traced into the unfastened V. And he waited. She opened her eyes and looked into the cobalt depths of his.

"Marry me," he suggested quietly, his thumb moving side to side, skimming just under the swell of each breast.

"No," she said, and swallowing, watched his mouth lift at the contrast between those words and her tone. "I love to see you smile," she whispered.

"You will," he promised. "And I don't think we need this." The gown was lowered over the cream of her shoulders, pushed by hands that were dark and demanding against the smooth slide of the fine cotton that slithered softly to fall on the carpet. And then he smiled.

He held out his hand as if he were escorting her onto the floor of some ballroom, and she rested hers in his and stepped out of the small pool of material.

But he didn't lead her to the high bed she had been aware of since she had entered the room.

He looked at her a moment, his eyes caressing the entire trembling length of her slim figure.

"Not at all boyish," he teased softly.

At the tension suddenly released, she laughed.

"You can't be afraid of me, Julie?" he asked softly, having felt her shivering anticipation. And he was reassured when she shook her head.

"You know I'll never hurt you," he whispered.

"I know. I'm not afraid."

He bent again and allowed his lips to touch beside the

pink-tipped bud of her breast. He moved his tongue slightly
against the silken skin, and her breath caught and held until
his mouth finally closed over the hard nipple and pulled
teasing gently.

"Dev," she said, her breath released in a whispered plea
that consisted only of his name.

He concentrated first on the prolonged adoration of only
one perfect globe, and then with the trembling direction of
her fingers, moved to the other. And then both. Endlessly
teasing, deserting and returning until the quivering waves of
sensation that grew upward from between her legs threatened her balance. Her fingers dug into his shoulders as she
felt him go down on one knee, still caressing with his mouth
nipples that were now swollen and aching and wet with
what he was doing. And then to the other knee. Until his
hair was caressing the valley between her breasts, his strong
fingers kneading the outside of their aching swell as his
tongue trailed lower.

It found at last her navel, and buried there, his teeth biting
gently around the edges, while his thumbs rubbed over and
around the throbbing peaks his mouth had created and then
deserted.

Her body was one long flame, wanting something she
couldn't find. Wanting what his mouth was doing everywhere. And not really knowing where. Wanting something.
Everything.

And at the first knowing flick of his tongue over exactly
what she had wanted him to touch, she arched against him,
her body exploding inside. She would have fallen had his
hands not held her hips, cupping and supporting, as she was
lost to anything but the sensation of his mouth moving with
sure command against the most sensitive part of her body.

He held her imprisoned by the pressure of his hard fingers
as the shivering torrents shattered and then, under his
mouth's assault, built again. And again. He wouldn't let her
go, demanding her response. And she was powerless to do
anything but convulse against the force of her love for him.

She hadn't known. Hadn't imagined. And finally he wrapped his arms around her waist and held her as she leaned, exhausted and sated, against him. She cradled his head to her, the silk of his hair moving against her skin as her panting eased. And when her knees finally gave way, her shivering body slid down beside him. And they knelt together in the moonlight.

"If this isn't temptation," he said softly, "then God forgive me, I don't know what would be."

She couldn't speak, couldn't think, but her fingers moved across the harsh landscape of his back and delighted in the roughness of the marred skin. Devon. Always Devon.

"Marry me," he said after a long time. After her body had stopped trembling, its cold warmed against the heat of his skin.

And he waited.

"No," she said, and put her lips against his eyes. "I'm still the dancing girl. The faro dealer. And the only hand I've ever held is carte blanche."

"I'll never ask you again," he said softly. "If you don't know... After that, if you don't know you're mine..."

"I know," she said. "But I won't marry you. I'll be your mistress, Dev, your lover. I'll live with you openly or in some discreet address on a quiet London street. I'll be whatever you want me to be. But not that. I can't be your wife."

He held her. And she hoped. At last he rose and helped her to her feet. Her knees were still weak and she felt fragile, brittle. As if she might fracture if she moved beyond the strength of his arms.

"If I accept what you're offering," he said softly, "then you'd eventually believe that I have also accepted your evaluation of your place in my life. And you mean too much for me to do that. It's all or nothing, Julie. And I'm not going to make love to you. Not beyond what happened tonight. And I didn't know..." He stopped, the memory of her response still shaking the foundations of what he thought he knew about making love. "But some day you're going

to decide that I'm right, that none of what you fear reall;
matters, and you'll want to be my wife. And I'll be waiting
I'm not leaving that choice up to you so that you'll have t
give in or give up or admit your feelings. But because i
has to be what you know is right. Your decision. Do yo
understand?''

''No,'' she whispered. ''I want you. How can you jus
deny what's between us?''

She waited, and in the moonlight, she saw him shake hi
head.

''I can't believe I'm saying this,'' he said softly. ''I
sounds like… I don't know what it sounds like. The sheeres
stupidity. Or the blindest arrogance.''

She waited, and finally he whispered what he had bee
thinking.

''I love you too much to make you anything less,'' h
said softly.

He didn't touch her, and he didn't wait for her respons
to something he had thought she must have known as lon;
as he had. Instead, he turned away from the strongest temp
tation he had known in his life and left her alone in th
seductive spill of moonlight. Inside her head she heard th
echo of the words he had spoken. Hearing them again an
again as her eyes filled with tears that this time spilled un
checked.

Chapter Fourteen

Julie didn't think she had been awake the next morning when the soft knock sounded, but so nearly so that she wasn't surprised by the entrance of the smiling chambermaid. She had been dreaming, she thought, or remembering the trembling response of her body to Devon's touch last night. He had known how to touch her in ways she had not been aware were possible between a man and a woman. And he had read her response and fed on it, stoked the fires he'd created as if he shared her mind.

But the cheerful entry of the servant put an end to that pleasant reverie. She could smell the rich aroma of the chocolate the maid carried in the blue-and-gold porcelain pot. She thought, after the hardships of the last months, that it was very welcome to be waited on.

"Good morning, my lady," the maid said briskly, carefully depositing the heavy tray with its Sevres chocolate set on the table beside Julie's bed. She moved to the windows and pulled back the draperies to let in the morning sun.

"I'm to be your ladyship's maid, as soon as you're ready to get up and dress. And the colonel gave me a letter. Said you was to have it as soon as you was awake," she carefully repeated her instructions, searching the voluminous pockets of the heavily starched apron she wore over her neat serge until she found the missive, a single sheet folded and sealed with a wafer and the seal Devon had borrowed from Avon' desk.

"Thank you," Julie whispered, her pulse racing suddenly at the thought of what he might have written. But she waited until the maid had left the chamber to break the wax.

My Darling,
I'm returning to London to provide Whitehall with information concerning the Emperor's current situation and conditions in France. After that, I hope to join Wellington, who, Avon's servants inform me, left for Brussels on the fourth. You should have plenty of time to decide what you want before I see you again.

Devon

"To join Wellington," she read aloud. "My God, Dev what have you done?"

Unmindful of her state of undress, she threw off the covers and, taking the letter, fled to the only person who might have some hope of stopping him.

Avon's majordomo was serving the duke his morning coffee and could not prevent a small betrayal of his surprise at her entrance, clad as she was in only her night rail. The servant's mouth gaped slightly, but he was too well-trained to allow the reaction to be anything other than brief and quickly hidden. Especially before the duke.

At the quick gesture of dismissal from Avon, who rested against the banked pillows of the bed in which he and his father and his father's father had been born, the butler departed without the least appearance of haste or embarrassment. As soon as they were alone, Julie handed Devon's letter to the duke.

"They won't let him, of course," Julie argued, as she watched him read it. "Surely he can't just rejoin his regiment."

The gray eyes lifted to rest consideringly on her face

"But he can," he corrected her softly. "You and I have cause to know that he most certainly can and will do whatever he sets out to. Believe me, Julie, Wellington will welcome Devon with open arms, one of his beloved staff with considerable combat experience. Most of the Peninsular veterans are in America now. And in his gratitude, Wellington won't look too closely at whatever strings Dev has to pull in Whitehall to be put back on active duty."

"But he's doing this..." She stopped because she couldn't discuss what had occurred between them last night. She was no longer sure of the validity of her reasons in refusing Devon. But even if he were convinced he could overlook her background, would London let him? God, she thought suddenly, what does it matter? Dev's gone, back to the hell that war is. He had warned her last night that the next move must be hers, and then he had left her no way of making it.

"I'm sorry," she said finally. "I don't know why I thought you could stop him. I know Devon well enough by now to know that if he's made up his mind, then nothing will prevent him."

"In spite of my inability to help, I'm glad you came to me," Avon said. Having nothing else to offer her, he held out his hand.

She walked to the bed and took his long fingers, which gripped her own, reminding her bitterly of Dev. She sat down suddenly on the edge, her fear for him making her knees as weak as they had been last night. She had already seen the horrors of what Devon was about to face forever imprinted on his back.

Avon, remembering all she had endured, pulled her against his chest and allowed his arms to enfold and comfort her. He was offering her the only consolation he was capable of. Devon was gone, and if he were determined on this course, then nothing either of them could say would convince him that his rightful place was not in Brussels with the forces that were massing for an attack against Bonaparte.

Lost in the unpleasant realization of how little they could do, neither heard the opening of the door or saw the sudden check of the figure who had rushed up the stairs past the majordomo, whose efforts to intervene in that swift ascent had been made far too late.

"My God."

Julie freed herself from Avon's hold and sat up to face the door. The duke's only reaction to that shocked voice was a quick dilation of black pupils in the silver eyes.

Julie waited for him to speak, to order out of his room whoever this was who had dared to interrupt his privacy without even knocking. But as the duke's eyes calmly met the intruder's blazing green ones, the tension grew until finally she spoke.

"I'm afraid there's been some mistake," Julie said politely to the slim figure who stood rigidly in the doorway. Mud-splashed breeches and riding boots seemed almost a desecration of the elegance of the chamber. And on second glance, curiously out of place with the jade velvet cloak thrown back over one shoulder and the hat, which was suddenly ripped off to reveal a spill of long, red-gold curls.

"And you, madame, have made it," the Duchess of Avon said scathingly, advancing toward the bed.

Julie stood quickly to face the fury of that accusation, perhaps even to protect the duke from the obvious hostility, but she couldn't help but admire the coldly brilliant beauty rage gave the woman who stalked across the chamber.

"And in *my* nightgown," Emily said bitterly, reaching out to flick the priceless lace at Julie's throat. "Really, Avon, you might have had more taste than to dress her in my rail."

"But it's so becoming," the duke said softly. "Or don't you think so, Emily? I had always considered that that particular shade of ivory set off your complexion to perfection, but now, seeing it on Julie, I wonder..." He let his voice trail off suggestively.

"Julie?" his duchess repeated icily. "You should at least

have found someone with a real name. Is this the very best that Paris had to offer?'' Furious emerald eyes traveled contemptuously down and then back up the small figure standing before her.

"I beg your pardon," Julie said dangerously, her own temper beginning to flare in response to the mocking insults of the tall, slim redhead standing before her.

"Julie," Avon said from the bed behind her, his voice as relaxed as if making introductions at a garden party, "I would like to present my wife, the Duchess of Avon. Emily, my dear, this is Juliette de Valmé."

"Get out of my husband's bedroom," the duchess said with great dignity.

"Your wife," Julie whispered, realizing what Emily thought, and that Avon, for some reason, was encouraging that belief.

"Oh, God," Emily jeered. "Don't tell me. He forgot to mention he's married." She laughed, but they both had heard the small, revealing break in her voice.

"This has gone far enough," Julie said furiously, turning to the duke. "What are you doing? Why are you doing this? Whatever she's done, surely she doesn't deserve to be treated like this."

"Whatever *I've* done?" Emily repeated. "What the hell do you mean, whatever 'she's' done?" she demanded hotly.

"I'm sorry," Julie said. "I don't know what you've done. I don't know what you *could* have done that would make him decide not to come home. I told him he was wrong to treat you this way, but it's not—"

"You told him? Good God, Avon," Emily said. "Must I be forced to ask this chit in *my* nightgown to offer an explanation for *my* husband's betrayal? Why are you doing this?"

Julie, recognizing how muddled her helpful intervention had become, once more faced the duke. "Tell her," she demanded. "Tell her who I am, Dominic."

"You tell her," he said, his face absolutely expressionless, but his eyes were fastened still with that strange intensity on his wife's features.

"Yes," Emily said, smiling rather bitterly. "You tell me. I can't tell you how impatient I am to hear this explanation."

"I'm the duke's—" Julie stopped, realizing suddenly that if she had thought Avon's proposal was ridiculous, how his wife would feel, especially since she had just been discovered in his bed.

"The duke's what?" Emily questioned sarcastically at her hesitation. And in unconscious imitation of her husband, one perfectly shaped brow rose in inquiry.

"Ward," Julie finished truthfully, unable to come up with a more acceptable lie.

"His ward," the duchess repeated softly, and then more loudly, incredulously, "his ward?"

"Yes," Julie whispered.

"Dominic?" Emily questioned suddenly.

"My ward," the duke agreed calmly.

"My God," she said again. "I could think of a better story than that, even caught *en deshabille*. Really, Avon."

"That, my dear, is one story you had better never have cause to create," her husband threatened softly.

At his tone, something in the emerald eyes flared and then eased, so that they rested, with considering intelligence, on his face. And softened unexpectedly.

"Dominic," she began, seeming to notice for the first time his thinness and the increased spread of silver in his midnight hair.

"If the duke's story is perfectly unbelievable, then it's probably the truth," Avon's valet said from behind Emily. He had heard most of the conversation, although he had proceeded more sedately up the stairs, given the difference in the ages of the duchess and himself.

And when he had arrived, Moss had taken time to study his master, always his first consideration. The signs of

Avon's illness, signs that Emily was just becoming aware of, had already been carefully noted.

"After all," he continued to reason calmly, "Dominic could certainly have thought of a better explanation than that. You know he could, Your Grace."

"How old are you?" Emily asked suddenly, her eyes returning to the delicate features of the woman who stood between her husband and herself.

"Why?" Julie countered softly. "How old are you?"

Emily smiled, but there was no humor in the movement of her lips. "*My* husband, *my* house and *my* nightgown. So I think I'll ask the questions."

"Old enough not to leap to conclusions," Julie answered challengingly.

The green eyes studied her face a long time, and Julie calmly allowed their scrutiny. After all, she had nothing to hide. There was nothing between herself and the duke beyond friendship.

"Who are you?" the duchess asked again, and there was only politeness in the careful voice.

"Juliette de Valmé," Julie answered.

"And why are you in my husband's bedroom?"

"Because Devon's going to Brussels, and I hoped Avon would stop him."

"Devon? To Brussels?" The duchess's voice had lost the polite control again.

"To join Wellington," Julie explained, recognizing in that loss of control a possible ally.

"My God," Emily said, no longer listening. "How can he? After all he's been through. All that we've been through together. How could you, Dev?"

"Because he's a soldier. It's who Devon is. You know that, Emily," her husband said quietly. "It's all he's ever wanted to be. And what's shaping up in Europe is—"

"I know what's shaping up. Another bloody damned battle where men get blown up like cinders in a chimney. I damn well know what's going to happen. Don't patronize me, Dominic. I've been there. And so has Devon. Don't you understand? First you're gone. And I thought— And now Dev. Or don't you care? Either of you? Don't you care what you do to the ones you leave behind?''

"Of course they care," Moss said quietly, putting a comforting arm around her shoulders. "You're overwrought, Your Grace."

Avon's valet pulled his mistress protectively against his chest and held her there tightly.

"And as for you, boy, I don't know what game you're playing here, but you ought to be ashamed. She's ridden all night to come to you. And how do you greet her? With tricks and riddles. What the hell's wrong with you?"

"I don't know," the duke said softly, meeting the furious eyes of his valet, which narrowed suddenly at the sincerity in that unexpected response. But in obedience to Moss's demand, Avon's gaze returned to the blanched face of his wife.

"I'm sorry," Avon said.

"Why would you do this? Why would you pretend that she's…" Emily asked.

"Because I'm a fool," he said, hearing the hurt that echoed in her broken question.

"You've never been a fool," she whispered.

"Only about you. I've done some remarkably foolish things because of my feelings for you."

"And was that what this little scene was all about? How you feel about me?" Emily asked.

"Believe it or not."

"I'd much prefer to believe it. But why?"

His eyes fell, and he forced his fingers to stop playing with the edge of the sheet.

"Because I needed to see exactly that response," he acknowledged finally.

"And what other response could you possibly expect? God, Dominic, you're frightening me. Please, my darling."

The duchess stopped again, waiting for an explanation that would make sense of this entire episode.

At what was in that whisper, the duke met her eyes. And then the same hand that had been extended in friendship to Julie was offered to the duchess. But the simple gesture was eloquent this time with some other emotion. When his wife's slender fingers were placed on his outstretched palm, Avon conveyed them to his lips with something that, to Julie, looked very much like worship.

And then the duke lifted his silver gaze to find his ward's dark eyes glazed with tears that she was forced to blink to control.

"Julie, forgive us. The worst kind of family contretemps. I can offer you no excuse. Only my apologies. And those of my wife, which, I assure you, you'll have when I've made mine to her. Moss, if you'd take Mademoiselle de Valmé back to her chamber and make sure that she has everything she needs. And Emily, I'd like to talk to you. A few overdue explanations. If you'll be kind enough to hear them."

"Of course," his duchess said, still studying her husband's face. "Moss, please provide whatever my husband's ward requires from my wardrobe." There was no suggestion of mockery in the quiet appellation.

"I'd be delighted, Your Grace," Moss said. It wasn't clear which of their Graces he was addressing, and it didn't matter. He stretched an inviting hand in the direction of the chamber door, and Julie, after a quick glance at Avon, smiled at the valet and allowed herself to be led from the room. After what she had seen in the duke's eyes as they rested on his wife's face, she knew they were definitely *de trop*.

When the maid had finished altering one of Emily's morning dresses, Julie put it on and waited for someone to tell her what to do. She knew that they had probably forgotten all about her, but she wished she could do something to make up for that scene in the duke's bedroom. Although, of course, it had been his fault. And deliberately done, she'd decided, but she couldn't begin to imagine why.

Finally she wandered out into the silence of the wide upstairs hall and was surprised to find the duchess sitting at the top of the grand staircase. The door to her husband's room was closed behind her, and she was alone, her head resting against the tall post of the banister. From where she stood, Julie could see that Emily was still dressed in the stained breeches and the shirt she had worn before.

Julie hesitated a moment, looking down at the surprising Duchess of Avon. She couldn't see Emily's face, but she watched her surreptitiously wipe at her eyes, and she knew by those furtive efforts to hide the fact that she'd been crying that the duchess was aware of her presence.

"Pritchett wouldn't let me stay while he examined Dominic. I don't know why. I already know every inch of his body. I would know, better than that damned doctor, what's wrong."

"Maybe that's why he put you out. Professional jealousy," Julie suggested and was pleased to hear the slightly watery laugh in response.

"I'm sorry about this morning," Emily said. "If Avon wants a hundred wards, he can have them. As long as he's all right."

Julie eased down to sit on the step beside her.

"That's really all I am. I know how it must sound, but when he offered and when I accepted— The situation was— Neither of us saw any solution to what was happening. And I'm still grateful that he offered. But I'm no threat to your relationship," Julie explained and saw the amusement in the tear-washed emerald eyes that were raised in response.

"I know that. If I hadn't let my temper get the better of me, I would have known it when I walked into the room. But he's never before given me cause to be jealous. He always let me know that I was—" The duchess stopped and shook her head. "I don't know why I'm telling you all this. You can't possibly be interested. It's just that I can't stand this damn waiting. It's taking Pritchett too long. I'm going to kill him. And Dominic, too. Damn them all,'' she said again, feelingly.

Julie was surprised when the slender white fingers found her hand and held it tightly.

"Have you ever been in love?" Emily asked after several more endless minutes had passed, the door behind them firmly shut.

"Yes," Julie admitted, and she was unaware of the pain revealed in that word.

"Not with Dominic?" the duchess asked softly.

"No," Julie said and smiled. "I'm sure you can't understand that, but no, not the duke."

Emily's answering smile was, for the first time, given with its usual warmth.

"I'm sorry," she said softly. "What happened?"

"Happened?" Julie repeated.

"To the man you love? What went wrong?"

"Well, nothing, I suppose. But considering he's on his way to Brussels…" she said and waited.

"Dev?" Emily breathed. "You're in love with Dev?"

"I know nothing can come of it. I told him. But I can't help how I feel. I promise you I understand how impossible it is."

"I think—" Emily began, and then shook her head. "You're going to have to explain all that. If you love Devon, then why can nothing come of it? You make it sound as if—you're not married?"

"No, of course not. What do you think I am?" Julie asked.

"Avon's ward," Emily replied. "That's all I know about you. And that you're in love with my brother. Who's lost his mind and is going to rejoin the army. As soon as I've finished killing Dominic for going to France, I'm going to do the same to Devon."

"I'll help," Julie promised grimly.

"And does Dev love you?" the duchess asked.

"Yes," Julie said, and her eyes were very sure when she met those of Devon's sister.

"Then why would you say that nothing will come of it?"

"Because no matter how much I want to, I know I can't marry Dev. And he won't let me be his mistress," Julie added, almost an afterthought.

"Then I take it that you've offered," Emily asked, fascinated by the idea that her brother might inspire that kind of sacrifice. "To become his mistress."

"Yes," Julie answered, without any explanation to soften the effect.

"So that's when Avon made you his ward?"

Julie hesitated and then finally admitted, "It was a little more complicated than that. We thought Fouché might still be looking for me in France, especially after what we'd managed to accomplish in rescuing the duke. And Jean, who was going to take care of me, thought I'd— He believed Devon and I..." Julie's voice faltered over confessing what Jean had believed. "So I accepted Avon's offer because I had nowhere else to go," she finished truthfully.

"And Devon?" Emily asked.

"He wanted to marry me. And I told him I couldn't, and then he left for Brussels. So if anything happens to him there, I suppose it will be my fault," Julie said, putting into words what she had felt since she'd opened his letter.

"Can you tell me why you can't marry my brother?" Emily wasn't making much sense of this disjointed narrative, but she had always been able to focus on the essential.

"Because I'm the daughter of the Viscount Ashford. If you don't know the story, I'm sure there will be any number of people in London eager to tell you. And because I've spent the last five years of my life as a dealer in one of the largest and most notorious casinos in Paris," Julie said calmly. "Either situation seems insurmountable to me, but together..." She gave a small and very Gallic shrug. "And so I told Devon no. He seems to think that all those things don't matter and that eventually I'll realize that and change my mind.''

''And you, on the other hand, are very sure they matter a great deal?'' Emily said softly, and she couldn't hide the pity in her eyes.

''Aren't you? You know London. I saw what the viciousness of the ton did to my father. And Dev will be forced to overhear the same whispered remarks, endure the same cuts and snubs, the open insults. It broke my father. He never recovered from losing the world to which he had once belonged. To which he still desperately wanted to belong. And I couldn't bear to watch that happen to Devon because of me.''

''But Dev... Don't you know how little Devon cares about those things? I don't know your father's situation. But I do know Dev, and I don't think all your reasons put together amount to a row of pins as far as he's concerned.''

''Not for himself, perhaps. But do you think Devon would tolerate any insult to his wife? Or his children? I've seen his reaction,'' Julie said softly, remembering his fury with the drunk's taunt at the fair and with Jean's accusation. ''And I *wasn't* his wife. I wasn't really anything to him then. How many duels do you think he'd survive? And he'd fight them. You know he would. And eventually he'd either kill someone or be killed.''

''And so you'll refuse to marry him because you're afraid he isn't strong enough to deal with your past.''

''It's not a matter of strength,'' Julie began to deny, but Emily's assertion that that was the essence of what lay between them was something she'd never considered before.

''What you're really afraid of is that Devon's love isn't strong enough to deal with all that without turning into something else, the same bitterness that ruined your father's life. But Devon isn't your father. And I think you must trust that he *can* handle every objection you just expressed. If that's all that stands between you, surely...''

"I wish I could believe you. You don't know how much."

"Then believe me. Because I know him very well. And when Devon asks you again—"

"But he won't. He told me that. I have to ask. I have to know that it's right. And now, even if I were convinced that that's the right course for us both..."

"Dev's gone."

"And it's too late."

"Why don't you let me see to it your place in the ton is so assured that when Devon returns, all your doubts will have been laid to rest? And you'll be free to make the offer, and Dev will accept. That won't be an exactly novel approach in this family," Emily said. Julie saw the softly remembering smile, but couldn't know the significance of that memory.

"You really think so?" Julie asked, wondering.

"No, I really know. We'll let Avon..." The pause recalled the situation that had brought them together at the top of the elegant staircase. Hearing the sudden doubt in the low voice, Julie put her arm quickly around the Duchess of Avon and held her as tightly as Moss had before.

Pritchett's face was unreadable when he finally opened the door. Emily stood to meet him, still holding onto Julie's hand. Julie could see the sheer terror in the emerald eyes of Dev's sister, and she supposed the doctor could, too, for the first words he said were intended to be reassuring.

"I can find nothing too seriously wrong with your husband, Your Grace. Beyond a troubling weakness of the lungs and a loss of strength caused by prolonged malnourishment and mistreatment. Considering the conditions of his imprisonment and the virulence of the pneumonia that resulted from it, I think he's very lucky. But I've prescribed bed rest. A month, at least. With nothing more strenuous to occupy his time than an occasional game of chess. I don't want his man of business or his estate manager to have access to the duke at all. I mean complete rest. I'll check on him periodically and have the local man look in between my visits. And I think if that regimen is adhered to carefully, he may, in time, recover fully. The lungs don't seem to be irreparably damaged as yet, but I'm sure you know how tricky such things can be. Even the slightest chill,'' he suggested ominously and then shrugged.

Realizing from her face that he had made his point, he kindly and rather unthinkingly patted Emily's shoulder. It was a familiarity he normally would never have allowed himself, but somehow this mud-stained duchess seemed far less intimidating than she should, considering the ancient title she bore. The women watched as he made his way down the steps and allowed the majordomo to help him into his coat.

"Do you know how to play chess?" Emily asked.

"No. Do you?" Julie answered.

"Not yet, but I intend to learn," the Duchess of Avon said, and turning, went into her husband's room, closing the door firmly behind her.

Chapter Fifteen

London—July 1815

The temperature of the crowded ballroom was enough to make several young debutantes swoon, and the officers who had unwisely worn their woolen uniforms were already regretting that decision. But somehow it had seemed appropriate that the military should turn out for these celebrations in full regalia, even if it were nearly August. Had it not been for the Duke of Wellington's stunning and decisive victory over the French five weeks before, none of these lavish entertainments would now be taking place. London, at this particular time of the year, should have been empty of members of the ton. But not this year. Not in the summer of 1815.

This was a time to glory in being English. In spite of the cost of that victory, named Waterloo, after Wellington's custom, for the village where he had established his headquarters. Even the name inspired a thrill, except in the hearts of those whose loved ones had appeared on the extensive casualty lists. But tonight society was attempting to forget the darker side of battle in honoring those who had assured the final defeat of the Emperor. Tonight was for celebration, and the swirl of uniforms and fashionable ball gowns that decorated the floor seemed to argue their success in forgetfulness.

The tall man who stood watching those waltzing couples had arrived more than was fashionably late. He had, however, been greeted with pleasure by his host and hostess, despite the fact that he was also uninvited. And he alone, it seemed, had chosen not to appear in uniform tonight, although he was certainly entitled. He was dressed instead in the somber black of formal evening attire, unrelieved except for an onyx stickpin and the fall of his snow-white cravat.

His blue eyes had searched the floor only a moment before finding the small, whirling figure held too closely in the arms of a handsome young hussar. The cap of gleaming ebony curls was longer than when he had last seen her, almost four months ago. But even the cropped hair was becoming the rage. Because, despite the whispers that still followed her passage through a ballroom, whatever the beautiful ward of the Duke of Avon had chosen to do or to wear since her arrival in London in the middle of May had ultimately set the mode.

Anything Juliette de Valmé did was charming in the eyes of her many suitors. It was rumored by those who knew about such things that Avon had already refused a half-dozen offers on her behalf from the few men who were courageous enough and deemed themselves eligible enough to brave the duke's cold reception.

Devon found he had been unconsciously supporting his left elbow with his right hand, and he knew his decision to discard his sling had not been a prudent one. But he'd be damned if he'd show up at a victory celebration like Banquo's ghost. There were enough painful reminders in the room of the realities of war. He didn't intend to be another.

"Devon?" A voice interrupted his reverie, and he turned to find an old Peninsular comrade considering him with questioning eyes. "I'd thought you were still, that is, I'd heard you hadn't yet come back to town."

"This afternoon," Devon said easily. "I'm afraid I wasn't invited. I've made my apologies."

"Which were unnecessary, I'm sure, considering your current reputation and the occasion."

"Our hostess very graciously forgave me," Devon said, ignoring the knowing smile that answered that unnecessary comment.

"I should imagine she would. Have you seen Emily? She's here. And even Avon. Guarding his treasures."

"His treasures?" Devon questioned.

"His duchess and his ward. The Divine Juliette. I suppose, being part of his family, you'll be in a position to cut us all out. Somewhat of an inside track."

"I'm afraid—" Devon began.

"Of course, you may be too late. You'll have to line up behind half the bachelors in the city. But I'd forgotten. You'd already joined Wellington before Juliette rescued Avon. Surely Emily wrote you?" his informant asked, seeing the confusion in the colonel's features.

"The post was uncertain. I don't seem to have heard about the rescue. Perhaps you'd be so kind," Devon suggested, the faintest smile beginning to hover about lips that had lately had little to smile about.

"Damned most romantic thing I've ever heard. I understand you knew about the duke's role in the war, that you even worked for him while you were...incapacitated."

At Devon's nod, his informant continued eagerly, "Well, it seems Juliette was Avon's agent in Paris. Or rather, originally, her father was. The Viscount Ashford. The government needed someone in position in France to spy on Napoleon. Avon approached Ashford, despite the circumstances under which he'd left England, and he agreed. And then later, when he became ill, his daughter took his place. She provided Avon with invaluable information that she acquired while running her father's casino in Paris. The duke went into France to get her out when

Bonaparte finally discovered what was going on, but she ended up rescuing him.

"I don't have all the details. It's been very hushed, as you can imagine. Only the barest bones of the story. They say Avon was furious that his role in the war has finally become public knowledge. But too many people knew about Mademoiselle de Valmé's bravery to keep it quiet. Although, to be honest, I doubt half of the men that are buzzing around her give a fig about her patriotism. I would imagine most of them are attracted by her far more obvious attributes. You really hadn't heard the story?" the man asked suddenly, recognizing Devon's fascination with his tale.

"No," the colonel assured him softly, "I hadn't heard it. But perhaps I can convince Emily to present me. Familial consideration, if nothing else."

"Well, good luck. But you won't manage a dance. They're always spoken for in advance. Even Emily won't be able to help you there. It's good to see you back," he said, punctuating his words with a friendly tap on Devon's left shoulder.

As he had already turned away, he missed the quick grimace that light touch had caused. Devon unobtrusively eased his palm again under the elbow of the aching left arm and wondered where Emily could be. It was amazing how quickly he'd found Julie, considering the throng. The dark blue eyes watched her laughing figure a few minutes longer, unaware that his sister, who had found him despite the crush, was quite accurately reading his thoughts from the grimness of the smile that played over his lips.

"What's wrong with your arm?" she asked, and he only then became aware of her presence at his side.

"Nothing," he said, quickly removing the supporting fingers.

"Liar," she returned with assurance, but without rancor, and they smiled at one another.

"Are you really all right?" she asked, when he finally

met her eyes. The deep blue of his was too bright, a brightness whose cause she recognized, and the flush across his cheekbones was not caused by the sun. Sisterlike, she put the back of her hand against his temple and could feel the heat of his fever.

"Don't," he said softly, and with his right hand he caught and lowered her fingers. He smiled at her again to take the sting out of his denial. "Just leave it alone, Emily. I'm staying only a moment, I promise."

"Dev…"

"Where's Dominic?" he asked, forcing a change of subject.

"In the card room. Have you seen Julie?"

"Only from a distance," he answered, waiting for whatever sisterly advice he knew she would want to give.

However, she surprised him. The green eyes rested on his face with concern, but she didn't say whatever she was thinking.

"Is Dominic recovered?" he asked and knew by her smile, knew before she told him, that her husband was again Avon.

"He's fine. He's wonderful."

"Thanks to Julie," Devon said, his tired blue eyes filled suddenly with humor.

"You've heard the story, I take it. One of Dominic's better efforts. I'm sorry your share in the rescue was lost somewhere in translation from the French. We decided that it might open questions as to the time you and Julie had spent together, and so, my dear, you were never in France. In case anyone asks."

"Of course," her brother said gallantly. "I'm delighted not to have been there."

"I'm glad you're home. Despite hearing about your exploits from half the army, I really wanted to see for myself that you'd survived. Did you have to go about proving whatever it was you were trying to prove with such recklessness?"

"Yes," he said, not bothering to explain the emotion that had driven him at Waterloo, an emotion he'd not acknowledged, even to himself, for a long time. He had gone to Brussels to prove that he was the same man he had always been, that the unthinking courage that had served him in countless battles in Iberia had not deserted him because of what had happened to him there.

"And did you accomplish whatever you set out to do? Or will you go haring off to the next war we become embroiled in?"

"If," he started softly, his eyes returning briefly to rest on one of the dancers.

She waited, watching his face until he again became aware of her presence.

"If," he began again, "I have my way, I'm going to be raising babies."

"I beg your pardon?" Emily said in surprise.

"Babies," her brother repeated. "You know. You have one. Little Gypsy girls and..." He stopped at the look on her face.

"Babies," she echoed faintly. In spite of the fact that her own son had always adored his uncle, Emily had apparently never thought of Devon with children.

"But first," he said, "I have to acquire a wife." He had come tonight because he had to see Julie. But he had also come hoping that she'd finally realized nothing stood in the way of their marriage except her own fears. He had never cared about the opinion of the ton, but according to his recent informant, even that hurdle had been overcome. Perhaps tonight.

"Any advice, my only and well-beloved sister?"

"No. No advice, but I'll wish you luck. I like my husband's ward very much. And she plays a very skillful game of chess."

"Chess?" Devon asked in surprise.

"Never mind. I'll explain later. The music's ending. You might just catch Julie between partners. If you hurry."

"No, I don't think so," he said and smiled at her raise brows. "I think I'll join Avon in the card room. I hav something of his I need to return," he continued, remem bering the duke's emerald seal, which he carried once mor in his pocket. And, of course, the next move must be, per haps now more than ever, Julie's.

The Duchess of Avon watched her brother stroll throug the crowded ballroom toward the small antechamber wher the gentlemen who chose not to dance were occupied wit their card games. He never glanced at the floor where he husband's ward was surrounded by the usual bevy of hand some men.

It was Emily who was waiting for Julie the next time th music ended. She used her prerogative as her chaperone t charmingly dash the hopes of the young man who owne the next dance and sent him callously on his way. Whe she turned back, Julie was smiling at her rather question ingly.

"I thought you deserved fair warning," Emily said.

"He trods toes," Julie suggested. "I know. But poo dancing isn't a reason to…"

"Devon's here," Emily said simply, and was well re warded by what was suddenly revealed in the dark eyes.

"Avon said it might be weeks before he concluded hi duties with the army of occupation. I don't know why every one else seemed to have had leave to return, and Dev ha to stay."

"There apparently was a reason for that delay. I'm afrai my husband has been as deceptive about Dev's duties a about your background."

Julie wondered why Emily was being so cryptic if Devo had been working again for Avon. Since the fabricated stor about her past that Avon had "revealed" to carefully se lected sources—sources the duke was sure wouldn't be abl to keep such a delicious and slightly scandalous secret— everyone was aware that espionage was Avon's vocatior

ut that, of course, was not the pertinent part of Emily's
formation.

"Where is he?"

"He went looking for Dominic."

"But not for me?" Julie asked softly.

"Well, to be fair, you were rather surrounded. And I
ink, from what you've told me, Dev's still waiting for your
ecision. Avon's in the card room. Shall I dance with your
ext beau?"

There was a long pause, and then Julie smiled serenely.
'I don't think so. Thank you, Emily, but I'll attend to my
wn obligations."

She turned to find her next partner standing patiently at
and, and with a smiling apology, she allowed him to sweep
er into the waltz that had already begun.

And so it wasn't until later, during a respite from dancing
emanded by the heat, when her partner had been dis-
atched for refreshment, that Julie looked up to find
evon's blue eyes resting calmly on her face. He was thin-
er and deeply tanned from the summer's maneuvers, the
ne lines around his eyes a pale contrast to the darkness of
is skin. His hair was streaked with gold burned by the sun,
nd she thought he had never been more handsome.

"Julie," he greeted her softly.

"I've never seen you in uniform," she said, glancing at
is quietly elegant evening dress, starkly understated in the
ea of military paraphernalia. The smile she loved began to
ft the corners of his mouth.

"I had thought," he said, looking around him, "that I'd
y to fit in. I didn't realize that parade-ground wear had
ecome de rigueur for an evening in London. My apolo-
ies."

Then the silence between them stretched uncomfortably.
here were no social niceties to be exchanged. And they
ouldn't talk about anything else here.

"Would you dance with me, Dev?" she invited. It was

an acceptable way to have his arms around her. She though from his smile that he knew exactly what she was thinking

"I was told that the beautiful and popular Mademoisell de Valmé never had an open spot on her card."

"I don't," she answered, her dark eyes flashing with mischief. "But I'll lie to my partner if you'll dance with me."

His eyes left hers to watch a waltzing couple sweep gracefully by. And then returned to smile at her regretfully.

"Forgive me, Julie, but I've been traveling most of th day, and…" He took a breath, but he didn't finish the ex planation.

"Of course," she said, embarrassed by his refusal. The seemed almost strangers. "Then…perhaps another time."

"I'd give an arm to be able to dance with you tonight, he said, and the old, familiar teasing note was back in hi voice. "Would you like the heart of a one-armed suitor t go with all these others you've managed to collect whil I've been gone?"

"No," she answered, smiling at his flattery, "I don think I would like that at all. But I would like your promis that we'll dance together. If not tonight, then eventually, she begged, hoping for something.

Dev seemed so contained, and into her joy at seeing hir again, a faint prickle of unease moved. Devon had alway been so sure of the depth and permanence of his love. Surel in the long months they'd been separated he hadn't decide that he no longer wanted her. Her hand involuntarily foun his, seeking reassurance that he still felt the same.

"We have an audience," he reminded her softly, but h lifted her fingers to brush his lips across them, and he foun that it was suddenly hard to breathe. "And I think we'v given them more than enough to talk about for the eve ning."

"You're not leaving?" she asked, correctly interpretin that last remark, in spite of what the touch of his lips o the back of her hand had done to her emotions.

"Yes, my darling, I'm going home," he said and then dded, "I'm at my father's, Julie, if you decide—"

"Devon?" a beautifully modulated voice inquired softly, reaking into whatever he had been about to tell her.

Julie forced her mind from its fascination with what was n Dev's eyes. Something was definitely wrong. But before he could formulate any coherent explanation beyond that rst terrifying thought, she became aware that Devon's atention had shifted, rather gratefully she suspected, to the all, slender blonde at his side.

Elizabeth, now the Countess of March, extended a hapely white hand, and her lips smiled in what Julie, at east, recognized clearly as an invitation.

Dev's gaze fell to the small fingers of the woman he had uarded so tenderly through France as they rested, still afely held in his. Julie gently began to extract her hand rom his hold and felt an unfamiliar tremble in his strong ingers as he reluctantly released her. Again the flicker of nease stirred in her consciousness.

"I wanted to introduce you to my husband," Elizabeth aid. "Since you are my oldest friend in the entire world, I vould very much like the two of you to be friends. It would nean so much to me if, Dev, in spite of everything…" Her oice trailed regretfully.

"I'd be very honored to meet March, Elizabeth," he said the lovely woman at his side. He kissed the hand she ffered and then released it. But her fingers tucked familarly into the crook of his right arm.

"I hope you'll excuse Colonel Burke, Miss Valmer," lizabeth said charmingly, making Devon's excuses for im. "We haven't seen one another in several months, and ny husband is so seldom in London I'm afraid I won't have his opportunity again for some time." Her eyes smiled into)evon's, clearly conveying information she wanted him to ave. "March much prefers the country, although I'm genrally bored to tears there. But he's most generous in sharing ne with my family. I often come up to town without him."

"De Valmé," Julie corrected softly, watching the interplay.

"Of course. Mademoiselle de Valmé. I remember. Forgive me, but I have a dreadful memory for names. Devon had to prompt me throughout my season, or I should never have managed at all. When someone approached, he was always there to whisper the proper title in my ear." Her smile to him was deliberately intimate, and then, to avoid rudeness, was redirected at the last possible second to include Julie. "And French names," she said, shaking her head helplessly over their seeming impossibility. The softly clustered curls bobbed gently, releasing a breath of lavender. "While you're in London, perhaps you might consider using your— Oh, forgive me, my dear. I'd forgotten that your father's name might not be something that you wish to remind people of."

"Why not?" Julie said, smiling easily. This was certainly not the first derogatory reference to her father she'd endured in London. It was, however, the least veiled. And clearly for Devon's benefit. "I loved my father very much. I'm not ashamed to be his daughter."

She met Dev's blue eyes, which were resting consideringly on her face. He had said nothing in her defense. But of course, nothing was really needed. She had already dealt with the worst London could offer and had found that even the most pointed remarks had gradually lost their power to wound.

She had thought that when Devon returned it would all fall into place. Emily had been so sure that he would be able to deal with the ton's lingering doubts about her suitability to be included in their small, tightly knit circle— doubts only the feminine guardians of that sacred *beau monde* seemed still to harbor.

But nothing was going as she'd planned. Devon was so different, so reserved. And all the old fears began to resurface. Was he acting so strangely because he was ashamed of her? Or wondering what the countess thought about her background? Apparently Emily had been wrong, she decided bitterly, and all her confidence about the future began to ebb in a wave of panic. Devon's distaste for her notoriety was exactly what she had feared.

"If you'll excuse me," she forced herself to say, "I need to find my next partner. I'm being extremely rude. Devon, I'm glad you're back. I'm sure I'll see you again soon at Avon House."

He looked down briefly at Elizabeth's hand resting possessively on his arm, and then back up at Julie.

"Until then, my Lady Luck," he said softly, and smiled at her. It was the old smile. There were no shadows there. And her lips moved unconsciously to answer it. Their eyes met again, and then he was gone, guided across the floor, still looking into the smiling face of the beautiful Countess of March, who was probably reminding him of all they had once shared. "My oldest friend," she had said.

Julie stood a moment, allowing her eyes to follow him until the somber black of his evening attire was swallowed up in the swirling sea of crimson and green and blue uniforms. She turned and blindly threaded her way through the dancers. At some point in that near-headlong flight, she felt Emily's fingers catch her arm, but she didn't pause until she had reached the safety of an alcove, sheltered from the ballroom by its ornamental greenery.

"Who is she?" Julie asked bitterly, knowing Emily well enough to know she would have been very aware of the interrupted reunion.

"The Countess of March," Emily answered, the tone of her answer as caustic as the question. "Didn't Dev introduce you?"

"Dev said barely three words to me," Julie said. And then, "She's very beautiful."

"Yes."

"And she seems very popular. I've noticed her before, but I never knew that she and Dev..."

"Why wouldn't she be popular?" Emily said, but the

small laugh that accompanied the question was mocking. "She has everything the ton admires—birth and breeding, wealth and power. She's beautiful. She married well and produced the required heir within the year. The Countess of March has done everything that London considers necessary for perfection."

"You don't like her," Julie said softly, comforted by the obvious loathing that had been in Emily's voice as she had spoken those compliments.

"Like her?" Emily repeated in surprise. "My dear, I once came nearer to murdering that woman than I have ever come to killing anyone. I despise her. She's the woman—" Seeing the sudden pain in Julie's eyes and realizing what she must think, Devon's sister decided on sharing the truth about the Countess of March, a truth she had told no one but her brother.

"When Dev was wounded, he made me write to her, to destroy whatever commitment had been between them. But then we brought him home from Spain and we were so afraid he was going to die. So I went to her. I broke my word to him, but— I know it's difficult to believe, seeing him today..." Emily's voice faded with the remembrance of those dark days.

"Emily?" Julie probed softly.

"I begged her to go to him, to tell him that it didn't matter. That she loved him still, despite what the doctor said."

"And she refused," Julie guessed.

"In order to marry March." Emily shook her head slightly in disbelief. "And then, when Dev—after the surgery, when he found out, he thought her family had forced her to marry the earl. I told him the truth. I wanted him to know exactly what she is. So why my idiotic brother would allow himself to be kidnapped by her tonight, I shall never know."

"Dev seemed so— I don't know what he was. He went

with her, but I thought… His hand trembled when he released mine. He was so strange.''

''I don't know what's going on. But I know someone who will. After all, Avon has very good sources of information. And as for Elizabeth, I doubt my brother will be taken in again. She has everything she wants except, apparently, Dev. But that's one game at which she won't succeed. My brother is not that big a fool.''

Emily pressed a swift kiss on her cheek and went to find her husband who, she seemed to feel, would have all the answers.

It was very early the next morning, after a night spent endlessly reliving the few minutes she had been allowed with Devon on the crowded ballroom floor, that Julie had dressed and sought out Emily, hoping for the promised explanation for Dev's behavior. But the duchess was not in her room, and Julie never considered seeking her in Avon's. Her questions would simply have to wait until her host and hostess rose and joined her downstairs.

Unless Emily was out on one of her early-morning gallops, she thought suddenly, and in that case, she might already have returned and be downstairs, breakfasting alone, as was her custom on those occasions.

Julie hurried down the long staircase, one hand holding up her gown so that the slender ankles of the Gypsy girl were again exposed. She halted at the raised voices in the dining room. Avon and Emily, obviously engaged in some argument. That alone was enough to cause her hesitation. She had never before heard them even disagree.

She had turned and begun to steal back to the upper levels of the vast Mayfair mansion when something Avon said caught her attention. And after that, she could no more have stopped listening to what was, undoubtedly, a very private conversation, despite the raised voices, than she could have ceased to breathe.

"Because Devon didn't intend for Julie to know. And gave him my word, Emily."

"But why? That's ridiculous, Dominic, and you know it Dev's my brother, and I love him, but this makes no sense.'

Avon's answer was too low for Julie to hear, but Emily's denial rang clear.

"Oh, God, Dominic. Poor Dev. It's so unfair."

The rest was muffled, inaudible, and in spite of the chaos of her shocked mind, Julie was certain that the duke had taken his distraught wife into his comforting arms.

Avon's explanation was softly spoken, so that Julie, trying desperately to hear, caught only broken sentences. But those were enough to force the suddenly trembling knees to bend, and eventually she sat alone on the massive staircase and learned the truth that Devon had hidden from her last night.

"...too widely spread...amputation...very dangerous in his condition...near the shoulder," and then clearly, "this afternoon, but Pritchett thinks he may have waited too long..."

Julie swallowed the fear that had grown as her mind began to make sense of those scattered phrases. And she remembered Devon's question. *Would you like the heart of a one-armed suitor to go with all the others?* And her laughing denial.

She took a deep breath and rose, forcing her numbed body to begin again to react, as she had forced her mind. She calmly retraced her steps to the landing and then down the winding servants' stairs and out into the humid heat of the London morning.

The ride in the hackney coach seemed endless, Avon' words echoing painfully over and over. *Amputation...near the shoulder...waited too long* repeated in her head until she thought she would scream. Not Dev, Emily had protested. Not Dev, her own heart agreed.

But Julie knew exactly what his reaction would be, the

smiling pretense that it didn't matter. That it was nothing, as the devastation she had seen before on his back was nothing. Shrapnel, he'd said. Nothing.

She knew how he'd hate this. The forced dependence. The brutally obvious imperfection of his body. But she'd make it up to him, she'd show him that it didn't matter. That she loved him in spite of...

And if he would hate the other, how he would despise that. I've refused you when you were whole and strong, and now that you no longer will be, I'm rushing to tell you that I want you. At least that's what you'll think. Because last night, last night when I had the chance to ask you, before I knew... Before I knew, she repeated, struck by that thought, because she had suddenly realized that no one could know that she knew. Not Avon nor Emily nor Devon.

Dev would marry her if she went to him now, full of loving concern for what was about to happen to him. The doubts about his love, which had been created by his behavior last night, were banished by the revelation of what he had been hiding from her. He hadn't wanted her to know. That's why he had come last night. He hadn't told her then because he had given her one last chance to come to him simply because she knew it was right. Her decision, he'd said, one that he hadn't wanted forever tainted by her pity.

She remembered again the teasing, off-hand question, *Would you like the heart of a one-armed suitor?* And her denial. If only she'd asked him last night. But now he would always doubt her reasons. Somewhere would always be the thought that it was pity or guilt for sending him into that battle that had brought her, full of regret, to ask him to marry her this particular morning.

He didn't need to be weakened today by her tears, her concern. He didn't want her pity. He didn't need it. Not Dev. He needed all the strength he possessed to endure, with his smiling confidence intact, the blow that would fall today.

And from somewhere, like a miracle, Avon's words to Emily came into her head. *I needed to see exactly that reac-*

tion. And Emily's reaction, which Avon had cherished in circumstances similar to Dev's, was jealousy. Bloodthirsty fury. And an open declaration that no one else would have the man she loved.

The carriage jolted to a stop, and the jumbled confusion of her mind cleared. Deception, she thought. No one can possibly be aware that I know. One more deception, my darling. And this one not for the hand, but for the game. A simple bluff to win the game that will last the rest of our lives. And I *am* the professional.

She scrubbed at her cheeks to remove any lingering trace of the tears that had been her first reaction. She bit her lips to give them color and pinched the pale skin over her cheekbones. She ran shaking fingers through her tumbled curls, thankful for the summer's humidity, which ensured their spring.

She glanced down at the pale pink morning gown she had so carelessly chosen. She hadn't known she would be dressing for the most difficult role she'd ever undertake. Far harder than the urchin or the Gypsy girl. Far more important. She gave a mental shrug and tugged the short sleeves farther off her shoulders so that the neckline scooped as low as the peasant blouse she had worn so long ago. The material skimmed the top of ivory breasts that heaved once with the deep, fortifying breath she took. And then she grasped the driver's hand and stepped out before General Burke's home.

Chapter Sixteen

She knocked imperiously on the front door, then pressed trembling hands against the skirt of her simple dress. She dried the telltale moisture from her palms and wished she had gloves. He would never believe she had left the house without bonnet or gloves and wearing what was obviously—

The aging butler opened the door in response to her knock, and suddenly the calmness she had sought settled over her. Like the almost supernal calm of that endless moment before the ball in the roulette wheel stops, or the dice fall, when the betting is heavy enough to ruin the house. Then, as now, there was no need for fear. Whatever the outcome, it had already been decided by the fickle gods of chance. My Lady Luck, he'd called her last night, and unconsciously, she raised her chin and allowed the full force of her smile to dazzle the old man.

"I'd like to see Colonel Burke, please. And would you pay my driver. I seem to have come away without my reticule."

She didn't wait for his response, but swept by him and into the hall. In spite of her air of confidence, she closed her eyes in relief at the conversation behind her, evidence that she had been obeyed.

"I'm sorry, my lady," the butler said as he reentered the house through the front door he hadn't bothered to close behind him, "but the colonel isn't receiving guests this morning."

He glanced rather pointedly at the hall clock, and she was surprised to find that it was only half past nine. Since most of the ton went to bed at four and seldom rose before the early afternoon, she realized how bizarre he must think this call. A woman scorned, she reminded herself grimly of the role she was playing, will do any number of bizarre things.

"He'll see me," she said aloud. "Tell him..." She paused and then knew her inclination was right. "Tell him Lady Ashford would like to talk to him."

"But, my lady—" he began to protest.

"And I'll wait." She raised questioning brows and allowed her eyes to consider the doorways that stretched on either side of the central hall.

"I'll ask," the butler said grudgingly, but he tottered ahead of her and waved her rather ungraciously into the main salon. When she was safely ensconced there, he disappeared, and somewhere from across the hall she heard a door close.

She shut her eyes, trying to think what she was going to say to make him believe her. She remembered Emily's furious eyes that morning at Sandemer, but she was afraid that when she saw Dev, she'd betray herself. Afraid that her eyes would stray, searching for evidence of the injury. Banishing that thought because she could feel the sting of tears, she pictured instead the Countess of March's graceful white hand against the black of Dev's sleeve.

Not the right arm, she thought suddenly. He had used his right arm to hold her hand. To raise it to his lips. She shut her eyes, trying to visualize the few minutes she had spent with him last night. The left, she knew without a shadow of a doubt. He hadn't moved his left arm at all. It had hung awkwardly at his side the entire time. And that's why he hadn't danced with her, she realized. Because he couldn't. Or she would have known immediately.

''The colonel will see you, my lady. But he's dressing. He asks if you'll wait. And I'm to offer you tea.''

Tea, she thought vaguely. Why would I want tea? Because the English drink tea for breakfast. And because I've come calling at the crack of dawn. I wonder what he'd do if I asked for brandy, she thought irrationally, but she controlled that impulse and simply shook her head. After all, Devon might be suspicious if she reeked of brandy. Or, she thought daringly, it might be a nice touch. But before she could make that decision, the old man had disappeared again.

She wandered aimlessly to the windows overlooking the street. Her coach had disappeared, and there was no traffic so early in this quiet residential neighborhood. The trees were green, and their leaves drooped heavy in the summer heat, but their vividness faded as other scenes filled her mind. The caravan where she'd shaved him. The kiss beside the stream. The shadowed barn with its reaching fingers of light. Her father's room above the casino. And Sandemer.

Lost in those images, she was unaware of the entrance of the man she was waiting for. He stood watching a moment as her fingers traced the edge of the window. He wondered who had told her. Emily, he supposed. Avon had known, of course. And whatever Dominic knew was eventually shared with Emily. It didn't really matter.

Only one more thing to be faced, to be endured. And there would be compensations. But first the concern, the dark, tear-glazed eyes trying to avoid looking at his arm. And then eventually he'd be allowed to hold her. And he knew, despite his reluctance to face her pity, that holding her this morning would make the afternoon bearable. And perhaps she would be there when it was over. Compensations. But first...

Somehow she became aware that he was there. She knew suddenly that he was watching her. She bit her lips as she had in the coach, and forced herself to visualize again

March's beautiful wife laughing up into Devon's face. And his answering smile.

She turned to face him, to begin the deception she'd planned.

"A late night, Colonel Burke?" she asked softly. "And whatever did you do with the lady's husband?"

She walked away from the window, the simple gown swaying gracefully as she crossed the floor that stretched between them. Away from morning sun that had created a corona behind the ebony curls, so that finally he could see her face clearly. And in the dark eyes were none of the emotions he had dreaded. They were the flashing eyes of the Gypsy girl—and they held no tears. And no pity.

"The lady's husband?" he repeated questioningly. He was leaning against the frame of the doorway, his pose perfectly relaxed. His right shoulder was propped on the wooden molding, and his left arm was bent at the elbow, the slightly curled fingers resting near his waist. He had hooked his left thumb in the last buttonhole of his blue silk waistcoat to support the injured arm, but the back of his hand hid that. His long legs in tight doeskins and gleaming Hessians were crossed at the ankles, and although he wore no coat over the snow-white shirt and waistcoat, he looked as elegant as any London gentleman she had yet encountered. And as much at his ease. Her lips almost lifted at his deception. Bluff and counterbluff, my darling, she thought, as she had once before.

"The Countess of March," she said haughtily, forcing her mind back to the game.

"Elizabeth?" he asked, and she was pleased to hear his disbelief that she could imagine there might be anything between them.

"And was she as entertaining as before?" she asked boldly. His head tilted slightly, questioning something in her tone or in her wording. Something that must have rung false. Careful, she cautioned herself. Don't overplay.

"She must be very talented indeed. Somehow she doesn't

look that...passionate,'' she finished carefully. ''But we both know looks are deceiving.''

''Julie, that's not—''

''You walk back into London after all these months,'' she interrupted furiously, ''after the time we spent together, after that night at Sandemer...'' She allowed a small, throbbing catch in her voice before she continued her angry tirade. ''And all she has to do is to crook her finger, and there you are again, her devoted slave. Emily was sadly mistaken in her judgment of her brother.''

''Emily?'' he questioned in surprise.

''She said you weren't that big a fool. Apparently,'' she added sarcastically, ''she gave you more credit than you deserve.''

He shook his head, and his eyes dropped, hiding his sudden amusement. Elizabeth, he thought in amazement. God, she's jealous of Elizabeth. If she could only know how little he cared. He straightened, intending to put an end to Julie's misconception about what had happened last night after he had forced himself to walk away from her. But the pain occasioned by even that slight movement of his arm reminded him of what he had steeled himself to face when Ashton had announced her. And instead...

''She can't have you, Dev,'' Julie whispered, and the blue eyes of the man she loved raised again. They looked so tired, she thought, so ill. *Maybe already too late.* Avon's words echoed, but she blocked them. ''She had her chance, and now you're mine. And you always will be.''

''Julie,'' he said again, and at what was in her face, he knew his long wait was over.

But before her control broke, she had succeeded in what she had set out to do. When her lips trembled and her eyes filled, he never thought it was out of pity. He accepted at face value what she was offering. He believed that she had come today only because she thought he still cared for Elizabeth.

''She may be more experienced at... She may know more

ways to please you than I do," Julie said, stumbling a little
over the admission. And her lips trembled again. "But I'll
learn, Dev. You can teach me. Like you did at Sandemer.
And you'll never regret it. I swear to you, my darling, I'll
make you happy. She can never give you little Gypsy girls,
and any sons she bears you will all carry his name. You
said you didn't want a mistress," she argued, knowing she
was losing control.

"Don't cry, my darling," he said, helpless in the face of
the tears that were streaming.

"Oh, God," she said, wiping at her cheeks with the back
of her hand. "I never cry. I darken my lashes, and if I cry
they run," she explained disjointedly. "I never cry," she
protested again, and raised her eyes to meet his.

And found he was smiling at her. He had straightened
away from the support of the doorway and stood watching
her.

"Oh, Dev, don't still be in love with her. I couldn't bear
it if I thought you cared about someone else. I've been so
stupid. But I've always loved you. You knew that. Please,
don't want her instead of me. Not when I love you so very
much."

"Enough, Julie?" he asked softly.

And knowing what he wanted, what he had demanded
from the first, she took a deep breath, feigning a moment's
hesitation. And the blue eyes again waited.

"Devon Burke, will you please, please marry me? I don't
give a damn what anyone says—about my father, about
Paris, about anything. Finally, I know that you don't, either.
I just want to be your wife. And I hope I'm not too late.
You do still want me, Dev?"

He opened his right arm invitingly, and somehow she was
across the room, being crushed fiercely against the strength
of his body. Where she had always belonged. She never
thought about the left arm that had not moved to welcome
her. It meant nothing. Less than nothing that it rested, caught
between their bodies.

And finally he released her enough to look into her eyes, searching them briefly and finding only love.

"Yes," he said unnecessarily, crushing her against him again. "And Julie," he added, whispering the words into the gleaming softness of her fragrant curls, "I have no idea where the Countess of March spent the night. But it wasn't with me, my darling. I was very busy dreaming." He paused, and she pulled away to look into his eyes.

"Dreaming?" she questioned, knowing what he would say.

"Gypsy girls," he whispered, and lowered his mouth to hers. There was nothing gentle about the invasion of his tongue. He was hungry for her, had been hungry through too many long, lonely nights. But her need was as great as his, and she answered as he had hoped she would. Her arms circled his neck, and he lifted her with the sure strength of his right arm. Her mouth clung, warm and demanding.

The fingers of his left hand moved between their straining bodies. He touched the nipple of her breast through the soft cotton of her dress and felt the gasping response of her mouth against his. He caught the hardened bud between his fingers and caressed its tip with his thumb. But even that small movement sent tremors of agony up his damaged arm.

He needed to tell her. He knew that it wouldn't matter, but she deserved to know. She belonged to him now, but it would be some time before he could make her completely his. And he needed to explain that to her.

He bent to let her toes touch the floor and loosened the grip of his right arm. He heard her murmured protest, and welcomed the clinging refusal of her mouth to release him.

"No," she protested, her fingers locked in the sun-streaked chestnut of his hair, pulling his head down to follow the unwilling descent of her body.

"Julie," he said against her lips. His right hand caught the fingers of her left, which circled his neck, and he removed them, holding them tightly in his own. "Julie," he said again, laughing, as she pressed her small body more firmly against the hard erection that was so reassuring of his feelings for her.

"Listen to me," he said, his amused response to her demonstration of how much she'd missed him clear in his voice.

"No," she said again, struggling to gain the release of that tightly held hand.

"Julie," he repeated, and then finally, knowing what would demand her instant attention, he whispered against her forehead, "You're hurting my arm, darling. Please, let go."

She stepped back as if he'd slapped her, released him so suddenly she might have fallen if he had not still held her trembling fingers. He supported her a moment, hating the terror in her eyes.

"It's all right. Just a small souvenir from Boney, but it's still a little uncomfortable."

She swallowed suddenly, and finally allowed her eyes to trace down the length of the left arm, from the broad shoulder to the slightly swollen fingers, once more curled rather unnaturally against his body.

His smile was as quick and readily given as it had always been when she finally raised her eyes to his face.

"No tears," he whispered, releasing her fingers to catch her chin between his thumb and forefinger. "Remember what they do to your lashes. Promise me, Lady Luck, no tears." He released her chin, and smiling, wiped at a small, dark smudge beneath her eye. His fingers trembled suddenly when they touched the velvet of her skin.

"No tears," she promised, willing herself to calmness to hear him say finally what she already knew, what she had known before she had come. She would never confess that her performance had hidden that knowledge. Only a small deception between them. And the only one, she vowed silently, that I shall ever be guilty of, my love.

He remembered, through the daze of pain and weakness and laudanum, that Pritchett had explained it to him. They had found what was contaminating the wound. And had removed it. A thread, he thought the doctor had said. A gold thread from his uniform, driven deep into the gash by the downward force of the saber. And suddenly he was back in the choking smoke of Waterloo, watching the saber's slow, dreamlike descent, watching the blade strike over and over into his arm. That must be what was hurting so badly. That must be… He awoke again to be violently ill. The laudanum always made him sick. He hated it—what it did to his brain, to his control. He thought he had cried out when they'd helped him to lean over the basin. God, it hurt so bad. But that was good. The arm was there, and the pain was reassurance. They hadn't taken it, and maybe now they wouldn't have to. He thought that's what Pritchett had said.

"Yes," Julie's voice came softly into his confusion. "It's still there," she whispered. He opened his eyes and found hers, smiling at him.

"Gypsy eyes." Somehow he managed to form the words as he thought them, and saw her smile.

"Go to sleep," she whispered, and he felt her lips on his forehead. He closed his eyes in response to that command, but he needed to know, and so he forced his lids up again. They felt as if they weighed a thousand pounds.

But it wasn't Julie who was holding the water to his parched lips. He sipped gratefully, and then his father eased his shoulders back against the pillow.

"Julie?" he asked.

"Avon came for her. She has to sleep. It's almost midnight. You'll be better in the morning and she'll be back. You can tell her everything then."

"I'm going to marry her," Devon said to his father and was surprised at the smile that remark occasioned.

"I know. You've told me. At least a dozen times. I'm glad. And I know all about the babies. Go back to sleep, Dev. You can tell me again in the morning."

"Then you don't mind?"

"Mind? I may be an old man, but I'm not an old fool. And I don't think it would matter to either of you if I did. But no, Dev, I don't mind."

He lost the struggle to keep his eyes open. It was after midnight, his father had said, and Julie would be back in the morning. And they hadn't taken his arm. He thought that's what Pritchett had said. Maybe he should ask his father, to be sure.

"No, my darling," Julie said, and he could feel her touch his fingers. They were cold, and hers were warm against their numbness. "Stop worrying. I'm here, and I'm holding your hand."

"And you're going to marry me?" he asked again. He watched her lips slant suddenly, and then she laughed.

"Yes, Dev, for at least the hundredth time, I am going to marry you. Now squeeze my fingers," she ordered gently, and was relieved to feel the slight movement of those swollen fingers against hers. Pritchett had been afraid the surgery had been so extensive it might have limited whatever use he would have of the arm. She felt the tears start at his successful obedience to her request.

"Why are you crying?" Devon asked.

"I don't know," she said. "Maybe because I'm happy," she whispered, smiling at him through her tears.

"You never cry," he said, closing his eyes, satisfied by the smile that she was really all right.

"Maybe," she began, and then realized how true it was, "maybe I've just never been happy before."

She knew he hadn't heard her because she had felt his hand relax into unconsciousness before she had told him that. But it didn't matter. She'd tell him again later. They would have a lot of time later to talk. She smoothed the curls off his forehead and touched the stubbled cheek. You need a shave, my darling, she thought idly.

He mumbled something in his sleep, and she glanced up to make sure his eyes were still closed. And they were, the lids resting without moving, hiding the cobalt eyes. Because what she thought he had said, what he could not possibly have whispered in response to that thought, had been a very softly spoken, "Yes, dear."

Julie could never remember much of her wedding. Only the warmth and strength of Devon's hand holding hers and the look in his eyes when he repeated the ancient vows, his voice as firm and commanding as it had been the day she had met him in the French village. She hated the whispered responses that were all her treacherous throat was capable of producing, but no one seemed to think it was unusual for a bride to be emotional. And perhaps they were especially forgiving of a bride who was so beautiful.

Later, at the reception at Avon House, Devon had finally danced with her. She alone had been aware of the slight awkwardness of his left arm. To the watching guests they had moved together in perfect unison, surrounded by an almost visible aura of happiness.

She glanced up finally to find Devon's eyes on hers.

"My father says you have the Ashford eyes," he whispered, thinking how grateful he was for the general's unfaltering steadiness today, for his support through the difficult weeks of his convalescence. He had allowed them privacy, precious moments that had sustained them during the enforced wait.

"Most people think they're from my mother because she was French, but for those who knew my father..." Her voice faded, and despite the watching throng, she laid her cheek against Devon's chest and relaxed into the pleasure of floating across the polished ballroom floor, securely held in his arms.

But his words reminded her of all the kindnesses the general had shown her since she had come that morning to ask Devon to marry her. He had treated her as he treated Emily, like a much-loved daughter.

And it had been the general who had finally told her the story that explained so much about her father's bitterness, a bitterness that had been for reasons very different from those she had always imagined.

Devon's father had secured her promise to accompany him to the last ball of the extended victory celebration, feeling, like his son, that she'd spent too many long hours in the sickroom. No one in his family had attempted to deny her right to care for Devon, despite what the ton might think. Only Devon's insistence on his full recovery before the wedding had prevented their immediate marriage.

And so she had stood beside the general in that sweltering August ballroom and watched again as the Countess of March floated gracefully across the floor in the arms of almost every man but her husband.

"She's very beautiful," the general said, clearly reading her thoughts.

"Yes," she agreed, smiling at him.

"You're not imagining that Devon still feels anything for her, are you?"

"No, I think Dev was quite clear on that point."

"She committed the unforgivable sin, you know."

"The unforgivable sin?" Julie questioned, wondering why they were even bothering to discuss someone who mattered so little to their lives.

"Cowardice," the general said, his eyes returning to watch that graceful figure. "The one thing Devon could never forgive."

"But I was a coward, too. And he forgave me," she said.

"But you were afraid of quite different things."

"I was afraid that Dev would eventually feel the same bitterness my father felt at losing his place in this world." She glanced around the magnificent room, wondering how she could have been so foolish. Dev didn't want this at all. He had told her how little he cared, but she hadn't believed him because her father had, apparently, cared so much.

"It was March, you know."

"March?" she said, wondering what the general meant.

"That night in White's. It was the earl. Didn't he ever tell you?"

"The night my father cheated? He cheated March?" she asked, thinking how ironic that would be.

"Your father never cheated anyone. I can't believe Arthur never told you. But, of course, knowing him as I did, I should have realized that he wouldn't. That was part of who and what he was. He made his decision that night and he never reneged. He gave everything up rather than betray the woman he loved."

"The woman he loved? I don't understand. What woman? What are you talking about?"

"The Earl of March's sister. Your father was in love with her. And he knew what would happen to her family when it was discovered that March had been cheating. So instead of allowing that to happen, instead of permitting her life to be destroyed, he took the blame. He 'confessed' that the marked deck was his. No one but he and March could be sure which cards had been used. And the earl was very willing to let Arthur assume his guilt. Another damned coward. They deserve each other," the general said bitterly.

"And his sister? She never knew what my father had done for her?"

"She knew. I told her. I thought she'd go with him. We all knew that leaving England was the only possible course open to Arthur. And I thought, if she knew—"

"But she didn't," Julie said softly. "In spite of what he'd done for her brother, she didn't. And so he went alone. No wonder he was so bitter."

"But he never told you."

"No. England was very dear to him. He talked about all this. It all meant so much to him." She shook her head, wondering what there could have been about this hollow show that he'd never forgotten. "But we never talked about that night. I never knew more than the stories I heard from the Englishmen who, despite believing the old scandal, were quite willing to play at his tables in Paris."

"I'll tell them, Julie, if you want me to. Only my promise to your father has prevented my speaking out before. But Arthur's dead, and you belong to my family now. I can clear your father's name. And yours."

"At the cost of March's," Julie said, wondering how the countess would deal with that blight on all that she'd accomplished. On everything that the ton considered important. She was perfect, Emily had said. And now Julie knew it was all built on a lie and a sacrifice.

"No," she answered the general's offer, not even tempted. "It's what my father wanted. But I'm glad you told me. I'm glad he didn't break his code, after all."

It was somehow comforting to know that her father's life had not been a lie. Jean had been wrong, she thought. Wrong about my father and wrong about Dev. And I hope you find someone someday, my friend, who will restore your faith that there are people who are truly noble.

She'd looked up to find the general's blue eyes on her face, and they reminded her of Dev's.

"Dance with me, please," she asked him, and smiling, he led her onto the floor. And his arms had been an acceptable substitute then for Dev's, which finally held her today as tenderly as she had always known they would.

Epilogue

And on their wedding night, deserted at last by both their family and the discreet servants, they were finally alone. The decor of the chamber to which Devon guided her was decidedly feminine, its hangings and draperies done in soft rose, the matching tones of the carpets deep and rich against the dark wood of its furnishings.

"And this is yours. My father had it redecorated. His wedding gift for you, Julie."

"It's beautiful," she said softly.

"But I'd like to invite you to share my room tonight, my Lady Luck."

"You haven't called me that in a long time," she whispered, remembering the night of the ball when she had been so afraid what they would share tonight might never happen.

"But you are. You always will be."

"Give me a few minutes then, and I'll join you," she promised softly.

"Only a few. And if you're longer than that, I feel I should warn you, I've had a great deal of experience storming citadels."

Devon caught her hands, holding both tightly for a long minute while he studied her eyes. Finally he turned her hands over and, almost reverently, kissed the palms. And then releasing her, he entered his adjoining room, closing the connecting door behind him.

He had nearly decided to launch the assault he'd threatened when the door opened again.

"That's almost as beautiful as the moonlight on your bare skin," he said, as she stood poised hesitantly on the threshold, dressed in the ivory silk nightgown Emily had had made for her, the exact shade of the one she had been loaned at Sandemer.

"Avon has impeccable taste," Emily had assured her with a laugh, "and if he says this is your color, then trust me, my dear, it is."

"Avon picked it out," Julie said and smiled at Devon's expression. "Well, not really," she amended. "Only the color."

"But how could he know," Devon said, crossing the room to stand before her. "He's never seen the moon's glow caressing this," he continued, his lips touching her shoulder, bared by the daring design of the gown.

"But you have," she said, and smiled at him again.

"All too briefly."

"And then you left."

"Do you think I could have spent another night under the same roof with you after what had happened between us and not make you mine?"

"I am yours. I was then," she argued.

"Not as completely as you're going to be."

"I couldn't be any more yours, Dev, if we'd been married a hundred years."

Devon took her fingers and kissed them, but when his eyes returned to her face, they were no longer teasing. He pulled her against him and simply held her close, his chin against the top of her head. And smiling slightly to herself, she slipped her hands into the opening of his dark dressing gown to touch the smooth warmth of his chest. She could feel the increased pounding of his heart as her fingers explored the skin exposed by the V of the lapels. She pushed open the robe as far as the material would allow and then began to struggle with the knot of the belt.

"Knotted, Dev?" she mocked, still smiling, and finally the cloth gave under her determined fingers. She released the belt, and as the garment parted, she put her arms around him inside the robe and leaned against his exposed body.

"You feel so good," she whispered. Her dark curls brushed his chest as she turned her face to rub her cheek into the fragrance of his skin. And then his hands caressed her back to pull her up into the hard arousal she had already been aware of.

"Yes," he said in agreement.

She slid her palms up to his shoulders, watching his eyes. They were the same smoky navy as they had been at Sandemer, slightly narrowed as they waited for whatever she intended. She pushed the robe off his shoulders, and it dropped to lie at their feet, only the silk of her gown separating them.

She gently touched the angry red scar that extended almost completely around his upper arm. She hadn't dreamed that it would be as extensive or as ugly. No wonder the doctors had despaired of saving his arm.

"Surely you're not going to quibble about one more mark on my less-than-perfect body, are you? Coals to Newcastle, my darling. Or something to that effect," he said, smiling. "And no, it doesn't hurt."

Julie said softly, "Liar."

As if to prove his contention, he suddenly scooped her up in his arms and carried her to the huge bed. She again enjoyed the sensation of being in Devon's charge, and of being therefore totally and completely safe.

He laid her on the bed and leaned over her, his left knee bent to rest beside her and the other foot still on the floor. He seemed completely unconscious of his nudity, but her blushing fascination must have been obvious, because he said softly, "As always with the French, my darling, you seem to be overdressed for the occasion."

"Or perhaps, always English, you think dress doesn't matter," she suggested, willing her eyes to his face.

"Well, it certainly doesn't matter here," he said, solving the mysteries of ribbons and design with an expertise that fascinated her. His hands managed to brush all the most sensitive spots with teasing accuracy as he expertly divested her of Emily's gift.

"You did that..." she began, and paused because the rough pad of his thumb was moving over her collarbone with tender wonder.

"What?" he asked, but clearly his mind was on something besides her words.

"Emily said you had always been popular with the ladies, but that show of knowledge of intimate apparel was rather—"

"Emily said? My God, Julie, what else did you and my sister discuss about my disreputable past?"

She was sorry she had brought it up, because the movement of his hands against her body had stilled.

"Only that when you fell in love, you... Something she said made me think that you hadn't... That it had been a long time since..." She stopped, sorry she had begun that particular line of thought.

"It has been. Far longer than you can imagine. There was Elizabeth. And then I was wounded. And then there was you. And then I was wounded again. That's rather frightening, don't you think?"

"That you seem to have a propensity for attracting violence?" she asked, smiling at his relaxed tone.

"No, I meant the possibility that I might have forgotten whatever...expertise in lovemaking I'd acquired in my misspent youth," he suggested.

"No," she said, remembering Sandemer and the responses he had called forth so easily.

"No," he agreed, his mouth lowering to find the peak of her breast. She had not been prepared for the sensation, and her body arched uncontrollably. His hand found her hip, and he soothed the force that had moved within her.

"I want to please you, Dev, but you'll have to teach me, as you did at Sandemer. Just be patient. I want to learn everything."

She realized suddenly in the middle of that breathless invitation that he was simply watching her, his eyes shadowed in the subdued lighting of the chamber.

"You said that before. About Elizabeth. That she might have more experience in pleasing me."

"Did you make love to her, Dev?"

And he smiled at the scarcity of any really intimate moments in the long history of his relationship with the Countess of March.

"I don't think Elizabeth was interested in the physical aspects of love. I don't remember her ever even touching me in any way that might—" He stopped suddenly, aware of what he was discussing with his wife on their wedding night.

And felt her small fingers steal to touch his chest, to skim downward across the ridged muscles of his stomach, and lower. She tentatively explored with a lightness that revealed far more than she could know, especially to a man with as extensive a misspent youth as Devon had enjoyed.

But for some reason, he didn't allow her to continue that hesitant exploration. He caught her fingers and raised them as he had done so often to the gentle caress of his lips.

"I think—" he began.

"No," she whispered, freeing her fingers to touch the fan of small lines at the corner of his eye. "Not tonight. Don't think. Only feelings, sensations. But no thoughts," she urged.

He allowed the movement of her hand against his face, but his eyes were considering, remembering, and suddenly she was afraid.

"Dev, what's wrong?"

"I don't..." He swallowed, and the dark blue eyes again considered the worried concern in hers.

"I think you're going to have to explain what you meant, Julie. I'm beginning to believe... My God, my darling, I'm beginning to think I've been a very great fool."

"I don't understand," she whispered. "Explain what, Dev?"

"What you meant about Elizabeth having more experience than you. And that I'll have to teach you how to please me. Believe me, Julie, nothing could change the way I feel about you, but I'm beginning to think that perhaps I've been mistaken. Would you please tell me, Lady Luck, *why* I'll have to teach you to make love to me?" His soft question stopped and, waiting, he lowered his head and touched his mouth again, as reverently as he had kissed her palms, to the pulse that fluttered erratically at the base of her throat.

Her hand found the soft silk of the hair that curled at the nape of his neck. His head was still lowered over her body, and her eyes were wide and dark as she thought about what his words implied. And then she realized what he thought, what he had thought through the long weeks he had sought to make her his wife, and finally she knew how much he loved her.

"Oh, Dev," she whispered. "I didn't know you thought there had been someone else. Someone before you. Only one man has ever touched me. Only one man ever put his mouth against my body. In Paris and at Sandemer. Only you, Dev, and I thought you knew. I thought you must have known or you would never have asked me to be your wife."

"Forgive me, Julie. I thought that was part of why you refused. Because you were unsure—"

"That you could love me enough to overlook that? There's never been anyone else, Dev. My father may have allowed me to run his casino because his illness necessitated that, but I was as protected from his customers' advances as if I'd been the cherished English girl he would have liked me to be. Protected by him, and then later, of course, by Jean.''

And in the darkness, with the sudden upward slant of his lips, hidden by their glide over the velvet softness of her skin, he released, at last, his jealousy of the scarred Frenchman, an emotion he had not even been aware intellectually that he still held.

''Then,'' he told her softly, the moist warmth of his breath tantalizing between her breasts, ''I will be very careful with you, my heart, because you gave me something very precious a long time ago. Then you gave me your trust, that I was the man you'd chosen. And tonight—'' he paused, thinking about what he wanted this night to be for her ''—I may hurt you, my darling, despite the care I intend to take. I don't think I will, given your responsiveness and my intent. But I want you to want me.''

''I want you, Dev. You have to know that.''

''I know. But not like you will. Not when I'm finished,'' he vowed softly, and when his lips again found her breast she knew that she truly didn't understand all he could make her feel. But he was right. Before the night was over, she would know just how right he had been.

With the tenderness of his fingers and with his worshiping lips, he took her again to the place he had shown her before at Sandemer. But this time he allowed her no release. Again and then again he drew her slowly to the edge of the precipice that she now longed to soar over. And slowly, with tantalizing cruelty, he retreated. His hands moved to gentle or to soothe, to touch her cheek, her shoulders. And his lips deserted the flame he had ignited to brush against the corner of her mouth or over the tears he drank from her lashes or to touch the perspiration that gathered under her breasts. But never to release her.

And then he began again. Almost taunting her with his power over her body, which was now totally in his control. She had lost the will to do more than move in response to what he was making her feel. Her hands had found his shoulders and gripped too hard, making their own appeal, which he also ignored. Her fingers fell between them to catch his hard nipples, which moved involuntarily with the roll of the underlying muscles caused by the hard, gasping breath that suddenly shook his body. He said her name then, whispered it into her mouth.

But when she touched him, his fingers paused in what they had been doing, and so she arched against them in her need, demanding, wanting.

"Dev," she begged. Her mind was incapable of any coherent thought. He began to touch her again, and she knew that what she sought was very near, and she wanted it so. And wanted him.

"What, my heart?" he said softly, his lips finding hers.

"Don't stop again," she breathed.

"Stop what?" he whispered.

"Loving me," she said, having no other reference. Her body had begun to shiver, to tremble, and it was very hard to think of the words he wanted.

"You have to tell me," he commanded, but there was only love in the soft demand.

"I don't know how," she whispered.

"Yes," he said. "You know what you want."

"You," she said. "Only you. Forever."

"How?" he asked. But as he spoke, the implacable demand his touch had made had cruelly stopped again. And he waited.

"With me?" she asked, hoping that it was what he wanted. Her body moved again, involuntarily lifting to seek his fingers. "Within me?"

"Yes," he agreed and touched her. But the focus of his caress had shifted. His fingers slid suddenly into the pulsing need he had created, into the warmth and dark sea of her desire. Her breath stopped, held by the wonder of that movement. And then his thumb touched, caressed again, demanding, and the chasm was there. But before she could plunge, both his hands had shifted under her hips, and as the air gathered around her soaring body, he entered her, hard and strong, thrusting into her even as she fell. And again. Slow and sure, and she convulsed into his strength. Held secure by Dev's arms so that she could fly without fear.

And when it was over, her body no longer racked by the force of its surrender, she opened her eyes to find his blue ones watching her face and what had been reflected there. She knew he had watched throughout her response to his gift, to this miracle that he could create within her body. And he smiled. And then he began to move again, to push deeper within her. She could feel him exploring the walls that no longer had any barrier to what he sought.

She became aware that her hands were on his hard buttocks, her nails pulling him even closer into her. There was something else he was trying to teach her, something beyond what he had already given her, but she didn't understand how there could be more than the swirling disappearance of the universe that happened when he touched her. But something was happening. Building. Changing. Melting. And she knew she wanted this, too.

And finally he said, "Open your eyes, my darling."

And so she watched, as long as she was able, as what she had given him in return began to happen. He held her eyes until he felt her join him there, and the waves of sensation that swept through her sent him over the edge of her imagined chasm also. And so they fell together.

She didn't know how long they lay entwined, his weight deliciously warm and heavy against her slenderness, almost as heavy as the languor inside her body. She felt the hard thud of his heart against hers, and she smiled because she had been aware of the gradual slowing of that measured rhythm.

And finally he shifted to lie beside her, and although she protested the desertion, she was comforted by his hand that moved over her, spanning the moisture that dewed her breasts and stomach. And finding the different wetness below. His fingers stroked, almost in memory, with no intent to arouse, but she convulsed, an aftershock to the eruption that had drained them both. And she felt the small spurt of his laughter her involuntary reaction caused.

"You are," he said softly, his lips in the fragrance of her disordered curls, "probably going to be the death of me, poor wounded veteran that I am."

She smiled at that, having no doubts about his strength. And then she said, the thought having come to her sometime before, but she had not had the strength then to utter it, "I'm very glad that you were wounded before, my love."

His lips hesitated briefly, and then knowing that whatever she was about to say was not something to be feared, he asked, "And why would you be glad of that?"

"Because that must be when you learned patience. All that wonderful patience," she said in remembrance, and turned her small body so that it pressed against the entire long length of his. "But, Dev," she continued softly, "I've never learned patience, so I'm afraid that, like a child, I want my pleasures immediately. Do you suppose..." she asked.

His fingers found hers and conveyed them gently to the answer to her question.

"In some things patience is considered a virtue, but in others, I believe you're right. If pleasures are immediately at hand, why shouldn't they be enjoyed?"

"But pleasures are always more meaningful when they're shared," she suggested, and his body moved to fit into hers like two halves of a broken coin rejoined.

"Like this?" he asked softly a few minutes later.

"Exactly like this," she whispered, her fingers moving over the scars on his back that were as familiar to her now as the blue eyes and as the smile she had loved from the first.

* * * * *